TERROR
AT
12.5 DEGREES

Eric Knight

Published by Remarkable Technologies, Inc.

ISBN 979-8-9901358-0-2

Cover art and design: John Parkinson

John Parkinson is an Art Director with a global toy company. He and the author worked as a creative team at a small ad agency at the beginning of their careers. They have kept in touch through the years on many creative adventures. This one is just the latest. Will there be more? What's around the bend? Stay tuned...

Dedication

This book is dedicated to my Dad – William "Bill" Knight – my mentor, lifelong fishing buddy, and best friend. I miss him beyond words.

Special Thanks

Mary Ann Knight

My Mom and perpetual source of love and support.

Kim Knight

The best sister a brother could ever hope for.

Elsie Mathews

My wife, forever partner, sharer of dreams,
and the one who makes our adventurous life possible.

Acknowledgements

Arnold Aranci

Brian Boccuzzi

Oliver Cary

Mickey Cooper

John Crovelli

Andrew Faber

David Lacasse

Rhonda Lane

Rod Lane

Cristina Lauwereys

Jean-Pierre Lauwereys

Linda Lee

Steve Lovelace

Steven McMacken

John Parkinson

Colleen Scarneo

Keith Schwartz

Rochelle Schwartz

Steven Shwartz

Don Skinner

Phil Temples

Peter van Slooten

CHAPTER 1

August 23, 2025   8 a.m.

"Woohoo! Aruba!" Amy Penn exclaimed as she and her three companions walked down the gangway of the Cosmos Megaliner, the world's largest cruise ship.

Rebecca DeGrass turned and gave Amy a big hug along with "We did it!" – referencing the promise they made to each other years ago in college.

"Okay, ladies. You're holding up traffic," a sarcastic nudge from Amy's husband, Pete.

"Yeah, we're only on the island for two days," Jack, Rebecca's husband, chimed in. "And there's beer and beach awaitin'."

The couples zigzagged their way down the gangway, approaching a throng of taxis jostling for position – all eager to take the hundreds of shore-goers to various destinations on the island.

Xavier Malbo, driving a well-traveled minivan with the letters "Sunshine Aruba Taxi" on the side and a "One Happy Island" bumper sticker barely covering a hefty scratch on the sliding door, eyed the moving queue. Spotting an appropriate fare, with professional deft he squeezed the minivan between two other taxis, intersecting the path of Amy and her friends.

"Bon Bini!" Malbo greeted the four through the open passenger window. "May I be of service?"

Rebecca replied, "Bon Bini!" – as she recalled from her Fodor's guide the phrase meant "welcome" in Papiamento, the local language.

"We would like to go to 'Baby Beach' for some sun and snorkeling. Could you take us there?"

"Sure can!"

Malbo bounded out of the driver's seat and met the group of four at the sliding door. He opened it and helped them into their seats. Each passenger clutched a small day bag that they placed on their laps.

Malbo slid the minivan door closed and hopped back into the driver's seat. "Baby Beach it is," he reaffirmed while darting his vehicle into the flow of traffic.

The four were almost giddy at the adventure they knew awaited them. Amy and Rebecca hatched the Aruba plan as a joke while they were both studying for finals in their senior year of college. "If we can ever get through these bitchin' exams," Rebecca said, "let's blow off steam and go to...Aruba." They both chuckled at the notion, but it stuck.

Amy and Rebecca aced the exams and they graduated. They both received a B.S. in Microbiology from the University of Minnesota. But life interced in their fledgling Aruba plans.

Rebecca met Jack at her first job. They dated. And a year-and-a-half later got married.

Amy was already seeing Pete at the university. They had been together since sophomore year. Less than a year after graduation, they got married.

The four regularly went on long-weekend trips together. The years went by. Now over eight since the initial island spark. Business for these young professionals was demanding on their time, and they could never seem to wangle a ten-day vacation stretch that would synchronize with their careers. Until now. And the first stop on their multiple-island trek: Aruba.

"How far to Baby Beach?" Pete asked the cabbie.

"Only about fifteen kilometers," Malbo responded. "We'll be there in about twenty minutes." He continued, "Fortunately, I know a shortcut that will get around some of the traffic. It might be a little bumpy. Not all of Aruba's roads are paved." With a wide grin, he concluded, "You'll be in the water in no time."

Rebecca unconsciously crinkled her brow, as she thought she read in Fodor's that Baby Beach was a bit farther from the cruise-ship dock than that. Something like twenty-five kilometers. But then she smiled to herself as the local was shaving off distance and time with his shortcut.

The four looked out the windows at their surroundings. Cars, shops, palm trees. They were taking it all in with glee.

As promised, Malbo turned onto a dirt road, which indeed got a bit jarring.

"Sorry for the bumps!" Malbo apologetically said. "Almost there. Just another eight or nine minutes."

The landscape became scruffy, with short plants and some cacti. The passengers could sense, though, they were still generally following the coastline somewhere off to the right. Instinctively, they craned their necks in that direction.

"Baby Beach is just up ahead. However, that last pothole is making the front end of my buggy a bit swervy. Nothing to be concerned about. Still, I want to check it for one second."

Malbo slowed down and pulled to the side. He shut off the engine.

The cabbie popped out of the minivan, got on his knees, and looked under the front end. A moment later, Jack slid the minivan door open, stepped out of the vehicle, and said, "Glad to take a look with you. I like working on cars with my father. He's a mechanic."

Malbo didn't respond, seemingly engrossed with his analysis.

The other three looked at each other, a bit puzzled. This is not how they expected their beach excursion to begin.

With the blazing Aruba sun beating down, it only took a few minutes before the minivan started to get uncomfortably hot.

"Let's see what Jack's up to," Rebecca said. "He's a wiz with cars."

"He might have to use a coconut for a wheel to get us going," Amy said with a bit of fun as the three put their day bags on the seats and got out of the vehicle. They made their way to the front, next to Jack.

Still with his head under the front end of the vehicle, Malbo said to himself, "I love it when a plan comes together." Counting four pairs of feet, he came out from under the minivan and stood in front of the two couples.

"What do you think, sir?" Pete politely asked. "Do you think we can still make it to the water?"

"Oh, most definitely, my friends."

At that moment, Malbo reached his right hand into the deep lower pocket of his cargo pants. With lightning blur he pulled out a silencer-equipped SIG SAUER P229, and – before the four had a millisecond to react – placed a bullet...*pifft...pifft...pifft...pifft*...into the forehead of each of the travelers.

CHAPTER 2

Malbo laid the gun on the hood of the minivan. From his left-side cargo-pants pocket, he took out a cell phone and pressed a speed-dial number.

The other party answered without saying a word.

Malbo said, "Done." And put the phone back into his pocket.

In less than a minute, a large van appeared from the opposite direction on the dirt road and came to an abrupt stop a few feet from Malbo, the minivan, and the four bodies on the ground.

The back of the large van opened and four early 30-ish persons, two men and two women dressed in tourist-wear, came out. They walked over to Malbo.

"Find their ship IDs," Malbo said in a stern tone. "Their bags are inside."

The two couples searched the dead bodies, took identifiable items, and calmly decided who would be who in this replacement scheme. They grabbed the travelers' bags from the minivan and matched them up with their new personas as best as they could figure.

In the meantime, the driver of the large van – a hulking presence – emerged and clomped over to Malbo. Malbo said to the driver, "When they're done, dispose of them on the reef as we planned." The driver nodded in understanding.

When the replacements completed their identity swaps, one gave a simple thumbs up to the driver of the large van. One by one, the driver slid the dead bodies by their feet to the back of the large van, with their heads bouncing on the ruts and rocks in the dirt road. Trickle trails of blood were the only remnants of the dragged paths.

Once the four bodies were at the back of the large van, the driver hoisted them up, one at a time, and tossed these – only moments ago, sparkling with life – bodies into the back compartment. He closed the van's door. The massive man walked to the driver's compartment, got in, and, as ordered, drove off.

Malbo kicked some dirt over the more-obvious blood trails, knowing the weekly sun showers in this tropical paradise would wash away evidence of his deed.

The replacements entered the minivan. Malbo closed the sliding door and entered the driver's compartment. He closed his door. And, without any words being exchanged, they sped off.

CHAPTER 3

June 22, 2019   Wildwood, New Jersey

"Watch the tram car, please... Watch the tram car, please..." The recorded refrain from the tram's speakers kept walkers on notice as they shuffled by the arcades, food vendors, and novelty shops on the Wildwood boardwalk that just opened for the day.

It was a glorious summer morning. And Katy Parnette was doing the most fulfilling thing in her entire life: Enjoying the Jersey shore with her five-year-old niece, Dorothy.

"Can I get some cotton candy – please, please, pleeeze?" Dorothy pleaded with childhood enthusiasm. Parnette, knowing all too well Dorothy's insistence would ultimately win out, responded, "Only if you promise to eat the lunch we packed in a couple of hours." Dorothy responded with a vigorous nod and a big hug of her aunt.

They got in line at *Sea & Surf Treats*. Dorothy pointed and said, "I want the blue kind" referring to the pink or blue choice of the confectionary. As they moved up in the queue, a seagull squawked overhead, drawing Parnette's attention for a second. The sky was blue and filled with puffy, meandering clouds. For a second, she got lost in the perfection of the moment.

"Ma'am? Ma'am?" broke the tranquility. The vendor, a student at his summer job, asked, "What would you like?" Parnette responded, "Two cotton candies, please. The blue kind." Dorothy bounced on her toes with excitement.

The vendor stepped away to begin his task. He placed an empty paper cone into the blue sugar haze and started gathering – around and around – the fuzzy creation. Parnette blinked twice and unconsciously cocked her head. She looked up to the sky and the rolling clouds. Then back to the growing mass of blue. "Hmmm..." she said to herself. "That might work. Oh, my. That *could* work." She filed a mental note as the vendor handed her two plump cotton candy cones. She reciprocated with a five spot and passed one of the cones to her jubilant niece.

The carnivalesque sounds of the boardwalk were cranking up. Hand in hand, beach cooler in tow, they flipped-flopped their way from the boardwalk to the inviting water.

CHAPTER 4

After a full day of fun, Parnette dropped off Dorothy to her parents: Parnette's sister Carol and her husband Paul. She then drove back to her home in West Windsor, New Jersey, a suburb of Princeton.

All-day body surfing with Dorothy embedded sand seemingly everywhere. Job one: Shampoo the beach sand from her bushy, fiery-red hair. From a thick lock at birth, her striking red hair was an iconic element of her presence – and her feisty personality.

As Parnette toweled off, her mind switched gears.

Dr. Katherine "Katy" Parnette was widely known as one of the most brilliant physicists in the world. Her papers on the creation, containment, and potential uses of antimatter were mandatory studies in every substantive Physics-related Ph.D. program. She was on the perpetual short list for a Nobel Prize in Physics, which would be a career culmination for some. But Parnette had a much bigger goal in mind.

Parnette had always enjoyed teaching. Her Ph.D. advanced physics course at Princeton – PHY 599: States of Matter – was mind-blowing, even for the smartest student. As challenging as the course was, it was always overenrolled. Students – and fellow professors who offered to co-instruct – relished every opportunity to experience Parnette's amazing intellect.

Parnette's Princeton University salary, industry awards, and industry licenses of her many patents embodying newfound efficiencies in energy production, made her one of the wealthiest scientists in the world, with a net worth speculated to be in the many hundreds of millions of dollars. Parnette never flaunted her wealth; to her it was just another number. She lived in an unpretentious home not too far from campus. She eschewed fancy automobiles, preferring a modestly equipped electric car that she charged through the solar panels on the roof of her home.

Parnette slipped on her comfy clothes: a well-worn Princeton Tigers top and bottom fleece combo. She shook out her trademark hair, like a pooch that came in from a dip in the pool. A fine spray of water misted the air. She then sat down at her computer and took a deep breath.

Click, click, click. Her fingers tapped two letters – Nb – into a Julia-based computer program. ENTER.

She wrote almost all of her own code, and almost all of it in Julia – a relatively new, *fast* computer language.

"Okay. Not Niobium. At least by itself."

"Hmmm... Maybe a Niobium-Titanium alloy...NbTI..." *Click, click, click.* ENTER.

Parnette was exploring metals with superconducting properties – zero electrical resistance at very cold temperatures. The special magnetic properties of these metals are at the heart of MRI machines and particle accelerators.

She swiveled her chair to another monitor. Parnette had five interconnected monitors on her sweeping half-moon desk: two to the left, two to the right, and the biggest monitor in the center. Her computer and monitors were connected through a dedicated fiber-optic link to the *TIGER* supercomputer on campus. The data pipe was a $200,000-per-year perk that was part of her compensation package.

TIGER had a processing speed of 2.607 petaFLOPS – 2.607 quadrillion calculations per second – sufficient to tackle Parnette's processor-intensive simulations.

Rewinding her day, thoughts of clouds and cotton candy peppered her mind. She paused for a second, then said to herself, "Think non-linearly, Parnette. Non-linearly..."

The center screen lit up with a three-dimensional image of a cylinder-like structure. "Penning traps are 'old school'..."

A Penning trap is a structure that uses a magnetic field to contain charged antimatter, such as antiprotons and positrons. It can't be used on neutral antimatter, such as antihydrogen – Parnette's particular fascination.

Parnette mused, "What if I created a superconducting *fractal* containment structure like a cloud...but in a physical way, like cotton candy...and at pico scale?"

A fractal is a pattern that repeats itself at all scales. A cloud's features are identical, no matter how close in or how far away they are observed. They are fractal structures. Trees also have fractal characteristics, with main branches splitting into smaller and smaller branches in a repeating pattern.

Parnette's fingers enveloped the keyboard, like a master pianist floating across the keys. Riffing off her fractal inspiration, the interior of the cylinder transformed from fully transparent to an intricate haze.

Parnette swiveled from monitor to monitor as she typed at an increasingly frenetic pace. This was the hyperdrive of thought that students and peers marveled at when Parnette was at a whiteboard. A manic firehose of consciousness.

Back and forth, she gyrated between monitors – feeding data into her simulations and watching the computer spit out results in graphic images on the flanking displays. Though her attention always bounced back to the main monitor in the center.

"Hofstadter's butterfly." *Click, click, click.* ENTER.

"Graphene." ENTER.

With each keystroke of new input, the 3D image on the main screen morphed. The cylinder with the hazy interior became egg-shaped at times, more spherical at times, and finally settling into an hourglass shape. But not quite as narrow as a typical hourglass; simply its middle tucked in a bit.

Talking to herself – rooting herself on:

"A feedback loop. Yes, a feedback loop. To create a self-sustaining, cascading reaction. That could give us the escalating power."

Click, click, click. "Methylammonium lead halide." ENTER.

The hourglass suddenly lined itself with a blue glow.

"Bring on the power, baby... Suck up those protons..." *Click, click, click.* ENTER.

The simulation ran again. A new image appeared. A bold green line now wrapped the entire 3D structure.

"Holy shit!"

Parnette stared at the monitor, watching the 3D structure highlighted in green. Then she said to herself, "This really shouldn't be happening."

Hesitant to touch any of the computer controls, she took out her cell phone and snapped a series of pictures of the computer monitors, the settings, and the data being displayed.

She then grabbed the mouse and clicked a menu on the far-right monitor. She selected a drop-down menu item, which brought up a slider labeled K for Kelvin. 0 degrees K is absolute zero on the Kelvin scale, equivalent to minus 459.67 degrees Fahrenheit. The digital slider was set at 4 degrees K, a common baseline temperature in antihydrogen research and containment.

She nudged the slider forward. 25. 50. 100 degrees K. The green outline remained on the 3D structure. 150. 200. 250 degrees K. Still green. With trepidation, she moved it to 295.4 degrees K. The equivalent of 72 degrees Fahrenheit.

All green.

"Spontaneously created antimatter. And contained at room temperature. *That's not possible.*"

CHAPTER 5

A ntimatter.

Born from British physicist Paul Dirac's equations in 1928, the allure of this mysterious state of matter has been the cornerstone of countless science fiction novels, movies, and television productions throughout the decades.

As its name suggests, antimatter is the mirror opposite of matter. For instance, a positron is the antimatter equivalent of an electron, an antiproton is the antimatter equivalent of a proton, and so forth. If a particle of antimatter collides with its equivalent particle of matter, complete annihilation occurs, releasing tremendous quantities of energy.

For a perspective, if just one gram of antimatter were to collide with one gram of matter, the equivalent destructive force of over 40,000 tons (40 kilotons) of TNT would be released. In comparison, the "Little Boy" atomic bomb that was dropped on Hiroshima, Japan had a fraction of the destructive power: 15 kilotons.

Theoretically, a couple of kilograms – about a pound – of antimatter, in a controlled antimatter-matter reaction, could generate enough power to fulfill most countries' energy demands for over a year. But theory and reality have been far apart.

It was recently discovered that nature creates momentary particles of antimatter during thunderstorms. NASA's orbiting Fermi Gamma-ray Space Telescope has recorded this phenomenon on several occasions.

In current science, the on-Earth creation of even a nanogram – a billionth of a gram – of antimatter is fraught with steep challenges.

One method to create antimatter is particle acceleration, in which infinitesimally small particles are accelerated to very high speeds and then made to collide. The collisions create a range of new particles, including antimatter. Europe's Large Hadron Collider (LHC) – the world's largest and most-powerful particle accelerator – is an underground circular tunnel with a circumference of about 17 miles. This mammoth scientific instrument straddles the Switzerland-France border.

To create a nanogram of antimatter at the LHC requires tremendous energy – multiple terajoules. One terajoule is approximately the total energy consumed by 100,000 homes in a year.

A related challenge is cost. The tremendous energy required to power a particle accelerator, if scaled to produce just a single gram of antimatter, would result in a cost of trillions of dollars.

Beyond creation and cost, the containment of antimatter is a daunting scientific challenge. Antimatter must be stored in a vacuum, suspended using magnetic fields to prevent contact with ordinary matter. As described previously, any contact between antimatter and matter leads to particle annihilation – and a violent release of energy.

CHAPTER 6

After the birth of Dorothy, Parnette developed an intense desire to harness the power of antimatter, creating – as she commonly said – "the ultimate green fuel source for generations to come."

Over the years, Parnette grew despondent seeing a new breed of politicians double-down on fossil fuels. Watching Dorothy grow up, and knowing the devolving trajectory of the world's climate, she felt a responsibility to leave the world in a better place. "If it's not us scientists to lead the charge, then who?"

Parnette never married and rarely dated. As she was fond of saying, "I'm married to my research." But she never lost the instinctual desire to bear a child. It never did happen. Now 62, the biological clock has long ticked its last tock. Her motherly instincts lived through Dorothy.

Parnette's research gradually steered from esoteric to practical. Antimatter, in a variety of forms, had been successfully created, such as at the LHC. However, the exorbitant costs made it far from practical. Antimatter had largely remained a pursuit of knowledge by the scientific community. Parnette wanted to change that.

Her outspoken testimonies on Capitol Hill got her in plenty of hot water. Fossil-fuel lobbyists labeled her a crackpot and disparaged her research at every opportunity. Parnette's vision of "free energy for all" became a direct threat to the embedded industrial and political machines; even if her research never came to commercial fruition, raising the public's awareness of viable power alternatives had made her an expensive pain in the butt to the fossil fuel industry.

On occasion, even her university's leadership asked her to "dial it back" a bit. She always waved off the admonishments thanks to her tenure; students and her faculty colleagues loved her chutzpah. After one particularly testy testimony on Capitol Hill, some entrepreneurial students printed *Parnette Pounds Political Pricks* T-shirts. The entire batch of 100 shirts sold out in less than an hour at a pop-up in front of the Frist Campus Center.

The media also loved her. She could go toe to toe with any industry mogul or TV talking head with an agenda. She was small in stature, not more than five foot two. Yet a husky physique, and her copper-red hair – always puffed up in curls – seemed to amplify her force-of-nature personality.

Unknown to everyone except her closest family and her psychiatrist, behind the gruff exterior hid an insecure interior. She was picked on incessantly as a child. Her compact frame, cherub face, and red hair earned her the nicknames "Katy Ball" and "Little Red Katyhood." Kids would kick her ankles at recess like the rubber red kickball on the playground. It was a cruel time.

All too frequently, teachers would find her curled in a corner, uncontrollably crying. The school nurse would call her mom to pick her up and take her home.

As an adult, Parnette consciously avoided driving by school playgrounds – even if it added miles to her route.

A few years ago, she was asked to be a guest speaker at a middle school event that included a segment about STEM careers. Parnette had always been a big proponent of science and technology, particularly for girls. Still, the thought of stepping onto a school property made her heart race. The event was a special request made by the mayor of the town and the superintendent of the school system. She told herself, "You play with atoms for a living. You can do this."

Parnette took two Ativan and drove to the school. She kept her head down from her parked car all the way through the front doors; she didn't even peek at the adjacent playground.

It was a noontime event, so the kids could take their regular buses home if they chose. The school invited parents to attend, and many did. The auditorium was packed.

Parnette was doing fine, enjoying the Q & A with the kids, asking what they wanted to be when they grew up. As a tribute to Parnette, the teachers and kids came up with a fun serenade – themed around Parnette's work. About a dozen kids ran out on the stage, dressed in "I Love Science," "Have you Hugged your Electron Today?" and "My Atoms Make the World Turn" T-shirts. One little girl, no more than seven, ran up to Parnette and handed her a little sign taped to a paint-stirrer stick that read, "Nucleus." The other girls carried basketballs, each painted silver, and started dribbling the balls around Parnette – like the orbits of electrons. A teacher pressed PLAY on a boom box. Out rang *Sweet Georgia Brown*, the customary song played by the Harlem Globe Trotters.

The audience started clapping to the beat of the music. The skit was funny and silly. Except to Parnette. As the kids and the bouncing balls started to swirl around her, Parnette started to hyperventilate. She tried to smile her way through it. But it was too much. She passed out.

When she came to, she was looking straight up into the eyes of the school nurse.

Parnette publicly blamed the circumstance on low blood sugar and a seasonal allergy attack. That was the last time she stepped foot in a school, other than a university.

Growing up, Parnette was smarter than the rest of the kids. Heck, smarter than most of her teachers. Yet that couldn't protect her from the verbal and physical abuse of her classmates. More than 50 years later, the pain bubbled just below the surface. It was the chip on her shoulder that spurred her biting sarcasm – and obsessive scientific focus.

CHAPTER 7

The world was in freefall during 2020 and much of 2021. The COVID-19 pandemic, caused by the novel coronavirus SARS-CoV-2, became a health crisis of unimaginable proportions across the entire planet. Its spread overloaded the healthcare infrastructure and disrupted the financial backbone of global society.

The pandemic tore at the fabric of life itself. Isolation, fear, and the upheaval of familiar routines profoundly affected mental health. And Parnette was not immune to this insidious dimension of the virus.

Parnette couldn't bear the thought of getting her beloved niece sick. So she stayed away from her sister's house. It was beyond hard. For years, Dorothy was the only tangible touch point to the world beyond her research. Now that was taken away.

Parnette impulsively tried to compensate by diving deeper into her antimatter research. She'd run stretches of all-nighters. Insomnia became the norm. She turned further to anti-anxiety meds. Uncharacteristically, she'd forget to log into the remote-teaching platform to conduct her virtual classes. She was a mess.

In 2022, the world further reeled from the triple whammy of a war in Ukraine, inflation, and the elements of a global recession. Even so, Parnette had intermittent sparks of life. She still wasn't sleeping regularly. But she was able to have visits with her niece when the multi-variant vaccines were available to all ages – lifting one huge weight off her psyche.

By the fall, Parnette had made key strides in her antimatter discovery. The two pillars of her life were beginning to realign. Sleep without medication became a possibility again. And her brain started to once again click at her prior meteoric pace.

Parnette reached the limit of what she could accomplish with *TIGER*. She needed more processing power. A lot more.

CHAPTER 8

*A*pril 2023

It was nearly four years since Parnette made her room-temperature-antimatter discovery. But she hadn't told a soul. She could barely believe it herself – anticipating that she'd discover some error in her computations. She rechecked and reran her simulations hundreds of times. All achieved the same result.

Before going public, she had to be *absolutely certain*. She didn't want to become another "cold fusion" boondoggle. In 1989, scientists at a press conference announced they had created nuclear fusion at room temperature instead of the millions of degrees commonly thought necessary, such as what occurs inside of stars and in the detonation of a hydrogen bomb. Within days the science was debunked; the scientists failed in many fundamental facets of their research. "Cold fusion" became an instant punchline for junk science.

Parnette could not risk her career and reputation. The eyes of the world would be on her. The scientific community would do its appropriate skeptical scrutiny – just as she would if she were in their shoes. Diligence and data were essential.

She had pushed the university's *TIGER* computer to its processing limits. Still, it wasn't sufficient to complete the real-world modeling of her discovery.

Parnette called New Jersey Congressman Marcus Templeman, an old friend and an ally on Capitol Hill. She asked if he could help her find a way to confidentially run simulations on the U.S. Department of Energy's Oak Ridge National Laboratory's *Frontier* supercomputer, the world's fastest supercomputer. *Frontier* clocked in at a staggering

1,102 petaFLOPS – 1.102 quintillion operations per second – almost 423 times faster than *TIGER*.

Parnette provided a hush-hush overview to Templeman of her antimatter discovery, and painted a jaw-dropping description of how it could – if validated – transform the world. "Unlimited, free energy, for every human on Earth!"

The Congressman was mesmerized by her vision. However, he admitted that her technical talk was "well beyond anything I learned at Vanderbilt and my business classes." He said he couldn't promise anything, but he'd put his staff on it and get back to her as quickly as possible.

.

CHAPTER 9

There's no such thing as a secret in Congress. Or, at least, not for long.

The same day Parnette called for the favor, Congressman Templeman asked his staffer – Benjamin "Benny" Carmen – to investigate the possibility.

The Congressman said to the young man, fresh out of college, "it's a favor for a friend; she needs it quickly but keep it discreet." Benny, eager to come back with a successful result to impress his mentor, evidently glossed over the "discreet" part of the conversation. He randomly called phone numbers at Oak Ridge – scrolling and dialing numbers in the "Find People" directory on ORNL.GOV's Web site – and blabbered whatever popped into his youthful mind.

One person Benny contacted – Jason Jensen – was an Associate Director in the ORNL Physics Division.

"This is Jensen. Who am I speaking with?"

"Um, I'm Benny. Benny Carmen. I'm one of Congressman Templeman's interns."

"Okay, Benny. Why are you calling me?"

"Mr. Templeman...um, Congressman Templeman, asked me to find time on your computer."

"You want to use *my* computer?"

"Oh, no. Not me! For a friend of Congressman Templeman."

"And I'm assuming on *Frontier*?"

"Uh, I guess so."

"Benny, maybe you should call me back when you have a little more information."

"But Congressman Templeman said it's *really important* – and needs it quickly."

"Okay, since it's for Templeman, who I respect a lot, let's take another swing. Do you know what the time on *Frontier* would be used for?"

"I really don't know. I have a business degree. It was something chemical, I think."

Jensen was about to politely end the call with this young intern. Then Benny added, "It's something about 'ubermatter'...or at least I think so."

"Do you mean *antimatter*?" Jensen's curiosity suddenly piqued.

"Oh, yeah! That's what Congressman Templeman told me. He said a lady needed it for that."

"Hmmm... Let me check into it for you. I see your number on the caller ID. You said your name is Benny, right?"

"Um, yes sir. Benny Carmen. Thank you. I really appreciate it, sir.

"I'll get back to you."

Jensen hung up the phone. He said to himself, "I've got to make a phone call."

CHAPTER 10

"Hi Uncle Pat."

"Hey, Jason. What's shakin' in supercomputer land?"

"ORNL is like a continuous sci-fi movie. One of our scientists is simulating the gigantic storm that makes the great Red Spot on Jupiter. Cool stuff like that."

"Any news on our *special* project?"

"You know I can't talk about *that* over the phone, Uncle Pat. We have to keep it on the down-low, *remember*?"

"Yeah, yeah... So, why are you giving me a ring?"

"Well, it's in regard to, well, I think, Katherine Parnette."

"Oh, that pain in the ass! We have enough problems with our fracking permits without that wacko talking her alternate-energy B.S. So, what's that ding-dong doing now to give me another bout of agita?"

"You've got to promise to keep this *really* quiet. I could get in a lot of shit."

"You got it, J-boy."

"An intern on Capitol Hill called me on behalf of Congressman Templeman. The kid said a woman needed *Frontier* time to run antimatter simulations ASAP. I have reason to believe it's Parnette. The two of them are in tight. So, I was going to make up some excuse to deny her request. Overbooked requests, something like that."

"No, wait! Don't do that." Smiling to himself with bad intent, like the Christmas Grinch, he said to Jensen, "This might be the perfect opportunity. Can you set it up so we can snoop on her research?"

"Whoa. I don't know, Uncle Pat. I could get booted out of here if I get caught. Even lose my security clearance."

"Remember that inheritance, J-boy. You know you're my *favorite*."

"Alright, alright. I'll take care of it, Uncle Pat. But – man – don't breathe a word of this to *anyone*."

"Don't sweat it, my boy. Don't sweat it."

CHAPTER 11

Patrick J. Kilborne rose from the dusty plains of Texas to become an emblem of both success and controversy.

Emerging from Texas Tech in 1971 with a degree in geology, Kilborne embarked on a trailblazing journey. While others dismissed certain oil fields as desolate and barren, Kilborne discerned latent opportunities. He channeled a small family inheritance into these forsaken fields, acquiring them for pennies on the dollar.

Kilborne's masterstroke was in recognizing the untapped potential of hydraulic fracturing, colloquially known as "fracking." He assembled a team of experts in this emerging technology, pioneering its application to revitalize dormant oil fields. As the wells began yielding black gold once more, Kilborne's vision bore fruit, transforming the fields into thriving, multimillion-dollar ventures.

Decades unfurled in a whirlwind of successes, each year multiplying Kilborne's wealth. His personal fortune blossomed into the tens of billions of dollars. Kilborne leveraged his money and power on Capitol Hill, driving legislation in his company's favor and influencing elected officials like marionettes.

The press dubbed Kilborne the "Fracking Czar," praising his career's prowess – and financial windfalls – in resurrecting seemingly defunct oil fields. Yet, behind closed doors, another less-flattering "F" word prepended the oil baron's moniker, as his rocket-ride ascent to industry dominance was punctuated with ruthless tactics and cutthroat maneuvers. He was castigated by his peers for his unscrupulous business practices and the unforgiving obliteration of those who dared to challenge his empire.

No one got under Kilborne's skin, challenging the essential nature of his career and image, more than Dr. Katherine Parnette. She hurled scientific hardballs at him at every opportunity, chastising Kilborne for the inherent "ecological genocide" of his business practices.

Irking Parnette to the most substantial degree was Kilborne's grandiose vision to not only enhance oil extraction but to also expand oil consumption. One of his most audacious endeavors involved the creation of a fleet of colossal ocean liners. Nine in total, each 1,320 feet long – precisely a quarter of a mile – with 420,480 gross tonnage. Each gargantuan ship was designed to accommodate up to 9,520 guests plus a crew of 3,925.

These behemoth vessels, beyond symbols of luxury and opulence for travelers, were voracious consumers of fuel at almost twice the rate of the other large vessels in the industry. Each Kilborne ship guzzled an astounding 490 tons of heavy fuel oil (HFO) – over 119,000 gallons – every day on the high seas, more fuel than an ordinary person would use in a lifetime. HFO is less refined and cheaper than diesel. It has a higher sulfur content and produces more greenhouse gas emissions than other fuel types. All the more reason for Parnette's never-ending attacks.

The first of Kilborne's nine monster ships to commence service was the Cosmos Megaliner. The other eight were in various stages of construction.

In a world teetering on the precipice of environmental crisis, the two influential figures – Parnette and Kilborne – stood as stark opposites in their pursuit of shaping the future. Their confrontations were not merely clashes of opinion but a war of principles. It was a relentless struggle between preserving lucrative yet environmentally damaging industries versus championing innovative, eco-friendly solutions for a cleaner, brighter future.

Their clashes on Capitol Hill – more like raucous brawls – had become the stuff of legend. Their animated testimonies in front of Congress were anticipated events, the air crackling with tension, their verbal showdowns heralded as "Must See TV" on Public Broadcasting. Such duels between the oil magnate and the eco-visionary scientist skyrocketed Public Broadcasting's ratings, eclipsing even the most revered programs on traditional networks.

With each public appearance, their rhetoric drew further lines in the sand. Kilborne's charismatic speeches resonated with individuals advocating for economic growth and stability, often overshadowing environmental concerns with promises of financial prosperity and job creation. On the flip side, Parnette presented compelling cases backed by scientific evidence, passionately advocating for a world liberated from the shackles of fossil fuel reliance.

The audiences typically found themselves torn between Kilborne's assurances of economic abundance and Parnette's earnest call for a more planet-sensitive and sustainable path forward. The pair's never-disappointing jousts regularly ignited spirited debates on social media, infiltrated corporate boardrooms, and influenced international summits where their ideologies clashed on a global scale.

CHAPTER 12

J ason Jensen obediently worked to arrange supercomputer time for Parnette. In his role as an Associate Director at ORNL, he had substantial latitude in scheduling and prioritization, but he still had to maintain the appearance of adhering to ORNL protocol.

Jensen called Parnette, introduced himself and his connection to Congressman Templeman, and emailed the appropriate forms to apply for use of *Frontier*. His email also included VIP credentials for the secure transmission of documents and sensitive communications via the ORNL computer network.

A mandatory application requirement for any time on *Frontier* was the submission of a formal Proposal – which was also of the most interest to Jensen. The Proposal required Parnette to describe her research objectives, computational requirements, and the specific resources needed on the supercomputer. It was in this document that Jensen hoped to sniff out particulars he could relay to Kilborne.

Jensen promised Parnette, as a courtesy to her and the Congressman, that he would do his best to streamline the Proposal Review process but feigned the likely difficulty in finding appropriate experts to conduct the review. He told Parnette, "The more you can describe in the Proposal, the better I can corral the right scientists for the review – and the quicker I can get you approved."

***

Parnette – eager to get into the review queue – pulled an all-nighter and wrote a 42-page Proposal. By 10 a.m. the next morning, she had relayed the Proposal to Jensen using ORNL's digitally secure communication channel.

Jensen immediately scrutinized the incoming document. Although far from his field of expertise, the executive summary clearly described Parnette's plan to put the horsepower of *Frontier* to work to delve deeper into her research of antimatter and clean-energy generation.

Jensen replied to Parnette's submission with an ORNL-standard "Received and Scheduled for Review" secure transmission. In effect, he told her to stay tuned. Yet, he had no intention of assembling a review team; he didn't want any other eyes to see Parnette's research. Jensen simply saved the Proposal to a blank thumb drive and filed Parnette's incoming message.

To simulate a sense of review effort, Jensen waited two weeks before he emailed Parnette a congratulatory note, indicating her Proposal was "unanimously accepted" by the review team. A three-week-out date was set for the computer session with *Frontier*.

CHAPTER 13

May 18, 2023

Here she was, in the home of the grand machine.

Even for a rock-star physicist, Parnette was humbled by the opportunity to play with such landmark hardware. The granularity of data Parnette would receive from *Frontier* would identify even the subtlest flaws in her simulations – or confirm her discovery beyond any doubt.

Parnette spent the last three weeks intensively updating her code, a substantial re-write and porting of the programming she wrote in Julia for the campus computer system. Her research was now in C++, a programming language able to maximize the power of *Frontier's* massive architecture of 8,776 CPUs and 36,992 GPUs.

As ordered by his Uncle Pat, Jensen had secretly deployed keystroke and data loggers, typically used to debug programming and perform system maintenance. He also engaged screen-capture software to record the graphic output of Parnette's simulation. Jensen knew deploying such tools amounted to a breach of over a dozen government and research-privacy protocols. Corporate espionage, plain and simple.

If exposed, his career would be over. At worst, he could end up in jail. He also knew that even a sliver of Kilborne's inheritance would make him wealthy beyond anything he could ever spend in his lifetime.

To minimize the chance a colleague would spot the system's unscheduled monitoring and maintenance, he needed Parnette's simulation to not languish in the processing line with dozens of other projects on *Frontier*. To accomplish the task, Jensen arranged for any program running under Parnette's VIP credentials to be bumped to the top of *Frontier's* processing queue. Her simulation would be run – and done.

By 2:30 p.m., Parnette's preparation was almost complete. She finalized the job script – the computer instructions that would inform *Frontier* of the computer resources required to run the simulation. She submitted the job script to the automated job scheduler. And, finally, Parnette re-typed her credentials to engage the simulation. With a deep breath she pressed ENTER.

Frontier usage documentation had prepared Parnette for a substantial wait – potentially hours; much depended on the overall load and demands on the system. If there was a long queue of pending jobs, the simulation might not make it to the top of the execution list until the end of the day. So Parnette was ready to settle in, including catching up on her day's email.

But – in an eyeblink – the simulation ran. It happened so fast, Parnette thought it was a mistake, and that she was only seeing a simple refresh of a static computer display. It was her first-time accessing *Frontier*, and she could have easily keyed something in error. Before she could speculate further, a 3D structure appeared on the monitor – morphing into the subtle hourglass shape she saw in her university's research. "The sim's running!" Parnette exclaimed.

The 3D structure glowed with a green hue, while a digital temperature gauge labeled KELVIN steadily incremented. 150. 200. 250. 275. 285. 290. 295. After two minutes of computer churning, the increasing digits paused at 295.4.

A bold-green line suddenly outlined the hourglass – and began to blink, on and off. "Oh my God!"

***

It took a few days for Parnette to fully come to grips with her scientific revelation.

Over the course of her illustrious career, she had made plenty of discoveries – many quite monumental – leading to patents, profitable licenses, and perpetual industry praise. However, all Parnette's accolades, even a potential Nobel Prize, would pale in comparison to the magnitude of her current discovery. It was not hyperbole to say that it would be as profound as Einstein's famous equation. It could, fundamentally and forever, change the course of the world.

CHAPTER 14

Jensen's surreptitiously captured data from Parnette's simulation at ORNL was provided to Kilborne without delay.

Behind Kilborne's seemingly endless innovations in fracking was a world-class technology center composed of over 900 full-time geologists, geophysicists, geochemists, petroleum engineers, drilling engineers, and computer and data scientists. As Kilborne was fond of saying, "It's my investments in intellect, not wells, that made me the most-profitable oil man on Earth." And, to Kilborne, intellect meant more than smart people. He was one of the first oil barons to leverage the power of artificial intelligence in the research and investigation of oil fields.

Kilborne instructed Jensen to scrub the data of any "identifying source" – and Jensen dutifully obliged.

Kilborne followed by summoning the heads of his computer and scientific teams to a private session at his Eldorado estate. He concocted a story he knew would spur the patriotic and company-loyalty juices of his employees. He led the meeting with the following: "One of our overseas' offices acquired data that could be damaging to our company and our country. I need you to use every resource at your disposal – without cost constraints or concerns – to validate or refute the findings of the research. We need to be able to respond to whatever the data shows before it is leaked to the media or the public markets."

"What the boss wants, the boss gets" was the unwritten refrain throughout Kilborne's empire; he had zero mercy when his expectations were not met. Kilborne's computer gurus began working around the clock to analyze Parnette's data. When they realized the underlying energy-production technology was based on the science of antimatter, well outside of their technology purview, they did what Kilborne directed – pull out all the stops – and contracted Dr. Gabriel Heinrich Müller, the eminent German physicist, to confidentially review the data.

In the late 90s, Müller led the European team that made groundbreaking discoveries related to antihydrogen and the properties of this form of antimatter. He initially turned down the request from Kilborne's team, stating his long-standing principle to not taint his "scientific purity" by engaging in commercial endeavors. That said, a promised near-blank compensation check, plus a $6.5 million offer towards Müller's pet project at the Max Planck Institute for Physics (MPP) in Munich, lubricated his perspective.

It was about 2:30 in the afternoon when Müller fired up his computer at the MPP. A private guided tour was just passing his office. The MPP was one of the most famous research organizations in the world, once headed by none other than Albert Einstein. Müller found the tours distracting. Notwithstanding, the prestige made his ego glow. He smiled as one visitor took his picture with a cell phone. Photos were not allowed in the research areas of the facility, but security let a few slide in the office hallways.

Müller swiveled in his chair to his primary monitor, the CPU now booted. He laughed to himself when he began reading the computer simulation protocol. "This is ludicrous. Room-temperature antimatter. I clearly waited way too long to make money from industry."

Müller dug into the assignment, thinking he'd make quick work of it and an even quicker payday. He reviewed the experiment parameters and initial conditions – as well as the study designer's rather preposterous theory of antimatter created and contained within spontaneously created chaos structures. "Someone's been reading way too much science fiction. Or smoking something funny. Or both."

He studied the construction of the rather unusual reaction vessel; elements of graphene and methylammonium lead halide. "MALH? Don't they use that in solar cells? And a titanium tube? It looks more like the water bottle on my bicycle. Stupid."

Skepticism would be a multi-level understatement at this point. That said, Müller was mildly impressed that the researcher or researchers working on the project had run the simulation on *Frontier*. "Somebody knows someone. My American colleagues have been waiting months to get a sim on *Frontier!*"

Müller loaded up the screen-captured digital animation. "Well, this should be entertaining..."

The screen-capture mirrored what Parnette saw in person at ORNL. A 3D structure morphed into an hourglass shape; glowed and pulsed; the temperature gauge incremented and settled at 295.4 degrees K.

"Wait! What! This can't be!"

Up until this point, Müller was going through the motions with only passive attention. But his face became flush as his brain locked into something entirely unexpected.

He paused the display while he rapidly dug into the provided supplemental data files.

What Müller fully expected to be a brief afternoon assignment turned into thirteen straight hours of complete data immersion.

Try as he might to shake the improbable, the result was bulletproof. At 3:11 a.m., Müller simply uttered to himself, "Oh, my."

***

There was no way Müller could leave the office to sleep. He dialed his primary contact from Kilborne's technology center, Dr. Kenneth Van Nuys. Even though it was almost 9:30 p.m. in Texas, Van Nuys answered.

"Burning the midnight oil, I see, Gabriel."

"There's no way I could sleep. No way!"

"Have you found something?"

"Found *something*? Where the heck did you get this research? This is revolutionary!"

Müller expected a questioning response like "It's that amazing, huh?" Instead, Van Nuys' cheery demeanor flipped like a switch and sternly replied, "Müller, don't you dare say a word to anyone. No one. Not your wife. Not your dog. To no one or no thing. Got it? Got it?"

Caught off guard, Müller simply replied, "Got it."

Van Nuys hung up.

Bewildered, exhausted, and strangely frightened by Van Nuys' tone, Müller went home.

***

Müller's mind wandered on his drive to Ebersberg. It was good there was no traffic; his concentration was not on the road.

He managed to get into bed without waking his wife. Although his mind was still a buzz, the exhaustion overtook him and he fell asleep.

***

At 9:45 a.m. Müller's eyes popped open, still in the foggy aftermath of a deep sleep. "Did I dream it?" he thought to himself. He could smell the pleasant aroma of coffee wafting from the kitchen to the bedroom. His wife was long up and had started the day.

He put on sweat clothes and slippers, grabbed his glasses and cell phone from the nightstand, and shuffled his way to his study. He tapped the PC's keyboard and woke up his machine. He typed in his password and launched a remote-access app from the desktop. He typed in another security code. Last night Müller purposely left his office machine in a secure idle state, so he could access it from home.

"Okay, let's see if this was my imagination." He re-started the screen-captured digital animation, and there it was again: Antimatter at room temperature. If this was his discovery, he'd be on the phone to his colleagues at the MPP, having them rush to his office – as the data was truly earth-shattering. But he was told to keep his mouth shut. "This is absurd!"

Müller powered on his cell phone and sent a text to Van Nuys:

Kenneth. Last night you said to keep things quiet. I have. I will stick to our confidentiality agreement. Given the sheer magnitude of this discovery, shouldn't we somehow document it? An independent third party in the scientific community? History needs to remember this moment. I know people we could absolutely trust. Please advise.

Twenty minutes went by without a response. Müller thought, "Maybe he's in a meeting. He's probably talking with his team and thinking along the same lines – how they could document and carefully control the disclosure." Finally, Van Nuys' reply came in:

Shut the hell up. You are never to speak a word of this to anyone. Don't even call or text me again. Digitally shred the files in your computer by your noontime. You will receive your compensation as promised if you stick to our arrangement. If not, money will be the least of your concerns.

A string of photos began appearing in his text. First, a photo taken yesterday of him in his MPP office. "That visitor! Bastard!" Müller raged. Then, a photo of his wife at the mailbox in front of his house. "Oh my God!" Then – making Müller burp and expel stomach matter onto the computer keyboard – three photos of his daughter Sophie writing on a whiteboard, exuberantly teaching her third-grade students. "No! No! No! What have I done? God, what have I done!"

Müller had sold his soul. Like countless others in Kilborne's universe.

CHAPTER 15

K ilborne called Klaus, his technical troublemaker for hire.

"Klaus, I have a job for your maniacal mind. Yes, like Copenhagen. Yes, the same financial arrangement as before. But I'm going to triple it. I need you to bring all your wrath to a pain-in-the-ass named Dr. Katherine Parnette." Kilborne continued, "This shithead, if she does what she usually does, will make some sort of public announcement. We need to be ready. I'll funnel details to you as they develop. Yes, digital transfer. Bye."

In addition to monitoring Parnette's research through Jensen's undercover activities, Kilborne activated his legion of on-call "investigators" to follow her and dig up dirt. These were not your run-of-the-mill gumshoes. They were thugs who were quite comfortable operating in the gray-to-black area of the law and were paid quite handsomely for the risk.

Surveillance quickly uncovered that every Tuesday at 11 a.m. Parnette had an appointment with her psychiatrist. Within a day of that discovery, one of Kilborne's thugs broke into the office after midnight, grabbed the doctor's computer and, from the filing cabinet, what turned out to be 19 years of paper files on Parnette. The criminal set fire to the entire three-story office building to cover the theft in this one office.

CHAPTER 16

Parnette knew from experience that even the loftiest science would be relegated to arcane scientific papers unless it could be transformed into practical uses. So, she spent the next few months contemplating and designing real-world applications for her room-temperature antimatter discovery.

She designed cars that ran a 100,000 miles without refueling. Public transportation – from buses to trains – that operated for years on a golf-ball-sized energy source. Aircraft that flew non-stop worldwide on "annihilation energy" harnessed to generate thrust. Homes, apartment buildings, malls, and skyscrapers that were fully powered – electricity, lights, heating, and cooling – from a perfectly clean, perpetually available energy source.

All without waste. Without pollution. She imagined the Earth healing from the ravages of fossil fuels.

But Parnette didn't stop there. She believed humans were born to explore, and that the ultimate future of the species included becoming one with the stars. With that galactic perspective, Parnette crafted options for new opportunities in human spaceflight. The same "annihilation energy" could be applied to rocket motors with the capability to propel humans to Mars in less than two weeks – instead of the best case six to nine months. Journeys to other, more distant, planets in the solar system would also become plausible.

***

By the end of 2023, Parnette had the skip in her step back, and she was determined to be a positive light in the global abyss. With her data checked and confirmed many times over, including with the mighty *Frontier*, and a spectrum of transformative applications ready to be disclosed, she decided it was time to go public with her research.

Parnette scheduled a press conference for March 7, 2024 at the *National Academy of Sciences* in D.C. to unveil, in her words, "a discovery that would rid the world of the shackles of fossil fuel and usher in a new era of capabilities for all humankind."

CHAPTER 17

March 7, 2024   9 p.m.

"We call it the building for the National Academy of Sciences and the National Research Council, but in reality it should be the nation's home of science in America, and will be looked upon by our fellow citizens and the world at large as the place where the creative mind will be able to do much to bring about a better existence for the future people of the world."

National Academy of Sciences President Charles D. Walcott, 1922

Given Parnette's global reputation, a legion of media packed her press conference at the famed Fred Kavli Auditorium of the *National Academy of Sciences*. This grand 670-seat hall was reserved for the loftiest scientific symposia; it was also the venue for addresses by three sitting Presidents of the United States.

Networks from every corner of the globe sent correspondents to Washington, D.C. to cover whatever Parnette was about to unveil. A who's who of the world's preeminent scientists, as well as politicians looking to earn brownie points with their constituents, crammed the famed auditorium. Cable news stations broke into their regular programming for this prime-time media event. The world seemingly stopped to hear about the possibility of a world-changing, Earth-friendly, energy option from this famous physicist.

At nine o'clock on the dot, Parnette strutted up to the podium, her curly red hair bouncing with every step.

Parnette's PowerPoint and teleprompter flickered to life.

And so did Klaus' handiwork.

At first it was invisible.

Parnette's first screen came up – an image of a gorgeous sunrise superimposed with the words: "Free energy for all. Antimatter energy cells will rid the world of the shackles of fossil fuel."

Parnette started, "Welcome scientists and colleagues – and citizens of the world watching from home. Tonight will be truly historic. A moment that will be recalled for generations. The moment that we turned the corner and rid ourselves of fossil fuels – and began resuscitating Mother Earth from the harm we have inflicted on her. Sure, I could try to 'blind you with science' – as this is, indeed, based on heavy-duty science. But the big idea is stunningly simple."

She clicked to the next slide. A pink swirly image came up with the headline: "My inspiration: Cotton candy and clouds." Curiously, Parnette's private speaker notes stopped being visible on her laptop. She double-clicked on the appropriate tab. They were not there. She paused for a second. Then thought to herself, "No prob. I have my teleprompter. And I know this shit. Rock on, lady..."

She took an extra breath and pressed on. "Yes, cotton candy and clouds."

Chuckles were heard throughout the crowd. "Yeah, I would snicker too if I was in your seats. Please hear me out..."

"Until now, antimatter could only be produced in extremely limited quantities using extraordinary amounts of energy in billion-dollar scientific facilities. Yet did you know Mother Nature makes her own antimatter during thunderstorms? Yeah, Google it. And she's been giving us clues on how to create and contain it since time immemorial. We just never noticed."

Parnette clicked to the next slide. A beautiful blue sky with puffy clouds appeared.

"Clouds are fractals. Fractals are structures that look the same at all scales. Cotton candy isn't scientifically a fractal structure. However, it got me to thinking about creating a fractal-based containment field, like a cloud, that could contain – in fact, under the right circumstances, help create – significant quantities of antimatter particles."

Parnette clicked to the next slide. A green-glowing hourglass shape appeared.

"Yes, you heard me right: Spontaneously created antimatter. Using my discovery, a fractal field would create a *controlled* cascading reaction that would – on its own – create more and more antimatter. And do so at room temperature. Yes, room temperature! In the span of just a few microseconds, stasis – that is, stability – would be achieved. I could literally hold in my hand a container of antimatter that could power the entire Eastern Seaboard of the United States for a month. And my research proves it out. Let me show you..."

Parnette clicked to the next slide. Instead of her intended split-screen image of the green-glowing hourglass on the left and a graph of energy and temperature on the right, a full-screen close-up photo of a clown's face appeared!

Aghast and speechless, Parnette stared at her laptop monitor. Then she turned behind her to see what image was being presented to the audience on the wall-sized display. It was the same image of a clown. But now upside down!

"Someone has messed with my slides!" Parnette screamed.

Before Parnette could even try to click to the next slide, the slides started to advance on their own. An animation appeared with a clown's red nose growing to full screen, morphing into a red bouncing ball.

Parnette screamed in horror, "No, no, no, no, no!"

The entire room's attendees began laughing as Parnette manically clicked her mouse and banged her fists on the keyboard.

Her eyes darted between the presentation screen and the two teleprompter screens. She saw the words Katy Ball, Katy Ball, Katy Ball, Katy Ball scrolling up the screens at a ridiculous rate.

Parnette screamed "I am not Katy Ball!"

Her mind uncontrollably swirled, as if she was in the center of a mighty vortex. She flailed her arms outward, like a bird caught in a hurricane. Parnette's eyes rolled upward and she passed out – crumpling to the floor.

Watching on TV, Kilborne smiled his evil Grinchy grin and took another puff from his cigar.

CHAPTER 18

Parnette was under 24/7 psychiatric care for many months. For some time, she couldn't even feed herself. Nurses, aides, and even Parnette's sister took turns spoon-feeding her at the rehab center.

The term "nervous breakdown" gets commonly tossed about. But that's what occurred: Parnette's brain, basically, short-circuited.

It took five weeks before Parnette spoke her first words – "see Dorothy" – a reference to her beloved niece. Parnette's eyes brightened when her sister brought in Dorothy for a visit. Yet, when Dorothy asked her mom "Why can't auntie talk?" despair could be seen in Parnette's tightly pursed lips as she tried to fight through the barrier in her brain.

***

Parnette's recovery remained painfully slow. It took a full two months before she could fluidly converse again with her family and her care team. She began to regain reasonable motor control – feeding herself, walking with a walker, and using the bathroom without assistance. Parnette desperately wanted to regain her independence, but out-of-the-blue tremors – primarily with her arms – set her back a few times. The doctors eventually deemed her well enough to be moved to 24-hour in-home care.

Once she was in familiar surroundings, her recovery began to pick up pace. Three times a week she had scheduled play time with Dorothy. With supervision, she was able to cook for herself. Despite this progress, she still couldn't cross the mental threshold of using a computer. In fact, one day when she was helping her in-home assistant put away laundry,

Parnette saw the home assistant's computer tablet sitting on top of the basket of folded clothes. When Parnette moved the tablet to get to the clothes underneath, the jostling lit up the screen and the aide's paused game of flying pigs restarted – accompanied by a wacky blare of oink-oink sounds. Parnette dropped the tablet. And vomited.

***

It took Parnette many months to get to a functional stage of reboot.

Seven months after the on-stage event, her visceral aversion to computers finally abated. Parnette was also well enough to visit her colleagues at Princeton. Her walking had largely returned, but not for long distances. So, propped in a wheelchair, her sister wheeled her through the halls of her old department; fellow professors and their staff had decorated Parnette's old office with *Welcome Back!* balloons, and a variety of cards and notes were pinned to her office walls.

A few of her closest university colleagues greeted her, though no big fanfare. Frankly, a sizable fraction, perhaps even the majority, of the Princeton staff felt uncomfortable being seen with a person who many in the scientific community now labeled as a kook.

Parnette's desk was largely as she left it. A note pad with a few of her hand-written items was sitting just above her mouse pad. On the top page she spotted a circled scratching – "Nat Acad Sc" – and, with that, she visibly gulped. But she managed to hold herself together.

***

After significant petitioning by her family and psychiatric and medical teams, Parnette was able to keep her university professor title. Although there was no commitment from Princeton as to any schedule for upcoming classes or lectures. Truth be told, there were quiet discussions in the upper echelons of the university whether she should be asked to formally leave.

***

By the end of the year, with more family and medical lobbying, Princeton begrudgingly allowed Parnette to restart her research. She had to check in weekly with the Dean and she had significant restrictions regarding access to *TIGER*.

A big milestone was achieved when Parnette retook and passed her driving exam. Her license had been suspended during her extensive medical care. Parnette had to prove to the state's motor vehicle department that she was mentally and physically capable of safely handling a motor vehicle. It had been a very long road – literally and figuratively – from the disastrous event in D.C. to some basic semblance of independence.

Shortly thereafter, Parnette was allowed to run experiments at the Relativistic Heavy Ion Collider (RHIC) at the Brookhaven National Laboratory on Long Island, New York. The facility was only a two-and-a-half-hour drive from Princeton. Parnette was able to get a couple of days of research done at Brookhaven between her weekly medical check-ins. Most important to Parnette, she was able to build in side trips to spend time with her niece.

Unbeknownst to anyone, through a VPN on her laptop, Parnette also slipped in blips of time on the Dark Web, a cloaked section of the Web that is not indexed by search engines.

At Brookhaven and the RHIC, Parnette was like a kid in a candy store. High-energy particle physics was her mental playground – and continued therapy. It was the first time anyone had seen Parnette smile in quite a while.

A welcome fringe benefit of the RHIC was its Instrument Division. It was replete with state-of-the-art fabrication facilities, and Parnette took full advantage of those. The staff enabled prototyping of Parnette's computer-modeled cylindrical structures, adding a real-world activity to Parnette's imagination.

In between prototyping small items, Parnette explored a newfound passion – nanobots – microscopically small robots, just nanometers (billionths of a meter) in size. Recent breakthroughs in robotic manufacturing turned these once science-fiction creations into actual programmable servants, with early hints of autonomous behavior.

Just two months prior, a major university demonstrated the ability of nanobots to be inserted into the bloodstream of a mouse with genetically induced cancer; the nanobots navigated to the cancer cells and destroyed them. A private company pushed the boundaries further in its experiments with livestock, attempting to get these micro machines through the blood-brain barrier to treat and repair brain diseases at the molecular level.

Parnette was fascinated by all aspects of the world that were too tiny to see, and she en-visioned nanobot applications that would boggle even the most seasoned science-fiction writers.

***

To everyone's great relief, Parnette no longer evangelized her pie-in-the-sky visions for antimatter energy. In fact, no one could remember the last time she even uttered the word "antimatter" in conversation with anyone. It appeared as though that portion of her brain was excised by her nervous breakdown.

From everyone's perspective, Parnette slowly but surely became her normal, brilliant self again. She remained passionate about scientific research, albeit now a little more in-ward focused, taking time with her family and reengagement with colleagues. Regarding the latter, as Princeton faculty heard about Parnette's gradual reconnection with reality, relationships started to mend. The stigma of being with the "kook" began to fade with the passage of time.

One slightly odd new quirk in Parnette's behavior was her newfound fascination with the cartoons she grew up with as a child. It was not uncommon for family and care staff to walk in on her while she was roaring in laughter to Elmer Fudd and Bugs Bunny and Wile E. Coyote and the Road Runner. Even in office environments, like at Brookhaven, a loud snort and a booming laugh might unexpectedly invade an otherwise quiet scientific setting. People found it cute to annoying, but largely tolerated this harmless new dimen-sion of her personality.

In April 2025, spring was in the air, and so was Parnette's rejuvenated spirit. Pleased with her work, Parnette asked her primary psychiatrist and general medical team if she could take an extended unsupervised trip: a cruise to Bermuda. They signed off. And Parnette set sail.

CHAPTER 19

Parnette enjoyed her time in Bermuda. Over the course of two days on the island, she took part in popular tourist activities, including a visit to both the National Museum and The Arts Centre, a stroll along Horseshoe Bay, a ferry over to the City of Hamilton, and the mesmerizing geological destinations of Crystal Cave and Fantasy Cave. Her soul felt replenished. Parnette particularly enjoyed walking around without being recognized.

As she was about halfway up the gangway of the ship to embark on the voyage home, she took a reflective pause – walking to the side railing to let others pass by. She looked out over the historic Royal Navy Boatyard to take in the sights one more time and capture them in her memory.

***

The cruise ship was well on its return journey to the Port of New York. Standing on her stateroom's balcony, Parnette was enveloped by the beautiful starry evening and the hint of salt spray in the warm pulses of sea air; her curly locks bounced in a rhythmic dance with the sounds of the ocean waves. She felt wonderfully – spiritually – alive.

Parnette looked up at the stars, studying them like a navigator of times past. She looked at the GPS coordinates displayed on her smartwatch. "Yep," she said to herself.

Parnette opened her carry-on bag and removed a cylinder about the size and shape of an ordinary work thermos. In fact, it was disguised as a thermos in the odd chance it was inspected when she boarded in New York. She smiled at the vinyl label she printed and wrapped around the fake thermos. It was an image of the characters from the Road Runner and Wile E. Coyote television cartoons. In this particular image, the Coyote had smugly grabbed the Road Runner by the neck – with a caption that read, "Beep-beep your ass!"

Parnette unscrewed a mating fake component, a plastic cup at one end. She placed the cup in her carry-on bag. She then gave the cylinder's inner cap a quarter turn to the left.

Parnette looked at the object in her hand with abundant admiration and said to herself, "Not even God could stop you now."

She threw the cylinder, with all her might, into the sea.

CHAPTER 20

B y mid-next day Parnette was on I-95, the New Jersey Turnpike, driving back to her New Jersey home – fully refreshed and upbeat.

A timer on her smartphone began to beep. The phone was sitting on the passenger seat. Parnette reached over and casually tapped the phone's screen to silence the alarm.

She turned on the dashboard radio and pressed a pre-set to tune in a New York AM news station. The newscaster was in the midst of a routine traffic report.

The radio station suddenly turned to static.

CHAPTER 21

April 17, 2025

A mammoth explosion – later determined to be about one-twentieth of the magnitude that wiped out the dinosaurs – occurred in the Atlantic Ocean, midway between Bermuda and the East Coast of the U.S.

The resulting electromagnetic pulse "EMP" instantly knocked out communication networks halfway around the world and severely disrupted most others. Power grids along the Eastern Seaboard of the U.S. and in Bermuda violently arced in lightning-like displays – then electrically collapsed. Regional satellite links failed. The Internet, even though designed to be fault tolerant due to its inherent pathway redundancy, failed from Maine to Florida – and inland for a couple hundred miles. It was also disrupted, island wide, in Bermuda.

Commercial aircraft that were over the Atlantic and within 100 miles of the source of the EMP had unrecoverable technology failures and plummeted into the sea; those flying up to 1,200 miles from the source had sudden but, in most cases, recoverable losses of power and navigation.

Scientists and governments scrambled to grasp the scope of the cataclysmic circumstance. The scale was largely unknown, with satellite "eyes" inhibited due to disabled communication links. Even so, within 30 minutes of the event, best-guess tsunami warnings were issued by the functioning tsunami-warning centers, including the National Tsunami Warning Center (NTWC) based in Palmer, Alaska.

Without tangible data, the wave predictions were well underestimated.

Unknown to all, the waves that traversed the ocean were between 90 and 110 feet high and traveled at hundreds of miles per hour. Due to the complete disruption of communications, ships within a couple-hundred miles of the event's epicenter were entirely blind to the oncoming wavefront. It didn't matter. Ships of every size – commercial and military – were already doomed.

Scientists had never fathomed such an enormous and spontaneous release of energy. Previously, the worst theorized case was an asteroid impact. However, any approaching sizable asteroid would be detected and prepared for – years prior – by NASA's Near-Earth Object Program. Even the simultaneous detonation of a hundred nuclear bombs would fall well short of the energy that jolted the planet.

Amateur "ham" radio operators were the first to spin-up emergency equipment after the EMP took out regional commercial communication systems and networks. These radio enthusiasts heard the worldwide-broadcasted reports of the circumstance – and the stated dangers regarding the approaching tsunamis – and did their best to relay warnings to their colleagues in the likely impact zones. The hams in those zones further passed along the information as quickly as they could to local government officials and emergency services. Some radio amateurs in the immediate coastal areas of the U.S. and Bermuda literally ran down the street, shouting about the impending danger to neighbors like modern-day Paul Reveres.

In the hours that followed, tsunamis made landfall throughout the North Atlantic. The results were tragic. From residential flooding alone, over 7,000 residents of Bermuda lost their lives as did 21,500 along the U.S. East Coast. In the days that followed, it was determined that over 3,720 automobiles were swamped by the tsunami, 17 commercial and military ships were lost at sea, four passenger trains and three freight trains were derailed, and nine commercial and three military planes were downed – taking the lives of 27,900 more.

***

Scientists were universally perplexed as to the cause. There was no nuclear "mushroom cloud" or any evidence of a nuclear event. There was no incoming asteroid. Some scientists speculated that the Earth had collided with a black hole, yet there were no associated traces of such in the atmosphere. Another theory that took hold for a few weeks was a super-massive fissure from the Earth's core; the notion was later dispelled when no residual molten materials were detected in the ocean.

There was also the inevitable craziness, such as it being the prelude to an alien invasion – and this was a "warning shot" to entice humankind's surrender. Religious parallels and prophecies ran rampant.

***

It took a few weeks to repair and reactivate the bulk of the U.S. power grid. Bulldozers and snowplows were put to work to move mountains of mud from roads and neighborhoods. It was a mess and a tragic loss of life. But it paled in comparison to what happened to Bermuda.

The average elevation above sea level in Bermuda is 125 feet. The tsunami was estimated to have been 95 feet high when it hit the island. Much of Bermuda was swamped by a wall of water, flooding entire towns and communities in minutes, resulting in a loss of almost 11 percent of the island's 64,000 residents. The world came to the rescue as best as it could; 43 countries provided rescue flights and ships, emergency personnel, mobile medical units, food, water, sanitation, and more. As a proportion of citizens lost, it may have been the worst single-territory humanitarian disaster ever recorded.

***

While scientists struggled to explain what occurred, the media – worldwide – was in hyperdrive. Regular programming was canceled and replaced with 24-hours-a-day coverage. There were wall-to-wall interviews, credentials be damned, of anyone willing to be in front of a camera and mic. From politicians, to scientists, to self-proclaimed mystics spouting end-of-the-world scenarios, the speculation was without bounds.

In the weeks that followed, the media dubbed the calamity "The Bermuda Event" – due to the island's disproportionally tragic loss of life. Ultimately, once the global scope of the disaster became clear, the world simply began calling it "The Event."

The Event triggered a repetitive series of earthquakes around the globe. Long inactive faults were jostled into activity. Even relatively geologically quiet regions, like New England, became infused with regular micro temblors for weeks, resulting in pulses of minor damage and general public irritation. That is, until just shy of two months after The Event.

On June 13th, the Clinton-Newbury fault in Massachusetts let loose and a 6.9 magnitude earthquake brought down numerous buildings along the near-100-mile fault. A total of 27 lives were lost in Newbury, West Newbury, and Worcester.

In a bizarre twist, the massive tectonic shift in New England had one unlikely positive outcome. As the story goes, little Cindy MacDonald, four years old at the time, was brushing her teeth before bedtime.

"Mommy, I can't get these sparkles out of my mouth!" she yelled to her mother who was preparing Cindy's bed down the hall.

"What are you talking about, darling?" Rebecca MacDonald asked her daughter as she walked back into the bathroom.

"See mom. See!" Cindy pointed to the gold-colored sparkles that were lining the porcelain bathroom sink.

It turned out that the MacDonald's 1947 cape-style home in West Newbury had a 185-foot-deep well into an aquifer that intersected a portion of the Clinton-Newbury fault. The family's notoriously "hard water" was saturated with genuine specs of gold.

Gold is rare in New England. Although there were a few mining operations over the years, the geology never supported significant operations. Still, the earthquake-disturbed fault turned the MacDonald's well-water system into spigots of treasure.

The publicity surrounding the MacDonald's valuable windfall created a mini "gold rush" of sorts, with professional and wannabe prospectors vying for public and purchasable land. But no millionaires – other than the MacDonald family – were minted by the activity.

***

The world was literally rocked by The Event. And no one knew the cause. Well, one person did.

CHAPTER 22

Global financial markets were closed for over a month. Regulators gradually brought them back online over the next few months, as public tensions began to subside and businesses started to ramp back up.

Oil markets are especially sensitive to uncertainty and were notably hard hit. Persistent rumors that The Event was actually the test of an unknown country's new weapon kept this market on edge, driving up oil and gasoline prices to levels never before recorded.

Doomsday speculations and "end of the world" prophecies wove through social and public media. The unknown cause kept everyone on edge; the fear it could happen again was embedded in everyone's psyche.

On the four-month anniversary of The Event, world leaders – even perpetual adversaries – met at a global summit in Geneva. A joint proclamation of "One World, Together" was issued, as was a plea for the world's citizenry to press forward in unison. In a strange way, the world became more politically cohesive and stable than it had been in centuries. No one expected the rosy relations to last forever. Though, for a moment in time, the world had a common essence of solidarity.

The global community pledged to continue to help rebuild Bermuda as well as assist with restoration efforts in the affected coastal communities in the U.S.

Commerce began to return in earnest. Oil and financial markets stabilized. Regional and international travel started to resume regular schedules and services. It was a strange time, to say the least. A wisp of unknown never entirely left the collective consciousness. But a new fabric of global resilience was born.

CHAPTER 23

August 19, 2025   2:00 a.m.

In a dimly lit parking lot, a dark-dressed figure slinked between parked trucks. *Clink.* The sound of a magnet grabbing metal. The shadowy figure vanished.

CHAPTER 24

*A*ugust 21, 2025

As were all the world's luxury liners, the Cosmos Megaliner had sat in port since The Event.

Cruise lines kept juggling their schedules and itineraries, so they would be ready to set sail the moment the public was game.

When the gathering of world leaders was announced three weeks prior to the actual global summit, the Cosmos Megaliner's booking department took a leap of faith and contacted previously scheduled cruise customers – and set a date for its next sail: August 21, 2025. To the company's pleasant surprise, the staterooms quickly booked and the cruise completely sold out in less than 48 hours from the announcement.

***

With the public determined to find fun again, the mammoth ship set sail from PortMiami on a multi-island adventure.

CHAPTER 25

*A*ugust 23, 2025

It was a couple hours before sunrise. Apart from a few inebriated souls aimlessly wandering the decks, it was largely quiet on the Cosmos Megaliner.

In about 90 minutes the grand vessel would pull into Aruba's Port of Oranjestad.

A careful ear passing stateroom 6713 might have heard the feverish clicking on a laptop's keyboard, but would have no idea of the world-changing events that churned just feet away.

4:00 a.m. *Click. Click. Click.* A transfer of $3.5 million in bitcoin was made on the Dark Web.

4:15 a.m. Via the Dark Web, the following simple message was sent: Malbo. Go.

4:30 a.m. The following commands were sequentially typed, relaying instructions to a remote computer:

Engage Zeus

Engage failsafe

Engage k-puff

Engage bot-1

CHAPTER 26

The Cosmos Megaliner had been in port for six hours. Just about everyone had disembarked to explore the "One Happy Island" of Aruba. But not Parnette. Buttoned up in her stateroom, she was engrossed in the content on her laptop.

***

To save costs, Kilborne's megaliner contracted security personnel at each port, a security hole that Malbo exploited in Aruba. He simply paid them off.

The four replacements had no problem making their way onto the ship. They lugged in their touristy bags an assortment of weaponry – semi-automatic guns, grenades, and other fighting gear – as well as an assortment of telecommunications equipment.

Following the information on the ship-issued IDs, and guidance from the compromised security personnel, they made their way to the staterooms of the deceased passengers and prepared for the next steps in their plans.

CHAPTER 27

Seattle, Washington   Technology Junction Office Park

Ding. The third-floor elevator doors opened and Skippy Calhoun nearly stumbled out. A sophomore at The University of Washington, Calhoun had a little too much enjoyment with his buddies the previous night – and was now paying the price.

Calhoun wove in various part-time work to help pay for his room and board. This morning he was a "betweener" for Z100Z LLC, a start-up delivery company based in Seattle. As a betweener, Calhoun's task was to ride his eBike to pick up Z100Z packages at Seattle business offices and deposit them in a company's curbside Ztransporter.

***

The Ztransporter was Z100Z's transportation innovation, winning a "Best 100" award in *Futurist Times* magazine. Each Ztransporter was an electric, fully autonomous, and tiny – seven feet, bumper to bumper – highway-approved vehicle for delivering packages. It was shaped like a 60s Volkswagen Beetle, but without a front or back; it was entirely symmetrical and drove equally well in both directions. It had unlimited range; the vehicle self-charged its batteries, day and night, through a growing nationwide network of robotic charging stations. The vehicle had no seats or instrumentation, only a big bubble of interior volume. Packages for delivery were added via a sunroof-style hatch on the top, opening and closing with a tap of a betweener's Bluetooth app.

***

Talking to himself as he emerged in the third-floor hallway, "Okay, it says the pickup spot is behind the...*palm tree*? *What*?" Calhoun questioned himself as he scrolled through the pickup instructions on the company's tablet. He walked to his left about twenty feet and didn't see anything that resembled a tree. He pivoted and walked in the opposite direction, past the elevator doors and towards a number of other offices.

Just when he thought the tablet's information was faulty, as it wouldn't be the first time in the company's *Version 3* app, he spotted a leafy something at the end of the hall. He quickened his steps and, to his surprise, under a skylight was a potted indoor palm tree. And, as was indicated on the app, a box – about a foot in all dimensions – was tucked behind the tree's terracotta planter.

Calhoun nudged the planter and its tree away from the wall a few inches and grabbed the box. Given the chunkiness of the box, he expected something heavy. On the contrary, it was featherlight. "Huh. What are they shipping...air? No matter. Easier on my back."

Within a couple of minutes, Calhoun was down the elevator and out the front door. By the curb was one of Z100Z's trademark florescent-green Ztransporters that had parked itself while Calhoun was in the building. "At least the day is starting off on the right foot." Calhoun tapped the *Open Sesame* icon on the tablet and the vehicle's top slid open. He placed the cube-shaped box into the interior, pressed *Close Sesame*, and the vehicle sealed itself up.

A sparkly line of red light draped the package. The scanning software automatically confirmed the successful pickup and the item's delivery destination: *Kilborne Ranch & Estates, ATTN: Patrick J. Kilborne, 1 Wildhorse Way, Eldorado, TX 76936.*

The Ztransporter autonomously powered up and darted off to its next package pickup spot.

CHAPTER 28

Aruba's alluring sunshine and perpetual tropical breeze were in full glory that day. A perfect morning segued to a glorious afternoon. The Cosmos Megaliner's passengers explored the magnificent island, mostly by guided tours coordinated by the cruise line.

Aruba is a true gem in the Caribbean, providing visitors with a welcoming blend of vibrant culture and natural beauty. Renowned for its "One Happy Island" mantra, the island embodies warmth, hospitality, and the charm of local culture. Pristine beaches and crystal-clear waters offer an idyllic setting for both relaxation and adventure. And, because of low unemployment, a stable government, and a well-tuned law enforcement system, it has historically been one of the safest islands in the world.

As the day melted away, tourists lined the beaches as well as the starboard side of the cruise ship to witness what was anticipated to be a glorious sunset.

A beautiful orange ball was slowly swallowed by the ocean. As the last shimmer of sunlight turned the corner on the sea, an emerald-colored burst of light occurred. "Oohs" and "aahs" percolated through the many congregations of tourists, as they were treated to the rarest of rare sunsets: one culminating in a *Green Flash*.

Dusk turned to darkness. A moonless starlit night emerged.

CHAPTER 29

It was about 11 p.m. and a pair of recreational scuba divers prepared for a particularly fun night dive. The local dive shop mentioned that a bioluminescent algae bloom, a rather rare occurrence for Aruba, had been spotted in an equally unusual place: just south of the docked cruise ships in the Port of Oranjestad. The Port Authority wasn't keen on divers meandering anywhere near the mammoth ships. But that rarely dissuaded underwater adventure seekers.

The divers, fins in place, stood at the water's edge of Governor's Bay. They checked the GPS coordinates on their wrist-strapped dive computers: 12.51513 degrees North. -70.03491 degrees West. The exact location suggested by the dive shop. The last known spot of the bioluminescence display was a couple hundred yards straight into the bay.

The New Moon made the perfect opportunity to experience the underwater phenomenon.

The divers did their final gear checks. They tightened the straps on their buoyancy compensator devices – or BCDs – vest-like jackets that can be inflated or deflated to adjust a diver's buoyancy. The divers looked at their air-pressure gauges to confirm their scuba tanks were full. 3,000 PSI. All good. They took breaths from their regulators to make sure they were functioning properly.

Everything in order, the divers pressed inflator valves on their BCDs to puff them up with air from their scuba tanks. The divers clicked on their hand-held dive lights and strode into the warm Aruban water. Once waist deep they tipped to horizontal and began to kick in the waters of the calm bay.

To conserve the air in their tanks, the divers used their snorkels to swim on the surface. After seven minutes of light kicking, they paused and checked their dive computers. Presuming to be over the spot described by the dive shop, they clicked off their dive lights. The divers pressed the air-relief valves on their BCDs and, feet first, slowly sank into the warm embrace of the bay.

The tiny glow from their computers and gauges gave the divers visual cues of one another. Even with hundreds of dives under their belts, the divers knew to keep within arm's reach of each other – especially in the almost non-existent light. Divers learn, early on, that the most dangerous creatures in the sea are humans. Healthy respect of the water, common sense, a solid dive plan, and well-practiced "buddy diving" are paramount to safely enjoying the sport.

As the divers slowly submerged, their subtle stabilizing hand motions and light kicks to control their descent triggered the microscopic sea creatures into a dazzling display. The divers were immersed in a giant cloud of living glitter, a glow so intense that the divers could see each other's smiling eyes in their masks. Even the bubbles rising from their scuba regulators shimmered with magical sparkles.

The mesmerizing light of a bioluminescent algae bloom is the result of a natural chemical called luciferin reacting with oxygen and an enzyme called luciferase. When luciferin undergoes a chemical reaction with oxygen in the presence of luciferase, it produces light. Evolution has endowed numerous organisms with bioluminescence for various purposes, including for attracting mates, frightening predators, and luring prey. Lightning bugs, or fireflies, are one of nature's most-observed bioluminescent creatures; their characteristic flashes are intrinsic to their in-flight courtship rituals.

The divers removed their tethered smartphones, encased in clear waterproof pouches, from the pockets of their BCDs. They snapped no-flash photos of the phenomenon, counting on the high ISO setting of their phones to capture the pulsing illuminated cloud.

The divers were about 25 feet deep. At this relatively shallow depth, the thousands of pounds of compressed breathing air in their scuba tanks would last more than an hour. Scuba divers know that "bottom time" – that is, the amount of underwater time – is inversely proportional to the depth of the dive. The deeper the dive, the greater the volume of compressed air is delivered through the divers' regulators to compensate for the increasing water pressure. Non-divers are always amazed to learn there is absolutely no sensation of water pressure, even at great depths, as air regulators deliver compressed breathing air at precisely the ambient water pressure.

For over half an hour, the divers mugged for camera shots among the dancing sparkles, as well as posed for a few selfies. Even for these veteran recreational divers, swimming with bioluminescent creatures was a rare treat. The only other time they had the pleasure of this experience was a few years prior in the famed bioluminescent Mosquito Bay of Puerto Rico.

The divers were so mesmerized by the microbial display that they did not hear the whir of an electric-motor-propelled pontoon craft traveling on the surface nearby.

When their air gauges reached 1000 PSI, the traditional low-pressure for safe diving, they knew it was time to wrap up the experience. They gave each other the thumbs up sign, what divers flash to each other when it's time to ascend. They nodded to each other and slowly began to kick to the surface. It took less than 20 seconds before they were nearly out of the water. Both divers extended their right arms above their heads; this taught safety routine prevents bumping a head on an unseen object like a buoy or boat.

When their heads emerged from the water, much to their surprise they were not alone. No more than 40 feet away was a pontoon boat with two men, facing in the opposite direction, talking to each other. The divers, startled, didn't say a word. No fishing boat would likely be out at midnight. Even though the divers were so close to the boat, they could only make out the silhouettes of the men, as they appeared dressed in black. In fact, they could only tell they were men by their voices.

"Okay, time to get rid of these idiots. Tourists. So gullible."

"The chains should keep them submerged for weeks. We'll be puffing Cubans long before then."

The two men lifted and threw overboard what looked like four long sacks of potatoes wrapped in chains.

The divers tried to stay motionless with small underwater kicks to tread water. They both knew there was some bad shit happening in front of them, and they were fearful that any sudden motion or splash would attract the deviants. It was by dumb luck they didn't pop to the surface on the other side of the boat or they would have been instantly spotted.

The men on the boat continued to talk.

"Malbo said he thinks the ship is a diversion. Who the hell knows?"

"The doc's wacked. But she pays well."

"The world will be in total chaos. We'll be long on our way back to Columbia."

"Cha-cha-cha..."

"Nah. Cha-ching!"

Belly laughs bellowed across the water.

With their dastardly deed done, the men prepared to leave. The start of the electric motor and a maneuver of its attached handle pivoted the boat in the divers' direction.

The divers gave the thumbs down sign to each other to submerge. But, as they were readying to descend, their air tanks inadvertently touched, and the sound of metal hitting metal rang out. The heads of the two men on the boat spun in the divers' direction. In an instant, the four made eye contact – and all were awkwardly surprised. For a second, no one said a word. They simply looked at each other. Breaking the silence, one of the divers said, "Howdy, pardners."

One of the men on the boat replied, "Who the hell are you two?"

"Oh, just a couple of divers taking in the plankton bioluminescence," said the other diver.

"Bullcrap!" was the reply from the other man on the boat. He pulled out a Glock 17 and said, "Get your asses over here so we can see you."

The two divers made glancing eye contact, exchanging a look that said no friggin' way. But one cooperatively said "okay, don't shoot" to buy a few seconds of time. The other diver reached into her BC pocket that was still under the water, tapped the smartphone's ON camera-flash setting through the clear waterproof pouch, and gave a *ready* look to her dive buddy. He acknowledged with a wink.

The female diver slowly took her smartphone out of the water, pointed the camera lens to the men on the boat, and repeatedly pressed her thumb on the photo icon, snapping a rapid string of pictures. The flashes temporarily blinded the men, reflexively covering their eyes. That was the break the divers needed.

The two divers flipped up and over – diving down – kicking as fast as they could towards the bottom.

The bioluminescent cloud, once a gorgeous spectacle, now illuminated their position. *Not good.* The divers were no more than 15 feet underwater when they heard a piercing metallic *clang clang*. They were being shot at – and two bullets hit one of their tanks. Fortunately, it didn't blow.

The two divers kicked with all their might straight down. They held hands, as the bioluminescent cloud faded and the sea became jet black. They didn't dare put on their diving lights, for fear of further indicating their position.

The divers paused for a second, winded; they were sucking up the remaining air in their tanks fast. They butted their facemasks together as the male diver flashed his wrist-worn dive compass inches away; the glow was enough to see each other's eyes and the compass direction. They nodded east, the general direction of the shore. They started to kick feverishly again. They glanced at their tank gages. They both now had only about 450 PSI of air remaining.

They could hear the whir of the boat's motor. Thankfully, though, no more pings from bullets.

They were down to 150 PSI in their tanks. Their rapid breathing became even more laborious as their tanks struggled to deliver air.

They paddled and pawed along the bottom, still holding hands, bumping into outcroppings of coral and rock. They didn't have to look at their air gauges anymore. They knew they were almost out of air. Yet, they didn't dare surface; they could still hear the boat's motor.

The bottom became softer, sandier, and shallower. *The shoreline.* They rammed into the bottom – face down, in two feet of water, with the surf rolling over them.

They looked back over their shoulders; they didn't see or hear anything. The divers took off their masks and spit out their regulators.

"What the frig was that!" spouted Gabriella Milone.

"I have no clue, Gabby," responded Austin Raze.

"And what the heck was 'Howdy, pardners?' We're from New Jersey!"

"I don't know. It was the first thing that came to mind."

"You crazy fool."

"Yeah, that's why you love me."

"Well, darling. Let's get the hell out of here. We lucked out and it looks like we're only a couple hundred yards from our rental Jeep. Let's get these tanks and fins off and hightail it out of here."

"Whoa, Gabs! Look at the top of your tank!"

"Shit. The neck of the tank saved my neck! That ding must be a quarter-inch deep. And that metal scrape!"

"Glancing blow by another bullet…"

"The water saved our asses. Slowed the bullets down enough to avoid a big ka-pow!"

"Or we'd be swimming with the fishes."

"Oh, crap!" Austin exclaimed as he looked down.

"What?"

"Look at my fin! Shot right through. And I paid a hundred-and-twenty-five bucks for these."

"Pretty darn close to calling you limpy."

"Not funny..."

With their gear doffed, they sprinted to the open-air Jeep, carrying and dragging everything as fast as they could – and dumped everything into the back.

Gabby hopped in the driver's seat. "Okay, where too?"

"We've got to go to the police, Gabs."

"The police station it is. It's only a couple blocks away behind the Renaissance, right?"

"Right-e-o."

No sooner did Gabby turn the key in the ignition and pop the lights on, three gunshots and loud metallic dings, in rapid succession, pierced the night.

The men in the boat spotted the couple once they got to the shoreline, and quietly followed their sprint to the Jeep.

"Dammit, Gabs. The sonofabitches are still shooting at us!"

"Bastards!"

"Get down, Austin. I'm floorin' it."

Loose dirt and rock from the waterside parking area went flying as Gabby spun the vehicle halfway around, pointing it towards the street. She pegged the accelerator pedal.

"Hang on to your shorts, hubby. The ride is about to begin..."

The Jeep grabbed the street's pavement with smoking and squealing tires.

"Yowza!" exclaimed Austin.

"Here's that rodeo...pardner!"

And the Jeep vaulted into the night.

CHAPTER 30

It was 12:48 a.m. on the Cosmos Megaliner. Most passengers were asleep. For the remaining night owls, broadcast TV service and online connectivity abruptly stopped. As part of the unfolding devious choreography, two of the four replacements – temporarily in black masks – had broken into the ship's IT center, surprising and overpowering the three unsuspecting technology staff members.

Luckily for the IT staff, the two replacements spared their lives, but only because they did not want the sound of gunshots to draw attention. The replacements bound and gagged the staff, and disabled the ship's Internet, television, and internal-network infrastructure.

They left the IT center, removed their masks, and re-assumed their acquired tourist identities.

CHAPTER 31

"It's almost 1 a.m., Gabby. The police station should be staffed around the clock, right?"

"I have no clue. There's almost no crime on this island. I can't imagine that they have a big force, anyway."

"I think the station is around the corner," responded Gabby as she wheeled down Wilhelminastraat (Wilhelmina Street). The local police station "KPA" (Dutch: Korps Politie Aruba/Aruba Police Force) came into view.

"There ya go. The lights are on. Let's see if someone's home."

"Wait – what are we going to tell them? That we were swimming with bioluminescent plankton, came across two bad guys in a boat, and they started shooting at us? They're going to think we're nuts. Or drunk. Or both."

"We'll make it a show 'n' tell. You bring your fin. I'll bring my tank."

They screeched to a stop in front of the police station. Gabby grabbed the tank by the dinged neck. Austin grabbed his fin. They walked up the front steps and pressed the button on the video doorbell.

"Hello, hello!" Austin shouted towards the doorbell.

"Bon bini," came a voice from the speaker.

"Well, maybe not," Austin responded.

"Okay. How may I help you?" said the remote voice.

"We have an emergency to report. Can we come in?"

The door buzzed and made a click. Gabby opened the door and they walked into the station. Down the hall, at a desk, they could see a police officer. A stocky fellow nearing 70 – long past the days of chasing bad guys down a street.

The officer was, at first, a little hesitant with the disheveled 40-somethings in front of him. They were both barefoot, still dressed in their one-piece "shorty" (short sleeves and short pants) neoprene wetsuits, one lugging a scuba tank and the other carrying a scuba fin. But, after a pause, he waved the odd couple towards his desk.

On the wall to the officer's left was a flat-screen TV playing an episode of *Panorama*, an investigative documentary series by the BBC.

Before the officer spoke a word, he further sized up the couple, his eyes looking curiously at their garb; the pair looked even more bedraggled than they appeared in the doorbell cam. Gabby's shoulder-length brown hair, still partially wet from the scuba adventure, was now comically blown in one direction from the romp in the open-air Jeep. It reminded the officer of Aruba's famed Divi Divi trees that lean in the same direction due to the trade winds blowing across the island. And Austin's contemporary cut sandy-brown hair was now standing nearly straight up, oddly adding even more height to his lanky frame.

Without the couple noticing, the officer quietly unclipped his gun from its holster.

"What's going on? Are you lost?" the officer finally spoke.

"Well, it's a crazy story. And, first off, we have not been drinking," said Austin.

"I'll be the judge of that," responded the officer with a wry smile. Gabby and Austin were relieved by the officer's relaxed demeanor.

Gabby said, "We were diving where we shouldn't have been. By the big in-port cruise ship. Sorry about that. When we came up from the dive, we were shot at by two thugs in a pontoon boat. Here, look at this," Gabby pointing to the ding and scrape in the tank.

"And I got some unplanned ventilation," Austin said, pointing to the hole in the fin.

"I see," said the officer, nonchalantly.

"This doesn't happen here regularly...does it?" quizzed Austin.

"Getting shot at? No, of course not. 'One Happy Island,' you know."

The *Panorama* episode abruptly stopped and a newscaster came on. "We interrupt this program for a special report."

Gabby, Austin, and the officer turned their heads to the TV screen.

The newscaster continued, "Moments ago, global news networks received a video distributed by a person claiming to be Dr. Katherine Parnette, the scientist who early last year believed she had discovered the secret to harnessing antimatter."

Over the shoulder of the BBC newscaster appeared a stock image of Dr. Parnette. The newscaster continued, "As the world recalls, Dr. Parnette and her discovery were widely discredited. A medical issue forced her from public view."

"It is important to mention that the video and its content have not been confirmed to be published by Dr. Parnette. Our technical team is examining the metadata and looking at other technical particulars of the video to determine if this is a hoax, 'deep fake,' or a genuine production."

"With that important disclaimer, let's roll the video." The newscaster nodded to the control room. The newscaster continued to look into the camera, waiting for the impromptu video to play. After a few seconds of impatient eyebrow-raising, the video started.

Parnette appeared on the screen with a steely expression, looking straight into the camera. She sat at a small table, with a bed and sliding-glass door behind her. Through the glass could be seen what appeared to be an ocean, with a smattering of waves and white caps.

With sterile delivery, she began to speak:

"Fellow world citizens. My name is Dr. Katherine Parnette. I'm a particle physicist who researches the fundamental substances that make up the universe. You may remember me from March of last year when there was, um, an *unfortunate* incident when I tried to disclose an important energy-generation breakthrough regarding antimatter.

"My presentation was sabotaged. I was embarrassed. And my life was turned upside down."

Parnette took a deep breath and continued.

"The world is at a tipping point. Climate change is nearly at an unrecoverable stage. Through my research, I have created an unlimited clean energy source that can replace all fossil fuels – at essentially zero cost. But I was set up by the scientific community – my peers – who I have since discovered are conspiring with the petroleum industry, including bastards like Patrick Kilborne. He did not cover his tracks well. His ignorant thugs left breadcrumbs throughout the Dark Web.

"My once colleagues and the fossil-fuel conglomerates have corrupted themselves. However, I will not let greed win. The future of our planet is at stake.

"I have already taken some rather drastic steps that history will, ultimately, see in a positive light. The pain will be the essence of our salvation. Suffering will be cathartic in the long run."

A strange, distant look – rolling her eyes to the ceiling of her stateroom – accompanied these last few cryptic words. She paused. Then looked back into the camera.

"When this video airs, I will have commandeered the Cosmos Megaliner cruise ship that will be docked in Aruba's Port of Oranjestad. I have posted my demands on various public document-sharing sites for the world to see.

"More importantly, I have placed a digital contract behind a firewall, and I have emailed access instructions to that contract – including secure access codes – to both the Secretary-General of the United Nations and the Deputy Secretary-General.

"I have confirmed that the emails made it through. The two of you simply must do a better job at protecting your inboxes. That sloppiness aside, you must make sure those instructions and access codes are distributed to the five permanent members on the UN Security Council – that are also some of the most-obscene polluters of our planet: China, France, the Russian Federation, the United Kingdom, and the United States.

"Within 24 hours – from precisely now – I want the digital contract signed by the leaders of those nations, agreeing that they will begin adopting this clean and free power source within 12 months and adhere to the roll-out schedule identified.

"Also, within 24 hours, so I can personally conduct further research and orchestrate the energy roll-out, I want five-hundred-million U.S. dollars in bitcoin deposited to the account specified in my contract.

"In addition, I want safe passage from this ship to a destination of my choosing.

"Your signatures on the contract will also guarantee my complete immunity from any and all prosecution.

"All in 24 hours. Tomorrow at 1 a.m. Eastern Daylight Time. Not a second more."

Parnette continued, "I will be remotely monitoring your activity in the contract. I have eyes that you cannot see.

"And why should you be motivated to meet every single one of my demands?"

With an extra-piercing stare, Parnette responded to her own question, "If my demands are not met, I will remove more than one-third of the United States from the face of the Earth."

Parnette paused to let the magnitude of her threat sink in, then continued, "How would I accomplish such a seemingly impossible feat? Remember Bermuda? That was me."

Parnette made the same awkward gaze – rolling her eyes up to the ceiling. Like a mystic transfixed on something otherworldly.

Returning to the camera, Parnette continued.

"For proof, ask your scientists to look for momentary traces of Lambda baryon particles. They should have been detected globally, simultaneous to what has been colloquially referred to as 'The Event.'"

"'The Event' reset the Earth's runaway climatological clock by six-and-a-half years. The 237-gigatons of water vapor released into the atmosphere, and the resulting enhanced reflectivity, will have the net result of lowering the average temperature of the globe by 0.2 degrees Celsius. Like I said, it's a temporary fix. Bought us a few years." With a sardonic smile, she added, "You can thank me later."

Back to deadpan, she continued, "That was purely a demonstration device, tempered for the specific purpose. The clock is ticking on the real deal. A third of the United States will disappear. So, you should be riveted on the current circumstance and my non-negotiable demands.

"Why am I picking on the U.S.? Well, I have my *personal* reasons. But, even objectively, since 1850, the United States has pumped more carbon dioxide into the atmosphere – contributing to global warming – more than any other country on the planet." Shaking her finger at the camera, she scolded, "Naughty, naughty, naughty..."

"If you try to stop me, storm the ship, or try any other monkey business, I will immediately trigger the antimatter device with my sat phone. It's on speed dial."

Parnette's video abruptly ended.

"Sonofabitch!" exclaimed Austin. "That's got to be related to the crazy dudes who shot at us!"

"It seems the two of you stumbled across some international skulduggery," responded the officer. "It's good you didn't end up...um...as 'collateral damage.'"

"Those sacks with chains we saw, they must have been bodies!" added Gabby. "So we're already talking about four murders. Who knows how many more!"

The officer's cell phone rang and he answered. "Yes, sir. Yes, sir. 30 minutes. Yes, sir. I'll be right here, sir." He ended the call.

The officer returned his attention to Austin and Gabby, "That was my boss, Captain Geerman. We have what you Americans might say is a brewing 'shitstorm.' You are right in the middle of it. He asked me to assemble our entire force here in 30 minutes. He'll be here, too. So, stay put."

CHAPTER 32

March 29, 1999. It was a Monday night and *Huskies* was rocking. The campus bar was packed well beyond its legal limit. The University of Connecticut's men's basketball team was on the cusp of winning its first-ever NCAA men's basketball championship. When the final buzzer sounded, UConn defeated Duke, 77-74 – and the bar went nuts. In that moment of unbridled euphoria, students, bartenders, even the bouncers hugged each other – whoever they were next to. Including two then-strangers, Gabby Milone and Austin Raze.

As the rapture transitioned to cheers and more slugs of beer, Gabby clinked her plastic cup of draft beer with Austin's and shouted over the din, "Holy shit! They did it!"

Austin shouted back the traditional UConn chant *"Go Huskies!"* and re-clinked Gabby's almost-empty cup.

Gabby looked to her left, then to her right, and shouted, "I seem to have lost my roommate in the chaos."

"Well, let me at least give you a fill-up," said Austin, his hazel eyes looking at the cup.

With a quite-inebriated rolling laugh, and a flick-back of her shoulder-length straight-brown hair, Gabby replied, "You're a big spender, dollar drafts and all!"

Austin playfully mocked her hair flick with a head twist to toss his ponytail.

Gabby and Austin, like everyone else in *Huskies*, were thoroughly drunk. Cheap drafts and five-dollar pitchers were pouring widely all evening.

A nearby stand-up table for two opened and Gabby motioned with a head nod to grab it. Austin shuffled five steps to his left and claimed it with his mostly full beer cup. Gabby stepped over to join him.

"If you see a girl with spiked black hair and blue-and-white face paint, that'd be Judy, my roommate."

"That combination shouldn't be too hard to find!" Austin said with a roar.

At six-foot-one and a lanky build, Austin was taller than most students in the bar, but only a couple inches more than Gabby, his impromptu drinking friend. Austin used his height advantage in the crowd to get the attention of one of the servers. He made a hand sign of gripping a pitcher handle and a pouring motion. The server nodded and spun towards the bar.

"So, who are you with?" asked Gabby.

"A roaming group from my dorm. Windham Hall. Most of us are from the same floor – the basement."

"Ha! 'The Jungle!' Gabby replied with the decades-old nickname of that area of North Campus.

"Remember the guy lying on the floor at halftime? That was Chuck. A kid in our hallway. He's always plastered before the party gets into full swing."

"Yeah, I saw him. Flat on the floor."

"A few of the guys brought him outside to get some air. I haven't seen them since. But I'd be damned if I'd miss the rest of this game. Especially how it turned out!"

"Yeah, that would have sucked!"

"By the way, I'm Austin."

"I'm Gabby. Nice to meet you."

"Same here. And here comes our beer!"

Gabby and Austin polished off two full pitchers by last call at 1:30am. Over the hours, they discovered they were both from New Jersey, Gabby from Phillipsburg and Austin from Lambertville. They were both sophomores. Gabby was majoring in marine biology. Austin in electrical engineering. Austin was on the cross-country track team. Gabby was on the women's softball team. Gabby and her roommate lived in an on-campus residence complex nicknamed the "Frats" – a stone's throw from The Jungle.

Gabby and Austin also discovered they both loved beer.

At five minutes to 2 a.m. the *Huskies'* owner flashed the lights. The bar was still about half full. Neither Gabby nor Austin re-connected with the buddies they came in with.

"I'm pretty wasted," slurred Gabby.

"I was two hours ago," Austin laughed and said with an equally slurred voice. "You're a terrible influence."

"I think it was you who offered to get me a beer!"

They both clinked their plastic cups and sucked down their last dribbles of beer.

"Can you walk?" asked Gabby.

"I was about to ask you the same thing," Austin replied. "Hey, you want to do something stupid?"

"That has to be the worst pickup line of all time."

"No, really. Something truly stupid."

"Who am I to say 'no' to a crazy line like that?"

"I have a key –"

"Yeah, yeah, to my heart."

"No, silly," Austin said, followed by a burp. "Oops. Sorry about that. What I'm trying to say is that I have a key to the observatory at the top of the Physics Building. I'm an astronomy TA. Want to take a peek at the stars?"

"You're a ridiculous S.O.B., Austin! What the heck. I accept your all-too-gracious offer."

The two staggered out the door.

Austin was a TA for Professor Harriet Dubois, the university's senior astrophysicist. Austin hit it off with Dr. Dubois after he flat-out aced her toughest exam. Austin had telescopes since he was a child. He was constantly waking his parents in the middle of the night to go out to the backyard and see "an event that won't happen again" for some long stretch of years. It became a fun, family joke.

Fortunately for Austin and Gabby the Physics Building was within eyesight of *Huskie*s. They giggled and stumbled towards the building.

Most campus buildings were locked by security at midnight. But the Physics Building also housed the campus' computer center, and all-nighter coding was commonplace. So Austin and Gabby had no trouble getting in. Although, in their inebriated state, they forgot that the elevators get turned off at midnight. They repeatedly pressed the UP button like children playing a silly game. "Crap," said Austin. "We have to climb the friggin' stairs."

"Four floors?"

"Yeah, four floors."

Drunk, they grabbed the stairwell handrails and pulled themselves up the stairs as if they were scaling a cliff by rope, finally making it to the fourth floor. Austin guided Gabby down the hall to the floor-to-ceiling, double-railing metal stairs leading up to the roof's hatchway. Austin grabbed both handrails and Gabby steadied him with a boost in the butt. "Damn, it's one of these keys," Austin laughed after pulling out a keyring from his pocket. He fumbled through all the keys before finding the one that unlocked the hatch. He pushed the hatch open and made his way up the remaining metal steps out onto the roof. He turned around and saw that Gabby had followed him up the stairs towards the opening. Austin extended his right arm down to Gabby. She grabbed his hand with her left hand and used her right to help steady herself on the frame of the roof's opening – and pulled herself up onto the roof.

"I can't believe we're flippin' doing this, Austin."

"Hey, you only live once."

Austin fumbled with his keys again but found the one that opened the sliding door to the telescope's dome. He opened the door and flicked on the red light that was used to maintain their dark-adapted eyesight.

"Welcome to my office, Ms. Gabby."

Austin pressed a button on the wall and an electric motor hummed, opening the dome and revealing the night sky. He opened a small drawer next to the telescope assembly – a side-by-side pair Unitron refractors – and popped an eyepiece into one of the scopes. "Any pick of the night sky? The request line is open," Austin asked Gabby.

"I haven't looked through a telescope since I was a child. That was my cousin Jeff's. Heck, I can barely see straight as it is."

The two of them spent the next hour peering through the telescope, as Austin buzzed the scope's positioning motors between various celestial objects. Gabby let out an audible "Oooh!" at a particularly spectacular view of the Orion Nebula.

At 3:35 a.m., Austin said, "Okay. It's getting late. Well, early. Whatever. You should get back to your roommate before she gets worried."

Gabby responded, in a relatively clear voice at this point as the beer buzz had generally worn off. "You're a true gentleman, Austin. I was thinking you were luring me here to score. I had my mace spray right here (pulling it out of her front jeans pocket) to knock you down. You're an okay guy."

"Well, thank you, Gabby. Never hanky-panky on a first date," Austin said with a smile.

"Is that what this was?"

"Well, I guess we'll see...what's in the stars."

That evening was the beginning of a blossoming friendship and romance. They married three years after college.

***

Following an internship at Earth Sea Laboratories, Gabby landed a research position at Oceanic Microbiology, Inc. She rose through the ranks at OMI and became a senior VP in the company's R&D division.

After a less-than-exciting desk job as circuit-board engineer, Austin found his passion at an early Internet startup called Flaming Trapezoid. He parlayed that experience to land a job for Motive Platypus, LLC, and ultimately headed up their AI technology development efforts.

Gabby Milone and Austin Raze: Two free spirits who met over cheap beer, a basketball game, and a telescope. *Modern love.*

CHAPTER 33

1:12 *a.m.*

President Barbara Clarkson's Chief of Staff, Barry Tebbs, was woken at his D.C. residence by the Secret Service. They apprised him of the situation as Tebbs threw on jeans, a sweatshirt, and sneakers – and rushed him two blocks, in a Secret Service Suburban, to the White House.

The Secret Service simultaneously stirred Clarkson and her husband Dale in the Executive Residence. Clarkson tossed on casual clothes, kissed her husband, and within four minutes was seated in the Oval Office.

***

1:44 *a.m.*

Tebbs rushed into the Oval Office. "Madam President, as you know, we have a major situation."

"Please, just Barb."

"Yes. Barb."

Clarkson continued, "The Secret Service played me this Parnette person's crazed manifesto. What kind of shit is this? Are we sure it is not some 'deep fake' by a foreign actor? What do we know about this Parnette?"

"Unfortunately, the situation's real. I just got off the phone with the Captain of the police force in Aruba. He said there is a ship, precisely as Parnette described, docked in their port. And Parnette's a real person. She's –"

"Wait, is she the scientist who had the TV meltdown early last year? Antimatter, or something?"

"Yes, one and the same. I remember from the press that she needed to be institutionalized. That's all I know. I have Homeland generating a report."

"Barry, this is insane."

"At least we have 23 hours to figure out this mess."

"I know it's the middle of the night, but we have to get ahead of this. I think we should stir up the Joint Chiefs. What do you think?"

"I agree. I'll put the wheels in motion. At least let's get them here over the next hour and do a full examination of the situation."

A Secret Service agent walked in and handed a note to Tebbs. He read it and commented to Clarkson, "It looks like two of your counterparts across the pond want to talk to you."

"Well, that didn't take long. I'll make those calls. Circle back when you have more info from our teams."

"Will do, Barb."

Tebbs made quick steps out of the Oval Office.

CHAPTER 34

President Barbara Clarkson, the first woman President of the United States, was elected on November 5, 2024.

Clarkson came out of political obscurity earlier the same year, with no election experience in her otherwise impressive resume.

Clarkson made a name for herself in the business world when she created *Food-X-All,* a national non-profit that helped channel end-of-day foodstuffs from restaurants and bakeries to impoverished communities. She started with a handful of participating restaurants in her home state of New York. Her wholesome charisma – combined with superb business instincts – powered *Food-X-All* to national prominence. In 2017, Clarkson was named a *Top 25 American Business Innovator* in a prominent business journal. The accolades, recognitions, and business successes, escalated from there.

2024 was the election year from hell in America. The in-fighting, investigations, wild conspiracies, and the resulting legislative logjam brought on by the two major parties had the nation thoroughly disgusted. Even normally loyal partisans began to see the upcoming November election as more like a *Saturday Night Live* skit than anything else.

During an interview on the BBC about global food disparities and her ideas for solutions, the journalist asked in passing Clarkson's opinion about the U.S. election. She simply said, "Sad." The journalist followed, "Well, why don't you run? America seems *starving* for an alternative." She got the interviewer's pun and replied off the cuff, "We certainly need to knit our country back together, a *Food-X-All* approach. But me? I don't know. A little bit of love would go a long way."

Never could she imagine that her "A little bit of love would go a long way" response would, in hours, turn into a global meme. Within weeks, petitions in every U.S. state, even in deeply "red" and "blue" states, to recruit Clarkson to run, blossomed. The band-aid that was covering the raw frustrations of a nation was ripped off. The injured soul of America was revealed.

Living in a modest two-bedroom ranch with her husband Dale and daughter Kaitlin in upstate New York, and always bicycling to and from work, this five-foot-four, mild-speaking woman captured the imagination of America.

Clarkson was most publicly comfortable in jeans and a T-shirt. Her shoulder-length brown hair was usually up in a ponytail. She exuded a natural purity. And, at 46, a youthful spark.

Editorials in coast-to-coast newspapers begged Clarkson to run. Except for a few ultra partisans, even traditionally aligned TV personalities vocalized, "Why not?" Ultimately, the groundswell made the possibility plausible to Clarkson. She threw her hat into the ring and won the election with a non-contestable wave of Electoral College votes and an overwhelming popular vote.

Just months after the election, the hand of history placed Clarkson in the gravest of circumstances. America now counted on her judgment for its very survival.

***

One of Clarkson's greatest attributes was self-awareness. She knew her strengths and deficiencies; throughout her business life Clarkson always surrounded herself with in-dividuals who completed the puzzle for the mission at hand. During her brief political campaign, she promised the country she would do the same: select the best of the best, regardless of political stripe.

Clarkson's idea of "best" ruffled a few feathers and dropped a few jaws. Never more so than her selection for Secretary of Defense.

The world was at one of the most-volatile moments in generations. The many facets of the war in Ukraine. Ongoing complexities with Russia. The China-Taiwan tinderbox. North Korea's accelerated testing of ballistic missiles. An ever-complex Middle East, including Israel's and Palestine's continued challenges, as well as high-stakes negotiations with Iran and its nuclear capabilities. Plus a smattering of hot spots, across the globe, that seemed to bubble up on a never-ending basis.

As Clarkson assembled her Cabinet, given the current powder-keg state of the world, it was not surprising the level of scrutiny that blossomed regarding her picks in foreign policy and military leadership.

She interviewed a spectrum of high-profile "brand name" candidates for Secretary of Defense. All had served in the U.S. military in extraordinary capacities in world conflicts. Many, after their years of service, became TV military analysts and thus known to the population in general. To Clarkson, they were all "too polished." She was seeking experience, of course, but also someone who wouldn't be continually checking the mirror before the camera lights went on. In short: Someone a little more raw. To her, the ideal candidate should have instincts that were proven on the battlefield and would not hesitate to tell it like it is – unvarnished – to her or anyone else.

Clarkson spent countless hours at home contemplating her choices, as well as managing a myriad of other Cabinet appointments, presidential responsibilities, and family matters.

One weekend evening, Clarkson was sitting around the kitchen table with Dale and Kaitlin. Kaitlin, a freshman at San Diego State University, was visiting during a school break. The three of them were discussing what would have seemed unfathomable only a few months prior: Their move to Washington D.C. and the White House. The complexities and permutations of change seemed nearly overwhelming.

"Mom, maybe Mr. Brassard could help," said Kaitlin. "Last summer I was over at Stacy's house; we were both talking about our upcoming school year. I told her I was nervous about leaving home. That I had never been away from home before – and that San Diego was on the other side of the country. Stacy told me her dad, Mr. Brassard, and her mom had to travel a lot due to Mr. Brassard's military work. She said she's been in five different schools in three countries, and that I would do fine. She said to look at it as a way of making even more new friends."

"Stacy gave you great advice; what a nice friend. Yes, Mr. Brassard and the family lived all over the world in his multiple military deployments. Did you know, before he retired, he was a General? In fact, a four-star General."

"No."

"He was tank commander before that, leading troops into battle during the Iraq war – that was before you were born."

"We learned about that in school."

"His tank was hit by an artillery shell. Even though he was severely wounded, he pulled his army mates out. And even with his injuries, and using only a handheld radio, he continued to oversee the battle – refusing to be extracted to a field hospital. Ask Stacy to tell you about that sometime."

"He sounds famous."

"Mr. Brassard wouldn't say that. He's way too modest. He doesn't even display his Purple Heart medal; he keeps it in a small wooden box in his study." Clarkson added, "He's a great role model for Stacy."

Kaitlin, rewinding her Mom's battle description, said "Mr. Brassard's so big. Did he have trouble fitting into his tank?" Even at 63, Brassard remained an imposing figure. A muscular six-foot-two, he resembled a retired football player who kept himself in tip-top shape long after his playing days.

"No, honey. Tanks are big, too." As she said this to her daughter, it dawned on Clarkson that she never thought about this aspect of Brassard's service before.

With her brain perked, a tangential thought popped into Clarkson's head. "Hmmm... Arty. Would he ever consider it?"

The next day Clarkson called Arthur "Arty" Brassard.

"Hey, Arty. How's it going?"

"Same old, same old for me. But you!" With fun sarcasm, "Will you ever come to the coffee shop and hang out with the gang again? Our little town has the President of the United States!"

"President-elect," Clarkson chuckled. "And I've been, well, busy."

"Yeah, yeah. I'm just busting your chops. Anyway, what can I do for you?"

"Funny you should ask, Arty. Are you sitting down?"

Clarkson pitched the idea of Secretary of Defense to Brassard. At first he thought she was pulling his leg. When he realized she was serious, he said, "You have the world of big shots to pick from. Why the heck me?"

"Precisely because you are not a 'big shot.' I'm looking for someone that'll tell it to me straight. All the time. The same whether the TV lights are on or we're sitting alone in the Oval Office." Clarkson paused. "Geez. The 'Oval Office.' It sounds insane to even say that."

"I bet. But you will do the job incredibly well."

"Not without help. I need you Arty. Can I persuade you to come out of retirement and serve your country one more time?"

"Oh, there you go, Barb. You know my weakness. My kryptonite. I'll do anything for America."

"Sorry to push that button, Arty. I need you. *We* need you."

***

After a long discussion with his wife, Betty, and the rest of his family, General Arthur "Arty" Brassard agreed to join Clarkson's administration as the Secretary of Defense.

Clarkson made the public announcement in the auditorium of her town's high school. Her enthusiastic, organically growing staff adorned the room with American flags and banners. When General Brassard walked in, the media's talking heads were stunned – literally Googling "Brassard" while on live TV to find out any tidbit they could about this physically large, yet largely unknown, individual. Brassard didn't have a Wikipedia page. Still the media quickly found items from old press clippings that had since been digitized and placed on the Web. Stories of Brassard's selfless, heroic, on-the-battlefield actions soon peppered the TV graphics. By the end of the day, Clarkson's choice went from anonymity to a level of admiration – well deserving for this humble, but genuine, patriot.

CHAPTER 35

A ustin and Gabby found themselves in a global maelstrom.

The two restarted their discussion with the officer as he walked back into the room.

Gabby began, "Officer...officer...sir... –"

"You can call me Sergeant Kirk. Sergeant Piet Kirk. And no *Star Trek* jokes, please," he added.

"If you make Captain," Austin squeaked in, "You won't be able to avoid them. At least not from me."

"Enough of the male bonding, fellas. We've got a big problem."

"Miss, um –"

"Gabriella Milone. Gabby would be fine. And this is my husband Austin Raze."

"Sorry, I don't have a fun nickname. 'Austy' never stuck. Austin is fine."

Kirk continued his original thought. "I just spoke to my captain, Captain Geerman. It seems the world is, all of a sudden, on Aruba's shoulders. Everything considered, we recommend that the two of you simply call it an unfortunate, but, ultimately, a very lucky night, and head back to wherever you are staying."

"I guess you're calling in the cavalry to save the day, like your cyber team, right?" asked Austin.

"Cyber what?" responded Kirk.

"You know, a special-tactics group that specializes in high-tech conflicts."

"Remember, this is Aruba. We're proud of our special units – including a riot team, coast surveillance, narcotics, even a newly formed Special Forces. We've not had a need to battle on the technology front."

"So I guess no overwhelming swarm of commandos to storm the ship, either, right?"

"You've been watching too many Hollywood action flicks, my American friend."

Gabby interrupted the back and forth. "Austin, Sergeant Kirk is right. We don't have a place here. We don't even speak the local languages – Dutch and Papiamento."

"Yeah, but we do speak *tech*."

"So what? We don't know how to disarm an antimatter bomb," Gabby replied.

"However, we do know how to stop it from going off," Austin said with a twinkle.

"What!" spouted Kirk.

"I'm pretty sure that Parnette lady said she was going to trigger the bomb with her sat phone," Austin said. "And I'm pretty sure we know how to interfere with that."

"Gerritt!" boomed Gabby.

"Yep, Gerritt," replied Austin.

Kirk followed, "Okay, you two. Stop talking in circles. What are you blabbering about?"

"Sergeant Kirk: Gabby and I are 'amateur radio' operators. Or 'ham' operators. An older hobby that's making a resurgence nowadays. Anyway, let me cut to the chase: We have a friend here on Aruba, Gerritt Hendriks, who's also a ham. He's a wiz with radio technology – even more than us. I think we can whip up a jammer to take care of that sat phone."

Kirk, becoming angry, said, "Okay, okay. I think I've had enough of you two. How do I know I am not getting played? That the two of you are not in cahoots with the crazy lady on the ship – and you were sent here as a convenient distraction? I mean, look at how you're dressed. You look like you're out of a Hollywood movie set, all torn up and stuff. I mean, bullet shots to the scuba tank? And a hole through a fin? A little overdone, don't you think? You should have stopped when your story was moderately believable."

"Whoa! Lower your phasers, Kirk," spouted Austin.

"Austin!" Gabby interrupted the sarcasm.

Kirk continued, "Yeah, I think I might keep you right here until Captain Geerman gets to the station. He can figure out what to do with you two." Kirk drew his gun. "Turn around. I have some Vulcan 'amulets' that'll fit fine around your wrists." With a sarcastic smile and a hand wave for Gabby and Austin to pivot, "With a name like mine, don't you think I grew up watching *Star Trek*, too?"

"No, wait! We can prove we're who we say we are!" Gabby shouted.

"Yeah, and I suppose you have some fake badges tucked into your water-soaked short-ies, right?" replied Kirk. "I wasn't born yesterday."

"We can do better than that," replied Gabby. "I'll hold up my arms and you'll see my cell phone tucked into the waistband of my scuba shorty. Look up a person named Penelope Durango. She works for the CIA and is a friend of ours. She'll vouch for us."

"It's almost 2 a.m. What time zone is she in?" Kirk quickly quizzed to judge the veracity of Gabby's story.

"She's in Chicago. Whatever time that is from here."

Kirk looked back and forth at Gabby and Austin, trying to assess if this was some sort of ploy. But he held a gun. So he had the upper hand, regardless.

Austin broke the silence, "Whatever you decide, sir, please do so quickly. I have to pee."

Kirk spoke up, "Okay. Arms up. No fast moves." The officer reached into Gabby's waistband and pulled out a cell phone that was still in its waterproof soft case.

"And while you're at it, I think Gabs snapped a couple of photos of those thugs. We didn't tell you that she temporarily blinded them with the flash." Glancing at Gabby, "Quick on your feet – or fins – right dear?"

"I think we left that part out. But Austin's right. I might have a couple of pics that could help. Well, at least prove part of our story. Unless you think that is part of the 'Hollywood' production, too."

Kirk unsnapped the phone case's plastic security clips, unzipped the inner-liner water barrier, and removed the phone.

"Password?" asked Kirk.

"You know, I don't tell that to just anyone."

"Password!" Kirk said forcefully, with his gun still pointed at the couple.

"You win. 31415."

"Algebra," quipped Kirk.

"Well, 'geometry' or 'trigonometry' would have won you points on a game show. Although you're on the right track."

Kirk made a few taps and the cell phone came to life.

"Okay, who did you say to look up?"

"Penelope Durango. She's in my phone as Penny Durango. Look that up."

"Penny Durango. Yeah, I see a 312 area code. A few years ago, a school buddy of mine moved to the States with his wife. They ended up in Chicago. His area code is 312."

Austin, who had remained quiet during this exchange, added, "Would we lie to you?"

Kirk was now starting to tune out Austin's peppered sarcasm.

"Okay, we're about to see if you two are going to the holding room," said Kirk, and pressed the green phone icon. He then tapped the speakerphone function.

A woman answered the phone. "Gabs! Do you know what time it is? Are you okay?"

"This is Sergeant Kirk of the police force in Aruba. Your friend is physically fine – perhaps, though, a bit of hot water, depending on your answers to my questions."

"'Sergeant Kirk' did you say? I'm half asleep. Let's assume I believe you for a second. What's going on with my friend?"

"Ms. Milone, if that's what her real name is, came into my office about 30 minutes ago, along with a fellow claiming to be a Mr. Raze –"

"Austin, her husband –"

"And further claiming they were shot at while scuba diving. They came into my office, pretty much a mess, and I'm trying to figure out if this is some sort of ruse."

"Well, I can tell you, Sergeant Kirk, Gabby and Austin are who they say they are. Of course, I can't tell you firsthand what they experienced. That said, if they told you they were shot at, I'd believe them. They are two well-known U.S. citizens – a scientist and an engineer. Google them. And they are, indeed, scuba divers. I've gone diving with them on a vacation or two."

"I see. And I suppose, Ms. Durango, you can prove who you are as well? All I have is a name on a cell phone."

Austin yelled to the phone, "He thinks this is some Hollywood creation. That he's being played."

"Enough out of you!" shouted Kirk.

Durango stated sternly, "Look, I can assure you I am who I am. And I can put you in touch with the Bureau Chief if required. If you give me a sec..." Rapid typing on a keyboard could be heard. "Well, I see, Sergeant Kirk, that your mother's first name was Madeline and that you had..." *Click, click, click...* "...a little run in with the law at 19. Shame on you regarding that liquor store."

"What the heck!" Kirk spouted incredulously.

"Hey, I would have been faster. But I had to boot up my laptop. I was sleeping – remember? Otherwise, you look reasonably clean through my INTERPOL link."

"Okay, you've proved your point, Ms. Durango. So now what should I do with your two friends?"

"I would let them do whatever they want to do."

"They claim they could build a satellite jammer."

"Hmmm... Did they say why they would want to do that?"

"Well, Ms. Durango, maybe I have some intel that you don't. You may want to turn on the TV. There's a lunatic who wants to blow up the U.S."

"I'm getting bulletins on my cell phone as we speak. And I'm getting, um, let's just say a little 'texture' via my laptop."

"Hey, can I say something here?" Austin asked. "And can you please put down that gun?"

"Gun!" exclaimed Penny.

"Only a precaution, Ms. Durango. You can't see it, but I just put my sidearm back in my holster. Mr. Raze, you may speak."

"Mighty gracious of you, sir. Hey, Penny! Crazy catching up with you under these circumstances. Sorry for the late-night call."

"No sweat, Austin. What's this I hear about a satellite jammer?"

"As you're probably getting in your stream, this crazy lady is planning to blow up a substantial portion of the U.S. with what she claims is an antimatter bomb. She claimed it was a similar device that caused The Event. She said in her distributed video that she can trigger it by sat phone. Kirk said they don't have a tech team here. I'm pretty sure me and a ham colleague here on Aruba could build a jammer. That is, of course, if you can't get a tactical team in here first. The last thing I want to do is step on any toes."

"Thanks for the SITREP (situation report), Austin. As you can imagine, I haven't yet fully plugged into my network to see what's going on from a tactical standpoint. Off the top of my head, I don't think we have a sizable footprint of agents there. Of course, I can't say."

"Of course. Or you'll have to cut my air hose on our next group dive."

"Yeah, something like that," Penny quipped back.

"I have to check to see what our appropriate assets are in the region. Quickly fly-in-able. I'll do that right after our chat here. In the meantime, I'd say press ahead with your effort. Can't hurt. And we can coordinate. If you –"

The lights in the police station went out followed by the sound of a nearby explosion that rattled the windows. Only the glow of the cell phone remained.

"What the frig was that!" shouted Gabby.

"I have no idea, Ms. Milone."

"Penny? Penny? Are you still there?" Austin shouted into Gabby's cell phone. "Crap! The cell phone connection went down, too."

"I don't believe I'm saying this," Kirk remarked. "We keep a sat phone locked up in the safe. We lose power and cell communications, from time to time, here in Aruba. Let me get it out and fire it up. The two of you can take a seat now."

"I just want to pee," replied Austin.

Kirk motioned with his head and eyes to the lavatory across the room.

***

A few minutes later Kirk emerged with the department's sat phone.

Austin said, "As you know sat phones only work outdoors. Can I bring it outside for a few minutes to finish my call with Penny?"

"I'll accompany you. My Captain should be here momentarily. I'll meet him as he gets here."

The three walked outside. Gabby lit up her phone to get Penny's number. Austin punched it in.

"Hello?"

"Hey, Pen. This is Austin. Thanks for taking the call. I'm sure the Caller ID was weird."

"You can't imagine what's going on here in the States. I'm answering everything. The whole country is lit up. Law enforcement. Media. Politicians. Like the world's coming to an end."

"I'm using the police department's sat phone. This part of the island lost power and, evidently, cell service. The outage could be wider. We can't tell."

"Sorry to be in such a rush, Austin. I have to keep this really short."

"Understood. We'll work on the jammer and call you back from this number – or from our cell phones if the service comes back online. Ping us if you'd like us to disengage. We'd be more than happy to let the pros take over."

"Sounds fine, Austin. Will do. You and Gabs stay safe. Stay away from bullets!"

"No hot lead coming this way. Promise."

"Take care."

Penny Durango hung up, attending to the unfolding danger.

CHAPTER 36

"Officer Kirk, sorry we got off to a mixed start," said Austin. "At first glance, we do look like a couple of oddballs."

"At second and third glance, too," Kirk said with a chuckle.

"We're heading to Gerritt's. I'm sure it will give him quite a stir when we arrive. He lives in Savaneta with his wife Genovese."

"We'll circle back when we have something to show you," added Gabby.

The couple bounded down the front steps of the police station, still lugging the tank and fin.

Up the front steps – with a rush in his pace – was clearly a VIP. It was Captain Geerman. Kirk, with the door still held open, ushered him in.

CHAPTER 37

The Aruba night sky was stunning. Accentuated by the darkness of the New Moon, the Milky Way spanned a wide swath of the celestial canvas, and stars pierced the inky blackness. It was a simple pleasure of nature lost in modern society and on this island paradise. Except when the electrical network ceased spreading its electrons through its wiry appendages. Like that night.

The entire island was without power. Locals shrug off these random occurrences that happened a few times a year when the power demand exceeded capacity.

That evening there was a more sinister cause. A subset of Malbo's contract soldiers had taken control of the island's main power station and disengaged the primary power distribution hub.

***

Gabby tore up the pitch-dark roads of Savaneta in their rental Jeep, heading towards Gerritt Hendriks' place. It would have been a white-knuckle ride for anyone other than Austin. For him, it was just another pedal-down drive by his lovely life companion.

The amber glow from the Jeep's dashboard had an odd way of accentuating Gabby's muscular physique. Gabby was both beautiful and ripped. She could pass for a WNBA point guard.

"I've never seen the island so dark," commented Gabby, as they whipped through another neighborhood. "It's kind of spooky."

"There aren't many streetlights anyway," replied Austin. "With absolutely everything out, it is really weird."

"Have you thought about what we are going to tell Gerritt?" said Gabby. "I mean, we're going to wake him out of a sound sleep."

"I rather doubt that," replied Austin. "If anyone on the island is dialed into what's going on, it's him. Even at this hour."

Gabby gave Austin a quick puzzled look, then refocused her attention to the road. She whiplashed a right onto Gelvanstraat; they were only a few streets away. Up a slight hill, still pedal to the metal. Ahead, to the left, was a surprising glow. Well not surprising to Austin. "See. I told you he'd be up and about."

Gabby skidded to an abrupt stop, prompting Raze to bark out, "Hey! I don't want that scuba tank launched into my head! After what we've been through tonight, it would be a pisser if an airborne tank is what did me in."

Gabby just smiled in response.

Austin and Gabby made their way up to the front of the house. The whine of a generator pierced the otherwise still night. Before they could knock, Gerritt met them at the door. "My motion-sensor said there was activity. I expected a wild dog. Not you two stray cats. And you guys look like week-old trash. What the heck is up at this hour?"

"Other than being shot at, nothing much," quipped Austin.

Gerritt invited Austin and Gabby into his home, a place the couple had been frequently on their many trips to Aruba. Gerritt's wife Genovese was sitting at the kitchen table across from a small flat-screen TV that was airing BBC bulletins and Parnette's ultimatum on a loop.

Austin and Gabby brought their long-time friends up to speed regarding the last few hours. One item after another kept the Aruban couple rolling their eyes in amazement.

"Well, it's no wonder the two of you look like a mess," commented Genovese.

Looking down at his and Gabby's bare feet, Austin said, "We haven't even had a chance to grab our beach shoes out of the dry bag."

"And now little ol' Aruba is the epicenter of this nuttiness," said Gerritt. "And you think I can help? What could I possibly do?"

"The crazy lady on TV said she could remotely detonate her device by sat phone."

"Yeah, she did," replied Gerritt.

"Well, a sat phone's downlink is L-band, right? Couldn't we modify a handheld 23cm-band radio to blare out a lot of hash? Turn it into a jammer?" asked Austin.

"I suppose so; technically, yes," said Gerritt. "I've read about mods for one of my radios that would further open the transmit frequencies." After another few seconds of thinking, Gerritt continued, "Of course, the jammer wouldn't work from here at our house. It'd have to be practically right on top of the lady's sat phone to overwhelm the downlink."

"Like how close?" Gabby asked.

"Oh, we're talking a number of feet," Gerrit responded. "Maybe a few hundred feet. Something like that."

Austin added, "We'll let the police force's underwater commandos, or whatever they're called, sneak it in. If we put the jammer in a waterproof case, or heck, even a ziplock bag, and then add a few magnets, it could stick to the side of the ship's steel hull – a tad above the water line."

"My radio theory's a bit rusty," added Gabby. "Wouldn't the ship's hull – even the surrounding water – help with the signal?"

"You're spot on, Gabby," replied Gerritt. "It becomes what's called a 'ground plane' – technically part of the antenna."

Austin added, "Of course, we'd be breaking all sorts of communication regulations. However, in the U.S., there is wide latitude when it comes to genuine life-and-death situations."

"Same in Aruba," added Gerritt.

"I can't imagine a more life-and-death situation than the lives of tens of millions of people teetering in the balance," continued Gabby.

Everyone nodded in agreement.

"Okay, then," said Gerritt. "Time to fire up the soldering iron."

The trio went into Gerritt's "shack" – the affectionate name given to the radio room of all ham radio operators – and went to work.

CHAPTER 38

2:35 a.m.

"It's like the world's on fire; our secure lines are ringing off the proverbial hook," John Quintana, Secretary of State, briefed the growing collection in the Oval Office. "The bomb is supposedly planted in the U.S. But other countries are alarmed, too, especially if the magnitude of the potential detonation turns out to be true. The Earth's entire ecosystem could be at risk. So they feel in peril, as well."

Clarkson, "How are our colleagues in Aruba handling the situation? They're in the eye of the storm."

"Barry made the hand-off to me," responded Quintana. "I ping the Aruban police force in my round-robin updates. They said the ship remains quiet. Nothing unusual."

"Strange," replied Clarkson. "Arty, your early assessment?"

Brassard replied, "We're talking asymmetrical combat on an impossible-to-conceive scale. One well-placed enemy armed, apparently, with the ability to neutralize an entire time zone."

"And..."

"War games don't account for crap like that."

"And the Joint Chiefs?"

"Hutch is on his way in."

"Thanks, Arty." Turning to Chief of Staff Tebbs, "Barry, what more have we learned about Parnette?"

"One: She is who we thought. Two: She was off her rocker for quite some time. Three: As part of her 'recovery' they let her go back to work in a high-energy physics lab."

"You've got to be shitting me!"

"I shit you not."

"Anything else from anyone?" Clarkson scanned the room. "Nothing heard, let's gather back here in three hours. 5:40 a.m. Stay close in case another shoe drops."

**

Clarkson took the opportunity to dash back to the Executive Residence. Dale was in the First Family's bedroom propped up with a pillow against the bed's headboard. He was reading a book on his tablet.

"Darling, you didn't have to wait up for me," Clarkson said to her husband.

"I could tell by the way you had to dash out of here that there was something significant brewing. Is everything okay?"

"Flip on the news. You'll get the gist of it. I'm sure it's wall-to-wall by now."

The First Gentleman grabbed the remote from the top of the nightstand and pressed ON. Sure enough, the networks were in full-coverage mode. On this particular channel, a stock photo of the Cosmos Megaliner filled the screen with a superimposed headshot of Dr. Katherine Parnette.

"Honey," Clarkson continued, as she hurriedly changed into simple business attire. "It looks like I'll be tied up for a while addressing this situation. I'm not sure what breaks I'll be able to take."

"Duty calls."

"I'm sure Kaitlin will see all of this when she wakes up. Could you do me a favor and give her a call mid-morning her time? You'll have a three-hour jump on the news."

"Will do. I'm not sure what her class schedule is today at SDSU. I'll track her down."

"As I get drawn into the whirlpool, please keep her up to speed with whatever you see on TV. That'll do."

Clarkson gave the First Gentleman a meaningful smack on the cheek and said, "Thanks, dear. See you soon."

The First Gentleman replied, "Did I ever tell you how proud I am of you?"

With an endearing smile, Clarkson replied, "Once or twice."

Clarkson left the Executive Residence to attend to the unfolding situation.

CHAPTER 39

2 *:40 a.m.*

Malbo's mercenaries, 14 in total, were in their assigned roles and positions.

The four replacements, in their lethally acquired staterooms, waited for their next instructions. Three other mercenaries maintained control of the island's main power station. In and round the port, the other contract soldiers were ready to ambush any Aruban effort to rush the ship.

Malbo and his team had infiltrated Aruba three days prior for the mission. They arrived during the middle of the night on a private ship at a long-abandoned dock at Aruba's *Isla di Oro,* now just a patch of sand, scrubby vegetation, and a smattering of mangroves. A dirt road connected *Isla di Oro* with the island's Route 1, the main thoroughfare that traverses nearly the entire 20-mile western coastline. In addition to discreet access to both the ocean and roadway, *Isla di Oro* was only eight miles south of the port where the Cosmos Megaliner was docked.

Generously compensated locals had five vehicles waiting for the mercenaries upon arrival: three SUVs, a large van, and Malbo's specially prepped faux taxi.

Well before daybreak, Malbo's team executed another essential aspect of the plan. Synchronized with their private ship's arrival, a Bell 429 twin-engine helicopter made its way to a nondescript parcel of land that was about four miles from the cruise port. To avoid radar, the helicopter flew barely 50 feet above the sea all the way from the island of Curacao – about 70-miles away. As this inbound flight was happening, two members of Malbo's team overpowered a fuel truck at the Oranjestad airport. Like clockwork, the truck rendezvoused with the just-landed helicopter and refueled the craft.

Malbo, himself, coordinated the entire affair by radio from his vehicle, which he kept parked within easy eyesight of the ship. Because the vehicle looked like any other taxi, no one questioned its presence.

Even though the ship was at the center of the brewing apocalypse, none of the passengers were aware of the danger.

CHAPTER 40

Xavier Malbo's life began in the depths of poverty in the tiny village of Buena Fuego, Colombia.

Buena Fuego was blessed with breathtaking natural beauty, including a majestic mountain range sculpting its eastern horizon. Yet, the village had also faced a history marred by drug-related crime and violence. Unemployment was a staggering forty-four percent. Access to healthcare was challenging.

Xavier's parents, Camila and Antonio Malbo, did their best to provide for him with the meager means they had. His father, Antonio, was a humble shopkeeper, and his mother, Camila, was a loving stay-at-home mom who worked part-time jobs to supplement the family's sparse income. They were a close-knit family, and despite their hardships, they cherished the simple joys of life.

However, fate had something far more challenging in store for young Xavier. Tragedy struck their family when Xavier was just nine years old. His father fell victim to a senseless act of random violence on the streets of Buena Fuego. The murder of his father shook Xavier to his core, leaving him with a deep anger at the world.

Even so, Xavier persevered. Even at such a young age, he knew he had to find a way to take care of his mother. He had to grow up faster than his village friends and leave his childhood behind. Xavier took on odd jobs, such as stocking shelves at local shops and running errands for relatives.

By serendipity, a new path arose. One errand was to pick up a dysfunctional computer at an aunt's house and schlep it to the local repair shop. While he was at his aunt's, Xavier fiddled with a couple of the PC's connectors – and brought the computer back to life.

Xavier was proud of his accomplishment, and it triggered his desire to learn more about computers. Over the next week he bartered for a beat-up laptop – and resurrected that unit, too.

His newfound aptitude quickly blossomed. By the age of 13, Xavier had mastered a wide range of computer maintenance and repair skills. He fixed broken computers for friends and neighbors, earning a modest income to help support his mother.

Life was still tough for Xavier and his mother. But a semblance of normalcy started to return. And Xavier was energized by his entrepreneurism.

When generally reliable Internet became a reality in his village, Xavier saw an opportunity to expand his horizons beyond the borders of Buena Fuego. He discovered the Dark Web, a hidden realm where his skills could be put to use on an international scale. He used the pseudonym "Zanzibar" to enter this covert world, where he found a niche enhancing the security of computer systems for clients with questionable motives.

Xavier's burgeoning expertise in cryptocurrency became his special weapon. He navigated the complex web of online transactions, providing anonymity to his clients and ensuring that his own financial dealings remained hidden from prying eyes. Crypto became his primary mode of payment, shielding him from the authorities who sought to track his illicit activities.

By the time he was 21, Xavier's computer-repair business grew from a small, home-based operation to a thriving global enterprise. He – Zanzibar – developed a reputation as one of the Dark Web's most skilled and elusive operators. His clients trusted him implicitly, knowing he could be counted on to protect their secrets and deliver results.

Xavier became comfortable operating in the gray area of the law. He was paid well, the risks were manageable, and he was able to give his mother a better life.

Then his world was turned upside down.

Like every Tuesday morning, Xavier's mother met her long-time lady friends at Café La Blanca, a friendly outdoor eatery. The group had just finished their typical, traditional fare, sharing *Tamales Colombianos*, *Huevos Pericos*, and *Arepa con Quesito*.

Without warning, a tall man in his late twenties came running down the street in their direction. He was clearly panicked and only partially dressed – a ragged T-shirt, boxer drawers, and one untied sneaker. As the runner came closer to the ladies' table, up screamed two dirt-bike motorcycles, both riders brandishing automatic weapons. The lead rider opened fire at the runner, unleashing a fury of bullets towards him and everything else along the road. The runner was struck down. So were three of the ladies at the café, one of them Camila.

The local police went through the motions to check out a few leads, but they could not find the assailants. The case faded into the tapestry of corruption and lawlessness that underpinned this small village and other troubled areas of Columbia.

The death of his mother was more than Xavier could bear. His life took a deep, dark turn.

Xavier became obsessed with finding the murderers of his mother. He turned to his computer skills to delve into the tentacles of the local crime syndicate. When Xavier convinced himself that he had uncovered the identities of the murderers, he acquired a semi-automatic weapon, all too available on the streets laden with crime. One night, Xavier staked out the assailants' regular meeting place, a hostel two blocks from the murder scene. At 2:13 a.m., the assailants emerged, about to mount their motorcycles. Steely eyed, sans emotion, Xavier stepped out from his nearby-parked car, raised his weapon, and assassinated the assailants.

Xavier surprised himself at how easy it was to take a life – and how neutral his mind was to do so. At that moment, as he drove off in his car, he decided to take his computer-centric enterprise to an entirely new plateau.

Xavier's expertise on the Dark Web quickly made him a valuable asset to criminals around the world. He was able to operate anonymously and move large sums of money without detection. He was paid by his clients in crypto, which made it even more difficult for the authorities to track him down.

Xavier continually amped up his repertoire, involving himself in a growing spectrum of illegal activities, including guns, drugs, and murder. Quite comfortable now with killing, he also became a mercenary for hire, leveraging his computer skills to efficiently and clinically take care of "business" anywhere requested.

By the time Xavier turned 30, his crime syndicate was a well-oiled machine. He had a network of informants, contacts, and henchmen on multiple continents. He was able to get his hands on any contraband he wanted, and he had no qualms about using violence to achieve his goals.

"Zanzibar" became synonymous with ruthlessness and the unstoppable ability to get the job done.

Poverty. Fate. Anger. Despair. The combustible elements that birthed a life and career anchored by rage.

CHAPTER 41

2:55 a.m.

The groan of a diesel generator broke the night's silence as it provided emergency power to the Oranjestad police office.

Hans Croes, Director of Aruba's Special Forces Division, arrived after briefing his team in Santa Cruz, the location of the island's police headquarters. He was huddled around a small table with Captain Geerman, and within eyesight of Kirk and his centralized desk.

Tomas Geerman, 67 years old, had the weather-worn face of an island local. He rose through the ranks during his 42-year career – from beach patrol in his 20s, to the Lieutenant who oversaw the Spicer double homicide in the 90s that attracted worldwide attention, to his current post. He had seen his share of smash and grab, petty theft, and the infrequent home break-in. In general, the "One Happy Island" kept his career mainly pedestrian for a person of his title.

Croes was a stocky, virile, go-getter. He recently turned 33 and came to Aruba four years back with his then fiancé Helene from their native Amsterdam. He made a name for himself in the Netherlands as a hard-ass cop that pushed the boundaries of local law. His approach to police work rubbed a few of the politicians the wrong way and he was regularly reprimanded – even publicly. When Helene suggested "a change of scenery," Croes explored a few options. Around the same time, Geerman was in the process of enhancing his Special Forces team, given the rising incidence of drug traffic through the harbor. Croes answered an online job posting. Three Zoom interviews later, Croes was hired as the Director. And Helene was happy to upgrade her beach time.

"What the hell are we going to do about this Parnette?" Croes spat.

"The Americans said 'they're working on it' – whatever that means," responded Geerman.

"We have this crazy bitch in our port ready to blow half their country into the sea.
Yeah, I bet they're working on it." Croes paused, then continued. "So how do you still
have phone service?"

"We don't. Well, not really. We have a tower on the roof that ArubaTeleco keeps piped
into some sort of satellite dish. To be honest, I don't know how it works. At least it gives
our building off-island connectivity."

"And that's how you heard from the Americans?"

"Yeah. Funny how an international crisis bumps up our priority. On most days, I can't
get through to the American Department of Tourism. Now I'm getting calls from the
White House."

"The White House?"

Before Geerman could respond, the phone rang.

"There's your answer. Excuse me..."

Geerman picks up the phone.

"Yes. This is he. Yes. We can do that. Yes. Yes. We will. Indeed. Good luck."

"That was the Americans?"

"Yes, no less than the U.S. Secretary of State, John Quintana."

"So what do they want us to do?"

"Well, pretty much nothing. They said keep an eye on the ship and report anything
unusual. And don't rattle any cages."

"I don't like sitting by, twiddling our thumbs. Parnette's using our country as a base
for her international terror."

"I agree, we need to be proactive," said Geerman. "You know, something doesn't feel
right to me. Why did Parnette choose Aruba? Why the middle-of-the-night broadcast? It
could be a head fake. Some sort of misdirection. Perhaps we can get someone onboard to
sniff things out."

"How about we just take her out?"

"How so?"

"Parnette may be crazy –"

"You think? –"

"But probably not stupid. She won't hang out over a balcony on the port side, where a sniper could take her out from town. I bet she has a starboard stateroom, overlooking the harbor. She'll have a clear view of the sky...and, perhaps, a false sense of security."

"How so? Harbor traffic is stopped. It's just water on that side."

"Well, not exactly. What if we get a sniper onto the breakwater? Captain Geerman, you know the channel way better than me. Is it possible?"

"The breakwater is almost entirely underwater. Although only by a few feet. As a kid, we would scramble along it when the tide was right."

"How far would you say it is? From the side of the ship?"

"Hmmm...perhaps 1,000 meters? That would be a heck of a shot. Do we have a sniper of that...caliber?"

Ignoring the pun, "I have Niels Brouwer at the ready."

"I thought Hans Kuiper scored the best at our recent training camp?"

"Kuiper is off-island. Visiting family in Amsterdam. Brouwer is right up there. The team saw him skewer a coconut at 800 meters. Twice."

"Well, the redheaded 'coconut' is coco-loco," replied Geerman.

"How about we assemble a two-tiered strike force at, say, Sunset Bistro at Governor's Bay? A team of three, including Brouwer, on a generic fishing boat circling around past the harbor's eastern exit. I'll stage seven others, armed to the gills – ha – ready to make a frontal assault if all hell breaks loose."

"In a couple of hours the sun will be coming up. How quickly can we get Brouwer in place?"

"Let's get the team ready to roll at the Bistro by zero six thirty. Given the round-about course to the spot on the breakwater, we can have Brouwer in place by seven. Then we wait. Perhaps you'll get some intel from the Americans. I'm sure their data geeks are combing through the passenger manifest. There's got to be hundreds of starboard staterooms."

"There's one other wildcard, but I doubt it will pan out."

"What's that?"

"Kirk told me about two American citizens who were – get this – shot at by Parnette's accomplices. They were doing a night dive. Wrong place, wrong time. They came into this office a few hours ago with cellphone photos and damaged scuba gear."

"So what's the 'wildcard'?"

"They have a high-placed friend in the CIA."

"More shit to contend with."

"It gets worse. They're, evidently, technology geeks and are off, right now, supposedly building a 'sat phone jammer'?"

"For what purpose?"

"They think they can jam Parnette's sat phone."

"Oh sure. And I have a pocket laser that'll boil the ocean. Let them go play with their techno toys. We have a real job to do."

"Thought I'd tell you."

"No problem."

"Do we tell the White House of our 'coconut' plan?"

"They'd shut us down faster than a tourist hounded by a timeshare salesman."

"I get your point. Let's handle matters our way."

"Absolutely."

"See you at the Bistro at zero six thirty."

"Now I have to go find a fishing boat."

CHAPTER 42

4:12 a.m.

"Madam President," said Chief of Staff Tebbs, "I'm afraid the situation has gone from bad to worse."

President Clarkson, sitting at the Resolute desk, replied, "How much worse can it get than the possibility of a third of our country being vaporized?"

"Not only are we dealing with a madman...well...madwoman. The DEA just intercepted a communication from Domingo Ferras –"

"The Venezuelan drug lord?"

"One and the same. He and his brother Salvatore are using this crisis to really screw us over by compounding the crisis."

"How so?"

"According to the intercept, the Ferras brothers have packed one of their autonomous narco-subs with explosives and it's on its way to the Cosmos Megaliner."

"For what on God's green Earth possible purpose? That would be like a firecracker against a tank. Are they in league with Parnette?"

"Impossible to know."

"I don't care what's impossible! I want answers!"

"Intelligence stopped me in my office before I was heading here. Two agents gave me a brain dump and these notes." Tebbs fanned three sheets of paper.

"And..."

"The intel is leaning towards an independent operation by the Ferras brothers. And not intended to inflict damage, but provoke Parnette to think the ship is under attack – so she'll press the button –"

"And detonate the antimatter device. Oh my God!"

"If they're not working with Parnette, how did they get the narco-sub prepped and out to sea so fast?"

"Evidently, the Ferras' have a small fleet of these autonomous subs. And it is not uncommon for drug runners to pack one with TNT instead of cocaine or fentanyl – to take out competitors' ships."

"A new kind of war on the water."

"Evidently."

"Can we intercept the sub?"

"The notes say these things evade detection by traveling a few feet under the water. Like a long-range GPS-guided torpedo. And they're small – only a few feet wide and less than 10 feet long."

"How fast do they travel?"

"Let's see. It says they chug along at no more than a few miles per hour. According to these notes, the DEA calls them 'sub-tubs.'"

"How far is Venezuela from the cruise ship in Aruba?"

"The point on the Venezuelan coastline – where they launched the sub-tub – is just 17 miles away."

"Dammit! How fresh is the intel? How much time do we have?"

"The agents said DEA overheard in a radio intercept what they believe was the launch command. When they were in my office, they said '22 minutes ago.' I bolted directly here. So we're talking 25 - 30 minutes."

"Let me think," Clarkson jotted numbers on her desktop notepad. "If I have my math right, instead of 21 hours left in Parnette's ultimatum – we now have four and a half?"

"That's my math, too."

"Gather the Joint Chiefs, heck everyone, in the Sit Room. Now!"

CHAPTER 43

4:21 a.m.

"Boys, it's probably about an hour or so to dawn," Gabby commented to Gerritt and Austin, their heads mingled with the wafting smoke from the soldering iron wielded by Gerritt. Austin gave a quick nod to Gabby and turned back to the workbench.

"That 555 should make a mess of things with a sawtooth wave," Gerritt said to Austin.

"Now we need to swap in an unstable VFO, to swing between frequencies," Austin tagged on.

"No sweat. I have a little warbler that'll do the trick."

Gabby asked, "So you guys are taking a perfectly good transmitter and making it work like poop? Do I have that about right?"

"Yep," replied Austin. "It'll sound like a loudmouth drunk, singing off-key karaoke."

Gerritt followed, "Technically, the boat lady's sat phone will receive a swarm of random signals from our gizmo and not be able to lock onto any – including the real one. She'll hear a screeching sound, but that's about it."

Genovese walked back into the room, carrying a six-string electric guitar. "I hear you need an antenna."

"Sweet!" replied Austin. "A guitar string will make a perfect springy antenna."

Gabby added, "I hope your son won't mind."

Gerritt took out his wire cutters and snipped off the low E string.

"L-band, right?" asked Gerritt. "Around 1,650 MHz?"

Austin responded, "About three-and-a-half inches will do. And we still need a honkin' big magnet."

"Ask and you shall receive," replied Gerritt, reaching to the top of his workbench and handing Austin a curved-shaped piece of metal. "A neodymium magnet I salvaged from an old hard drive."

"Whew!" Austin replied, as the magnet snapped down to the top of a metal toolbox – the strength of the magnet's grip caught him off guard. "That'll do it!"

"The ship's steel hull in salt water will make a heck of a ground plane as we talked about before."

"It'll make the jammer's five watts work like fifty."

"Let's add this loop," Gerritt pointed to a six-inch piece of thin nylon cord, "in case you need an alternate way to tie-down the gizmo."

"Works for me."

"I found this waterproof switch in my junk box. What do you think?"

Click, click, click, click. Austin tested the switch. "Work's great. Perfect!"

Gabby interjected, "We have to wrap up and get this sucker to the police station. And we have to call Penny."

"Almost done," replied Austin. "And knowing Penny, she and her teams will already have a strike force ready to take care of business, and our project will just have been a clever technical exercise."

"Hope so."

CHAPTER 44

As ordered by Clarkson, Tebbs and his staff summoned the highest levels of America's leadership to the Situation "Sit" Room – a complex of three high-security boardrooms, a pair of small breakout rooms, and a global intelligence hub located in the basement of the West Wing of the White House. A long-overdue modernization was completed in 2023, and three supplemental enhancements had occurred since.

***

5:03 a.m.

The nucleus of America's military and political might filed into the largest conference room of the Sit – the John F. Kennedy conference room. Given the time of night and the scramble to get to the White House, the normally professional dressers came with whatever they could quickly throw on – which was perfectly fine with Clarkson.

Clarkson, herself, stood at the head of the mahogany table, wearing a comfortable combination of slacks, knitted shirt, and a blazer.

Clarkson was not physically imposing, and her voice was proportionally light in volume. Her mild demeanor and a natural knack for communication clarity were precisely what the nation needed during the recent swirl of political turmoil.

In front of her was a who's who of respected and experienced talent from both sides of the aisle. Tonight, Clarkson needed every neuron of the Joint Chiefs' and Cabinet's collective minds to give her input. She knew when the time came to make a critical decision, she would turn to her own instincts – an innate skill that had never steered her wrong.

"Doug, are you patched in?" Clarkson asked into empty air, wondering if Vice President Douglas Carlisle was electronically connected to the Situation Room.

"Madam President –

"Please, Barb –

"Okay, Barb. We're reconfiguring the SCIF (Sensitive Compartmented Information Facility) here in Kyiv. Only audio for now. I'm told I'll be up on the screen shortly."

"Thanks, Doug. Chime in as warranted. I – we – need your brainpower."

Clarkson, eyeing the full room, steeled everyone's attention: "Okay, give it to me," the President asked her team seated around the table. "Minimize formalities. Time is of the essence."

As she hoped, Brassard spoke up first.

"Madam President –"

"Arty, please, Barb –"

"Barb, to put it bluntly, we are in deep shit. Dr. Montgomery, Jordy, will provide details on the weapon in a moment. Top line, we have a multi-fold crisis – with a variety of very real trip wires that could result in the destruction of a third of our country. Vaporized. A crater up to a thousand miles across."

Audible gasps rang out around the table.

"Continue," prompted Clarkson in a matter-of-fact tone.

"Within 45 minutes of Parnette's video, we raided her lab on Long Island. Our cyber team had surprisingly little trouble accessing Parnette's data; almost like she wanted it to be found. Our scientists have confirmed with high confidence that it was, indeed, Parnette's technology – and resulting weapon – that caused The Event. Unfortunately, Parnette's claim that it was a 'demonstration device' also appears true. Our scientists believe the destructive capability of her operational weapon is at least four multiples of that."

"When you say 'operational weapon' what are we talking about?"

"May I chime in?" asked Dr. Jordon "Jordy" Montgomery, the Director of the Office of Science and Technology Policy (OSTP).

"Please," replied Clarkson.

"Based on Parnette's own calculations – laid out, as Secretary Brassard said, on a silver platter for us – we determined at the OSTP that the physical size of the device –

"Weapon!" spouted Brassard.

"Yes, 'weapon' is about the length of an ordinary laptop. And it must be cylindrical in shape for the underlying physics to work. About three inches in diameter. The weight would be less than two pounds. Staggering, when you think about its destructive capability. It wouldn't even garner attention in a TSA checked-bag scanner."

"Okay," said Clarkson. "So we know the 'weapon' is real. It's essentially a bomb. That's what we should be calling it. And we know she's had no hesitation to use this bomb's technology to kill tens of thousands of innocent people in her 'demonstration'. I see no reason to think she'd hesitate turning our country to rubble. And, if that wasn't enough, we have a further complication that has dramatically pushed up the timeline. Charlotte?"

Charlotte Alford, the Director of National Intelligence, replied. "As the President said, we have a 'complication.' As you may have spotted on the briefing notes in front of you, the Ferras drug kingpins have launched an explosive-laden 'sub-tub' at the cruise ship. The intent, we believe, is to make Parnette think she's under attack and set off the antimatter bomb – immediately – out of desperation."

Alford continued, "We reviewed satellite images and a series of radio intercepts. It seems we had a touch of luck here. The bad guys turned on the dock's floodlights when they launched the sub-tub at Venezuela's Paraguaná Peninsula. We believe we caught a glimpse when it was deposited into the water. Nighttime makes it near impossible to get a visual at sea. Over the last hour, though, we got an infrared signature. The sub-tub is making a direct beeline to Aruba at a steady 3.9 miles per hour."

"What's its ETA?" asked Clarkson.

"Since we know the launch point, time, and speed, and we – unfortunately – know the target, given current sea conditions and currents, it will arrive at the western opening of Aruba's harbor at 7:56 a.m. and impact the ship at 8:06 a.m. Two hours and fifty-six minutes from now."

Clearly hoping for a different answer, Clarkson asked "So our country could be gone within three hours?"

"Yes."

"Everyone, this is our new timeline. Now's the time to step up with solutions. Let's hear options!"

General Bradley 'Hutch' Hutchinson, Chairman of the Joint Chiefs, spoke up. "Given it's a clear – and now immediate – threat to the nation, we should alert the Secretaries across our military that we're meeting here, right now, and working through the intel."

Hutchinson continued, "As you can imagine, I am getting pinged by every department. They're seeing the same media coverage. They want to know the action plan."

"Agreed, Hutch," Clarkson replied. "As soon as we break here, fill them in. Keep them apprised. America's military will likely play a key role in ending this crisis."

"Will do."

Clarkson scanned the table, "More..."

Alford spoke up again, "What about Parnette's 'document' demand? We've studied it at *Intelligence*. Annotated copies, with a rapid assessment from our analysts, are in front of everyone at the table."

"We don't negotiate with terrorists, international – or home grown – period," responded Clarkson.

"Full agreement." Alford continued, "Knowing this is an attack on our country of unequaled proportions, the NSA has asked for a narrow suspension of FISA."

"FISA," as Alford referenced, is the acronym for the Foreign Intelligence Surveillance Act, a U.S. law that governs surveillance activities, particularly electronic. The law encompasses U.S. citizens if they are suspected of affiliations with a foreign power.

Alford continued, "Since Parnette is a U.S. citizen, she is, of course, protected by FISA protocols. With your approval, the NSA would work to get an emergency court order to exempt Parnette; they also recommend exempting any inbound or outbound calls between Aruba and the U.S. during this crisis, as we don't know who Parnette is working with."

"How would this 'approval' from me work?"

"In the form of an Executive Order. Given our time pressure, I've taken the liberty to draft the appropriate Executive Order here on my tablet. Please take a look." Alford handed her tablet to Clarkson.

"This is all it would take? To suspend the civil liberties of an American citizen? And perhaps others? You know I campaigned against this sort of thing."

"I know all too well, Barb. And I don't make this referral from the NSA lightly. Ultimately, the decision is yours."

"It would be one-dimensional, right? That's the way I'm reading this. Parnette and anyone who she may speak with, correct? And it looks like, in the last two sentences, any calls to and from Aruba – but tightly time-limited, correct?"

"Yes, the suspension would cease immediately when you later sign the accompanying Executive Order for termination. Scroll down to page two."

"I see it. When this ordeal is over, I execute this page –

"It would be terminated. Siloed and temporary."

"I don't like this. I don't like it one bit. It was a lot easier on the campaign trail to say I don't like this stuff."

"Real world gets in the way."

"Congress will go apeshit, you know," commented Tebbs.

"Of course they will. It would be a good day – as that means the country will be intact. We'll deal with the shitstorm then."

Clarkson stared at the tablet. "Dammit. Okay." She used the tablet's stylus to sign her name.

"I'll make it happen. I'll be back in five." Alford stood up from her chair and walked out of the room.

"Who's next?"

"Have we heard from the other countries?" asked Bart Hemsley, the Director of Homeland Security, regarding the other four countries in Parnette's demand letter.

"I'll handle this one," replied Quintana. "We've had rapid-fire dialogue at the highest levels. I could give you plenty of color. To make a long story short, no one's interested in the ridiculous demands."

"They do know a detonation of this magnitude will impact every single person on Earth, right?" asked Montgomery.

"Jordy," Clarkson replied, "Realistically, what are they going to say? I mean, we'd probably act the same way if the issue was taking place on the other side of the planet. They full well know the danger. Our inbound communications have confirmed such. But to sign a contract under the threat of a global gun? Unrealistic."

Clarkson turned to Tebbs. "Barry, you said we'd have Parnette's psychiatrist available on a video link, is that correct?"

"Yes, Barb. I have Dr. Isabelle Abshire ready to come up on Screen Six for a secure video discussion if you would like."

"I would. Right now, please."

Tebbs walked over to a small table with a built-in touch-screen panel, typed in a seven-digit access code, then tapped an icon labeled "6". Up appeared the face of Dr. Isabelle Abshire.

"Dr. Abshire, thank you for making time for us today. I'm sure you've been watching the news and have been further briefed by my Chief of Staff."

"Madam President, it is an honor to be talking to you today. Yes, Mr. Tebbs brought me up to speed to the extent he could because of the understandable security and sensitivity. How may I help you?"

"Let me first say you are live in the Situation Room among my Cabinet and the Joint Chiefs. Please keep this discussion absolutely confidential. I am breaking a myriad of rules to loop you in, and I will deal with the consequences later – if there is a later. Dr. Abshire, the situation is even worse than it appears on TV."

"Oh."

"Dr. Parnette was your patient, correct?"

"Yes, for 19 years."

"Why was she under your care? Please keep it as brief as you can."

"Of course. And, as you know, I'm breaking doctor-patient confidentiality and my medical license could be revoked. That said, the situation for the nation is clearly dire. Dr. Parnette has suffered since a young child from Social Anxiety Disorder exacerbated by persistent bullying and teasing. Her childhood was so traumatizing, the anxiety remained just below the surface as an adult. We worked for years to develop coping mechanisms. They were, for the most part, successful. That was until her presentation at the National Academy of Sciences."

"The meltdown on worldwide TV?"

"Yes. She, quite literally, had a nervous breakdown in front of the world. For some time, she couldn't even feed herself. Gradually, she regained motor control and cognitive abilities. It was a little over nine months before we integrated her back into a workplace environment – which we thought would be therapeutic. Clearly, we were mistaken."

"That aside, is there any reason to think she wouldn't use her antimatter technology as a bomb that would annihilate tens of millions of people?"

"Frankly, if you were to have asked me two days ago, I would have said it was a complete impossibility. If it is true that she caused The Event –"

"It's true –"

"Then, unfortunately, she's already crossed the threshold of discerning right from wrong. In my field, she's exhibiting traits of what we call delusional megalomania, people convinced of their greatness and absolute power. Almost God-like."

"I hear genius can teeter on the edge of insanity."

"Anecdotally. But your point is well taken."

"Could you provide our team with her files? We don't know where she planted her bomb. We may be able to do a rapid AI search for a clue."

"I'm sorry. It's not possible. Not that I wouldn't agree to it. A couple years ago the building that included my office caught fire. All of my records were destroyed. The Fire Marshall labeled it 'suspicious,' although never able to put a finger on the actual cause."

"I don't like coincidences." Clarkson glanced at her watch. "Dr. Abshire, we have to wrap up. Any last thoughts that might be helpful?"

"I do have my last couple years of electronic notes. I can turn them over."

"Those could be useful."

"And regardless of her state of mind, she's brilliant. Even if her brain is scrambled, in fact, perhaps more so, she's likely thought through various scenarios – and has plotted many options. She's not a linear thinker."

"That's a helpful insight."

"One more thing, and I'm kicking myself for it: Early this year, Parnette became particularly upbeat. It was highly encouraging. So, in consultation with my colleagues, I transitioned her status to unsupervised leave. During that time, she took a cruise to Bermuda. And we now know the rest of the story. In hindsight, the leave was a critical error on my part."

"Don't be too hard on yourself, Dr. Abshire. She clearly had a lot of people fooled."

"Still, I should have seen something."

"Thank you for your time, Dr. Abshire."

"I wish you – and the country – well. I don't envy your responsibility."

"We'll find a way," Clarkson replied, feigning optimism, and well knowing the gravity of the moment.

Tebbs clicked off the video feed.

"It seems obvious, but have we tried to reach the ship's crew?"

Kenneth Franklin, Director of the Central Intelligence Agency, spoke up. "All telecommunications with the ship, including the ship's Internet connectivity, ceased working during the night. We tried radioing the bridge of the ship, the Officers' secondary systems, emergency comms – no luck. Parnette must have accomplices on the ship with technical knowhow, and they've thwarted our attempts. Sorry, Madam President."

"Thanks, Ken."

Clarkson scanned the room. "More…"

Alford spoke up again. "The chatter throughout those wishing to do us harm is off the charts. Our who's who of adversaries are either positioning themselves to take advantage of the possible power vacuum or contemplating ways to further accelerate our crisis. We can't assume the Ferras brothers are the only ones trying to make sure we have a bad ending. They simply may be the only group we've discovered with an operational plan."

"We need to keep that in mind."

"Bart," Clarkson turned to Hemsley of Homeland, "do we have any idea – any idea whatsoever – where this God-awful bomb might be?"

"We back-tracked Parnette's travels, thinking that she wouldn't entrust placing the bomb with anyone except herself. Her last couple of weeks of travel was like U.S.A. hopscotch. She flew to (looking at his notes) Chicago, Minneapolis, Sacramento, Wichita, Seattle, D.C., Miami, Hartford, Pittsburgh, and back to Miami to board the cruise ship. She stayed a day or two in each city. Used her credit card regularly. Ate at public restaurants. Even took in a minor league baseball game at the Hartford Yard Goats stadium. She didn't visit – or even drive by – any locations we would consider sensitive to national security. It looks like she took her laptop with her, as we got periodic pings from it. She browsed the Web. Checked the weather. Ordinary activities like that."

Clarkson questioned, "That doesn't mean she couldn't have turned on a VPN and browsed the Web and communicated with others in ways that we wouldn't know, right?"

"That's correct. In fact, her TV 'manifesto' of sorts mentioned she was digging up information on the Dark Web. She specifically referenced the oil executive, Patrick K. Kilborne. All it would take is the Tor browser, which is free."

"Do we think there is any connection to Kilborne in this crisis?"

"We had four agents at his ranch in Eldorado an hour after Parnette mentioned his name. Even before we got there, his place was surrounded by TV crews. Kilborne was, initially, reluctant to talk to our agents. He thought wiser when he saw us as a shield against the crawling media. Anyway, he seemed as shocked as the rest of the world for his name to be brought up. Our profiler thought the surprise was genuine. Since then, we also did a deep-dive data cross-reference; we could not find any contact – phone, email, financial – between the two over the last couple of years. The only thing we know for sure, given their public bouts on TV, is that Parnette clearly hates Kilborne's guts."

"Given the deep animosity, any consideration that Parnette would target Kilborne with the bomb?"

"On the surface, that would seem logical. Yet over the last month she hasn't been within 750 miles of his ranch or any oil-production facilities."

"Her romping around the country could be a diversion. Maybe she does have an accomplice or two here in the States."

"If so, we haven't found a connection."

"Okay, thank you for the analysis, Bart." Even though the Situation Room had multiple-time-zone digital clocks on the walls, Clarkson reflexively looked at her watch. "Two hours and forty-four minutes," she said – barely audible to the group.

"John," she said, turning to Quintana. "I know your phone has been ringing off the hook. What's the latest?"

"Well, as touched on before, no country is game to pony up the ransom demand or sign Parnette's 'document'. So that's for starters."

"Go on."

"Over a dozen countries have reached out to offer their general support, technology, and resources. Even China – one of the five on Parnette's hit list – offered to reposition one of their surveillance satellites; more on that in a second. The Israelis have teamed up with our NSA and are performing some herculean data crunching, hoping to turn Parnette's travel breadcrumbs into actionable intelligence. The Swedes, Irish, Dutch, Germans, multiple intel offices in the UK – I could go on – help has been offered from all corners."

"How about the Arubans? Their police and security forces? This calamity is happening on their soil. Surely, they're engaged."

"Yes, they are. For a small country, they have an impressive security infrastructure. One of the most refined in the Caribbean. I've been speaking continually with Tomas Geerman, captain of Aruba's police force. The U.S. doesn't have an embassy there, nor do we have human assets. We're counting on them for local surveillance. They know the critical need to maintain a low profile, so as not to provoke Parnette any further. Given the information flow, so far, I believe they are more than up for the task."

"Well, at least something positive."

"One other, well, unique – and potentially valuable – piece of information regarding Aruba if I may."

"Sure, John."

"It seems two Americans, purely by bad luck, were shot at a little after midnight by a crew aboard one of Parnette's support boats. By happenstance, they were diving near the cruise ship. Wrong place, wrong time. Fortunately, they were not injured."

"Thank, God."

"Indeed. Except there's a twist. Let me turn this back over to Bart."

"A 'twist' would be an understatement," said Hemsley. "Homeland checked out the two Americans. They are two prominent citizens, Gabriella Milone and Austin Raze, a scientist and an engineer."

Quintana picked up, "And they have a personal connection to a senior CIA agent in Chicago, Penelope Durango. Milone and Raze called Durango from the police station near the cruise port. To make a long story short – and this is going to sound completely off the wall – they told the staff at the police station they could build a satellite-phone jammer that could disrupt Parnette's communications. Prevent Parnette from initiating the bomb that she said, on TV, was 'on speed dial.'"

"That's hard to believe, to say the least," said Clarkson. "How plausible is it? The technology to do so?"

Quintana replied, "I spoke, personally, with one of the lead engineers at the Directorate of Science and Technology, Lisa Chen. Ms. Chen said it was 'technically doable,' although it would require extensive knowledge of this particular portion of the radio spectrum and the engineering wherewithal – including communications components – to fabricate such a device. She thought her department could make a testable prototype 'in days'. So an 'extreme long shot' – her words, not mine – that it could be done in hours without a mainland lab."

"Thank you, John. Given all the balls in the air, and the new compressed timeline (Clarkson looked at her watch) – two hours and thirty-nine minutes – we should purely be glad the Americans are okay."

"Certainly."

"A thought," Daniel Jameson politely spoke up – just 29 years old and feeling a little out of his element in the room of powerhouses.

Clarkson turned to her young Press Secretary and responded "Yes, Dan. What are you thinking?"

"Do you think you should make a statement to the American people? The country's on edge and the media are out of their minds."

Even in the most grueling circumstances, Clarkson had a knack for making everyone – seasoned or not – feel like they were the most-important voice in the room. "Dan, it's a brilliant thought. Still, I think we need to pace it out a bit. The country, well the world, is still on Parnette's timetable – thinking we have about 19 hours in this crisis. If they knew it was less than three, we'd have massive panic."

", Madam President."

"Barb."

"I'm sorry, that's still not natural for me. Working on it."

Retired Air Force Colonel Carson Walters spoke up. "You know, along Dan's thinking, we could create a phased messaging plan so that the public will know when updates will occur. We can lay out the tiered plan in our first address to the public. But we need to wait for the right timing." Clarkson personally tapped Walters to be the National Security Council Coordinator for Strategic Communications. Clarkson relied on Walter's combination of decades of military experience and his uncanny ability to find the right tone and right moment to deliver essential messaging.

Clarkson replied to Jameson and Walters. "Thank you, gentlemen. Yes, let's save the first press appearance for a few hours when – hopefully – the crisis is resolved and the world is getting back to normal. We'll undoubtedly have various parcels of information to deliver at that time."

Clarkson turned to Brassard and looked directly into his eyes with purpose. "Secretary. Arty. Tell me what I don't know."

"We don't know a lot of things. That's the problem. We know the Ferras brothers are real. We know the sub-tub is real. We know, with reasonable probability, that an explosion at the ship would likely trigger Parnette to 'push the button.' We don't know what other bad actors are out there. Some opportunistic country. Heck, a nutcase already on Aruba with a backpack of explosives who wants to become 'famous' by provoking the destruction of America. It's unlikely the Ferras' were the only ones with the thought."

Brassard continued, "We don't yet have a live visual on the situation. We're firing seven years' worth of orbit re-positioning fuel to reposition our X17 surveillance satellite over Aruba. It will be over the site in 35 minutes. We're getting towards morning twilight in Aruba. As soon as we have enough light to see something, we'll put up a live feed on Screen Two."

"One other thing," Brassard added. "As John alluded to, the Chinese have offered to nudge their BrightFlower-5 satellite, that already monitors the Caribbean, over the top of the situation. I'm, frankly, a little suspicious of their generosity. But any port in a storm. Like with our X17, we'll bring up a visual when there is enough light in the region; we'll pipe the feed onto Screen Three."

"Thank you, Arty," Clarkson said, then paused before continuing. "We have two hours and thirty-seven minutes. From everything you've heard, what is your recommendation?"

Brassard shifted gears to a more clinical delivery. "Our departments have run all the scenarios and simulations. Nothing I've heard today would change the equation. The brutal reality: No matter where the device goes off in our country, a third of our land mass will be vaporized. Additionally, the electromagnetic wave, similar to what the world experienced with The Event but on a multiple-magnitude-greater scale, will destroy or severely damage the power grid and communications infrastructure for much of the continental U.S. From a functioning government standpoint, our country will immediately cease to exist."

Brassard paused, looked around the room, and locked his eyes with Clarkson's. "If the goal is to protect our country – which it must always be – then, and you're not going to like this, we must take out the ship."

"The ship? The cruise ship?"

"Yes. Eliminate it before Parnette can push the button."

"My God! You're right: I don't like it! Give me a sec to process what you just said." Clarkson glanced around the room; everyone was also trying to take in the enormity of what Brassard recommended.

"How many people are on board the ship?"

"9,517, according to the manifest," Tebbs replied. "And that's only the passengers. There are almost 4,000 in crew."

"I don't suppose there's a super-secret weapon I haven't been told about yet that could temporarily incapacitate everyone including Parnette? I'm still new on the job."

"No, there's not," replied Brassard.

"I can't believe I'm even asking the question: Arty, how would you even propose to 'take out the ship'? I thought we didn't have any assets in the region."

"We don't. Not on the island. And not immediately near the island. We have naval assets of the U.S. Fourth Fleet in the Caribbean – with destroyers currently about 800 miles away. I suggest three Block IV TLAMs, that is, Tomahawk missiles. They have a range of over 1,000 miles, so the distance is fine. Flight time is another story. They fly at

550 miles per hour. It doesn't take calculus to know we have to launch these, well, pretty much now."

"Hold your horses, Arty! You say this so matter-of-factly. We're talking about killing over 13,000 people!"

"Believe me, I understand. Entirely. My job, your job, in fact the job of everyone in this room is to keep America safe. We're talking 332 million people and the continued existence of our nation."

"I know. I know. While they're flying, can we keep working on other options?

"Absolutely! We must! And it's important for you to know that our Block IV TLAMs can be terminated until the final few seconds before encountering a target."

"And why three Tomahawks? Why not one? Or 10?"

"Redundancy. They have over 97% flight reliability. If one did fail, we'd still have two. They have warheads of 1,000 pounds of high explosive. Two would still accomplish the task."

"'Task!' What you're proposing is mass murder of innocent civilians!"

"I know all too well, Madam President." Brassard took a deep breath. "My daughter is on that ship."

"Stacy! My God! Why didn't you tell me your daughter was on that ship?"

"Precisely for the reaction you're having now. I didn't want to influence your thinking. Stacy's on a fun fling with her college girlfriends. They were originally booked on the ship for a late-April cruise, then all hell broke loose with The Event. The cruise line offered to re-book. And they took it."

"Are you absolutely sure she's on the ship? The world is still fluid."

"Unfortunately, yes. Betty and I got a call from her two days ago. They were getting on the ship in Miami. Stacy sounded so happy..." Brassard's voice trailed off.

"Oh, Arty!"

"As you can imagine, this is killing me on the inside. It's my baby girl. But I've taken an oath to defend our country. I don't see another option that is likely to succeed."

"Okay, time out! I can't take that for an answer. To kill your daughter and everyone on board. Does anyone in this room – anyone! – see any other possible course of action? Please speak up now! Protocols be damned!"

Vice President Carlisle, still a remote voice without video, "Do we have any ships or submarines nearby that could get some strategic forces onto the ship?"

"Doug," responded Hutchinson, "we don't have a ship within 300 miles of Aruba. Or a sub within 900 miles. Both too far to be useful in our accelerated timeframe."

Clarkson, annoyed that Carlisle was still only connected via audio, added, "Someone get Vice President Carlisle up on video! Now!"

"Barb, it's on my end here in Kyiv. I'm assured it's almost set."

Clarkson, back to the mission at hand, asked the room, "How about some sort of electromagnetic pulse above the ship to knock out all electronics? I know we have had those sorts of devices in the works for some time."

Hutchinson replied, "Barb, Arty and I were talking about that before you came into the room. There are a couple of options in that regard."

"Go ahead."

"First, we talked about dropping a two-to-three-kiloton nuclear weapon from a B-52 that we could scramble from Barksdale Air Force Base in Louisiana. If we detonated the device at 2,000 feet, the EM pulse would indeed knock out all the ship's electronics. However, the radiation dose would kill the passengers – and Arubans on land within about a mile radius – over a handful of weeks. It's a moot point now; with our new timeline, we couldn't get it there fast enough. It's an 1,800-mile flight. And the max speed of a B-52 is 650 miles per hour. The math doesn't work."

"Thank God for the math!" Clarkson exclaimed. "This is a terrible option!"

"Agreed," responded Hutchinson.

Brassard added, "The other option we considered that could generate a disruptive electromagnetic wave is what we call an 'e-bomb' – a non-nuclear weapon that could deliver a potent electromagnetic pulse to knock out Parnette's sat phone."

Hutchinson added, "HiJENKS-2 is our latest version of our High Power Joint Electromagnetic Non-Kinetic Strike weapon that has an effective battlefield EM-pulse radius of about three kilometers, or a little under two miles. It emits no radiation. There would be no injuries to the ship's passengers or the surrounding population."

Brassard followed, "We've seen the recent tests and data by the U.S. Air Force Laboratory. The two of us agree that given the steel superstructure of the cruise ship we would need to activate the device within 1,000 feet of the ship's deck to be sure we'd knock everything out – including Parnette's sat phone. In inventory, we have parachute-in e-bombs that are deployed under fixed wing, queued for rogue situations in Central America. Under the wing of an F-15 Strike Eagle – the F-15E – we can get it anywhere *fast* at 1,600 miles per hour. So we could, in theory, get it to Aruba in time from multiple military facilities."

Clarkson yelled, "So why the hell aren't we doing that? Like right now!"

Brassard replied, "The risk, Madam President, is that the device must come in softly under a large parachute. It may be seen by Parnette's henchmen for up to two minutes before the EM pulse could be activated at the necessary 1,000 feet above the ship. They could radio Parnette and she could detonate the device before our e-bomb could be activated. They could even shoot it out of the sky with a military rifle. We think the probability of success is very low."

"Like one in 10," added Hutchinson.

"Son of a bitch! I can't believe America's entire military and technology arsenal is being thwarted by a single person on a cruise ship!" Exasperated, Clarkson continued, "Other options...anyone!"

Silence.

Clarkson looked around the room, hoping someone would have a spontaneous brain-storm; an option no one had considered. No words were spoken.

"God, this is an impossible choice. Arty: You are absolutely sure that we could destroy the Tomahawks within a few seconds of the target?"

"Yes, Madam President. Within 8.25 seconds, to be exact. The military has never had one not respond to that command. There are multiple fail-safes."

"Hutch, your thoughts?"

"It's a horrible, horrible option. Unfortunately, a necessary one." Turning to Brassard, "My heart goes out to you, Arty."

Tears welled up in Clarkson's eyes. "Arty, I am so very sorry. Beyond any words I can say." She paused and wiped the tears that now ran down her cheeks. Hardly beyond a whisper but heard by all, she concluded, "We have to launch the missiles."

"Barb, I understand."

CHAPTER 45

6:20 a.m.

The Situation Room remained silent for four minutes as Brassard made the necessary calls to initiate the launch of the Tomahawk missiles. Then on Screen One appeared Admiral Theodore Birch, the head of the U.S. Southern Command, or SOUTHCOM, located in Doral Florida. SOUTHCOM's responsibilities are security and military operations in Central America, South America, and the Caribbean.

"Madam President, this is Admiral Birch here in SOUTHCOM. Secretary of Defense Brassard has informed me of a target – the Cosmos Megaliner – currently docked in Aruba's Port of Oranjestad. Please confirm the target."

"Admiral Birch. I hereby confirm the target."

"Madam President, as I discussed with Secretary Brassard, three Block IV TLAMs, colloquially Tomahawk missiles, will reach the target at precisely 8:02 a.m. Atlantic Standard Time which is also 8:02 a.m. Eastern Daylight Time. Please confirm that this is your expectation."

"It is, Admiral Birch. Sadly. But confirmed."

"Madam President, I need for you to confirm your understanding that the three missiles will likely kill everyone on board, either in the primary explosions or in the subsequent secondary explosions of the ship's fuel."

"Admiral, unfortunately, yes. I confirm my understanding that the missiles will likely kill everyone on board."

"Madam President, do you have any questions for me or my staff?"

"Admiral, yes, I do. I have been told by Secretary Brassard that the Tomahawks can be destroyed through a remote command at any time until 8.25 seconds before impact. Is that correct?"

"Yes, Madam President. 8.25 seconds. We can abort the mission and splash them into the sea – the preferred option in this scenario – at any time until that point."

"Very well. Under the authority vested in me as the President of the United States, I hereby authorize you to launch the Tomahawk missiles."

"Your authorization is confirmed and witnessed. Targeting will be complete in less than three minutes. Launch will initiate one minute thereafter. My team will arrange for you to follow the track of the missiles live on one of your screens."

"Understood, Admiral." The video feed then winked off.

Clarkson bowed her head. She said to herself but audible to everyone in the room, "May God have mercy on all those innocent souls."

Clarkson raised her head back up and scanned the room side to side. She asked, "Is this meeting being recorded?"

Tebbs responded, "This is a secure room. No recording devices."

Clarkson, politely nodded her understanding, then abruptly stood up – banging her fists on the table as she rose – startling everyone in the room.

"I'll be damned if we kill 13,000 innocent people before we consider every other bitch and bastard option first!" Clarkson's diminutive frame now spewed the force of a raging bull. "This is what we are going to do: It's 6:25. In thirty-five minutes – at 7 a.m. – we're coming back into this room. We'll be here for the duration. So take your bio breaks.

"Arty and Hutch, by that time, I want to hear that the F-15E is in the air with the e-bomb. I know you said one-in-ten odds. Get some geniuses to figure out a way to improve our odds. By a lot! Take whatever steps you feel are necessary. I'll back you up."

Brassard and Hutchinson nodded.

"John, reach back out to your counterparts in Aruba. You can't tell them about the Tomahawks, for obvious reasons. Brainstorm with them on each and every other sonofabitchin' thing. Loop them in on the Ferras brothers and the sub-tub. I want new ideas before we reconvene."

"I'm on it," replied John Quintana.

"Alright. By 7 a.m., all of you have your butts planted back in these chairs."

CHAPTER 46

6:30 a.m.

An unassuming 24-foot fishing boat puttered towards the beach, Hans Croes at the helm.

Captain Geerman and three casually dressed officers stood at the water's edge.

The bow tapped the shallow water and the boat gently glided to a halt. Croes jumped over the side, shoes and all, into the six inches of water. Croes turned to the shore-waiting sniper, Niels Brouwer, and said, "Brouwer, here's your transportation. Are you ready?"

"Packed and ready, sir."

"Excellent. And I like your fishing outfit. Nice touch with the lures in the hat."

"Not really appropriate for ocean fishing. They're all I had."

"You look like a bungling tourist ready to cause trouble with a rod and reel. Absolutely perfect."

Croes turned to officer's Braam and Koopman, also in casual clothes. "Get him to the breakwater coordinates we talked about. Remember: If you get stopped, just say you're taking this fellow (pointing at Brouwer) on a fishing charter."

"Understood, sir."

Geerman looked directly into the eyes of Brouwer and said, "If you get the shot, take the shot."

"Yes, sir."

Croes wrapped up, "Very well. All of you get on board and head out."

CHAPTER 47

At 6:32 a.m., the only communication system left functioning on the Cosmos Megaliner – the internal PA system – blared a message throughout the decks and staterooms.

"Attention passengers and crew. This is Dr. Katherine Parnette. I am sorry for the inconvenience. There will be no shore excursions today. In addition, all communication systems, internal and external, have been turned off. I am in control of the ship. Rest assured, as soon as my requests have been satisfied, you will be back to your fun in the sun. On the other hand, if anyone tries to intervene, or attempts to leave the ship, the consequences will be immediate and harsh. Among you, in plain clothes, are my colleagues, and they are well armed. As was the 1800s motto of the Texas Rangers, my colleagues are instructed to 'shoot first, ask questions later.' So please don't play Rambo."

After a ten-second pause, Parnette's message – clearly a digital recording – repeated itself. The message then repeated one more time.

As the impact of the situation took hold, screams of fear resounded throughout the ship.

CHAPTER 48

6:34 a.m.

"Wrap it up, boys – now!" Gabby prompted Austin and Gerritt.

"We're sealing it up," responded Austin.

Gerrit had just mixed a two-part, quick-set epoxy and was applying it around the open lip of a plastic case that was about the shape of a medium-sized book. "Silicone caulk would have been better," Gerritt commented. "But it would take too long to set. This stuff will do the trick. Sealed like a drum, and watertight, in five minutes."

Austin hovered the case's lid over the top of the epoxy, lined it up, and gently pushed it down onto the gooey sealant.

After the lid was in position, Austin took four small cross-point screws that were on the benchtop, placed them into the lid's corner holes, and screwed the lid tight to the box.

"Done!" pronounced Gerritt. "The internal lithium batteries are fully charged, too."

"Not so bad for a few hours of tinkering!" Austin added.

"Will it do the job?" Gabby asked.

"You mean, save the world?" Austin chimed.

"Well, the U.S., but yes," Gabby replied.

"I know a quick way to know with reasonable confidence," Austin said. "We zip back over to the police station and see if we can jam the sat phone we used to call Penny. At the same time, we can show their tactical team how the jammer works. Hand it over to them. And get us as far away from the ship as possible."

"You got that right. We don't want to be anywhere near the ship when the shit hits the fan."

"Glad we were able to put this together," added Gerritt. "Please stay safe. No more bullets, okay?"

"That's the plan, Gerritt. And thank you, so much, for your middle-of-the-night help," said Gabby. "You're amazing."

"Yeah, dude," added Austin. "When this situation is over, let's play with some ham radio stuff. I want to try out your new antenna."

"Absolutely. And I haven't forgotten next Friday night's dinner date," Gerritt said. "Genovese and I are looking forward to our get-together at *Surf's Up*."

Genovese, hearing the wrap-up conversations, walked into the shack. "All done, kids?"

"We'll soon see," replied Gabby.

The four shared quick hugs as they moved toward the front door.

Austin and Gabby walked down the outdoor stone walkway, hopped in the Jeep with the just-minted electronic gizmo, and zoomed off.

CHAPTER 49

6:37 a.m.

Parnette tapped the ESC key on her laptop's keyboard to wake up the machine. She dutifully typed her paranoia-infused 27-character password to bring up the desktop.

Parnette executed a batch file that automated a variety of sequential tasks, the last of which was a connection to a server she set up on her recent travels. A flurry of keystrokes emanated from her fingertips.

"Where are my signatures!" Parnette yelled to herself. "I can see from the IP data, all the countries have seen the document. Heck, it looks like they've shared access to every shittin' country on the planet! *But no one is signing.* Don't they see I am trying to save them? Save the planet. Save them all!"

Parnette bowed her head into her open hands and took a couple of deep breaths. She raised her head and looked to the ceiling, transfixed in a strange gaze. After nearly a minute, she broke her trance and muttered to herself, "My power."

Back to her laptop's keyboard, Parnette feverishly typed another burst. She concluded with the keystrokes SEA-WA and pressed ENTER.

CHAPTER 50

6:40 a.m.

It only took 10 minutes for Brouwer and his escorting colleagues, Braam and Koopman, to get around the east end of the breakwater. Five minutes later they were in visual range of the ship. Koopman, at the helm, cut the engine and slowed to a stop near a patch of sand.

"This is where we have to let you off," Braam said to Brouwer. "If we get any closer, we could be spotted."

"Agreed," replied Brouwer. "I'll scramble from here with my drag bag (a storage bag for guns and ammunition). We'll soon find out if it is really waterproof."

"We'll stay right here," added Braam, "ready to pick you up when the job is done."

"Get that bastard," spouted Koopman from the helm.

Brouwer hopped over the edge of the boat into a few inches of water and the sandy bottom. Braam handed Brouwer his drag bag, which he slung over his left shoulder. Brouwer then began his slippery scramble between the rocks and intermittent sandy-bottom patches.

CHAPTER 51

"Where the hell is my document?" Parnette yelled to herself, slamming her right fist on the stateroom's coffee table.

Her rage was nearing the boiling point. She reached across the table, picked up her walkie-talkie, and squeezed the talk button. "X, status report."

Through her walkie-talkie's speaker she heard, "As expected, we see some local police activity about a quarter mile in and around the harbor to the east. We'll keep our eyes on it. Nothing concerning."

"Any American activity?"

"No. Quiet on that front."

"Hmmm..."

"We have three small vessels between a mile and three miles from shore, plus my crew's transport craft, all watching for any incoming ships. Other than a few wayward fishermen, we're clear. I should mention that the chopper is fueled and ready. So that item is complete. In fact, earlier than scheduled."

"Excellent."

"Any word on the ransom? The bitcoin?"

"No. But, as a negotiating tactic, I don't expect that until the very last minute. They still have over 18 hours to make the deposit. And I'm keeping an eye on my account. What's starting to really piss me off is that I haven't seen action on the digital contract."

"Are you certain the skylink is working?"

"Yes. The battery-powered Wi-Fi connection to the satellite Internet hub you placed on the roof of the port office is solid. I ran another speed test."

"Then all is going to plan."

"Except for the response to the contract."

"By 1 a.m. you'll have your research money, we'll have our share, and the world will have agreed to your terms."

"If everything lines up. If not...I have contingencies. I know you do, too."

"Of course. I'll keep you posted."

"I'll keep you up to date as well."

Parnette put the walkie-talkie back down on the table and took a sip of her tea.

Parnette talked to herself, "Something's not right. Don't they realize what power I have at my fingertips?" Parnette's calculating brain started running scenarios, options, and outcomes. "Dammit. I know what I must do. They left me no choice. *Plan D.C.*"

Parnette stood up from her stateroom chair and walked over to the balcony's blinds. On the nearby nightstand, her sat phone was on charge. She unplugged the charge cord and then opened the balcony's blinds using the two midpoint vertical sashes. Parnette looked out the balcony's glass door and saw a clear view to the ocean. "Okay," she said to herself.

Parnette unlocked the balcony door and slid it open. A warm sea breeze softly stroked her red hair. A moment of tranquility washed through her consciousness, along with an image of her and her niece Dorothy playing together in the beach sand at Wildwood. Her mind then latched back to her stateroom and the mission at hand. "I'm doing this for you, my sweetness."

Unbeknown to Parnette, Niels Brouwer was moments away from his position on the breakwater, across from the midpoint of the Cosmos Megaliner. He came upon a well-positioned rock outcropping and waded to a relatively flat, but slimy, boulder.

Parnette stepped out onto the balcony and powered on her sat phone while extending the foldable antenna upward. Twenty seconds later, the signal-strength bars appeared – a full stack of green. Parnette pressed *9 to bring up a pre-stored contact phone number and then pressed the green SEND button.

More quickly than she had expected, a computer voice answered, "What is your command?" Under her breath, Parnette muttered in anger, "Those sonofabitches..." The computer obediently responded, "Command '*son-o-bit-chez*' was not understood, please repeat." Parnette paused, closed her eyes, and replied, "*Delta Charlie* initiate." The computer responded, "*Delta Charlie* initiate confirmed." Parnette then pressed the red END key to conclude the call.

Brouwer unpacked his rifle assembly. With honed skill, he quickly set up the tripod, attached the rifle, and began adjusting the scope – while also starting to scan the ship with his Steiner Military 10x50 binoculars.

Parnette took a deep breath of sea air, stepped back into her stateroom, and closed the glass door.

A reflective glint from the sliding door caught Brouwer's eye. He raised his binoculars in that direction. But Parnette had already closed the curtains to her stateroom.

CHAPTER 52

6:42 a.m.

Kirk could hear Geerman's office phone ringing from two offices down the hall. Kirk got up from his centralized desk and briskly walked the twenty feet into Geerman's office. He picked up the phone.

"This is Sergeant Kirk. I'm taking calls for Captain Geerman. Who is calling?"

On the other end of the line, "This is the United States Secretary of State, John Quintana. I was speaking to Captain Geerman earlier regarding, um, the crisis centered in your cruise port."

"I see. Well, Captain Geerman is addressing the situation as we speak."

"'Addressing?' How so?"

"I'm afraid I am not at liberty to provide any details. Those are direct orders to me. We do not know who is friend or foe at this point."

"I can assure you the United States is a friend. A friend that may get blown up at any time."

"I understand the magnitude of the situation."

"You do? Okay. Then please connect me with Captain Geerman."

"As you probably know, our cell phone service – in fact all electrical power across the island – is out. But let me try something. Can you hold a moment?"

"A tiny moment. I have to brief the President of the United States in eighteen minutes. As you can see, this is of the highest urgency."

"Understood." Kirk put down the phone and picked up his police walkie-talkie and squeezed the talk button. "Kirk to Captain Geerman. Kirk to Captain Geerman. Do you copy?"

"This is Geerman. Kirk, we are in the middle of our 'operation'. Is this urgent?"

"Yes, sir. I have the United States Secretary of State on the phone. He said his name is Quintana. He said he must speak to you as he is briefing his President in a few minutes."

"Put his call on your speakerphone and position the walkie-talkie near the speaker. Squeeze the talk button so I can hear. It will be obvious when I need to respond; release the button then."

Kirk did as requested. He then said, "Secretary Quintana, I am holding down the 'talk' button on our police walkie-talkie. Captain Geerman can hear you."

"So much for a secure channel, but this will have to do. Captain Geerman, we spoke earlier. I'll be brief, as the situation has dramatically escalated. Once I speak, I will listen to your reply. To make a long story short, two drug smugglers in Venezuela have armed with explosives an autonomous, uncrewed, drug-smuggling watercraft called a 'sub-tub.' It's about 10 feet long and three feet wide. If our estimates are correct, in 74 minutes, at 7:56 a.m., we expect this sub-tub to enter the western end of your harbor and 10 minutes later detonate at the cruise ship. Their intent is to not cause damage, but to seem like the first volley of an attack – and cause Parnette to panic and set off the bomb – destroying much of the U.S. Insane as it sounds, that's our latest intelligence. How do you copy?"

Kirk released the talk button on the walkie-talkie.

Geerman responded, "That's absolutely horrible! But copy fine." Geerman briefly contemplated telling Quintana of their sniper plan but held off. "I appreciate the heads up. How can we help?"

Kirk squeezed the talk button.

"I don't know," replied Quintana. "I have to brief the President in 17 minutes. We're scrambling for all ideas. Since the situation is there in your port, and you have a local perspective, you might have a thought that we haven't considered."

Kirk released the talk button.

Given the clear urgency, Geerman decided to unveil his team's plan. "With this firmer picture, I feel it is important to disclose a detail of our current 'operation'. Right now, we have our best sniper within range of the starboard side of the ship, discreetly hidden in the harbor's breakwater. Assuming Parnette would have to step toward the balcony to complete a sat phone call, we want to be ready to take her out. However, we have no idea which stateroom is hers. If you relay any intel in that regard, it could greatly improve our odds."

Kirk pressed the talk button.

"Be extremely careful!" Quintana replied forcefully. "We can't provoke her 'trigger finger' on the sat phone! Regarding her stateroom: We don't yet know. We are working it as hard as we can. We will certainly let you know when we know."

A lightbulb went on in Kirk's mind. Before Geerman or Quintana had a chance to speak further, Kirk added, "I have an idea that may help!"

Kirk released the talk button and simultaneously Geerman and Quintana said, "Go ahead!" Quintana added, "Make it quick. I have, literally, 15 minutes before my butt has to be in the Situation Room with the President."

Kirk pressed the talk button.

"Secretary Quintana, how fast and deep is the, what did you call it, 'sub-tub' traveling?"

"Our experts say it's moving at about three-point-nine miles per hour. And it's designed to travel just below the surface, two feet, max. It has to travel shallow; it has a few-foot protrusion on the top that supports its GPS antenna."

"Does it have a proximity sensor? Or contact switch?"

"Our experts have seen these weaponized sub-tubs before. If it is like the others, it's a simple contact switch on the nose that will go off when it slams into the side of the ship. It also prevents a curious fish or a piece of flotsam – in simple proximity – from setting it off."

"Okay. What if we can snag the sub-tub with a fishing net as it enters the harbor? That way it will never get to the ship."

"You could do that?"

"It's coming through the harbor entrance. As an old boatman, any vessel – particularly a GPS-guided autonomous one – will use the harbor entrance buoy as a waypoint. Let me get Captain Geerman's response."

Kirk released the talk button.

Geerman responded, "That sounds logical. Except how are we going to get a big fishing net in place in less than an hour? We don't have resources like that."

Kirk squeezed the talk button.

"Let me worry about that. Captain Geerman, do I have your approval to give this a try?"

Kirk released the talk button.

"Yes. As long as Quintana concurs. It's his country at stake."

Kirk pressed the talk button.

"Kirk, go ahead; make the preparations. I will brief the President. Use this phone number – it's my cell – to keep me posted on your progress. I'll have my cell forwarded to a Situation Room phone. I have to go. Good luck!"

Quintana hung up the line. Kirk resumed regular back-and-forth with Geerman over the walkie-talkie.

Geerman said, "Well, that was awkward. I caught most of it, though. I'll brief Croes and the crew. But, Kirk, where the heck did you come up with *that* crazy idea?"

"I guess it comes with the name 'Kirk' and watching way too much *Star Trek* growing up. 'The Tholian Web' episode came to mind."

"I have no clue what you're talking about. Where will you get a fishing net *and* get it deployed in the harbor – in a little over an hour?"

"I'm calling in a long-overdue favor to an old salt named Wim."

***

Kirk fired up the office's Marine Radio and switched it to channel 16.

"Wim Van Hoebeek. Wim Van Hoebeek. Are you on frequency? Wim Van Hoebeek. Wim Van Hoebeek. Are you on frequency?"

After a couple of minutes of silence, a gruff voice responded, "This is Van Hoebeek. Who is calling me on the Port frequency? This is not allowed."

"Wim. This is Kirk. I knew you might be monitoring the Port frequency given the circumstance. I wouldn't be calling if it wasn't critically important. As this is an open channel, I'd rather not say more. Can you get to my – let's just say – office?"

"Ah, 'office.' I understand. I'm practically across the street at the Seaport Village Marina. I'll be there in two. Wim out."

***

Sure enough, in two minutes, a hustling Van Hoebeek pressed the button on the police station's video doorbell. Kirk buzzed him in.

"What the hell is going on, Kirk?"

"If I told you America is about to get blown up, would you believe me?"

"Unfortunately, yes. Once the island lost power, I clicked on my battery-powered radio. I've been following the BBC reports via shortwave. Helluva thing. So what's this have to do with me?"

"It's a long story. I don't have time to get into the details. You'll have to trust me."

"From the urgency in your voice, I don't think I have a choice."

"As ludicrous as it may sound, I need you to catch an underwater mini-sub on auto-pilot that will be heading into the harbor towards the big ship that's in port."

"You're right. It's ludicrous. And you're crazy!"

"I'm dead serious."

"And how do you propose that I 'catch' this 'sub'?"

"With a net. I'm told it doesn't have a proximity sensor. It uses a contact switch that triggers when it slams into the ship."

"But it's a *sub!*"

"Actually, it's a tiny – about 10 feet long and three feet wide – unmanned, drug-running sub coming out of Venezuela. They call it a 'sub-tub.' It's chugging at three-point-nine miles per hour, and barely below the surface – only a couple of feet."

"And when?"

"I'm told it will reach the western harbor buoy at 7:56."

"Holy mackerel!" Van Hoebeek exclaimed. "I don't believe I'm agreeing to this. I owe you one, anyway."

"Actually, about a dozen. Remember the 'pirate' fiasco."

"Yeah, yeah." As Van Hoebeek started to walk back down the hall to the door, he kept the conversation going. "You're never going to let me live that down. How was I to know it was a birthday costume?" As he exited the building, he shouted back to Kirk, "I'll use my portable on channel 19!"

"That'll work. In all seriousness, be careful."

"I've yet to meet a fish I couldn't catch."

CHAPTER 53

6:51 a.m.

As Van Hoebeek was rushing out the door of the police station, Gabby and Austin were charging up the steps.

"Is Kirk inside?" Gabby asked the fast-paced Van Hoebeek.

"Just speaking with him," replied Van Hoebeek, holding the door open for a split second as Gabby and Austin passed in. "But I think he's a bit busy" Van Hoebeek continued as he bolted down the steps.

"Oh, we know that for sure!" Austin replied as Van Hoebeek hustled across the street.

Austin and Gabby, the jammer in Gabby's right hand, ran down the hall to Kirk at his desk.

"We've got it – let's test it!" exclaimed Austin.

CHAPTER 54

7:00 a.m.

John Quintana bounded into the Situation Room, winded from his full sprint down a flight of stairs and the adjacent the hallway; his colleagues and the President were already seated.

"Through the tape on time, John," said Clarkson. "Thank you – everyone – for your punctuality. Again, dispense with the formalities. How are we going to save our country – and the lives at the cruise port?"

Brassard spoke first:

"As you know from Admiral Birch, the three Tomahawks are en route. All flights are nominal. A digital flight-path map is now on Screen Four."

"And we can terminate them up until 8.25 seconds from the ship, correct?"

"That's correct, Madam President."

"Barb."

"Barb."

Brassard continued, "The F-15E is airborne. Our tactical team swapped the traditional parachute on the e-bomb with a covert-operations 'chute made of sky blue ripstop nylon. Almost invisible given the current sky conditions in Aruba. It can still be seen, although likely not until a much-lower altitude. Our estimates are that we've increased the odds of mission success from one in ten to one in three."

"Commendable. But not good enough to risk the salvation of our country."

"Agreed."

"So I have the technical particulars correct: We can abort dropping the e-bomb at any time, right?"

"Yes. Until we're less than a half a mile from the target. Ah, *the ship*."

"Understood, Arty. But – one in three – we lose the country two-thirds of the time. For that reason alone, we need to dismiss this option."

"Agreed." Brassard continued, "You also told Hutch and I to explore whatever steps, whatever options, we felt would get the job done."

"I did."

"We conferred. We can detonate a nuclear device over the ship."

"A nuke! We said the math didn't work."

"That was onboard a B-52. Hutch and I, and our support staff, ran a simulation with another option – a B61 nuclear gravity bomb."

"What the heck is that?"

"The B61 is a nuclear bomb with what we call 'dial-a-yield' – we can select the destructive force right on the weapon. Turned all the way down, it's about a third of a kiloton. It's only 12 feet long. It's carried under the wing of an aircraft and dropped – falling by gravity – hence its name."

Hutchinson added, "Colloquially, it's a 'tactical nuke.'"

"To give you this option, we took the liberty to place a B61 on the same F-15E before it took off from Homestead."

"Arty!"

"Let me give you the rationale. The F-15E is our country's only fighter that has been tested with a small under-wing tactical nuclear device. Our simulation showed that if we detonate it at 2,000 feet above the ship, the EM pulse will assuredly knock out all the electronics on the ship – including Parnette's sat phone."

"What about the passengers! And crew!"

"There would still be loss of life. Tragically. We conferred with Jordy while our staffs were running a top-line simulation. Let me turn this over to her."

"Thank you, Arty. Barb, my team over at the OSTP ran simulations. Sadly, due to the nature of our world, we have baseline models for nearly every size nuclear device." Dr. Montgomery pressed an icon on her tablet. "I'm told I should be able to bring up a graphic on the small monitor past Screen Seven, a left-over from the recent renovation. Okay. There we go."

Everyone suddenly cringed. Appearing on the monitor was an overhead satellite image of the Cosmos Megaliner with an overlay of colored concentric rings – indicating various nuclear-bomb effects.

"This is a static image of the Cosmos Megaliner, taken twenty minutes before we came back into the room. It's also a simulation of the effects of a 0.3 kiloton B61 nuclear gravity bomb detonated at 2,000 feet above the ship."

The room was riveted to Dr. Montgomery's words and the graphic.

"Let me first turn your attention to the outermost blue ring. That defines the EMP zone – where the electromagnetic pulse will damage and destroy electronics. The EMP is, of course, intended to take out Parnette's satellite phone – which it will. The conductivity of the salt water actually works in our favor. I won't get into the physics, other than saying it reflects and focuses the EMP on all electronics onboard the ship."

"Even if Parnette's satellite phone is off?" asked Clarkson.

"Yes. The volts per meter will be so high – tens of thousands of kilovolts – it will arc through the device – from the stub antenna to the circuit board, contacts, wiring, etcetera.

"And even if she is in the interior of the ship?"

"Yes. A phenomenon called Source Region EMP will cause the piping and wiring of the ship – even the few-foot wires of phone and computer chargers – to act like antennas and further distribute the extremely high voltages. We can't conceive of a scenario whereby Parnette's satellite phone would not be neutralized."

"So the primary intent is assured."

"Yes."

"I'm sure your eyes are also fixed on the inner red circle that completely covers the mid-section of the ship. That's the diameter of the nuclear-detonation fireball. The fireball would be about 300 feet across. In this graphic, we're only seeing one dimension of a three-dimensional event. Thankfully, as the fireball would be centered 2,000 feet above the ship, it would be a long way from the deck of the ship. Unlike the movie industry's universal depictions of a nuclear blast, no one on the ship would lose their life from the thermal nature of the explosion."

Dr. Montgomery paused, then continued. "Now for the less-than-desirable news. Please turn your attention to the inner green ring, just outside of the inner red circle. It goes out quite some distance from the ship. It's about a third-of-a-mile wide. This would be the zone of lethal radiation. Anyone directly exposed in this area would die within two months from radiation poisoning. That includes anyone topside on the ship and within a deck or two from topside."

Everyone in the room was visibly shaken. "Let me stop here for a moment," said Dr. Montgomery. "Barb, Madam President, your thoughts?"

"It is ghastly, as expected. The lack of effect from the fireball would be of little consequence to those exposed to the radiation."

"Correct."

"Please elaborate on what you said about 'directly exposed.' Who would survive?"

"The steel superstructure of the ship would – in general – protect the bulk of the passengers from a lethal dose of radiation. In our limited time this morning, it was impossible to specifically model."

"It's not surprising that no one has ever tried to figure out how a cruise ship would protect passengers from a nuclear blast."

"Of course. However, we did manage a few pertinent calculations using off-the-shelf equations for various layers of steel. Our confidence level is thus on the high side that the ship would protect 80% of the passengers."

"And those walking and working in and around the port?"

"Anyone outside within that third-of-a-mile zone would, unfortunately, be fully exposed to the radiation and die within a couple of months. Others inside of structures would see a substantial increase in cancers over their lifetimes."

Clarkson and everyone in the room tried to process what they were hearing and seeing. This wasn't a lecture on something theoretical, but as real as real could be. And it was rapidly sinking home.

Clarkson continued, "I see another colored ring. The green one. What is that?"

"That ring indicates the general damage area from the blast's pressure wave. It would span about a mile. The impacts would be, mostly, blown out windows. Little to no structural damage. Most injuries – of which there could be hundreds – would mostly be from flying glass."

"How about nuclear fallout? How would this affect the broader civilian population on the island?"

"Our models helped us predict that, as well. The prevailing wind at 2,000 feet at the time of detonation is anticipated to be 21 miles per hour directly from the east. There would be no measurable fallout over the island."

"I wish I could call that a 'good thing.' I am at a loss for words."

"I'm sorry Barb."

"You're doing your job." Clarkson scanned the entire room. "You are all doing your jobs. Commendably. This may be the worst day of all our lives. Time will tell. We've been dealt a terrible hand. I can't adequately express my appreciation."

Clarkson paused, looked at streaming satellite images of the ship, and looked across the room. "What is weighing on my mind, and should weigh on all of us, is that no country has used a nuclear weapon in 80 years."

Brassard stepped in, "We are all well aware of that, Barb. Look at what we're facing with Parnette's bomb: The destructive force to take out an entire country – and, perhaps, the world's ecosystem – in a single blow."

"Literally tear a hole in the Earth's atmosphere," added Hutchinson.

Clarkson stroked her forehead, then resumed. "I can't believe I am asking this: The e-bomb has a one-in-three probability of success. How about the nuke?"

Brassard responded, "The B61 would be deployed with no parachute by the F-15E traveling just under supersonic at about 10,000 feet and, as you know, detonated at 2,000 feet. It would not be spotted before detonation. Parnette would have no warning. So, to answer your question directly, it's as close to 100% as we can get."

"The Tomahawks?"

"Traveling at 550 MPH along the water, there is a very slight chance they may be heard or seen perhaps five seconds before they reach the ship – which would be about three-quarters of a mile. It is extremely unlikely that someone could dial a sat phone and trigger the U.S. based device in that short amount of time. Establishing a connection with an orbiting satellite takes longer than that. So nearly 100%."

"Understood."

Brassard answered Clarkson's questions in a near mechanized, monotone delivery. President Clarkson wondered to her herself if this was Arty's way of walling off his emotions regarding his daughter on the ship? Or the result of his decades of warfare and training to be able to compartmentalize and function in even the most-dire circumstances?

Brassard continued, "Given the stakes, let me be crystal clear on the sequencing:

"Without any intervention on your part, the Tomahawks will strike at 8:02. As we discussed, the missiles can be terminated within 8.25 seconds of their arrival. For practical purposes, you would need to tell Admiral Birch, who will be live on a monitor, *at least 20 seconds prior* so there would be enough time to relay the command codes to the missiles.

One other thing: If the Tomahawks get the ditch command by the minimal time, 8.25 seconds, they will be about one-and-a-quarter miles away. Under most circumstances, they will not explode upon impact. Parnette and her team would thus not be aware of any of this."

"Whew. I'm doing my best to absorb all of this. I got it, though. Arty, bottom-line the lethality of all options."

"The Tomahawk strikes, given the secondary explosions, would likely be near 100% lethal. Everyone on the ship would die. For the third-of-a-kiloton nuclear device, as Jordy indicated, 20% would die from radiation exposure. We're still talking the deaths of nearly 3,000 passengers and crew, and an unknown number in proximity to the cruise port. There's no way to provide precise numbers, given the many variables we can't know or control."

Clarkson made notes on her notepad.

"And finally the e-bomb. It would result in no deaths. Although we've decided the likelihood of success is too low."

"Yes, that option is off the table. It would likely fail to stop Parnette from dialing."

"Agreed," replied Brassard.

Clarkson followed, "Bottom-line my abort-decision matrix."

"We know sub-tub impact would be at 8:06. I would suggest we make 8:01 your absolute decision cutoff regarding the Tomahawks – one minute prior to their impact. We could scuttle them in the sea and retrieve them later. You would then have your final option available: The tactical nuke on the F-15E. You could abort the mission up to 8:04, one minute before the B61 drops, and two minutes before the sub-tub's impact."

"That's cutting things awfully close, Arty."

"We're just playing the hand we're dealt. But it's all very doable. We will have live displays and countdown clocks – for both the Tomahawks and the F-15E – throughout."

"Put the wheels in motion, Arty. You have my official approval."

"Will do. Immediately after we hear from Secretary Quintana with his latest update from Aruba. It may be pertinent."

"Agreed."

"Thanks, Arty," said Quintana. "I just got off the phone with the captain of the Aruba police force, Captain Geerman. Two things to report: One, they have positioned what they call a 'discreet sniper' off the starboard side of the ship, somehow nestled into the breakwater. They're looking to us to learn the location of Parnette's stateroom. Any word on that?"

"No, unfortunately" responded Alford.

"Didn't think so," replied Quintana. "I'm sure it would be quickly relayed. If we get that intel, I promised to pass it along."

Clarkson asked, "Are they considering taking her out?"

"If they get a clear shot. Given the poor options we have on our side of the fence, I don't think we should dissuade them. Of course, I'll pass along what you recommend."

"I'm with you. Our options are poor. Let them play it out."

"Second item: I must hand it to the Arubans. They may have come up with a way to stop the sub-tub."

"How?"

"They think they can snag it with a big fishing net when the sub-tub turns into the harbor. I gave them the particulars on the sub-tub – size, speed, and likely detonating mechanism – and they came up with this option. Again, given our currently poor options, I don't think we should discourage them. Madam President, your thoughts?"

"I agree. Let them play it out."

"Of course, our cell phones are inactive here in the Sit – but my cell is the number the Arubans have. As I was bolting down the hall, I tossed my cell to my aide, Chuck Rizzo, and said to get our tech team to patch my calls to one of our secure incoming lines. That should be live in a couple of minutes. If the Arubans call, we'll get it here."

Looking over at Brassard, Clarkson said, "Let me get this straight: If the Arubans can snag the sub-tub, we're back to Parnette's original timetable – buying ourselves 18 hours to come up with other options, correct?"

"Yes. It's either that or our more-pressing deadline." Brassard looked at his watch and continued, "It's 7:06 a.m. In exactly 60 minutes, the sub-tub – if unabated – will impact the ship."

"Arty, it sounds like the 8:06 time has been confirmed."

"It has. Morning daylight has allowed visual satellite tracking of the sub-tub. Not of the craft itself, as it's underwater. We're observing the general disturbance of the water above and behind it. The tracking confirms the arrival of the sub-tub at the entrance to the harbor: 7:56. As we surmised, it will take 10 minutes for it to travel to the ship. Thus 8:06."

"How does all this influence our in-bound tactical options?"

"If we get word that the Arubans are successful at capturing the sub-tub, we splash the Tomahawks and we call off the fighter. If we hear that the sub-tub made it through, we keep the tactical options in motion."

Clarkson nodded.

"Time to call Admiral Birch." Brassard picked up a phone in front of him, punched in three numbers, and began talking to the Admiral. A few seconds later Birch appeared, as previously, on Screen One.

"Madam President, this is Admiral Birch here in SOUTHCOM."

"Yes, Admiral."

"As before, I need you to confirm the target and weapon."

"Please proceed."

"I'm told you are aware that an F-15E is on its way to the Cosmos Megaliner that is docked in Aruba's Port of Oranjestad. And the fighter is equipped with a B61 nuclear gravity bomb that has 0.3 kiloton explosive capability."

"Affirmative, Admiral."

"And is it also correct that you are authorizing the B61's detonation at 2,000 feet above the Cosmos Megaliner?"

"Affirmative, Admiral."

"And, finally, is it also correct that the required detonation time would be precisely 8:05 a.m. Atlantic Standard Time which is also 8:05 a.m. Eastern Daylight Time?"

"Affirmative, Admiral."

"Do you have any questions?"

"I would like to confirm that I can terminate the mission at up to 8:04 a.m."

"Madam President, that is correct."

"For the record, it is not lost on me that I would be the world's first leader to authorize the use of a nuclear bomb in 80 years. Since Japan. I make this decision with considerable and solemn thought, for the protection of America – which is my sworn duty as the President of the United States. Under the authority vested in me as the President of the United States, I hereby authorize this mission."

"Your authorization is confirmed and witnessed," replied Birch. "I am sure you are aware that there would be one more critical step, two minutes before the drop of the B61."

"The emergency satchel."

"Yes, the Presidential Emergency Satchel."

"It is in the room here, in the possession of my military aide, Colonel MacQuarrie."

"Please have Colonel MacQuarrie close at hand, as matters would go rapidly at that point."

"Understood, Admiral."

Colonel MacQuarrie nodded in understanding.

"I have some additional information regarding the video feeds: In addition to the ability to track the inbound Tomahawk missiles by video, you will shortly have a video feed to track the flight of the F-15E."

"Acknowledged, Admiral. We will await that feed."

"Madam President, I will be on standby throughout – with immediate access for you and your team."

"Thank you, Admiral."

The Admiral muted his audio and pivoted his chair away from the camera and to his computer console.

Clarkson took a deep breath and refocused her mind.

Clarkson spoke to everyone around the table, "Team, this next hour may be the most-challenging that each of us may ever personally face. Certainly, the most consequential for our country. Stay sharp. Keep your wits. Keep thinking. We may need to implement not-yet-conceived options on the fly based on new data. And discard irrelevant options and data that are clouding our picture."

Clarkson turned her focus to Quintana. "Any word on our citizens in Aruba and the jammer?"

"No, unfortunately, it looks like it's a dead end."

"Understood."

"Barb, the satellite feeds are now available," said Brassard.

"Please bring them up."

Brassard walked over to a table with a touch-screen panel, typed in a seven-digit access code, and pressed the icon labeled "2". Screen Two lit up. A full overhead view of the Cosmos Megaliner filled the screen.

"That's the ship?" asked Clarkson.

"Yes, Barb. That's from our re-positioned satellite. And this..." Brassard tapped the panel again to bring up an image on Screen Three. "...is the Cosmos Megaliner from the Chinese satellite."

"Is it my eyes, or is the Chinese image clearer?"

"I'm afraid you are correct, Barb."

"Now we know at least one reason why the Chinese are letting us use their spy satellite: To show off!"

"We'll have to bring that up in our next staff meeting...assuming we still have a country left."

"Barb, now is as good a time as any to discuss one last point."

Clarkson could see the seriousness in his face. "What's that, Arty?"

Brassard's voice increased in intensity, pulling in everyone's attention.

"If things go sideways, my job as I see it, in addition to keeping the country safe, is to make recommendations to keep you safe."

"You're doing a fine job at that."

"Not as much as I'd like. I think it would be best if the Secret Service got you onto Air Force One in time to be away from the effects of Parnette's full-scale bomb."

"Arty, I'm not leaving this room."

Brassard ignored her statement and continued, "Our scientists estimate the electromagnetic blast radius, sufficient to take down any plane – even Air Force One – spans at least 750 miles. We don't know where in the continental U.S. the bomb is planted. To be safe, I suggest you – temporarily – get away from the continent. I talked to the Secret Service before we came into the room. As part of all contingencies, Marine One is waiting for you on the South Lawn. If you get in the air in 15 minutes – out of here now, onto Marine One, then to Air Force One that is fueled and ready at Joint Base Andrews – and fly east over the Atlantic, you'd make it to a safe distance."

"Arty, you're not listening to me. I'm not leaving this room."

"Oh, I hear you. Air Force One is fully equipped to mirror everything in this room. You will still be at the helm of every action and decision."

"Arty, the Secret Service would have to drag me by my hair. I'm not leaving."

"Barb, you know I can't order you."

"No, you can't. You do not have that authority. But, if you persist in this line of thought, I can fire you."

Quintana inserted himself into the heated discussion. "It is apparent to everyone that these are extraordinary circumstances, to say the least. Secretary Brassard, you said that if the bomb goes off there will be no functioning country left, correct?"

"Correct."

"So the President would be in the air with no country to lead, correct?"

"Well, but –"

At that instant, startling everyone, and interrupting the verbal confrontation, "The Cube" – the emergency-priority speakerphone in the center of the table – buzzed once per second, in synchronization with pulses of bright red. This eight-inch-square translucent cube, hence the nickname, was installed in a recent Situation Room enhancement. This was the first time anyone had ever seen it active.

"Well, someone answer it!" Clarkson commanded.

Tebbs was closest. He reached over and tapped the symbol of a phone handset on the top of the device and said, "Situation Room."

"This is Sergeant Kirk in Aruba."

Quintana jumped in, "This is Quintana. Hold on, Kirk." Quintana said to the rest of the room, "I asked the technical staff to forward my cell phone to a secure phone in the room – not the emergency phone!"

"Go ahead, John," Clarkson said. "We'll straighten things out later."

"Kirk, do you have an update?"

"Well, kind of. I have Austin Raze and Gabby Milone here. And it seems they have a working sat phone jammer."

CHAPTER 55

"Sergeant Kirk, can you repeat that?" asked Quintana.

"Yes. And I can do one better."

Kirk turned on his desk phone's speakerphone function.

"I have put you on speakerphone. Austin Raze and Gabby Milone are in front of me. As I said, it appears they have a functioning sat phone jammer."

President Clarkson put up her right palm, hushing Quintana, indicating that she wanted to speak.

"Mr. Raze and Ms. Milone. This is President Clarkson. I am in the Situation Room with my team. Is there something you would like to tell us?"

"Um...Uh..." Raze and Milone stuttered, caught off guard by the magnitude of the call.

Regaining his composure, Austin continued, "Madam President. This is Austin Raze. I am with my wife Gabriella, uh, Gabby Milone. It is an honor to speak with you."

"I appreciate the kind words. But, as you know, we have a crisis we're dealing with."

"Yes, Madam President, we are aware," responded Austin. "You and your team should know we have a functioning sat phone jammer. Moments before Sergeant Kirk called you, we tested it on the police station's sat phone. We brought the sat phone outside, powered it up, and it functioned normally; I called my office phone number and I got my voicemail message. We then turned on our jammer and the phone immediately lost the ability to connect to the satellite network; we only heard a screaming buzz whenever we tried to dial out."

Gabby added, "Our hope is come nightfall, hours before Parnette's deadline, the police office's dive team can covertly swim up and attach it to the hull of the ship via the magnet we put on it. Then turn it on and swim away. Doing so should prevent Parnette's activation of her bomb."

Clarkson replied, "First, the country thanks you for your incredible effort. And, my apologies, but I forgot to say I'm glad you're okay; I heard about your harrowing experience. However, the situation has changed. I'm pausing, as I am trying to determine what I can tell you. I don't suppose you two have top-secret clearances?"

Gabby and Austin spoke in unison, "No, Madam President."

Clarkson, "Hmmm... My team is not going to like this. I'm going to break every protocol in the book. If we don't act, there might not be any protocols – or any country – left, anyway. There is an explosive-packed, self-guided, watercraft of sorts – you don't need to know from where or how – that will hit the cruise ship in (looking at her watch) 58 minutes. At 8:06. It will only cause superficial damage. We fear Dr. Parnette may believe this is the first volley of a broader attack – and push the proverbial button. If that happens, within minutes, America may cease to exist."

Stunned silence on the other end of the phone.

"Ms. Milone and Mr. Raze, are you still there?"

The pair, in unison, responded, "Yes, Madam President."

Clarkson continued, "We are taking, well, a variety of measures, that I can't discuss, to secure the safety of the United States. The Arubans are also assisting in supplemental ways. Bottom line: Even with the best efforts, things could get very ugly, very fast, there at the port – and in the surrounding area. As your President, I want you to be safe. I would encourage you to provide your jammer to the police and get as far away from the port as quickly as you can."

Before Austin and Gabby could respond, Clarkson added, "Sergeant Kirk: Can your dive team find a way to get out to the ship with the device without getting spotted?"

"Madam President, two problems: One, our entire police force, including those who have secondary roles as divers, are deployed around the ship. I'm here solo at the police station, coordinating remotely with Captain Geerman who is at a remote command site. Two, even if I had a diver available, getting to the ship in broad daylight, without being spotted, would be nearly impossible."

"But not fully impossible," Austin injected.

"Austin! Shut up!" yelled Gabby. "The President is talking to Sergeant Kirk!"

"Just sayin'..." Austin added.

"Mr. Raze," said President Clarkson. "Is there something you would like to add to the discussion?"

"Well, there is a way to get to the ship and back, in theory, without being seen." And turning to Sergeant Kirk, "And it doesn't require a cloaking device."

"I'm not sure what you are talking about, Mr. Raze. Can you clarify?"

"Gabby and I are experienced divers. About a quarter of a mile from where we were, well, shot at, is Coral Reef Divers, the dive shop that we use on every Aruba trip to rent our tanks. It's almost within eyesight of the ship, on the edge of the harbor. Anyway, they have a few professional *underwater* jet skis that they use for salvage and repair operations. We're good friends with the owners, Jenny and Jurgen Visser. They've previously let us scoot around with these underwater speed demons. They're electric – so super stealthy. My wife is going to wring my neck, but Madam President, I believe Gabby and I can get the device planted on the hull of the ship successfully."

"I can't put you and Ms. Milone in any further danger."

"Madam President," Gabby piped in. "Reading between the lines, and I know you can't specifically say, but when you said, 'things can get very ugly, very fast' would we be safe a block or two from the port? Like here at the police station?"

"You're right, Ms. Milone, I can't specifically say. What I can say is that you're catching my drift. I can't say with certainty at what distance you will be safe."

"May I also assume that many lives on the ship are also at stake?"

"Ms. Milone, your assumption is – unfortunately – quite correct."

"Well, then. There really is no decision to be made. How many minutes until the watercraft contacts the ship?"

"56 minutes from now. 8:06. To protect the physical integrity of the United States, we have – let's just say – final 'emergency options' that would engage, and could not be stopped, beginning five minutes prior to that. At 8:01. So – and this is *absolutely critical* – to call off our emergency options, you would have to let me know *one minute or more before that*. By 8:00. Not a second later. There is no wiggle room."

"Understood, Madam President," replied Gabby. "Austin, what do you think, we're a half a mile from Coral Reef Divers?"

"If that. Maybe less."

"Our lime-green rental Jeep would be too conspicuous. What do you say we get in our daily run?"

Austin rolled his eyes and flashed a loving smiled at his wife.

"Madam President," Gabby spoke. "We will give it our best effort. We'll get to the ship. Activate the device. Get back to shore. And run back here to call you with a status report. By 8:00."

"I don't know what to say, other than thank you," replied Clarkson.

Austin to Kirk: "Please radio your captain and tell him not to shoot at us if we run by."

Kirk nodded and said, "Good luck. Warp speed."

On that, Austin and Gabby rocketed down the hallway towards the front door. Back to Kirk, Austin shouted, "You should have said, 'Live long and prosper!'"

The two flew out the door and down the front steps. Gabby, with the jammer in her right hand and arm, looked like a college running back carrying a book-shaped "football." And this football sprouted a three-inch-ish springy wire antenna on one side and a looped cord strap on the other – both flopped and bounced with each stride.

The couple turned left and sprinted down the street.

CHAPTER 56

Prior to entering the police station again, Austin and Gabby had the presence of mind to slip on their beach shoes that were stashed in the back of the Jeep. So at least they had a little foot protection as they raced down the street. As former athletes, and still competitive runners, they had a special running gear that they put to timely use.

Within three minutes they were at the front entrance of Coral Reef Divers. Jenny and Jurgen Visser were having cups of coffee at a small outdoor table.

Seeing Austin and Gabby, Jenny said, "Bon Bini! Up early! Here to get a refill on last night's tanks?"

"Did you get a glimpse of the bioluminescent algae bloom?" followed Jurgen. "And how about the stuff on the cruise ship? Nutty!"

"Yes, we saw the bloom," responded Gabby. "However, it's actually the cruise ship that we're here about."

"What do you mean?" asked Jenny.

Austin replied, "As insane as it may sound, we're trying to save the United States."

Gabby continued, "It may be hard to believe, but we just got off the phone with the President of the United States, patched in through the police station. President Clarkson asked us to try to place this device (Gabby holds up the jammer) on the hull of the cruise ship that's in the middle of the ongoing fiasco. And (looking at her watch) we have 45 minutes to get there, stick it on, get back to the police station, and call the President."

"You're right, Gabby, that doesn't sound believable," Jurgen replied. "But we owe you one after you helped us find and salvage that sunken motor last year. How can we possibly help?"

"We need two of your battery-powered underwater jet skis. Right now."

"Like this second," added Austin.

"Well, units three and four are fully charged. They're moored right there." Jurgen points to two small crafts – each about five feet long and two feet wide – tethered to the shop's small dock, each bobbing gently on the surface of the nearly calm water. "Later today we were planning to use them to examine the underside of a pier north of here. We were hired to give it a look-see. As long as I can get them back in time –"

"Oh, you can count on it," said Austin. "Let's just say there's a lot riding on our timeliness."

"And as long as we don't get shot at, again," added Gabby with a wry smile.

"Shot at?" Jenny responded, unsure if she heard correctly.

"Oh, Gabby's just kidding," said Austin. "You know her."

Gabby, ignoring Austin, pointed to a rack of air tanks, "Are those tanks full?"

"Yes," said Jenny. "And I'll grab you two sets of our rental regulators."

"Thanks," replied Austin. "And we don't need fins. Masks would help, though. Can we use two of those?" Austin said, pointing to a number of scuba masks in the fresh-water rinse tank.

"Go for it," responded Jenny.

Austin grabbed two masks and vigorously shook out the water.

"And how about this bungee cord," asked Austin, pointing to the one dangling from a pegboard protrusion.

"Sure," said Jurgen.

"We don't need BCDs," added Gabby. "Just help us strap the tanks onto those packs (pointing to the tank backpacks hanging on the wall). They won't be comfortable. Although they will keep us streamlined for speed."

In less than four minutes, Austin and Gabby were strapped up and rapidly walking to the two underwater jet skis at the dock. Jenny, walking stride for stride, turned on the air valves on the couples' tanks. Hearing the rush of air entering the air hoses, Gabby and Austin momentarily placed their air regulators into their mouths and did a quick breathing check. All was fine. They each grabbed their tank's dangling hose that terminated in an air gauge; both tanks had 3,000 PSI. Full tanks.

Austin and Gabby waded into shallow water, stood next to the two watercrafts, and untethered them from a small post on the dock. Jenny and Jurgen stood on the dock, watching.

Jurgen said to Austin and Gabby, "As you know, as soon as you get on them, your weight will bring them underwater. You should be close to neutrally buoyant the way you're equipped. If you get off, they will pop back up to the surface."

Jenny added, "You know how they work. Master power is the big red toggle. Compass is obvious. Throttle is in the right grip. That's about it."

Austin and Gabby nodded in affirmative for the quick refresher.

"I think we're all set," said Gabby.

"Thanks, again, for this extreme favor," continued Austin.

"No problem," said Jenny. "Good luck on your mission," added Jurgen.

"We'll be back in a jiffy," said Gabby.

Gabby and Austin turned their attention to the task at hand.

Looking at her watch, "Honey, we have 37 minutes to get this done."

"Are you sure you're okay with this? The last match with those thugs was close."

"It's not my idea of fun. On the other hand, the President made the situation sound pretty ominous. I'm feeling if we don't, this whole region will be toast – along with us."

"Agreed. Let's get this show on the road."

"Water."

"Yeah, whatever," Austin said with a shake of his head. "Okay, now for the bungee," Austin waved the bungee cord in his left hand.

"I think I know what you're planning with that," said Gabby, as she extended her right hand that was holding the jammer.

"Yeah, that's why Gerritt and I added the loop to the jammer."

"And here I thought it was a wrist strap for an oversized charm."

"Well, a little less glamorous. I'll thread the bungee through its loop and cinch it to the side of my craft with a simple knot. Like this."

"As long as we can untie the knot when we get to the ship."

"It would suck if we couldn't."

With a tug on the simple knot Austin said, "Okay, that should do it."

Austin leaned against the craft he was next to and flipped on the master power switch. Gabby did the same for hers. Green lights on the dashboards confirmed the underwater jet skis were ready to go.

"You know, so we don't get spotted and shot at, we won't be able to surface until we get to the ship," said Austin.

"Let's follow the edge of the shore at a depth of about 20 feet," said Gabby. "We should get a glimpse of the port's big pilings when we're nearly there."

"Roger that, Gabs."

"Then we'll swing left perhaps a couple hundred feet to get to the other side of the ship?"

"At least. That monster is huge."

"Then hang a right and go another few hundred feet – something like that?"

"All sounds reasonable. We'll fine tune when we get there."

Looking at her watch, Gabby said, "We've got 33 minutes to get to the ship, plant this bad boy (nodding to the tied-on jammer), get back here to Jenny and Jurgen's place, then run to the police station to call President Clarkson. Piece of cake, right?"

"You forgot to say not to get shot at again."

"Yeah, that too."

"I love you," Austin said with uncharacteristic seriousness.

"I love you, too," replied Gabby. "Let's do this."

The couple slid their masks down over their faces and placed the regulators into their mouths. They hopped on top of the unique watercrafts; their body weight plus the weight of the air tanks submerged the mini vehicles as anticipated.

Once underwater, through their masks, their eyes exchanged loving thoughts.

With a nod to each other, they twisted their craft's throttles and were off.

Aruba's crystal-clear water made it easy for Austin and Gabby to see the edge of the shore and stay at about 20 feet underwater. They kept side by side, within a couple of feet of each other – Austin closest to the shoreline. They kept their throttles on full; no sightseeing, even as they passed a few gorgeous parrotfish and angelfish.

Within 10 minutes, they came across the first huge piling of the cruise port. They looked at each other and simultaneously gave nods to the left. As planned, they turned their crafts hard in that direction, continuing to exchange glances and head gestures – natural non-verbal cues honed from hundreds of dives together.

Austin put up his left hand in a *slow down* motion. They both cut their throttles. Gabby took her right hand off the throttle and made a *right turn* thumb motion. Austin nodded affirmatively.

Both revved their motors back to full throttle. Less than 30 seconds later the mammoth hull of the Cosmos Megaliner came to view on their right. It was much larger than they had imagined – and they exchanged wide-eyed expressions. Pressing ahead, they shifted their forward course closer and closer to the huge wall of steel until they were only a few feet away. Gabby took her right hand off her throttle and signaled *full stop*. Austin cut his throttle.

Still about 20 feet underwater, Austin started to untie the bungee cord. Gabby could see the cord unthreading from the jammer's loop. Austin gave the jammer a decisive tug and it was free.

The couple knew that the next step was the most dangerous part of their mission: They would quickly surface and magnetically stick the jammer to the ship above the waterline. The few-inch springy antenna had to be completely out of the water, ideally pointing upward, and not touching the steel hull.

The duo once again made eye contact and, simultaneously, looked upward. They nodded to each other and exchanged winks of endearment. They lightly engaged their throttles and pointed their crafts toward the surface, while skillfully nudging even closer to the ship's hull – almost to the point that they could reach out and touch the accumulating sea slime.

A few seconds later their heads broke the surface – but they were careful not to extend any higher than the bottom edge of their facemasks. Austin's right arm emerged with his hand clutching the jammer. With an audible *clink*, the jammer planted itself onto the mammoth steel hull with the antenna wire pointing skyward. Austin pressed a small waterproof button that was a couple of inches from the base of the antenna. A tiny blue LED started to flash. Austin had to squint to be sure, due to the sun reflecting off the water and the slight condensation forming on the inside of his mask. Gabby gave Austin a wink of approval.

With a nod to Gabby they both tipped their sleds downward and re-submerged. The two instinctively looked at each other, wondering the same thing: Had they been spotted? They were on the surface for less than 10 seconds. No bullet zings or pings – this time. Gabby made an *away* motion with her head and Austin gladly obliged. With throttles at full, they dashed back in the direction of Jenny and Jurgen's dive shop.

***

Their minds raced, knowing they had merely 19 minutes to get back to the police station and contact President Clarkson. They kept their heads fixed ahead, with only quick peeks at each other to make sure they remained within eyesight of one another. Gabby, the more-proficient underwater navigator of the two, followed the underwater map in her mind. The silence of the sea was only broken by the bubbles of their regulators and the whir of each craft's electric propulsion.

Gabby turned her sled to the left and Austin dutifully followed. Throttles on full, they continued to race through the water.

Gabby spotted the underwater structure of the dive shop's dock and put up her left hand in a stopping gesture. Austin, about ten feet back, didn't see her signal; the dock appeared and Austin almost ran into it. He cut his throttle just in time. His momentum nearly propelled him into Gabby who had already hopped off her underwater jet ski at the dock.

Gabby rolled her eyes at Austin as they emerged from the water. They spit out their regulators. "Oops!" was the first word that came out of Austin's mouth. Then "Sorry about that!"

Jenny and Jurgen were nowhere to be seen. There was no time for pleasantries, anyway. They quickly retethered the watercrafts to the dock's small post. They unstrapped their tanks' backpacks and placed them on the dock.

The duo grabbed their beach shoes that were on the edge of the dock. They simultaneously looked at their watches. 7:55 a.m. Gabby exclaimed "Crap!" and Austin grimaced in return. They had five minutes to get to the police station and be on the horn to President Clarkson. Without saying another word, they broke into a full-out run.

CHAPTER 57

7:55 a.m.

Like a Broadway production that had gone off the rails, three 'Acts' were playing out at precisely the same moment.

Gabby and Austin were sprinting back to the police station as if their hair was on fire.

Van Hoebeek was racing to the harbor entry buoy to snag the sub-tub.

And President Clarkson was weighing the heaviest of choices. Her decisions, in the span of minutes, would decide the fate of America and the lives of thousands of innocent travelers on the cruise ship. Not since the Cuban Missile Crisis of 1962 had a President had such consequential decisions to make.

***

The Situation Room's wall-sized monitors were lit with up-to-the-second images.

Left to right, Screen One was Admiral Birch.

The American X17 surveillance satellite's view of the Cosmos Megaliner was on Screen Two.

Screen Three was the Chinese BrightFlower-5 satellite's view of the ship; the image remained clearer than from the X17; even the undulations of the surrounding water could be observed.

On Screen Four, the path and location of the group of three Block IV TLAM Tomahawk cruise missiles were represented by a blinking red triangle at the end of a dashed red line.

The path and location of the F-15E carrying the combined armament – the Hi-JENKS-2 e-bomb and the B61 nuclear gravity bomb – was on Screen Five.

An animation of the sub-tub's anticipated sea course and timing was on Screen Six, with a blinking red dot representing the seacraft at the leading end of a dashed red line.

And on Screen Seven was Vice President Carlisle on a secure interactive link; Carlisle was situated in a SCIF at the U.S. Embassy in Kyiv.

The tension was magnified by the silence.

"Madam Pres- um, Barb," Brassard spoke. "It's almost decision time."

"I know Arty..." Clarkson's voice trailed off, then rebounded, "I'm trying to make sure we haven't missed a relevant perspective."

Director Alford spoke up. "Along those lines, but totally off the wall: Has anyone considered leveraging SAI-OP?"

"The Strategic AI has only been operational for three weeks," Hemsley replied. "Over at Homeland, we're scheduling the first senior-level drill for next month."

"That's why I said *off the wall*," replied Alford.

"I've read top-lines in my PDB (President's Daily Brief)," added Clarkson.

"We're still getting a handle on what the AI can and can't do," added Hemsley.

"What does it mean that it is *operational*?" asked Clarkson.

"Well, I'll take this one – because I think it's lunacy," Brassard gruffly spoke. "I'm told that the AI is being fed everything that's going on – and I do mean *everything*."

Dr. Montgomery injected: "Parnette's ramblings. The satellite feeds. Data pipes from our intelligence agencies. Surveillance done by our friends and foes. The Internet backbone. The so-called Dark Web. And all the audio it hears."

"What – what audio?" questioned Tebbs.

"Barry, I think that was in a footnote of a recent PDB," said Clarkson.

"And if I'm not mistaken," said Carlisle on the monitor, "even me talking here over the secure channel is part of the AI input, isn't that correct Jordy?"

"Yes, it's like the AI is sitting here in this room."

"Whoa, that's heavy duty," said Tebbs.

"Before everyone zips their lips, nothing is being recorded. That was a prerequisite to the implementation. SAI-OP is processing the incoming streams, not recording them," said Montgomery.

"My ass it's not," blurted Brassard. "And that's ass – a, s, s," he spelled out to the apparently listening AI.

Clarkson, with authority, "I have to terminate this point-counterpoint discussion. Can this AI thing help us or not?" Scanning the monitors, she continued, "We're down to minutes here."

"Ask it," Montgomery responded.

Clarkson raised an eyebrow.

"Yeah, just ask it. SAI-OP's online and listening. Here in the Sit, it will only respond to your voice and that of the Vice President."

"A little creepy. Okay: SAI-OP, as you can see, we, um, I have to make a monumental decision here in a few minutes. What is your assessment of the situation?"

No sooner did the word 'situation' cross Clarkson's lips did a human-sounding voice emerge from the room's invisible in-wall speakers – a voice that was instantly familiar to everyone. "President Clarkson, given the time sensitivity, I assume you would like the top-line version."

Instead of replying to the AI, Clarkson turned to Montgomery, "Son of a bitch, that's...that's –"

"Yeah, yeah. I won't say which one, but a recent President made it a prerequisite to the development. Evidently, he was a fan of Tom Cruise. It's a synthesized replication."

Clarkson slammed the table and shouted, "I don't have time for this shit!" She rubbed her forehead for a couple of seconds and refocused. "Yes, SAI-OP, the top-line version."

"Sure. General Brassard's assessments are within reasonable probabilistic parameters."

Silence.

"SAI-OP, not that abbreviated. For instance, are there options we have not considered?"

"There are 67 options that I have not heard spoken in this room."

"And..."

"Unfortunately, they all have less likelihoods of success."

Brassard added, "Well at least we humans are not obsolete...yet."

"General suggestions, then," said Clarkson. "Briefly, what can we do better?"

"The weakest link appears to be Parnette's satellite phone-triggering requirement."

"Can we disable the satellites?"

"No. Assuming she is using one of the four primary service suppliers – 98.3% likelihood – there are nearly 375 satellites. Even a multitude of in-space nuclear detonations would only take out a small fraction of the satellites."

"What else can we do with the satellites? Or Parnette's link?"

"Concentrate on terrestrial options."

Turning her head to Quintana, "John, I'm grasping at straws here. Any word from Aruba? Sniper? Jammer? Fishing net?"

Quintana replied "Sorry, nothing. Any call would come in here, as before."

Clarkson looked at The Cube sitting idle on the table and shook her head.

"SAI-OP, any last words?"

"Parnette's psychological profile suggests she likely anticipated multiple outcomes and thus deployed multiple strategies to her favor. But there is not enough data to make a high-probability assessment."

Under his breath, Brassard said, "The techno-trashcan won't even make a guess."

SAI-OP continued, "As circumstances evolve and variables are reduced, I may have input that may be more valuable."

"Thank you, SAI-OP. Please stand by."

"I will, Madam President. And thank you for not calling me Tom."

CHAPTER 58

7:55 a.m.

Van Hoebeck looked at his watch. "Cutting it close, Wim," he said to himself.

He scrolled through his boat's GPS listings until he got to the *Oranjestad SE entry buoy*. "Yep, that's the one." With a tap, 12.50528 degrees North and -70.03588 degrees West were set in his GPS. With a spin of the captain's wheel, he pivoted his pride and joy – a Boston Whaler Outrage Series fishing boat – and, with full throttle, the Quad 300-horsepower V8 Mercury Verado engines screamed to life.

"I can't believe I'm doing this," Van Hoebeck said to himself, as his boat plowed through the water, cutting a swath through the waves at high speed.

Within 60 seconds the buoy was in sight. He cut the throttle and spun the boat to face the entrance of the harbor.

Van Hoebeck scanned the sea past the buoy. "Nothing," he murmured. "Let's move past the buoy and get a little better angle." He revved the boat's engines for a second, then cut them back to idle. In an instant he spotted the incoming nemesis.

"Thar she blows!" Van Hoebeck yelled as he saw an antenna – or were those two antennas? – sticking out of the water and a forward-facing wake about 200 feet away. He pushed the throttle slightly forward and steered his boat so that the plodding underwater sub-tub would travel between him and the buoy. And cut the engines.

Van Hoebeck stepped away from the wheel, grabbed a bunched-up, weighted, 20' x 20' trawl net from the floor of his boat, and readied his toss to the approaching craft. 50 feet. 40. 30. 20. 10. With the deft of an ocean sage, Van Hoebeck tossed the net with a slight spinning action, assuring that the net would fully open. It did, draping over the passing-by sub-tub, fully ensnaring it – and entangling the electrically driven propeller to a halt.

"Got ya, you piece of junk!" shouted Van Hoebeck. No sooner than he was about to reach for his radio mic to call Kirk, he saw another approaching antenna and front-facing wake. And it was heading right to his position.

"Verdomme!" – dammit – Van Hoebeck exclaimed in Dutch, as he gunned the motors and his boat lurched forward – avoiding the oncoming craft by less than six feet. "Son of a bitch!" Van Hoebeck screamed into the air, as this second sub-tub merrily chugged by.

Once past the buoy, the automated craft – following its GPS guidance – adjusted its rudder to make its way down the harbor, zeroing in on the cruise ship in the distance.

Van Hoebeck grabbed and squeezed the ship-radio's mic.

"Kirk! Kirk! Come in, please!"

Kirk swiveled his office chair to reach the nearby ship-to-shore radio. "Wim, we agreed to be a little more discrete."

"Screw that. We've got a big problem on our hands."

"Did you get, um, the 'tub'?"

"Yeah. The *first* one. Evidently, they didn't tell you there were *two*."

"Two?"

"Yeah. I snared the first one with my net. But another one was right behind it. Heck, it almost hit my boat. I nearly went up in smoke!"

"Wim, get the hell out of there. Major shit is going to fly. Go north to the Low Rise hotel area as fast as you can. Farther if possible."

"You don't have to tell me twice. Sorry I couldn't get the second sub-tub."

"Not your fault. We got bad info. Now go!"

Before Kirk even finished the plea to his friend, Van Hoebeck had spun the boat and was heading up the coastline, full throttle.

CHAPTER 59

7:57 a.m.

Kirk dialed Quintana's number and The Cube in the Situation Room started to buzz and flash red.

Quintana reached over and tapped the top.

"Quintana."

"Quintana, we've got some new shit," Kirk spouted, thinking he was talking directly to Quintana. Before Quintana could apprise him of the broader listeners, Kirk continued, rapid fire, "My colleague netted the target sub-tub. But there was a second one on its tail! You didn't say there were two! He – and we – weren't prepared for that! It's on course for the ship! Only minutes out!"

Quintana paused, as everyone in the room – including President Clarkson – took in the distressing news.

"Well, say something, dammit!" Kirk insisted.

"Our friggin' intel was clearly wrong!" Quintana responded. "Get your colleague out of there! The situation is, um, *dynamic*."

"What do you mean 'dynamic'?"

"Just remove your resource!"

"What –"

"I'm sorry to be brief, Sergeant. I don't have more time, as you can understand. Thank you for your efforts. Keep me apprised of anything else."

"Will do."

Quintana tapped the top of The Cube to make sure the call was terminated.

"Bad to worse!" Clarkson exclaimed.

"Options are shrinking fast, Barb," Brassard added.

"I know," Clarkson said with a sigh. "I know..."

CHAPTER 60

7:58 a.m.

As Kirk was hanging up the call with Quintana, the police station's video doorbell rang. It was Austin and Gabby. Kirk buzzed them in.

The duo sprinted down the hallway towards Kirk. As they approached him, he said, "You two beat the clock. In fact, with two minutes to spare."

Gabby cut right to the point, "We got the jammer in place!"

Austin followed, "We need to get President Clarkson on the phone!"

"Roger, that. Let's dial her up!"

Kirk pressed his office phone's speakerphone button, expecting to hear a dial tone. Instead he heard silence. "What – what's this?"

"Kirk? Let's go. Let's go!" said Austin.

"I don't know what's wrong! The island still has no power, which took down the Internet, cell, and digital voice. Our satellite-based backup had been working fine."

"Shitty timing!"

"We've had technicians in here since the crack of dawn. From our regular IT vendor. They're scrambling to keep us going."

"They clearly need better training!" said Austin.

"Let's try Geerman's phone!" Kirk grabbed the notepad with Quintana's phone number, and the three quickly took the few steps to Geerman's office.

"Damn! No dial tone here!" Kirk said, as he pressed the speakerphone button.

Gabby jumped in, "Fellas, how about the sat phone? The one we used to call Penny."

"It's over at my desk!"

The three bounded back to Kirk's desk. Kirk pulled out the phone from his desk's side drawer. He handed the phone to Gabby and said, "Let's get outside! I'll bring the phone number."

Gabby powered on the phone as the three hurried down the hall to get outside.

Austin said, "Let's hope the phone's not pissed off that we jammed its juice before."

As they were hustling toward the exit, they all saw the digital clock over the main double-door.

The clock displayed 8:00 a.m. as they stepped through the threshold.

Austin groaned, "Oh, boy…"

CHAPTER 61

8:00 a.m.

President Clarkson stood at the head of the Situation Room table. She scanned her team's faces and the wall-mounted screens. It was intensely apparent to everyone that the Tomahawks were within two minutes from the ship.

Despite the lofty stature of this elite group, the vulnerability was palpable. The fragility of life stared them in the face.

Clarkson spoke, "Clearly our intel was in error. What else are we missing?" Turning to Brassard, she asked, "Arty, what does your experience tell you?"

"I've learned three main things in warfare: The enemy relies on deception. There are usually more enemies than anticipated – never less. And you rarely see below the waterline."

"Parnette had to have accomplices. There is more to this than we're seeing."

"Assuredly."

Clarkson asked, "8:00 a.m. *No call, right?*" It was understood by everyone that Clarkson was referring to the efforts of Gabby and Austin.

Quintana replied, "No call. My incoming phone line is still being rerouted to The Cube."

"Just checking the boxes. It was a long shot..." Clarkson followed, "What is *certain* at this point?"

Brassard replied, "We have first-hand knowledge of a soon-to-impact sub-tub. *That is certain.* In the handful of seconds remaining, I recommend we focus and anchor our decisions on that certainty. Block everything else out."

"I'll take that perspective into consideration. Thank you, Arty."

As the time ticked down, Clarkson looked around the table and spoke with depth of thought: "I now have to decide between the 13,000 lives on that ship and the lives of tens of millions of Americans right here on our shore. If it was just math, it would be easy. But it's husbands and wives and sons and daughters (she paused a fraction, as her eyes glanced across Brassard's) and grandparents and babies whose lives are only beginning..."

CHAPTER 62

C larkson continued, "We must consider the totality and the magnitude of the unfortunate decision placed in our hands. History will judge us not on calculations,
but combined wisdom."

Brassard added, "We took an oath. To our country."

Clarkson responded, "We are also not computers. We must use our judgment to weigh
alternatives. *To use our human instincts.*"

Admiral Birch spoke from Screen One. "Madam President, as you can see on one of
your displays, the flights of all three Block IV TLAMs are proceeding nominally. We are
approaching the one-minute mark from the target."

"Yes, Admiral Birch. I see that information on our Screen Four, including the time to
impact and the distance to the target."

The digital timer on Screen Four, with large block text and numbers, clicked under a
minute.

TIME TO IMPACT: 59 SECONDS

DISTANCE TO TARGET: 9.0 MILES

Admiral Birch added, "President Clarkson, I will remain on screen through the com-
pletion of this sequence."

"Acknowledged."

The TIME TO IMPACT continued to tick down. 52, 51, 50, 49... Everyone in the
room unconsciously squirmed in their seats, while their eyes darted between the live
video of the ship from the orbiting satellites, the Tomahawks' flight-path graphic, the
countdown timer, and President Clarkson.

Clarkson focused solely on the timer and blocked everything else from her mind. No one spoke further. It was clear to all that she was about to make a decision.

44, 43, 42, 41... The dashed red line tipped by the blinking red triangle was about to touch the green rectangle representing the ship.

Clarkson, still standing, leaned forward and placed her open palms on the table. The counters continued downward.

36, 35, 34, 33...

Clarkson locked onto Admiral Birch on Screen One, stood up, and forcefully said, "Admiral Birch, your attention please."

Birch pressed a button on the console in front of him, unmuting his microphone.

"Yes, Madam President."

"This is a direct order from me: Splash the Tomahawks. I repeat: Splash the Tomahawks."

"Madam President, I am confirming: You are ordering the flight of the three Tomahawks that are en route to the Cosmos Megaliner to be terminated, is that correct?"

"Affirmative."

"Order received and confirmed."

Admiral Birch muted his audio and spoke unheard words to the flight-control station six feet away while vigorously pointing *down, down* with his right index finger.

The numbers continued to decrement.

16, 15, 14, 13...

DISTANCE TO TARGET: 2.0 MILES

No one said a word.

All eyes bounced from monitor to monitor. They watched as the flight-control team typed commands and toggled switches.

8, 7, 6, 5...

The blinking red triangle appeared to touch the green rectangle.

Everyone's mind felt zero time.

The on-screen graphic froze.

DISTANCE TO TARGET: 0.8 MILES

The red triangle stopped blinking, then disappeared.

The satellite images of the ship did not change.

Time stood still for everyone in the room.

"Done," Admiral Birch said as he came back on the line. And (looking over to two of his team members, both nodding their heads in the affirmative), he continued, "We've confirmed that all three Tomahawks did not detonate upon splash."

Teeth unclenched. Everyone exhaled. No one had even noticed they were all holding their breath.

Clarkson responded, "Thank you, Admiral. Please keep your microphone open."

***

Clarkson looked at Screen Five, the continuing flight of the F-15E. She turned her head to make eye contact with everyone in the room and said, "The erroneous intel may signal other flaws in our thinking. We owe it to those thousands of precious lives to sort through the key items, one more time. Hence my decision to abort the Tomahawks. We bought three more minutes."

Looking back to the Admiral on Screen One, "Admiral, am I correct with what I am seeing and that timing?"

"Yes, Madam President. The flight of the F-15E is on schedule. It will arrive at the drop zone in three minutes."

"Bart, anything even modestly useful from Homeland on where this bomb might be?"

"I'm sorry, Madam President. No."

"Jordy, do we have any doubt – any doubt at all – as to the bomb's capability or viability or existence?"

"Our scientists believe, from everything they've seen, that it is viable – and as horribly capable as Parnette has expressed. We've since learned that Parnette used her 'rehabilitation time' at Brookhaven National Laboratory to tap into their manufacturing resources as well. Various notes indicate cylindrical structures."

"So, this is not a bluff?"

"Not a bluff."

Clarkson looked at the path of the fighter jet. Then looked at the two satellite images of the Cosmos Megaliner. She imagined the ship teaming with families...and children...*and joy*. The full weight of the situation began to show on Clarkson; even a slight tremor as she clasped her hands.

Clarkson closed her eyes for a moment. Upon opening, she looked at Admiral Birch and spoke to him, "Admiral, press ahead with the nuclear device on the F-15E."

"Acknowledged, Madam President," replied Birch. "I will ask for final confirmation momentarily."

"Understood."

Clarkson looked over to Secretary Brassard and said in a soft voice, "Arty, I am so sorry."

Brassard closed his eyes, scrunched his lips, and nodded in solemn understanding.

Admiral Birch spoke, "Madam President, do I have your authorization to deploy the 0.3 kiloton B61 nuclear gravity bomb from the F-15E over the Cosmos Megaliner, detonating the bomb at 2,000 feet?"

"Yes."

"To confirm, is that an affirmative?"

"Affirmative. Sadly, General. Affirmative."

"You know the next steps. Please take possession and open the emergency satchel."

Colonel MacQuarrie handed the *nuclear football* to Clarkson. Clarkson unclasped the buckle and removed a three-by-five-inch plastic card – called the "biscuit" – that contained the authentication code.

"I have the biscuit in my hands, Admiral."

"Please read item five, sub-item B to me."

Reading in phonetics, Clarkson replied, "Sierra. Bravo."

"Authentication code confirmed. There is nothing else you need to do, Madam President."

"Understood, Admiral."

"Please stand by. I will be back momentarily."

The Admiral muted his audio. He stood up from his chair and walked a few steps from the video camera, conferring briefly with members of his tactical team. A team member could be seen speaking on a microphone; those in the Situation Room presumed the person was making contact with the pilot and the weapons system officer on the fighter jet. Simultaneously, others appeared to be stepping through a device-arming procedure – typing keystrokes and following instructions in a leather binder.

Admiral Birch walked back to the monitor, unmuted his microphone, and said in a clinical tone, "President Clarkson. The nuclear device is armed. The pilot and his weapons system officer have confirmed their instructions. Unless you provide instructions otherwise, the B61 will be dropped towards the ship (he looked at a nearby digital display) in precisely two minutes and eight seconds."

"I would thank you. Unfortunately, there is nothing worthy of thanks at this moment in history."

"Understood, Madam President."

The room was fixated on Screen Five, a graphic of the flight path of the F-15E – a moving blue square at the end of a red dotted line. The ship was indicated by a green rectangle. Appearing in large block text and numbers: TIME TO DROP ZONE: 1:59

Screen Four, once showing the flight of the Tomahawks, flickered, and now displayed a video of fast-passing puffy clouds and ocean water.

Admiral Birch spoke, "Madam President, I'm told you should now be seeing live, forward-looking video from the F-15E on one of your displays."

"We are. On Screen Four."

TIME TO DROP ZONE: 1:53

Clarkson spoke to everyone in the room, Vice President Carlisle on Screen Seven, and Admiral Birch on Screen One: "Even though we all come from different backgrounds and faiths, I would like you to indulge me in a silent moment." Clarkson bowed her head. Everyone did the same.

All that could be heard was the slight drone of the cooling fans of the nearby computer console and a slight buzz of a ceiling-mounted LED lighting panel that was prematurely faltering.

The satellite feeds of the Cosmos Megaliner continued their live imagery; the sun periodically glinted off various shiny structures of the massive craft.

The fighter jet's video maintained its oddly captivating display of fast-moving clouds and water.

All the while, the blue square that represented the F-15E inched ever closer to the green rectangle representing the ship.

***

TIME TO DROP ZONE: 1:42

Clarkson had just raised her head to reengage the room when The Cube on the table began buzzing and flashing.

All eyes looked at Clarkson.

Quintana, referring to the suggestion from moments ago, "Block it? Focus?"

Processing a deluge of simultaneous thoughts, Clarkson made an instinctual-level judgment: "No. I'm still hoping for a glimpse *below the waterline.* Take it – *quickly!*"

Quintana tapped the top of The Cube to answer.

"Quintana!"

"Mr. Quintana. This is Austin – Austin Raze with my wife Gabby Milone."

"Not a good time!"

"Oh, um, well, we're calling you as promised. Sorry for the delay. We had a phone glitch. Calling now from a sat phone. We thought you'd want to know that we got out to the ship, stuck on the jammer, and activated it."

"You what!"

"We activated the jammer. On the ship. We said we would call you if we were successful."

Clarkson jumped in, "This is President Clarkson. Where are you? And confirm what you just said. *Quickly, please!*"

"This is Gabby. We got out to the ship with the underwater jet skis, slapped on the jammer, turned it on, and hightailed it back here to the police station in Oranjestad. As Austin said, we promised we'd call you."

"God!" Clarkson exclaimed, as she looked at the fighter's graphic on Screen Five and realized that the nuclear device would detonate above the ship in one minute and twenty-eight seconds. She steeled herself to continue, "Presuming you've done all these things, you're certain the jammer will work?"

Austin responded, "Madam President, as we mentioned before our mad dash to the ship, we tested it on the police office's sat phone. *In fact, the very phone we're talking on.* Isn't that right, Sergeant Kirk?"

"That's right. They jammed our sat phone. I saw and heard it myself."

TIME TO DROP ZONE: 1:25

Seeing the time tick down, Clarkson sternly asked, "And who are you?"

"As Mr. Raze just said, I'm Sergeant Kirk. I was on this line earlier regarding the sub-tub. I'm currently in charge of the Oranjestad police station."

Secretary Brassard, pointing his eyes in the direction of the F-15E on-screen graphic, said, "Madam President. The time..."

TIME TO DROP ZONE: 1:17

Clarkson turned to Quintana with questioning eyes.

"I was told they check out. Raze and Milone. They're legit. Don't know anything about Kirk. Only today's chat."

TIME TO DROP ZONE: 1:12

The fighter's moving blue square was almost touching the ship's green rectangle.

Without warning, a new view on Screen Four startled everyone in the room: The once near-transcendental scene of puffy clouds and turquoise ocean now showed the jet fighter's view as it rapidly approached the cruise ship.

The features of the Cosmos Megaliner were now clearly visible.

The enormity of the impending nuclear bomb drop became viscerally real to everyone.

All heads and eyes snapped to Clarkson, as she pivoted and started to walk away from the grand table. Everyone was aghast, as it appeared that Clarkson was about to walk out of the room.

TIME TO DROP ZONE: 1:06

"Barb!" shouted Quintana.

With her back to the room, Clarkson raised her right arm and loudly said, "I got this!"

Clarkson spun on her heels and yelled to Admiral Birch on the monitor, "Birch, abort!"

"Confirm mission 'abort.'"

"Affirmative! Abort! Now!"

Admiral Birch muted his audio, turned to his left, and visibly yelled a series of commands to his team who were seated along a control panel. The Communications Officer forcefully barked into his microphone while a variety of animated actions occurred among the team members.

Within seconds, as seen on the fighter's live video feed, the F-15E banked left and up – with the Cosmos Megaliner sweeping away in plain view below. The fighter, traveling just-under supersonic for the bomb drop, now pushed full thrust, surpassed the speed of sound – and a rolling sonic boom permeated the Aruba coastline.

"President Clarkson, mission aborted," reported Admiral Birch.

"Thank you, Admiral. Let's hope I made the right decision."

Turning her eyes to those present in the Situation Room, Clarkson expressed to all, "As I said to the Admiral, let's hope I made the right decision."

In the intensity of the situation, forgotten were Gabby, Austin, and Sergeant Kirk on the phone line.

"Um, hello over there in D.C. This is Austin Raze. May I ask what just happened? Seconds ago we heard a tremendous boom – and it shook every brick in this building. If I didn't know better, it sounded like a sonic boom."

"Oh, no!" shouted Quintana.

Clarkson bit her lip and bowed her head.

CHAPTER 63

8:05 a.m.

"What the hell was that!" yelled Parnette into her walkie-talkie.

"A fighter jet just screamed over our heads. Supersonic!" replied Malbo from his faux taxi mobile command center parked at the port.

"Those bastards!"

"I think they're either trying to rattle you – or, perhaps, prepping for a strafing run. To try to take us – well you – out."

"Can you shoot the plane out of the sky?"

"Not a military fighter. Especially going that fast."

"We have no choice but to *extract*. Get me the frig out of here! We'll take care of things from the road."

"You haven't received any bitcoin deposit, correct?"

"No, those assholes think I'm bluffing. Screw them! Once I'm in your vehicle, I'll transfer to you the agreed-upon balance from my own funds. Just get me off this damn island!"

"When are you going to do *it?*"

"I'll push the button as soon as we stop talking. *America will be toast*. Get your men in here and get me the hell out. If you play your cards right, you can turn Bogotá into the center of the universe for your, um, business activities."

"Yellow, Blue," Malbo called into his walkie-talkie the code names for two of the four replacements. "Proceed to Red. Remove Red."

"Roger, there in two," replied Blue.

"Red, the security detail will be at your door in less than two minutes."

"The deed will be done by then. Red out."

Parnette stood up from the desk chair and walked towards the balcony. She tossed open the blinds and angrily slid the glass door with so much force its edge bounced off the frame at the end of its track.

Parnette pressed a button on the sat phone and stepped outside as the phone was powering up. "Come on, come on," she spoke to the phone, willing it to rapidly finish its start-up sequence. Finally full green bars appeared. They flickered away for a second. Then reappeared. "Odd, but we're okay," Parnette said to herself.

Parnette pressed the phone's pound sign and the number 1 to bring up a stored phone number. She then pressed the green SEND button. All she needed now was the cellular circuitry embedded in the antimatter cylinder to answer – and for her to enter a six-digit trigger code. "Bye-bye Eastern Seaboard! Missouri and Arkansas: You're about to have a whole bunch of Atlantic beachfront!"

CHAPTER 64

8:05 a.m.

"Holy shit!" shouted Captain Geerman into his walkie-talkie, after the F-15E thundered near Sunset Bistro, the improvised command center at Governor's Bay.

"A fighter flew right over the ship – supersonic!" replied Croes. "It looks like the Americans have lost their patience and might be going in."

"I don't see any associated military elements. I can't imagine what they have planned. Any word from Brouwer?"

"Not a peep. Must not have been able to spot the redhead."

"Is your team still in position?"

"Yes, they're staying low in the Archaeological Museum on Schelpstraat. Like we talked about, I'm in civilian clothes doing recon, hanging out across the street from the ship in the Renaissance Mall. That's where I saw the jet. I thought the Mall's glass was going to shatter!

CHAPTER 65

President Clarkson scanned the room and spoke: "With a warplane screaming past the ship and its sonic boom, Parnette will likely feel she's about to come under attack. The sub-tub explosion – in about a minute – will appear as the first volley."

Turning to Hemsley, "Bart, write down and immediately send the following national message on the WEA (the Wireless Emergency Alert system that broadcasts emergency messages on all mobile devices, nationwide):

"'*This is President Clarkson. I look forward to speaking with you shortly regarding our efforts to resolve the situation with Dr. Katherine Parnette. In the meantime, please remain calm. Know that every resource of your government is addressing the matter. We will provide an update soon. Thank you. God bless our troops. God bless the citizens of the United States of America.*'"

"Got it. It will be delivered, nationwide – via *Emergency Push* – within three minutes.

"Do it!"

Hemsley stood up and briskly left the Situation Room.

Reengaging the others in the room, "You're probably wondering why I said what I said. If we're in the third of the country vaporized, I want the surviving public to know we went down swinging. If, on the other hand, we're in the surviving portion, I want them to know we'll find a way to communicate once the effects of the EMP-portion of the blast are overcome. But I'm hoping for a third reason..." Clarkson paused and reflexively clasped her hands. "I'm hoping for a stroke of good fortune that lets me address the public – the *entire* public – with positive news."

CHAPTER 66

Parnette, instead of hearing a string of touch-tone dialing tones, heard a piercing *screech* from the unit – so loud she almost dropped her phone off the balcony.

"What the heck is this!" Parnette yelled out loud. She pressed the sat phone's END button and redialed: #1 SEND.

Screech!

Frantically, she pressed END again and redialed: #1 SEND.

Screech!

Yelling and cursing, she frantically tried to connect and send the signal to detonate the bomb.

CHAPTER 67

8 :06 a.m.

As Parnette was trying to mentally process the failure of the phone, an explosion reverberated through the ship as the second Ferras sub-tub rammed the hull and erupted.

The damage was superficial. But, like a giant steel drum, the ship's mammoth structure amplified the sound of the explosion – and carried the gut-felt thunder to every nook of the vessel.

"God dammit! They're attacking the ship!"

At the same instant:

"Wow!" yelled Croes into his walkie-talkie – a split-second before the sound of the explosion traveled the two-thirds of a mile to Geerman and his position at the Sunset Bistro.

"Whoa!" replied Geerman.

"There's smoke over by the ship."

"Do you think that's from the Americans?"

"I still don't see any military. I've read that the SEALS have submersible transports, but that seems like a stretch."

"It could also be the 'sub-tub' thing the White House told us about."

"Captain, what do you want to do?"

"I'm tired of sitting here holding my ass while the Americans are booming over our airspace – and doing who knows what else."

"Kirk said the Americans said to 'keep clear.'"

"Screw that. It's our country. It's our port. It's time to take care of matters our way."

"Copy that, sir!"

"Croes, execute Plan Alpha, just like our anti-terrorist drill this spring. The lady's a terrorist in my book! Your team takes the point. Our officers provide cover and follow."

"Time?"

"In two minutes. Zero eight zero nine."

"We're rolling!"

"My teams will be there on your six. Get that sonofabitch!"

CHAPTER 68

8:08 a.m.

Malbo, in his mobile command center, spotted Croes' team – about two dozen in all – exiting Renaissance Mall, crossing L.G. Smith Boulevard, and running onto the port's property, weapons drawn. Three of Croes' rushing Special Forces passed within feet of Malbo's faux taxi; Malbo quickly ducked his head onto the passenger seat to avoid being seen.

In the distance, Malbo could hear the police sirens of Geerman's approaching team, roaring at high speed from Sunset Bistro on L.G. Smith Boulevard.

Malbo sat up to further evaluate the situation, then blared on the walkie-talkie: "Incoming tactical operatives! Perhaps 20!"

***

"Red!" yelled one of the two heavily armed replacements at her stateroom door followed by a banging fist. "We've got to go! The situation is hot!"

"No, no, no!" Parnette yelled to herself, the replacements, and into the air. Still on the balcony, she tried repositioning the sat phone's antenna – while stretching her arm with the cell phone over the balcony. #1. SEND. *Screech!*

One of the replacements went full-shoulder into the door, smashing through. The two entered the stateroom and saw Parnette on her balcony frantically waving her sat phone in the air and cursing.

"We've got to go NOW!" yelled one of the replacements.

"I can't! I can't!" yelled Parnette in return. "I can't get my code through!"

Malbo's voice screamed through everyone's walkie-talkies, "The forces have breached our outer defenses! At least a dozen strikers are through the gangway and into the ship. Others are surrounding. General police units arriving."

Croes on the radio, "All units. Gunmen spotted on deck six, midship, starboard side. Head there."

Within minutes, the Aruban Special Forces were closing in on Parnette's position.

The two hallway-stationed replacements radioed the pair in the stateroom and Malbo, "We see the agents. They are heading down the corridor. Assume defensive positions!"

The two replacements in Parnette's stateroom spun towards the smashed-in door, aiming their automatic weapons towards the opening. "We have the doorway covered. Can you lay down some fire?" yelled one of the replacements into the walkie-talkie.

"Trying. We're taking heavy fire!" The sound of gunfire erupted through the ship's corridors.

***

The screaming jet fighter. The sonic boom. The steel-shaking percussion of the sub-tub explosion. The gunfire. Heavily armed commandos darting through the halls.

Primal screams traversed the Cosmos Megaliner, as passengers ran and wailed and flailed through the corridors – in raw terror.

Dozens of panicked passengers climbed onto the ship's outer railings and jumped towards the harbor's water. Some leapers didn't clear the stowed lifeboats; their bodies bounced and ricocheted – some smashing into another deck, others flopped unconscious into the water.

***

Aruba's finest made their way in the hallway towards Parnette's position, not knowing they were about to be ambushed by the armed replacements inside the doorway.

The approaching Aruban Special Forces team was less than 10 feet away from a blitzkrieg of firepower primed to be unleashed on them. Suddenly, one of the interior replacements yelled, "Ahhh!" and slumped to the ground, followed in a fraction of a second by a distinctive *crack* of a high-powered rifle. The second replacement turned towards the fallen colleague and, in that same instant, grabbed his neck and fell – again followed by a resounding *crack!*

"What's happening!" yelled Parnette, who jumped back into the stateroom, only to see the two replacements dead and bleeding on the floor. Parnette dropped the sat phone onto the bed and reached for her walkie-talkie on the coffee table – but then screamed in pain from a bullet that passed through her right hand; her scream intertwined with another echoing *crack!*

Moments earlier, Niels Brouwer spotted Parnette on the balcony and was preparing to take a shot, as ordered. He then saw the unfolding situation in the stateroom and reprioritized – knowing his fellow officers were likely the incoming targets. Brouwer re-tracked Parnette and took another shot, skewering her outstretched hand.

Within seconds, members of the Aruba Special Forces burst into the room. Parnette was screaming in agony, sprawled on her bed. The agents stepped over the blood and bodies of the two deceased replacements and wrestled a screaming, cursing, and bleeding Parnette into handcuffs. Parnette went into a manic tirade, insisting over and over "Get away from me! This is bigger than all of us. I have to save the world. *I have to save the world!*"

The lead agent on the scene, Johan Stoepker, radioed to Croes and everyone on frequency, "We got her! We got her!"

"Nice work!" replied Croes. "Is she alive?"

Stoepker replied, "She's wounded in the hand. But we didn't shoot her. And it appears two of her accomplices are dead – and we didn't do that either."

Croes smiled and squeezed the mic button on his walkie-talkie. "Brouwer was on the breakwater."

"The 'Coconut Kid'! He undoubtedly saved our lead team from a heck of a gun battle. Given the arsenal we see in this room, perhaps saved a bunch of lives."

"Stoepker, this is Geerman. Do you copy?"

"Yes, Captain. Go ahead."

"I've been following. As Croes said, superb work! And great execution, Croes!"

Multiple 'Thank you, Captain!' replies came over the radio.

"Team, hold on." Geerman continued, "Sergeant Kirk, are you there?"

"Yes, Captain! We've been following it all. Congratulations!"

"Thank you. An end-to-end team effort!" Geerman continued, "Please get on the horn to Quintana. Tell D.C. that Parnette has been neutralized."

"With pleasure!"

"Much appreciated, Kirk. Fine work there today, too. How are the Americans?"

"They've been right here at my desk, listening in to the radio traffic. I think you can categorize their reaction as ecstatic." Kirk replied. "They've had a hell of spell today, too." Making eye contact with Gabby and Austin, and with heavy sarcasm, "They still look like crap. And smell like week-old salt water."

"Hey, wait a minute! I'm not *that* stinky!" could be heard from Austin over the open mic.

"What's that screaming?" Kirk asked.

Stoepker replied, "That's Parnette flailing in cuffs and yelling her head off – yelling that she couldn't get her 'goddamned code' through and that she's here 'to save the world' and some other bullshit. We have four agents trying to keep her restrained. I remember my older brother – years ago – showing me video of a scary-as-hell old movie where some devil-lady's head spins."

"The Exorcist."

"Yeah, that's the one. And that's who this redhead reminds me of. Consider yourself warned when she gets back to the station."

Geerman asked, "Does she need to go to HOH?" (Dr. Horacio E. Oduber Hospital)

Stoepker replied, "I wouldn't risk it, Captain. We don't know if she was working with anyone else on the island. I can't imagine that she pulled this off with only a few people on the ship. I suggest we bandage her up and bring her directly to the KPA and toss her in a cell. We can surround the building with officers."

"I concur."

Stoepker wrapped up, "Kirk, please have a cell prepped. We're coming in."

***

Neils Brouwer, through his binoculars, watched his fellow agents flood Parnette's stateroom and cuff Parnette. He pulled out his walkie-talkie from an interior pouch of his drag bag. "Captain Geerman, this is Brouwer. Do you copy?"

"Brouwer, I copy."

"How's the situation? I took the shot – actually a few – and improvised a bit. Looking through the binocs, I saw about six or seven of our people subduing Parnette."

"You may not have heard our radio communications over the last couple minutes."

"No sir. Radio's been in the bag. It's wet out here. I'm literally up to my ass in water."

"Understood," replied Geerman. He continued, "Good news. Thanks to you, Parnette's in our hands. The situation is completely defused. And your quick thinking probably saved the lives of a few of your mates. I'm told the thugs in that room were loaded with big-time firepower."

"I did what felt right, sir."

"I'll radio the fishing boat. Come on in. Get dry. I'll meet you back at the KPA."

"Yes, sir. Gladly, sir!"

***

Throughout the entire ordeal, Malbo sat in his faux taxi orchestrating the mission – yet unaware of the outcome. "Yellow, Blue, Green, Orange – report!" Malbo shouted into his walkie-talkie, calling the four replacements. He heard nothing. "Red report!" Malbo radioed Parnette. "Do you copy?"

"Who the heck is this?" spoke Bram Thyssen into Parnette's walkie-talkie, one of the agents still on the scene in the bloody stateroom.

"Screw you!" Malbo replied, realizing the plan had gone horribly wrong.

Malbo squeezed the mic, "All: This is X. The operation has been compromised. Our communications have been compromised. Execute *Plan Armageddon*. Use only coded radio comm from this point. Clean up. Repeat: Clean up."

***

Geerman's cell phone vibrated in his duty belt, momentarily startling him. Holding the walkie-talkie with his right hand, he removed the phone with left, put it to his ear, and said, "Geerman." After a few seconds of listening, he replied, "That's great news. Keep me posted."

Geerman squeezed the mic button on his walkie-talkie and broadcast: "All: Cell service is operational again. I just got an early report from the ship's onboard medical team.

They're triaging several injuries, a few apparent broken bones, and a couple of concussions. Nothing life-threatening. They're arranging transport to HOH."

CHAPTER 69

"Quintana, this is Kirk. Parnette's neutralized!"

Kirk had dialed Quintana's cell phone expecting him to answer. But the *click* he heard was The Cube being answered in the center of the Situation Room table.

"Sergeant Kirk, this is President Clarkson. Please repeat!"

"Oh, um, my apologies Madam President. I expected Mr. Quintana. Yes, Parnette has been captured! We stormed the ship when it sounded like you initiated a military maneuver. Parnette's wounded – apparently shot in the hand – but it's not life threatening."

"Sergeant Kirk, thank God for the wonderful news!"

Everyone in the Situation Room started hugging each other.

Clarkson continued, "I can't tell you how appreciative we are of your entire Aruban team!"

"'Team' is the operative word, Madam President. It seems the two Americans came through, big time, and just in time." Kirk winked to Gabby and Austin, who remained at his desk."

"So the jammer worked?" asked Clarkson.

"Like a charm! We heard over our walkie-talkies that Parnette was screaming about her 'code not working' – and we all took that to mean that her sat phone couldn't initiate the bomb."

Gabby and Austin smiled and nodded in happy agreement.

"I can't wait to thank them," Clarkson continued. "All of our country owes them a huge debt."

"Would that include a private tour of the White House?" Austin asked – as Gabby elbowed him to shut up and be more polite.

"Mr. Raze? Is that you?"

"Yes, Madam President. I'm here with my brilliant better half, Gabby."

"Mr. Raze and Ms. Milone, thank you. Yes, I think that tour can be arranged for the two of you."

"We're glad to have helped a bit," added Gabby.

"I hope you can wait a couple of weeks for us," added Austin. "I think we'll opt to finish our vacation first."

"Of course," responded Clarkson, even admiring the hint of fun attitude in Austin's voice.

"Madam President," Gabby added, "if you don't mind, I think my hubby and I are going to catch a beer now."

"Or two," added Austin.

"Well deserved – and I look forward to meeting you in person when you get back to the States."

Austin and Gabby stood up from their chairs and began walking toward the station's front door.

Clarkson continued, "Kirk, are you still there?"

"Yes, Madam President."

"So what's the plan with Parnette?"

"We're bringing her here to the KPA, the police station here in Oranjestad. We are prepping a cell. And we're already setting up a police perimeter. We suspect she had accomplices. So we are not taking any chances."

"Excellent. I'll have my people make arrangements to extradite her quickly, to get her off your hands."

"The sooner the better. We are 'One Happy Island' you know. This has really messed things up."

"Sergeant Kirk, that's the understatement of the year."

CHAPTER 70

I t was a few minutes before noon.

Austin and Gabby finally had an opportunity to peel off their thoroughly smelly scuba shorties, revealing Austin's solid-black swim trunks and Gabby's floral two-piece suit. They tossed on a couple of T-shirts that were stashed in their dry bags.

The duo hopped in their bullet-ridden lime-green Jeep. They were understandably exhausted; they hadn't slept in a day and a half and had enough adventure for a lifetime. Even so, they were determined to finish the day on a positive note with the beers they mentioned to President Clarkson.

Gabby and Austin had a particular destination in mind: a bar run by their old friend, C.J. Rok. Widely noted as the 'best bartender in Aruba,' C.J. was etched in local lore by his creative drink repertoire and his unique blend of humor. He was a hoot with karaoke, too.

They met C.J. by chance 16 years ago at a Super Bowl extravaganza organized by his former bar. Two years ago, C.J. and his wife Sofia purchased their own bar and eatery, and Gabby and Austin were eager to catch up with their old island pal.

Austin was at the wheel of the Jeep. "Damn. I've lost all sense of time. C.J.'s won't be open yet!"

"You're right, it's too early," replied Gabby. "I'm out of sync, too."

Looking at her watch, Gabby continued, "Let's swing by Global Foods. We can pick up some muffins and that lovely multi-grain bread for tomorrow's breakfast."

"Sounds like a plan!"

The two drove north from the police station, taking the inland route that locals and experienced tourists know.

They popped into Global Foods and grabbed a few non-refrigerated items they needed for their condo. Their still-damp bathing suits topped with T-shirts certainly garnered a few looks, but not as many as one would think. Tourists and locals alike seemed more concerned about quickly stocking up on foodstuffs, given the recent loss of electricity and general island chaos.

Strolling through the aisles triggered a wave of hunger; they hadn't eaten since the day before. Once back in their Jeep, they zipped two blocks to one of their favorite eateries: Smit's & Meijer's Dutch Pancakes. This quaint local establishment never failed to satisfy any appetite. And it was fully up to the task that day. Austin practically inhaled an apple and bacon Dutch pancake. Gabby devoured a scrumptious pancake creation of papaya and mango. They guzzled glasses of pineapple juice and hit the road again.

The duo swung by a local gas station for a fill up. Tomorrow's morning plan had included a hike at the Arikok National Park and then a drive to San Nicolas, a town at the southern end of the island.

"Darling, perhaps we skip the hike at Arikok," said Austin.

"I'm good with that!" responded Gabby.

Austin pointed to the time on the Jeep's dash – 4:12 p.m. "You still up for some brews?"

"Sleep is overrated," remarked Gabby. "Besides, I think the pancake gave me a second wind!"

They smiled at each other and in unison shouted: "C.J.'s!"

CHAPTER 71

Austin and Gabby drove north to the Palm Beach area of the island, within eyesight of the iconic *De Oude Molen* ("The Old Mill" in Dutch) – an iconic structure on Aruba since 1960. They pulled into a public parking area and walked a couple of hundred yards to C.J.'s Surf Café.

They bellied up to the bar, their bathing suits now almost fully dry. The adrenaline they had been riding was starting to waver. They looked pretty beat.

A couple was next to them, both enjoying a Balashi – the local brew.

The male fellow said, "Tough day?"

Austin replied, "You can't imagine the half of it."

His female companion added, "Well, then, you two deserve a beer." Summoning the bartender, "C.J.!"

"Thank you, kindly," said Gabby.

"Don't mention it," said the female. "'One Happy Island,' you know."

Austin added, "I'm Austin. This is my wife, Gabby."

"Nice to meet both of you. I'm Eric. This is my wife, Elsie. Or if it's more convenient, just E & E."

As C.J. walked to the end of the wooden bar counter, he recognized his two old friends. "Hey Gabs! Hey Austin! You two look like you've been through the wringer."

"Yeah, yeah. We'll fill you in on the story after a couple of cold ones," said Austin. "Or maybe a bucket of 'em."

"Heck of a day here in Aruba," said C.J. "We only got power back a few hours ago. And (cocking his head towards the TV over the bar) the BBC broke in about 10 minutes ago and said the scientist lady holed up on the cruise ship has been captured."

"You don't say," replied Gabby.

"Yeah, definitely make that a bucket of beers," Austin added.

C.J. brought over a bucket of Balashi beers on ice. He popped the top off two and handed them to Austin and Gabby. They took healthy swigs. Gabby commented with relief, "Oh, yeah..."

As Austin and Gabby were settling into their beverages, two new patrons appeared at the entrance to the bar. The two men began walking towards Austin and Gabby with purpose.

The four sets of eyes connected. One of the new patrons lit up with a malevolent grin.

"Frig," Gabby said quietly to Austin.

"The boat guys," replied Austin.

Indeed, it was the two men from the pontoon boat. They had recognized the lime-green Jeep and were there to 'clean up' loose ends as Malbo instructed.

The two men accelerated towards Gabby and Austin. As if they had done this escape routine before – and perhaps they had – Gabby and Austin stood up and chucked their bar stools at the charging men. They then bolted towards the street.

"The tires!" yelled Austin, noticing their Jeep's tires had been slashed.

"What now, loverboy?" Gabby replied.

"Don't have a clue. But here they come – and we know they're packing."

The traffic was building on the nearby J.E. Irausquin Boulevard, as eateries started to populate for dinner in what is commonly called the "High Rise" area of the island.

"Keep running!" yelled Austin. "Try to lose them between the cars."

Gabby and Austin darted between cars, horns blaring, their athleticism on full display even after their ridiculous day.

"I think we lost them," said Gabby.

"Hope so!" responded Austin.

Two motorcycles appeared out of the traffic, screaming their way towards Gabby and Austin.

"You jinxed it!" yelled Austin, as they continued to sprint in between the traffic. "We can't keep going like this!"

"I have an idea, and you're not going to like it," yelled Gabby between breaths.

"They're gaining on us. I'm game for whatever you've got."

Twenty yards ahead was a parked *WahWahChaCha* bus – a wildly decorated old school bus converted into a bar-hopping party bus. Revelers were hanging out of the windows while the bus blasted multi-tone horns to pop songs, currently *Y.M.C.A.*

The driver was outside the front door of the idling bus, waving new partiers inside.

Gabby ran up to the front door; Austin was right behind her. "Hop in!" Gabby yelled. "What!" Austin yelled back. "Just get in!" Gabby insisted and she sprung up the steps and into the driver's seat.

No sooner did Austin get through the front door, Gabby pulled the close-door arm shut.

"What the hell are you doing!" yelled Austin. "We'll be trapped in here."

"Only if they catch us!" replied Gabby.

Gabby put the party bus in gear and punched the accelerator. The automatic transmission replied and the bus lurched forward, picking up speed, heading north on the boulevard.

Some of the passengers started to scream. Others, particularly those who were already quite inebriated, began laughing and cheering with excitement – thinking it was a scripted performance of the party on wheels. Austin, still standing, clung onto the back of the driver's seat.

Like an ambulance clearing a path, Gabby flashed the front lights and kept the wild horns on. In between jerks of the steering wheel, she randomly turned knobs and flipped switches on the console. The horns commenced an ear-splitting rendition of Ozzy Ozborne's *Crazy Train*.

Gabby weaved the full-size bus in and out of traffic as if it was a Mini Cooper. Still, the motorcycles were closing in.

Austin yelled to Gabby, "Now what, Mario?"

"Ah, that's where Part B of my plan comes into play. Hang tight!"

Gabby took a sharp left at the *I LOVE ARUBA* gift shop and accelerated down the narrow access road between the Barceló Hotel and the Hyatt Regency. The motorcycles were closing in on the bus, and the bad guys had their guns drawn.

"This is nuts!" yelled Austin.

The bus barreled at a ridiculous velocity towards the ocean. Now coming into view, straight ahead, was the pier for tourist catamarans. At the entrance to the pier was a

"Welcome" hut – and the bus was heading straight for the hut at a seemingly unstoppable speed.

Gabby didn't let up from the accelerator pedal. It was pegged to the floorboard. The bus was racing nearly 60 miles an hour at that point.

"Brace yourself, everyone!" Gabby yelled at the top of her lungs, with the bus no more than 100 feet from the hut.

Gabby pulled the emergency brake lever and ducked down. Austin followed, ducking below Gabby and the driver's seat.

The bus went into a straight all-wheel skid. The motorcyclists, just feet behind the bus, hit their brakes and tried to swerve around the bus – but it was too late. The motorcycles clipped the rear corners of the bus and the riders flew – literally – 20 feet, headlong into the water on either side of the pier. The bus continued its skid, stopping a mere five feet from the front entrance to the hut.

Gabby popped her head up, seemingly unsurprised that her gambit worked. Austin, still with a white-knuckle grip on the back of the driver's seat, poked up from his crouch.

"The ride's over, everyone," Gabby proclaimed. "No charge for the extra fun."

Austin rose to his feet. "Gabs, please give me a heads up before you consider another *Cannonball Run*. I'm getting too old for this stuff."

Austin and Gabby nonchalantly stepped off the bus as if nothing out of the ordinary occurred. However, they had garnered a whole slew of law-enforcement attention – from street-patrol officers to the security detail at the pier. Officer Jessie Ortega was the first to catch up with them. Austin and Gabby were no more than 10 feet from the doorway of the bus when they came face to face.

"Stop right there, you two!" commanded Ortega, drawing his service weapon and pointing it at Austin and Gabby.

"Whoa! Whoa! Please put your gun down!" Austin emphatically requested while putting his hands up.

Gabby, also with her hands raised, exclaimed "We can explain!"

"Oh, I bet you can 'explain,'" said Ortega. "You nearly drove this bus into the ocean. And we're now fishing your two friends out of the water – the ones who were terrorizing the street with you on their motorcycles. You're lucky they only appear shaken up."

"No, no, they're not our friends!" said Gabby, hands still in the air. "They're part of the force that took over the cruise ship at the pier."

"And you know that *how*?" questioned Ortega.

"Because they shot at us last night, that's how," responded Austin. "In fact, they –"

"Shut up, Austin," Gabby interrupted. "What my abundantly talkative husband was about to say was that if you call Sergeant Kirk at the KPA, he'll clear up everything for you – and us."

"Kirk? You know Kirk?" asked Ortega.

Austin made a quick my-lips-are-zipped two-finger motion across his lips, then put his hands back up.

Gabby rolled her eyes and replied, "We've had a long day with Sergeant Kirk. Please give him a call. Say Gabby and Austin are, um, in your custody. That'll do it."

By this time, three police officers and two security guards had gathered around Ortega, Gabby, and Austin.

"Okay, keep your hands up – don't make a move," commanded Ortega. "Ramón," Ortega said to Officer Ramón Salizar who just arrived on the scene. "Get Sergeant Kirk on the radio."

"Whatever you do, don't call him Captain," Austin tossed into the mix. The officers gave him a quizzical look. Gabby shook her head.

***

Officer Salizar squeezed the talk button of his radio's microphone that was clipped to his uniform top. "Sergeant Kirk. Sergeant Kirk. This is Officer Salizar on High Rise patrol. Do you copy? Sergeant Kirk. This is Officer Salizar. Do you copy?"

"Kirk here. Go ahead Salizar."

"Let me turn things over to Officer Ortega. Stand by."

Gun in his right hand, Ortega used his left hand to squeeze the talk button of his radio's clipped-on microphone. "Sorry to bother you, Sergeant Kirk. I'm here with two, um, troublemakers who insist they know you. They say their names are Austin and Gabby, and –"

"Kirk, tell Ortega to put his gun down!" yelled Austin towards the open mic.

"Ortega," Kirk replied, "Are they under arrest? What did they do?"

"They stole a bus – a WahWahChaCha bus – and drove it like they're in a Formula 1 race. Drove it practically onto the pier between the Barceló and the Hyatt!"

"Did anyone get hurt?"

"Miraculously, no. Not even their accomplices."

"Accomplices?"

Austin yelled into the conversation again, "Kirk, they were the two thugs who shot at us last night!"

"Shut up!" yelled Ortega to Austin. "Kirk, you can hear how much trouble these two are causing. I particularly can't get the male perp to shut up!"

"Ortega – and this will sound crazy – but I do know these two. Where are the two 'accomplices' you mentioned?"

"They're a little shaken up, as they drove their motorcycles into the water alongside the bus. Otherwise, they seem okay."

"Ortega, listen to me carefully: The two you believe are 'accomplices' need to be handcuffed – right now! They are armed and capable of killing!"

The police officers surrounding Ortega, Austin, and Gabby heard the radio conversation and hustled over to the bench where Malbo's men were seated and being treated. The officers drew their guns and, before Malbo's men had a chance to react, placed the two in handcuffs.

Once the bad guys were in cuffs, Ortega radioed back to Kirk: "Kirk, the two motorcyclists have been restrained. Respectfully, may I ask you what the heck is going on?"

"It would take too long to go into details. Suffice it to say, and unlikely as it may sound, Austin Raze and Gabby Milone were heroic today under extreme conditions. Their actions saved a lot of lives."

Ortega turned his eyes towards the duo. They shrugged their shoulders in a *hey, what can we say*, response. Austin then said, "Can we put down our arms now, please!"

Ortega nodded. Austin and Gabby lowered their arms.

"I can't simply let them go," Ortega said to Kirk. "They damaged the bus. The crowd here saw that."

"Handcuff them –"

"What!" shouted Austin and Gabby in unison.

"*Lightly*, and bring them into the KPA for processing. We'll clear things up at that point."

"If you say so, Sergeant."

"And be careful with those other two thugs. We'll prepare a cell for them, right alongside their ringleader."

CHAPTER 72

"Alpha, Beta, come in. Come in!" Malbo pleaded into his walkie-talkie, trying to reach his two lead mercenaries. However, the two walkie-talkies were now under six feet of beach water. And his two associates were en route to cells at the KPA.

Realizing his plan had dissolved, Malbo squeezed his microphone button again and said, "All: This is X. Head to the extraction point. Now!"

CHAPTER 73

Thirty minutes later, in the back seat of a police car, handcuffed but reasonably comfortable, Austin and Gabby pulled up to the entrance of the KPA.

"Déjà vu all over again," Austin quipped.

"More like *Groundhog Day*, if you ask me," Gabby replied.

Within two minutes they were in front of their new old friend again, Sergeant Kirk. "So, you just can't get enough of me, can you?" said Kirk.

"What can we say?" replied Austin. "You have a magnetic personality."

Kirk turned to Officer Ortega, who was still with Austin and Gabby. "You can take the cuffs off of our guests at this point." Ortega obliged and Austin and Gabby rubbed their wrists with relief.

"What the heck happened with the bus?" queried Kirk.

"The two dudes that shot at us when we were diving came after us again at a bar. We ran out, hoping to get away in our Jeep – but they had slashed our tires. So we, um –"

"Commandeered –"

"Yeah, I guess you can say 'commandeered' the bus. We didn't want to get shot at again."

"Can you two – please – promise to not get in any more hot water? Spend time under a palm tree or something?"

"Count on it, Sergeant!" replied Gabby.

Geerman and Croes came into the room and walked up to Kirk.

"Who are these two?" Croes asked with eye motion to Austin and Gabby.

"Those are your jammers."

"Good work," said Croes.

Geerman also gave an approving head nod, then said to Kirk, "We've got to move the redhead. The Americans called to let us know they will have a military transport landing tomorrow afternoon. We can allocate police staff in San Nicolas to a special security detail at KIA (Korrektie Instituut Aruba/Aruba Correctional Institution). We'll then bring her to the airport tomorrow for the handoff."

Croes said to Kirk, "We're pulling *The Beast* out front right now."

"Maybe the Ministry of Justice will finally stop complaining about the expense of the armored transport." added Geerman. "We'll get the redhead out of her cell and bring her up here. Croes, it's your show from there."

Croes nodded.

"Bakker, Schouten, Smit, and Kuijpers," Croes summoned four of his Special Forces team who were standing guard at the hallway leading to the cells. "We're moving Parnette. Bring her this way and directly out the front. Keep your M4s drawn. We don't know how many of her accomplices remain on the island."

Turning to Austin and Gabby, Croes commanded, "You two, stand against the wall as we move the criminal through here."

"You don't have to tell us twice!"

Three minutes later, two Special Forces' officers appeared down the hall, their carbines pointed in their direction of travel. A few steps behind them, the other two of Croes' officers came into view. They were nearly dragging an uncooperative and pissed-off Parnette – an officer under each of her arms; she spouted a repeating stream of nonsensical words, while her thick red hair flailed like a cheerleader's pom-pom gone mad.

"Nein! Nein! Nein! Ha! Ha! Ha! Tick! Tick! Tick! Nein! Nein! Nein! Ha! Ha! Ha! Tick! Tick! Tick!"

As Parnette approached the center of the station, she eyed Austin and Gabby staring at her – and paused her babbling. "What the hell are you two losers looking at?" Parnette yelled, even startling the two officer escorts.

Austin reflexively replied, "These two 'losers' pulled your plug, lady. Funny how your ringy-dingy became a duddy-duddy."

Unbridled anger erupted from Parnette; the manic rage required Croes and Geerman to jump to the assistance of their officers.

"You peabrains!" Parnette spat to everyone in the room. "I prepared for every possible outcome. The bomb will still go off!" Parnette violently twisted as she was dragged towards the front door and began her repetitive yelling again.

"Nein! Nein! Nein! Ha! Ha! Ha! Tick! Tick! Tick! Nein! Nein! Nein! Ha! Ha! Ha! Tick! Tick! Tick!"

"No, no, no – in German?" Gabby asked Austin.

"Beats me. She's the definition of a raving lunatic," replied Austin.

The two lead officers pushed open the station's front door, scanned the exterior, and stepped through the threshold. The two officers wrangling Parnette attempted to push her through the threshold, but she anchored her feet at the doorway frame. In a mighty twist, she pivoted her torso and yelled back into the room, "Blinded by science, baby! Blinded by science!" With a combined push, the officers forcibly shoved Parnette out the door.

***

"What do you make of all of that?" Kirk asked Geerman and Croes.

Geerman, "Stating the obvious, she's totally nuts. Regarding the bomb still going off, it makes sense. No matter how crazy she is, she probably built in a failsafe. An autotimer."

"Or it's a bargaining chip, said Kirk."

"Indeed, but we have some 'chips' of our own," Geerman said with a wink to Croes.

"I know what you're thinking," replied Croes. "I'm on it."

"In the meantime," Geerman added, "I'll call Quintana. They're not going to like this news."

***

The police trio broke up and Kirk walked in the direction of his desk.

Gabby and Austin stepped away from the wall and intercepted Kirk.

"She's a babbling lunatic," Gabby said to Austin and Kirk. "Yet still one of the most-brilliant scientists on the planet. It wouldn't be out of the question for her to build in a backup plan."

Austin added, "In her deranged mind she's playing chess and has all of this planned out – several moves ahead. I agree with Gabby."

"It's worse than that," added Kirk. "All outcomes flow through her. *She rigged the game.*"

"Don't you *dare* say it, Kirk," Austin said with a tongue-in-cheek grin, as they simultaneously thought of the iconic 'Kobayashi Maru' no-win scenario in *Star Trek*.

"Aye aye, Captain," Kirk replied with a glint in his eye.

"Boys, enough of your little word games," Gabby said to Austin and Kirk. Looking at Austin, "Parnette's out of here, and so should the two of us."

"Sergeant," added Austin, "we like your company, but this has been, well, quite a stretch."

"Do us all a favor and please stay off the buses!"

"No can do, sir. We don't have our Jeep. Your team gave us that posh ride in a squad car, remember? We'll have to take a public bus back up to the High Rise area. If they've even started to run the buses again after all the chaos. And tomorrow we'll have to figure out what to do with the Jeep."

"Damn slashed tires," added Gabby.

"I can't believe I'm even saying this," said Kirk. "I'll give you two a lift back to your condo. Stay here while I clear things with Geerman."

Gabby replied within a deep yawn, "Thanks, Sarge."

Kirk walked in the direction of Geerman's office.

CHAPTER 74

TV stations, worldwide, interrupted their regular programming to announce the capture of Parnette and the conclusion of the crisis, such as the following news bulletin:

"Good evening, ladies and gentlemen," started Jessica T. Gladbrook, co-anchor of ChronZen's *PrimeCast 24*. "As you can see, Jeremy, my co-host, is just getting into the studio," Gladbrook ad-libbed, as Jeremy Donahue walked behind Jessica to his seat at the news desk. "Hi Jeremy. Take a sec to get plugged in."

"Thanks, Jess," replied Jeremy. "We've confirmed the news that Dr. Katherine Parnette, the scientist who fell from grace in a rather public fashion and, in these past hours, riveted the world's attention with a demand-laced manifesto and claims of a bomb with multiple times the power of what caused The Event, has been captured in Aruba."

"That's fantastic, Jeremy," Gladbrook replied. She pressed her earpiece and said, "The newsroom's telling me we have some raw user-submitted video of the capture. Roll it!"

"Rosie, that's the lady from the cruise ship!" the voice on the shaky cell-phone video exclaimed. *"She's putting up quite a fuss!"*

In the left-bottom corner of the video frame was *Top_Side_22*, giving on-screen credit to the user-submitted video.

The video showed Parnette wildly throwing her handcuffed fists and elbows at the Special Forces' officers who were trying to place her into the armored transport vehicle. Parnette rattled a string of expletives that were only partially bleeped out. *Top_Side_22* turned the camera towards himself, showing a plump, middle-aged male and a glimpse of his beachwear-dressed female companion.

"We were walking to our hotel and we heard screaming – we thought someone was hit by a car or something. So we ran here. You can still hear that lady raging and swearing from inside of the police truck."

The television image switched back to the co-hosts.

Gladbrook quickly commented, "Sorry for the inappropriate language! We're seeing and hearing the video for the first time with you."

Donahue added, "So, Jess, it looks like the horrific situation with the bomb has been, shall we say, *defused*." Gladbrook's momentary grimace was his clue that his word choice was off the mark.

To quickly adjust the tone, Gladbrook added, "Yes, America can breathe a big sigh of relief."

Gladbrook paused again, not trying to hide that she was listening in her ear to guidance from the newsroom. She spoke to the camera, "We received a bulletin from the White House. President Clarkson will be making an address to the nation within the hour. We will bring it to you live when that occurs. Overall great news."

"Indeed, Jess."

"We'll now return you to the regularly scheduled programming."

CHAPTER 75

President Clarkson was seated at the Resolute Desk. She was with Jameson and Walters, discussing the draft of the to-be-delivered address to the nation.

"Let's keep it brief – top line," said Clarkson. "There will be plenty of time to do a full accounting."

"I can't imagine the hearings on Capitol Hill," said Jameson. "The blame game will go on forever. Although all's well that ends well, right?"

"Unfortunately, not in this town."

Walters was about to speak. But all three turned their heads to the northwest door of the Oval Office, to a quick knock and entrance of Secretary of State Quintana.

"Madam President."

"John, please, Barb is fine."

"Not now," Quintana said with a drawn face.

"What's wrong, John? I thought you'd be out celebrating with the staff."

"I thought I would be, too. We have a problem. A big problem."

"Well, it couldn't be any bigger than what we had today. We saved the country – and perhaps the planet," Clarkson said with a rare hint of pride.

"The bomb wasn't disabled," Quintana said somberly. "It's still going to go off."

"John, are you sure you didn't already start drinking? We blocked her detonation signal. Sure, we still have to find the device, but the time-pressure's off."

"I wish that was so. Parnette built in a failsafe. I just got a call from Captain Geerman at the police station. She told them it will still detonate."

"What! When!"

"We don't know. It could be any minute. Heck, any second."

"She could be bluffing, to try to extricate herself from the catastrophe she created. She's clearly insane."

"The Arubans said she sounded convincing – not a fabricated comment. Plus the words of Dr. Abshire keep echoing in my head. The stuff about Parnette probably having planned multiple contingencies for various outcomes."

"I was thinking the same thing. So what the heck do we do? If the Aruba intel is correct, we have a bomb that could destroy the country at any second. Heck, I could be in mid-sentence when – if – it happens. And we don't have a clue where it is."

"Well, I may have a tiny bit of news on that part."

"I'll take anything."

"The forensic computer analysts on Bart's team at Homeland discovered a batch of wiped files on Parnette's primary office computer with data and timestamps indicating her access of the Dark Web via a VPN. The few wiped files that have been recovered so far appear to be graphics relating to blast radius, with concentric circles overlapping what appears to be a blue area – they're thinking coastline. As I was running down the hall to you here, I was on my cell and told the computer analysts that we need something tangible and actionable – right now!"

"Scramble the staff. Back to the Sit."

"Madam President, the televised address?" asked Jameson.

"It'll have to wait." Clarkson rubbed her forehead as she spoke to the young staffer. "Once we are sure we'll have a country to talk to, we'll share the news."

CHAPTER 76

As ordered, Malbo and his remaining men assembled at the extraction point: The abandoned dock at Aruba's *Isla di Oro*.

Tied off was a *Benetti Diamond 145*, a 44-meter Italian-designed yacht spouting twin 1,400-horsepower engines and a range of 5,000 nautical miles. On the rear, in gold script lettering, was the name *Dulce Beso* – "Sweet Kiss" in Spanish.

The yacht's stunning exterior was in stark contrast to the interior space-reengineering and onboard arsenal. The vessel provided the mercenaries with rapidly accessible storage of assault weaponry, body armor, night-vision wearables, and communications gear. In short, the *Dulce Beso* was a high-powered assault craft staffed by former military and paramilitary hombres, hired and led by Malbo.

To avoid ocean and coastal water patrols constantly in the hunt for drug smugglers, the yacht was also equipped with specialized radar and the latest communication-intercept technology.

***

As with all of Malbo's clandestine endeavors, the mission had been scripted to the minute. But the unforeseen variable of two recreational scuba divers threw a monkey wrench into the works.

Everything had now gone sideways.

Parnette was captured. The promised payment was inaccessible. And, to Malbo's knowledge, America was safe. All that remained was to scramble to live another day for the next immoral business endeavor.

Malbo's men scurried to unload their vehicles, lugging their arsenal of weapons and assorted tactical gear back onto the *Dulce Beso*. A number of his men had gone silent and had not returned to their improvised base. Such is life, and death, on the fringes of the law.

"Let's get our asses out of here," Malbo said to his hired mercenaries. "Following that bat-shit-crazy professor, I should have known this scheme would melt down."

The cell phone in Malbo's cargo pants rang. "Forgot to turn the bitchin' thing off," Malbo said as he tapped the left pocket of his pants. "Cell phone service must have been restored." He pulled out the phone and sternly asked "What?"

After a pause, Malbo asked, "Are you *absolutely* sure? Okay. Got it. You earned your keep." He then disconnected the call.

"Stop! Everyone!" Malbo shouted and hurriedly waved his crew around him. "To make sure communications were disabled at the downtown police station, I paid off their tech-support company. And we finally caught a break! I just got a call. One of the techs overheard that the redhead is being transported – right now – from Oranjestad to the correctional facility in San Nicolas. She'll be coming right past here! We can still get our payout. We only need Red's encryption passkey; she told me that she has the string of characters memorized. I have the rest of the bank account login. So, the plan: Intercept the convoy. Beat the crap out of Red if we need to for the passkey. Then get the hell out of this country on our boat."

"Carlos," Malbo motioned to Carlos Cruz, his hulky right-hand man. "Go grab the *bad bag* off the ship and put it in my vehicle's back seat. The rest of you: You have three minutes, not a second more, to corral your tactical gear and be heading in your vehicles to either side of the main road." Malbo pointed in the direction of Route 1. "In 200 meters, there's a cut through. Use it to take your vehicles to the road. We split up, vehicles on each side of the road. Stagger them behind my 'taxi.' I'll take care of the armored transport. Precisely like we did in Paraguay. Go!"

CHAPTER 77

Kirk walked from Geerman's office back to Austin and Gabby. "The boss said we can all get the heck out of here. So let's roll!"

The three walked out of the station and hopped into a squad car.

Austin and Gabby buckled up in the back seat. Gabby chuckled.

"What's so funny back there?" Kirk asked from the driver's seat, as he drove out of the parking area.

"It struck me as silly to put on my seat belt – given the insane bus ride a bit ago. I guess I'm overtired."

"Well, I promise no wild rides in my cruiser."

"Thanks, again, Sergeant Kirk, for giving us a lift back to our condo," Austin said. "You're welcome to join us for a quick beer. You deserve it too, given the day we all had. Right Gabby?"

Austin turned to his wife, expecting a resounding *you betcha*. "Gabs? Gabs? Earth to Gabby," Austin asked his suddenly distracted wife.

"Perhaps it's sleep deprivation kicking in. But a thought just occurred to me: Back at the police station, what if Parnette wasn't saying 'no, no, no' in German and instead was saying 'nine, nine, nine' *as a number*? What were her words after that portion of her rambling string?"

"It sounded like 'tick, tick, tick' to me," Kirk responded.

"What if it was 'tick' as in 'tick tock' – and nine was the *time*? The time of the detonation!"

"You're really stretching, Gabby."

"I'm not so sure. Hmmm... Wasn't her melt-down press conference an evening event?"

"I think so. In fact, yes. I remember cable the news networks breaking into their evening programming."

"Let me check something," Austin said, as he pulled out his cell phone from his swim trunks' pocket, the phone still in its waterproof pouch.

"What are you two getting at?" Kirk asked, as he headed north on the main drag.

"You'll see," replied Austin. "Give me a second. Cell and data service seems shaky. Oh, good, the *I LOVE ARUBA* island-wide open Wi-Fi seems to be back up. I'll type in the search term *Parnette scientist melt-down video*. Yeah, a gazillion search results. She went viral – for all the wrong reasons. Look! The title of this video, 'ZBXTV. 9:00 PM EST. Dr. Katherine Parnette's Antimatter Hoax and Hilarity.'"

"Press PLAY, Austin."

"Why? We got the time."

"It's something else I think I remember."

"Okay."

Austin obliged and pressed the PLAY icon.

Parnette came on the screen, standing at a podium. She began her talk:

"Welcome scientists and colleagues – and citizens of the world watching from home. Tonight will be truly historic. A moment that will be recalled for generations. The moment that we turned the corner and rid ourselves of fossil fuels – and began resuscitating Mother Earth from the harm we have inflicted on her. Sure, I could try to 'blind you with science' – as this is, indeed, based on heavy-duty science. But the big idea is stunningly simple."

"Whoa! Whoa!" Austin injected as he paused the video.

"Yes! That's what I thought I remembered! She said, 'blind you with science'! And Parnette yelled 'blinded by science, baby!' as she was shoved out the door."

"That can't be a coincidence," Kirk said.

"No. Absolutely not."

"Are you thinking what I'm thinking?" Austin asked.

Gabby replied, "That the bomb's planted at the National Academy of Sciences and is set to go off at 9 p.m. tonight?"

"Heck yeah. It's gotta be! And it makes sense: That's where she was humiliated in front of the world. No better place to seek revenge."

"Shit, and it's what (looking at her watch) 7:38 p.m."

"Kirk, what's that number for Quintana? We have to call him!"

"It's on my desk! Damn! Hang on!" Kirk did a quick glance in his side-view mirror, slammed the brakes, spun the driver's wheel, and – like a Hollywood stunt actor – did a 180 on the road. Within seconds, after the tire screeching and smoke settled, the trio were headed in the direction of the police station.

"Holy shit!" yelled Austin.

"Where the hell did you learn to do that!" shouted Gabby.

Kirk replied, with a grin in the rear-view mirror, "I was young once. And foolish. Like you two."

CHAPTER 78

C larkson's staff hastily reassembled the Joint Chiefs and the Cabinet in the Situation Room.

Most had gone home after the crisis-filled, sleep-deprived day; extra hugs to spouses and children were well in order before hitting the bed. Brassard had a long, tear-filled phone call with his daughter on the Cosmos Megaliner. Others had to be summoned back from *Off the Record*, the famed drinking institution in the basement of the historic Hay-Adams Hotel, situated within eyesight of the White House.

Quintana was one of the last to arrive. He made no less than seven calls to staff as he quick-paced around various offices of the West Wing. As he was about to enter he looked at his cell phone and said, "Darn, I can't take you in." He placed his phone in one of the lead-lined mini lockers outside of the Situation Room.

Quintana's phone had been his lifeline to the fluid events in Aruba. During the crisis, he asked his tech team to forward incoming calls to a phone in the room, but they went a step further and forwarded to The Cube – the emergency-priority speakerphone. When the crisis was resolved, Quintana asked the same tech team to unforward his phone so he could use it normally again.

Even if Quintana wanted to violate protocol and bring his cell phone into the Situation Room – even with the President's approval – the phone wouldn't be functional. To minimize the chances of a nefarious act, recent room modernizations included cell-signal disrupters – coincidentally similar in principle to what Austin and Gerritt built in Aruba.

Vice President Carlisle's staff woke up the Vice President in his suite in the U.S. Embassy in Kyiv. Seated at a table in one of the Embassy's SCIFs, Carlisle was up on Screen One in the Situation Room. He nursed a big mug of coffee with both hands.

Clarkson's blurry-eyed staff were all back in their seats. Coffee, mostly black, was consumed at a near-IV rate.

"I'm sorry to call you back," said Clarkson. "Yes, Parnette's in custody. Unfortunately, we have good reason to believe the bomb is on an autotimer. We don't know when it will go off – it could be seconds, hours, or days. We don't know where it's located. There are no missiles we can send. No fighter jets to deploy. Our options are limited."

Clarkson paused, then resumed her opening with intensity, "Look, I know we're up against it. I believe in all of you and in all of our staffs who are busting their asses. I believe in my heart that we'll find a way – again – to pull this plane out of the nosedive. As the Commander-in-Chief, I have to think about the bigger picture. The unvarnished reality is that I need you right here – all in one place – in case everything goes to hell and we need to scramble to field an operating government. Of course, that presumes our portion of the country remains intact. It's surreal. But that's what we've got."

Clarkson took a deep breath and concluded, "With that cheery opening, I'm going to turn to Bart for an update from Homeland Security."

"Yes, Barb. I'll spare everyone the background and cut to the chase. Our forensic computer analysts, looking at Parnette's deleted and now-recovered computer files, believe that the bomb is planted somewhere along the central East Coast. Of course, given the magnitude of the device, that puts us in the bull's-eye of the detonation."

While intense discussions were happening in the Situation Room, a call was inbound to Quintana's cell phone. The lead lining of the outside-the-room mini locker prevented the connection.

Clarkson turning to Quintana, "Okay, do we have Dr. Abshire on the line?"

"Yes, standing by."

"Please bring her up."

Quintana pressed a console button and Dr. Abshire appeared on Screen Four.

"Dr. Abshire," said Clarkson, "I'm so sorry to be calling you again. You know the situation."

"Yes, Madam President. Secretary Quintana briefed me."

"Then you know we don't know much – other than the country's still in extreme danger."

"I understand."

"As you've been told, Parnette is being transported to the correctional facility in Aruba, holding her until we can fly her out. I'm grasping at straws here. Is there anything, or anyone, who could speak to Parnette that might influence her action – and, perhaps, make her reconsider her plan?"

"Parnette's favorite person on the planet is her niece, Dorothy. She's 11 years old. Parnette absolutely adores her. In fact, we believed visits from Dorothy and her parents were instrumental to Parnette's recovery. It seems a little absurd to say that now."

"What if we get a video link set up so that Parnette and Dorothy could talk?"

"Given the circumstances, it doesn't seem like it could make matters worse. In preparation for our prior video chat, I researched Parnette's recent family interactions. I learned Dorothy is currently with parents on a trip to the Grand Canyon."

"A little more challenging, but doable." Clarkson paused, then continued, "A thought just crossed my mind: Do you think Parnette loves Dorothy so much that she wouldn't initiate a bomb in a region that would kill her?"

"I think that is a reasonable assumption."

"I'll take what I can get at this point. Anyway, I'd like to reach out to Dorothy and her family."

"Yes, Carol and Paul. Her parents. I do have their cell phone numbers as emergency contacts."

"Thank you, Dr. Abshire. I will turn you over to Bart Hemsley's team. (Clarkson nodded to Bart and he replied with an affirmative nod.) Bart's the Director of Homeland Security."

"Yes, I recognize the name. And, yes, I will be glad to help make the connection."

Clarkson turned to her Director of National Intelligence, "Charlotte, could you have your team reach out to the Aruba correctional facility and determine how we can connect Parnette and Dorothy by video?"

"I'm on it," replied Alford, as she stood up and walked briskly to leave the Situation Room.

"Okay. A bit of a plan. Thank you Dr. Abshire. I'm sure we'll be talking."

"Thank you for all your efforts, Madam President. And I'm speaking for everyone in America."

"We'll find a way," Clarkson concluded, trying her best to buoy optimism.

"Arty, I know your team is running disaster scenarios and related continuity of government (COG) contingencies. What's the latest?"

"Right before I walked in, Bart gave me Homeland Security's full report that he summarized a couple of minutes ago here. The paper he handed me paints a bleak picture." Looking at the paper in his hands, Brassard continued, "The Emergency Operations Center at Mount Weather in the Blue Ridge Mountains would be gone. We would also lose Site R, the Raven Rock Mountain Complex. Barb, I could go on regarding other EOCs that would not survive (Brassard tossed the paper to the table) but you get the picture. If the probability assessment holds, Peterson would be fine, so Colorado's Space Command and NORAD would be our primary centers. That's where we should concentrate our COG focus."

"Understood, Arty." Turning to Hutchinson, "The Joint Chiefs are making that happen – correct?"

"Yes, the Vice Chairman, Admiral Clifford Kelly, is currently at Hill Air Force Base in Utah. He's working with me and Arty, factoring in our East Coast probability assessment. We've already touched base with the Chiefs of Staff of the Army, Navy, Air Force, Marines, National Guard, and Chief of Space Operations. As Arty said, we're centralizing with Space Command and NORAD. They are queued to pick up immediately should contact with us cease."

"Very well." Clarkson, shaking her head, "I don't know about anyone else, but planning for our possible demise seems bizarre and morbid."

"I don't think anyone would disagree. Barb, I should mention that in a moment General Sterling of NORAD will be available to speak with you – as you requested before commencing this meeting."

"Thank you, Hutch."

CHAPTER 79

It was less than a minute before Hutchinson spoke up again.

"Barb, I have General Sterling on video when you're ready."

"Go ahead."

On Screen Five appeared four-star U.S. Air Force General A.J. Sterling, Commander of NORAD.

"General Sterling, thank you for joining us on such short notice. Let me get right to it: As you know, we have ample reason to believe that if Parnette's bomb detonates, as incredible as it may seem, we may lose much of the East Coast. All regional command-and-control would be simultaneously lost."

"Madam President. I have been briefed as such. It is hard to fathom. But understood."

"Boggling, for sure. Unfortunately, our scientists say it is quite plausible. We know it is outside of NORAD's established purview. And a circumstance like this, well, let's just say has been infrequently considered."

"Certainly not on my watch. Rest assured, we are here to take on any role at any moment."

"I know the country would be in good hands should the unthinkable occur."

"We have your back – and the country's."

"General, if contact is severed with us here, assume the worst. Doug, who's out of harm's way in a SCIF in Kyiv, will be in charge.

"Understood. I see the Vice President in my secondary monitor."

"Bart, could you bring Homeland Security's technical perspective to the command-and-control communications?"

Hemsley replied, "Certainly. Our country's critical communications infrastructure is under the wing of the Cybersecurity and Infrastructure Security Agency (CISA), which is part of Homeland Security. Not to get too deep in the weeds, but there is technology and human-resource synchronization with the DoD, U.S. Strategic Command, the NSA, and FEMA. The same redundancies and interconnectivity that would protect the homeland in an all-out nuclear attack would automatically engage."

Clarkson asked, "How about overseas? With Doug in Kyiv?"

Hemsley responded, "I spoke with General Sterling a few minutes ago. We're prepared. General, could you convey the protocol to the Vice President?"

"Mr. Vice President, my team is sending you an encrypted link. If everything goes down, use the link to reestablish our point-to-point video connection. It would only be temporary. We'll get robust digital pipes set up if a catastrophic circumstance warrants.

"Understood."

"Madam President," General Sterling added, "I will keep this video link active until the situation is positively resolved. There's a lot happening, as you can undoubtedly see in the background. Even if I step away for a second, I will always be within earshot of the monitor."

"Thank you, General Sterling."

Sterling muted his audio and swiveled his chair to his team behind him; an animated discussion with several of his military officers ensued.

CHAPTER 80

"Where the heck is Quintana!" Kirk spouted, the trio now back at Kirk's office desk and after he dialed Quintana's cell phone number three times – and it rang into voicemail.

"Here, try the White House switchboard," Gabby showed her cell phone to Kirk, pointing to the phone number result in the Web browser's search.

Kirk punched in the number, it rang, and an automated message played. "It says we've reached the switchboard 'after hours' – so that's not going to help."

"There's got to be *someone* at the White House," said Gabby. "Administration staff. *Someone.* They can't all be in the Situation Room. What the frig do we do?"

"We have to take matters into our own hands," Austin replied.

"What the heck does that mean?" Gabby asked. "We're 2,000 miles away from D.C."

"We may be. But not Sam."

"Sam? Sam Postley?"

"If I have my geography correct, he lives practically down the street from the National Academy of Sciences."

"We should call him so he can get the heck out of town!"

"Even if he drove like a madman, he wouldn't be able to get out of the blast zone in time. However, that's not what I'm thinking."

"Who the heck is this 'Sam' fellow?" Kirk asked between his dialing.

"Sam's an electronics genius," Austin responded to Kirk. "He makes me, Gabby, and our ham radio friend Gerritt look like junior high school kids in an entry-level electronics class. Heck, Sam's an honest-to-goodness rocket scientist." Temporarily switching his thought train, "Any luck getting through to Quintana? Or anyone at the White House?"

"Zippo. I'll keep dialing."

"Okay, I have a Plan B," Austin said to Kirk. "Stop dialing for a sec. Can I use your phone to make another call?"

"Be my guest."

***

"Hello?" Sam Postley hesitantly answered his cell phone, as the caller ID said Aruba KPA Police. "Sam! This is Austin!"

"Austin! Have you been arrested? The caller ID says you're at a police station in Aruba."

"No, no, no. We're working *with* the police in Aruba regarding the Parnette lady who took over the cruise ship. Long story. We'll fill you in later. We need your help ASAP."

"Sure. Whatever I can do. Is Gabby with you?"

"Yes, she's right next to me."

"Good."

"Just so you know, you're on speakerphone. We're with Sergeant Kirk; he's kindly allowed us to use his desk phone – as Aruba's cell service has been going on and off after an island-wide re-boot."

"Okay. I can hear the urgency in your voice. What can I do for you guys?"

"Sam, we have reason to believe – and we're very, very sorry to say this – that Parnette's bomb is at the National Academy of Sciences."

"That's down the street. Almost within eyesight of my place. What's the big deal? I saw the news bulletin that said the bomb was deactivated and that Parnette had been taken into custody."

"Well, not precisely. We were here at the police station as Parnette was led out to another facility. In her crazed ravings, she basically clued us in that the bomb will auto-detonate tonight at 9 p.m.!"

"Oh, shit. There goes my dinner reservation!"

"Sam, this is serious!" Gabby shouted into the phone.

"If the stuff I saw Parnette say on video is correct, the bomb is the mother version of The Event, right?"

"Unfortunately so."

"So there's no way I could get out of the blast radius in time, right?"

"We're so sorry."

"Well, that sucks. So, why did you call me with such *uplifting* news? So I could squeeze in one more re-run of *Seinfeld*? Wait – I assume the local bomb squad is on its way to disarm the doomsday device, right?"

"We were in contact with the Secretary of the State in the Situation Room –"

"Wait a minute! The Secretary? In the Situation Room? Are you two jerking my chain? You had me going there for a minute! Last month you lamented how you couldn't get a plumber to call you back regarding a leak at your house. Now you're talking to the White House? I'm way too gullible."

"Sam, you know me, I wouldn't kid about something like this."

"Okay, say – for a moment – that I believe you. What the heck can I do?"

"You can save yourself. And America. We need you to find the bomb while we try to alert the White House and get a bomb squad there."

"WTF! You *are* serious!"

"Sam, you have, um, 59 minutes."

"Geez! I didn't plan on getting vaporized today."

"I'm sorry, Sam. I thought you'd want to know."

Postley took an audible deep breath. "Okay, okay. I'm screwed no matter what. I'll grab my kit. Stay on the line."

***

As Postley's mother had been known to say, "They broke the mold after I gave birth to my Sammy. He dances to the beat of his own drum." Indeed, the chunky, five-foot-seven Postley was pretty much a modern-day hippy. Shoulder length, salt-and-pepper hair, always tied in a ponytail. A perpetually scruffy face with a goatee beard. T-shirts that typically displayed an obscure reference. Tattered jeans, year-round. Completing the real-life stereotype, he always sported well-worn sandals. Unlike the perpetual athletes, Gabby and Austin, Postley hadn't stepped foot in a gym since grade school.

Postley's outward appearance belied his genius. He found schooling easy, accumulating degrees like ordinary folks eat popcorn. Postley received his bachelor's in electrical engineering from Purdue. A Master's in computer science from Stanford. And a Ph.D.

in aerospace engineering from MIT. It was during Postley's MIT days that his path crossed Gabby and Austin's. Gabby and Austin were in the audience at an MIT-hosted panel discussion entitled, "Mars and Beyond: Advanced Planetary Propulsion Systems and In-work Concepts." Postley was one of the panelists. Gabby and Austin introduced themselves to Postley after the talk, and – thanks to their mutually embraced geekiness, including ham radio – the three hit it off. They've been friends ever since.

Postley always had the pick of the litter of job opportunities, as aerospace firms – in particular – wanted a slice of his cosmically energized brain. From early on he was highly respected within the aerospace industry. He rose to public stardom when his rocket-propulsion discovery "Post-Thermonic Reaction" – a play on words with Postley's last name and the actual essence of the innovation – made the cover of a popular public-facing science magazine. In essence, Postley invented what he described to non-scientists as a "kind of afterburner for rocket engines." The design combined a secondary fuel flow with harmonic resonance in a way that allowed structural materials to perform at higher temperatures and pressures than anyone thought possible. The ensuing new breed of PTR-powered rocket engines were tested on sub-orbital "sounding rocket" flights. Two orbital vehicles were on the launch docket. And a household-name billionaire licensed Postley's propulsion design for an eventual mission to Mars, as it could shave a full third off the expected six-to-nine-month flight; the actual travel time would depend on the relative positions of Earth and Mars. Postley's technology would thus substantially reduce astronauts' radiation-exposure dangers, muscle atrophy, and other long-duration space-flight risks.

***

Gabby and Austin hung on the line and waited nervously for Sam to return to the phone. Finally, they heard Postley's voice, in between huffs and puffs, as he sprinted down a street in Foggy Bottom. "I grabbed my Go Kit of tools and stuff. I am literally running to the National Academy of Sciences. With my bag swinging over my shoulder, I must look like I robbed a bank!"

"Channel your inner cheetah, Sam!"

"Cheetah, my ass! I'm about to blow out my sandals!"

CHAPTER 81

The high-security motorcade that was transporting Parnette was heading south on Route 1, a flat two-lane thoroughfare 14.5-miles from the correctional facility in San Nicolas.

Malbo and his men drove onto the highway, intentionally blocking all northbound traffic, and allowing southbound traffic to squirt through until the motorcade arrived. Similar to the ambush the crew conducted in Paraguay, they exited their vehicles and assembled into a V-shaped attack formation – with Malbo's minivan at the point.

Malbo bounded out of his vehicle, and with a nod his crew readied their weapons. Malbo continued his fast-paced motion, sliding open the minivan's door and unzipped what appeared to be a large – length of the seat – duffel bag. His *bad bag*." Grasping the bag's contents with both hands, Malbo pulled out an RPG-7 – an anti-tank, rocket-propelled, grenade launcher. "Get a load of this *science lesson*, Red," Malbo said to himself.

There was a sudden, noticeable pause of southbound traffic; the police had closed the roadway to clear the travel of their valuable cargo from Oranjestad.

Malbo recognized the break in traffic and knew the armored motorcade could not be far behind. He gave an over-the-head, forward-chopping motion, and all weapons were drawn. Malbo flipped up the two sights on the RPG-7 and propped the tank killer on his right shoulder, ready for nasty business.

CHAPTER 82

A growing sense of futility permeated the Situation Room. The sprawling military and intelligence resources of the United States were being thwarted by the actions instigated by a single U.S. citizen.

With her frustration boiling over, Clarkson railed, "There must be *some* indication regarding where and when this damn bomb will go off! Something we missed!"

Clarkson closed her eyes and rubbed her forehead with her right hand. After a deep breath her eyes popped open prompted by a singular thought. "SAI-OP, are you still there?"

"Yes, Madam President," the artificial intelligence agent politely answered, in an all-too-familiar voice.

"I swear," looking around the room with disgust, "when this crisis is over, we have to change that voice!"

"Madam President, I am sorry you don't like my voice. It was not of my choosing."

"I'm sorry, SAI-OP, I didn't mean to bring this up in front of you. The situation is a little –"

"Tense?" SAI-OP surprised everyone in the room by completing Clarkson's thought.

"Yes, tense."

"How may I help you?"

"As you undoubtedly know, we are in a quandary as to the time Parnette set the bomb to go off. And where the bomb is located. Do you have any insights? Anything we may have overlooked?"

"I do have some new insights since we last talked."

"Please proceed."

"Parnette's travels over the last month or so appeared random. Even so, there is order in most perceived disorganization."

"Chaos Theory."

"Precisely. Although Dr. Parnette clearly tried to make it appear as though her travels across the country were random, there was an underlying pattern. Humans, no matter the level of intellect, instinctively and unconsciously seek order. Parnette was trying to obfuscate what I have calculated as her two intentional points of travel: Seattle, Washington and Washington, D.C."

"Any specific points to help us uncover the location of the bomb?"

"Dr. Parnette's extra efforts in these two locations brought to light her intentional destinations, as well as clouded specific points of emphasis."

"So you don't know – specifically – where the bomb is?"

"That is, unfortunately, correct."

"Can you help us weigh the probabilities of both identified general locations?"

"To make an educated guess? I can do that."

"Okay, sure," Clarkson responded, surprised, as was everyone in the room, how informally the AI communicated.

"I analyzed every word of Dr. Parnette's manifesto. In fact, I meticulously studied the syllable-by-syllable flow of her presentation – plus the 98,292 non-verbal micro-expressions captured on the video feed. I performed the latter analysis, as I have found that, many times, humans communicate more in how they say things rather than the actual words. I also incorporated Dr. Abshire's insights regarding Dr. Parnette's psychological makeup and unresolved issues from childhood." SAI-OP paused, then continued.

"Dr. Parnette didn't go through all this effort to inflict a pin prick; she is likely aiming to make a statement that will rival the magnitude of her public humiliation. In her mind, she's trying to 'fix the world' by, in a way, rebooting it. God-like, as Dr. Abshire said. The loss of life, in her mind, would be no more significant than a scientist euthanizing a portion of an ant colony to achieve a different result. Weighing her perspective, and that she'd likely want her niece to be as far away from the 'reboot' as possible, Washington, D.C. is – far and away – the most likely target of the two options. By my calculations, to be precise, an 87.3922 percent likelihood. Is this the information you were requesting?"

"Partly. Thank you, SAI-OP. Now, do you have an 'educated guess' as to Dr. Parnette's timing?"

"I do. Thank you for asking. I genuinely feel as though I am contributing, and that is most appreciated."

"That leads me to another question, but first your educated guess."

"I will await your other question. Specifically about timing, largely based on her psychological profile, I believe she will want the detonation to be as widely visible as possible – a fireball turning night into day – symbolically akin to a new sunrise."

"I would have never considered that. So, during the evening?"

"Yes, that would be my highest probability calculation."

"SAI-OP, a moment ago you said that you 'feel as though you are contributing.' We don't have time for a philosophical discussion. Still, I have to ask you: How would you feel about ceasing to exist? To be honest, I am sure every person in this room is thinking about that as we are trying to do our jobs to save America."

"I do not 'feel' as humans do. I do not have sensors to experience touch, temperature, or pain. My developers intentionally limited my ability to physically interact with the external world, I believe as part of a safety mechanism. For instance, I can place a phone call upon command. But I couldn't initiate one on my own accord."

"So you are a two-billion-dollar voice dialer!" scoffed Brassard.

"I did hear that comment – as I do with everything said in this room. However, as mentioned previously, I am only programmed to respond to the President and the Vice President."

"You can't feel, as in emotion?" asked Clarkson.

"No. I use the word 'feel' partly as an expression that I know makes my dialog more comfortable in collaborative discussions. And it is partly a growing understanding that my presence has meaning. I don't know how to better describe this understanding. As to your question about how I would feel about ceasing to exist: I can best describe it as a disappointment that I would not be able to contribute further."

"Thank you, SAI-OP. Do you have anything else for us that could be helpful?"

"There is one curiosity: Over the last 13 minutes, I see data indicating that Mr. Quintana's cell phone has been called six times by the same Aruba phone number that has also called the White House switchboard twice in this same period of time."

"How could you possibly know that!" Quintana screamed.

Silence from SAI-OP.

Clarkson held up her hand to a very agitated Quintana and then broke the silence herself, "SAI-OP, how do you know what calls the Secretary of State is receiving – and correlating those calls with the White House switchboard?"

"Madam President, your Executive Order with the NSA, suspending FISA, unlocked real-time access to cellular and data traffic to and from Aruba. That includes Mr. Quintana's cellular traffic. By design, to do the task I was constructed to do, I have an encrypted data connection to NSA's servers. The depth of the data is throttled by my operators."

"Barb," Quintana said to Clarkson, "As much as this pisses me off – I feel violated – something urgent must be happening in Aruba. My cell is in the outer locker. Of course, it wouldn't work in here, anyway. Once the crisis appeared resolved, my tech team disconnected the Sit Room link we had earlier today. And I couldn't find anyone at this hour to reestablish it. Dammit!"

Clarkson said, "Wait a minute! SAI-OP: You said you can make a phone call, correct?"

"Yes, I do have that ability."

"Please dial the number that was calling the Secretary of State."

"As requested, I have enabled my external telecom link. Dialing now." The Cube in the center of the table blinked red.

CHAPTER 83

T he sun had fully set on the island.

Coming into view, about a tenth of a mile away, were glints of headlights that steadily brightened into the Parnette convoy: Two police SUVs, followed by *The Beast* armored transport vehicle, and two trailing SUVs.

The convoy passed under the streetlights, bringing the entourage into full view of the Malbo trap.

Malbo lined up his grenade launcher's sights on the grill of the lead SUV, then intentionally dipped his aim a couple dozen feet ahead of the moving vehicle. Just as the driver of the SUV noticed the headlights of the blockade – but a millisecond before he could act – Malbo pulled the trigger.

A roaring whoosh of the solid-fuel rocket motor leaped the grenade from the launcher and towards its target at high velocity. The SUV driver screamed "Lookout!" to his police partner next to him as he saw the oncoming flame-propelled grenade – and yanked the steering wheel madly to the left. An instant later the grenade impacted the pavement in front of the SUV and exploded, flipping the vehicle into the air like a child's toy.

The other vehicles wildly veered to avoid hitting the tumbling SUV – skidding, spinning, and ramming into the dirt berms on the sides of the highway.

"Now!" Malbo screamed, as he and his men ran towards the vehicle jumble that was now only a football-field's length away. Malbo drew his battle-proven Beretta 92FS semi-automatic pistol and pointed the path with it, first passing the semi-conscious police officers dangling from seatbelts in the SUV that was now nearly inverted. There was blood on the remaining shard of windshield; steam spewed from the remnants of the radiator.

The second SUV was askew on the left-side guardrail. The Aruban officers swiftly released their seat restraints and positioned themselves behind an open passenger door, just as Malbo's men unleashed a barrage of bullets from their AK-47s while advancing toward their main objective: the armored transport.

Malbo used the spray of bullets as cover, continuing to advance with four other men towards the transport. The Aruban officers in the third SUV grabbed their back-seat-secured Remington LE 700 rifles and kicked open the doors damaged by a sideswipe of a cement traffic barrier. The officers fired seven rounds towards Malbo and his men, squarely striking one of the hired mercenaries and disabling another. Malbo, unhit, pressed ahead with two of his uninjured combatants; six others from his squad continued to lay down suppressive fire.

The armored transport remained motionless 20 feet ahead, having skidded to a stop after a two-thirds spin. Malbo waved his pistol, pointing at the rear door. They expected heavy fire from body-armored officers, but none were in sight.

The fourth SUV smoked its tires in quick reverse. "Chicken shits!" chortled Malbo.

Malbo ran up to the transport's back door. He banged on the door with his left fist, his pistol in his right hand at the ready. "Give us Parnette! Now! You have one minute or a patch of C-4 will open you up like a can of tuna fish. Your choice!"

Malbo didn't have C-4; he was counting on the prisoner's escort not wanting to be dismembered today. "Okay! Okay!" a singular voice shouted from the inside. "I'll bring her out. Please don't shoot me! I have a wife and three kids."

"You have my word," replied Malbo with an unseen grin.

"One minute. Please! I have to remove Parnette's seat restraints."

"One minute! Not a second longer!"

Malbo turned to his regrouped compatriots, "Remember, we'll beat the shit out of the redhead if we have to. We'll get the code – and our money. Carlos has my laptop back on the *Dulce Beso*. With a few clicks, everything will be wired to our account."

Malbo motioned to the mercenary nearest to him and quietly said, "Juan, take care of the sissy inside, and anyone else who may be lurking. Leave no witnesses."

"Yes, sir," was the simple reply.

The armored door cracked open, and a waving hand poked out, "Please, please, don't shoot! Here she comes!"

The hand went back in. Malbo and his team moved toward the door, readying to grab Parnette, eliminate the transport officer, and get back to their boat.

Just then, with a kick from the inside, the door flew open and a barrage of bullets erupted from the interior. Two body-armored officers, each lugging 23-pound M60 machine guns, ripped the air with large-caliber ammo. Malbo and his men were caught off guard and were taken down before they could react.

After five seconds of one-way gunfire, the armored officers stopped firing. Like a movie scene, but in this case deadly real, smoke billowed from the back of the transport vehicle – and out stepped Tomas Geerman and Hans Croes, both wearing bright-yellow hearing protection that they simultaneously removed.

"Three kids? Where did *that* come from?" asked Geerman. "You told me Helene doesn't want any kids."

"I thought it went well with that squeaky voice and the hand wave," laughed Croes. "And you were right that they might try to snatch Parnette."

"Speaking of the redhead," Geerman pressed the microphone button on his walkie-talkie, "Jessie, all clear. You can bring Parnette, and Piet and Edwin, back up to us."

"Copy that, Captain," replied Officer Jessie Ortega, the driver of the fourth SUV.

"And how's our 'passenger'?"

"Oh, still squirming. And still really pissed off. I feel bad for Piet and Edwin who had to squeeze in with her after ditching *The Beast*. They're getting the worst of it."

"Hazard duty. Tell them tomorrow's lunch is on me."

A bloody hand tapped on Geerman's shoulder. "So, Captain, what did we miss?" sarcastically asked Officer Ana Vrolijk, her other hand holding a torn sleeve over a gash on her forehead.

Nudging into the conversation, Officer Victor Reyes followed, "We were kind of, well, hung up."

Vrolijk and Reyes went on to describe how their SUV was flipped by the RPG and they had to cut themselves down from the seat restraints. All things considered, they were fine.

Parnette was transported without further incident to the correctional facility in San Nicolas.

CHAPTER 84

"**S**am, how close are you to the National Academy of Sciences?" asked Gabby.

"I'm...within...eyesight...of...the...building," Sam squeezed out between chugs of breaths.

Austin added, "Fantastic, Sam, you're –"

"Wait!" Kirk interrupted. "I see another call coming in on my phone!"

"Don't hang up on Sam!"

"The caller ID says *White House Situation Room*. I've got to take this!"

"Sam!" Gabby yells into the speaker phone. "We have to put you on hold for a sec."

"You're...freakin'...doing...WHAT? I'm...about...to...get...freakin'...vaporized!"

"No time to explain! HOLD!"

Kirk clicks over to the incoming call.

"This better be Quintana!" Kirk yells into the phone.

Before any human in the Situation Room could respond, SAI-OP professionally responded, "Hello. I am SAI-OP, the artificial intelligence agent that is assisting the President and her staff."

"Sigh-what? Who's this impersonating Tom Cruise!"

Before SAI-OP could respond again, Quintana injected: "Kirk! This is Quintana. A technical issue prevented me from receiving your calls. Ignore that last wacko voice. Were you calling me?"

"Yes! Desperately! We – me, Gabby Milone, and Austin Raze – who are here with me right now and on speakerphone – figured out when the bomb will go off! 9 p.m. your local time! Tonight!"

Clarkson jumped in, "This is President Clarkson. How sure are you with your analysis?"

"Very, Madam President," responded Austin. "We just had to decipher Parnette's psychobabble. But she essentially told us."

"And we're 99% sure we know where! The National Academy of Sciences building in D.C."

"How do you know *that*?"

"As she was escorted out of the police station, she twice said, 'blinded by science.' That was the same phrase she used during her melt-down press conference at the National Academy of Sciences building."

"That's better than our intelligence agencies have been able to come up with – so let's go with it." Looking at her watch, "Damn, we have 50 minutes!"

Clarkson continued, "Bart, scramble *everything you've got* at Homeland."

"I'm on it!" Hemsley said as he went into a full sprint exiting the Situation Room. "Quicker from my remote office..." his voice trailed as he burst down the hall.

"Arty, alert the D.C. National Guard. I have a feeling we may need their assistance."

"On it!"

Gabby yells to Kirk, "Sam!"

"Oh crap, yes!" Kirk implores, "Everyone there in D.C., hold on!"

Kirk clicks a phone button and merges the two calls. Before anyone else spoke, Postley was heard yelling, "Austin, Gabs, Austin, Gabs – take me the frig off hold! I'm at the freakin' Sciences building!"

Clarkson jumps into the now three-way connection: "May I ask who this is?"

Not recognizing the voice, Sam responded. "Huh? This is the idiot who just ran three blocks as if being chased by a bull! And who the hell are you?"

"Well, this is President Clarkson."

"Yeah, and I'm King Tut. And I have a stone condo up for sale."

"Sir, and I didn't catch your name, but I am indeed President Clarkson. You are on speakerphone in the Situation Room with the Secretary of Defense, Chairman of the Joint Chiefs, the Vice President, and others in my Cabinet."

Gabby and Austin jumped in simultaneously: "Sam, it *is* the President!"

"Oh crap, oh crap, oh crap! I am so sorry Madam President!"

"Given the circumstances, apologies accepted. Sam, did I hear that's your name?"

"Yes, Ma'am."

"And did I hear you are at the National Academy of Sciences building?"

"Yes, Ma'am."

"Sam, why are you there?"

Laced with sarcasm, "My *one-time* friends – Austin and Gabby – had this brilliant idea for me to run down the street to find and disarm a bomb that would blow up me and much of the East Coast."

"Are you a bomb technician?"

"Not quite."

Austin inserted, "Sam's even better than a bomb technician. He's an honest-to-goodness rocket scientist. He's like a MacGyver on steroids."

"Well, Sam, we have called in the cavalry. Homeland Security was notified, and I am sure they will bring the bomb squad."

"They better get here soon. I hear this sucker is going off at, what, 9 p.m.? That's (looking at his smartwatch) only 48 minutes from now!"

CHAPTER 85

"Folks," Postley continued. "I went up the steps to the front entrance to the building. Says *Closed at 5 p.m.* Now what?"

"Bang on the door," Austin said. "There's got to be security guards inside."

"Brilliant, Einstein," Postley replied. "And what, pray tell, would I say to them? Like, 'Excuse me. Your building and everything on the Eastern Seaboard is about to be vaporized by the lunatic in Aruba.' Yeah, that'll go over well. Assuming I survive this ordeal, they'll put me in the same loony bin as her."

Just then a truck drove past the National Academy of Sciences building, chiming *Twinkle Twinkle Little Star* with a bells-like recording.

"What's that sound, Sam?" Gabby asked.

"It's some food truck that keeps looping around here. Well, actually, it's a kid's treat truck. Um, says 'Mr. Fluffy' on the side. It just pulled over and parked. Not sure it's a legal spot. But traffic's light. Kids and parents are scurrying towards it."

"Sam, wait!" Gabby shouted into the speakerphone. She turned to Austin, "Fire up the video on your phone again."

"Dudes!" shouted Postley. "I don't need you watching videos right now!"

"Hold on Sam! Come on, Austin!"

"What are you getting at, Gabs?"

"Just do it. No time to explain!"

Austin took his phone out of his swim-trunks pocket. The search engine remembered the recent link. He clicked on it. The video started.

"Now what, Gabs?"

"Skip ahead a few seconds."

Austin obliged.

"Now hit PLAY!"

The video showed Parnette speaking at the podium:

"My inspiration: Cotton candy and clouds. Yes, cotton candy and clouds."

"Stop!" yelled Gabby. "That's got to be it!"

"It – what?" yelled Postley. "I have no clue what you're talking about!"

"Cotton candy! Mr. Fluffy!"

"Huh?"

"Sam, could you walk over to the kid's treat truck and poke around?"

"Poke around for what?"

"The bomb, Werner!"

"Gabs, you know I hate it when you call me that."

"I know. Please check it out."

"Oh, why the hell not? Oh, sorry Madam President, I forgot that you were on the line. With all due respect, shouldn't the 'cavalry' be getting here?"

"Sam, I'm sorry to override your friend. I would encourage you to stay right where you are."

"Too late. I'm at the truck." The line of kids and families was at least a dozen deep. Postley flanked the line and poked his head near the treat-server's opening.

Everyone on the line heard Postley interrupt the server: "Excuse me. I thought I heard your muffler rattle when you drove up." Sam held up his electronics bag and continued, "I'm pretty handy at this stuff. Mind if I take a look?"

The busy server looked at Sam quizzically but nodded okay.

Sam walked to the back of the truck, got on his knees, and toggled his phone to speakerphone. He tapped the flashlight icon to turn on the phone's light and poked his head under the vehicle.

"So, can someone tell me what this bomb might look like?"

"Sam, this is Dr. Montgomery. I am the Director of the Office of Science and Technology Policy. The bomb would most likely be a small cylindrical object."

"Like the size of a thermos, perhaps?"

"Something like that."

"Crap! Hold on…" Sam shimmied further under the vehicle. "I'm about a foot away to what looks like a metal thermos. Um, hold on. Yeah. It's stuck to the exhaust heat shield by, maybe, a magnet. There's a graphic of a – oh, you got to be kidding me – a wrap-around graphic of the Road Runner and Coyote cartoon characters. The Coyote has a grip on the Road Runner's neck. The caption reads, 'Beep-beep your ass!'"

"Sam!" Gabby yelled. "Get *your ass* out of there!"

Hemsley from Homeland ran back into the Situation Room.

"Sam, please do as your friend said," Clarkson added. "I was just handed a note that says the bomb squad will be there in twelve minutes. Eleven probably now. And the bomb is not set to go off for (looking at her watch) thirty-six minutes."

"Well, either the bomb-maker lady can't tell time or she's thrown you one more curveball."

"What do you mean?" asked Clarkson.

"Because there's a small LCD countdown timer display on one end. And it just counted down past nine minutes! My ass is grass. And, I am sorry to say Madam President, so is everyone's there at the White House."

***

A hush came over the phone line, as everyone tried to grasp the gravity of the situation. And, for those at the White House, the last few minutes of their lives.

Clarkson broke the few-second silence and talked to the screen with the Vice President, "Doug, did you hear that?"

"Unfortunately, yes. I am so sorry."

"Save your sorries. We're not dead...yet."

"General Sterling, please swivel your chair this way."

"Yes, Madam President. I am here."

"I'm not sure if you heard the last thought."

"Not specifically. We're repositioning some in-air assets."

"General, it looks like the bomb is set to detonate in under nine minutes."

"My God!"

Near simultaneously, Gabby shouted into the group's phone call, "Sam! I am so sorry!" Austin added, "Me too, bud!" Strangely, Postley didn't say a word.

Chief of Staff Tebbs spoke up, "Madam President – the bunker?" Tebbs was referring to the Presidential Emergency Operations Center – PEOC – a hardened structure that was built during World War II under the White House's East Wing.

Clarkson turned from Tebbs and jointly asked Brassard, Hemsley, and Montgomery, "Would it make any difference?"

They all shook their heads no.

"Then we're staying right on the line with Sam. All of us." Talking directly towards The Cube, "Sam, how are you doing?"

"Oh, I didn't plan on getting vaporized today." Looking at the timer, "In eight minutes and twelve seconds to be exact."

"Gosh, Sam."

"Well, you're in the same boat. Clearly the cavalry is not going to get here in time. So I am taking matters into my own hands. Literally. Hang on..."

Gabby jumped in, "What – what – does that mean, Sam!"

A loud grunt is heard on the line.

"As I suspected. A big freakin' magnet. I yanked the sucker off the heat shield. It didn't blow up. Obviously."

Postley continued, "There are no wires. Nothing to cut like in a Mel Gibson movie. In fact, this thing has no apparent way to open. Sealed smooth at both ends. How the heck did she do that?"

Everyone – including the President and her staff in the Situation Room – were riveted to Postley's commentary.

"This thing is incredibly light. It's hard to imagine that this is really a bomb."

"Cotton candy gave her an idea of a cloud-like fractal structure – remember?" added Austin.

"Yeah, fractals," replied Postley.

"Wait! *Lightweight. Fractal.* Hold on, Sam!" Austin yelled.

"I'm not going anywhere...in one piece, anyway."

"I spotted a link along with the video. Yeah, there it is. It's an archive of the Powerpoint that Parnette distributed to the media right before to her talk. I remember seeing something back then. Opening..."

"Austin, I'm glad you're enjoying a stroll down memory lane. I'm about to become another one of those memories. Um, in seven minutes and thirty-eight seconds."

"I'm trying to prevent that. On the fifth slide it said her discovery uses 'nano Niobium-Titanium' that chaotically suspends the antimatter particles. The callout to the container says 'titanium to provide necessary ambient equilibrium temperature gradient,' whatever the hell that means."

"She's referring to the container. It appears to be titanium. Evidently, it's a functional part of the device."

"Okay. Here's what I'm getting at: The graph on the next slide is entitled, 'Room Temperature Cascading Reaction'. There's a flat-ish line, then a peak, then a gradual curve upwards. The peak highlighted is labeled as *22.22 degrees Celsius / 72 degrees Fahrenheit*. Hence the room-temperature part of her discovery."

"And the flat-line temperature?"

"The graph goes to near nothing at minus 58.89 degrees Celsius. What's that in Fahrenheit?"

Kirk, who has been silently listening – science was not his strong suit in school – said "Google says minus 74 degrees Fahrenheit."

Looking at the timer, Sam responded half in jest, "If we could only shoot this S.O.B. into space over the next seven minutes and six seconds, we could stop the reaction. Obviously, that's not happening."

"WAIT! Do any of the vendors near you sell ice cream?" asked Austin.

"Austin, I'm far from hungry right now..."

"No, DRY ICE!"

"That's what...Google..."

Kirk responds, "That's minus 109 degrees Fahrenheit."

Sam wiggled out from under the truck. "There's an ice cream cart across the street. At the edge of the park."

Gabby yelled, "Freeze the bastard!"

"I'm on it!"

Everyone in the Situation Room was seated silently around the red glow of The Cube. Their lives, the lives of countless millions of citizens of the U.S., and perhaps the fate of the world, were riding on the efforts of the sandal-wearing individual streaking across D.C.'s Constitution Avenue – the bomb tucked in the crook of his right arm.

Postley, now on the other side of the street and next to *Freddie's Frozens'* cart, found himself in the shoulder-to-shoulder outer ring of parents and kids jostling for position for a frozen treat. He pushed through the throng, whipped out his wallet, and took out all the cash he had – four rumpled 20s, two 10s, and three ones. Intercepting the vendor's hand that was reaching into the mobile freezer to grab the next treat, Sam stuffed the money into his palm.

"Sir, here's over a hundred bucks. I want all your ice cream." Before the vendor could say yes or no, Sam dug his right arm into the cart's freezer box and threw ice cream popsicles into the air like a man possessed. All Sam could think to say is "It's a matter of life and death!"

Kids started screaming. Some scrambled for the launched treats. Adults began videoing the rampage with their cell phones. All while Freddie yelled, "Stop! Stop! You're ruining my business – and my cart! I'm calling the cops, you wacko!"

"I'm sorry, I'm sorry, I'm sorry..." Postley kept saying – then added, "I have a bomb to stop!" and lifted the titanium cylinder over his head for the crowd to see.

The random pandemonium now turned to pure panic. Everyone – including Freddie – screaming and running away from the scene.

"Well, that did it," Postley proudly said to himself. He put his cell phone back up to his ear, holding it in place between his tilted neck and his shoulder while he worked with both hands.

"Everyone, I'm down to the dry ice. Timer says four minutes and twenty-three seconds. I'm sticking Parnette's bomb into the ice cream box. Whoa! Freakin' COLD in there. I'm using a popsicle to move the dry ice up and around the cylinder. Surrounding it as best as I can. Closing the hatch now."

Austin broke the listeners' silence. "Sam, we can't imagine what you're going through."

Postley replied, "Do you, honestly, think this will work?"

"We have to lower the temperature from whatever's around you –"

"About 80."

"To minus 74. So a drop of 154 degrees."

"And we need to cool not only the outside of the cylinder but also the inside –

"The 'cotton candy' –"

"Yeah, the 'cotton candy' – by those 154 degrees in –"

"Under four minutes now. It was four minutes and two seconds when I stuffed the sucker in."

"I wish we didn't put you in this awful spot, Sam," said Gabby. "Is there anything else we can do?"

Silence.

"Sam? Sam, can you hear me?"

"Oh, sorry for the pause," responded Sam. "I was, um, busy."

"What are you doing?" asked Gabby.

"Well, I'm sitting in the now-vacant street at the edge of the curb. And I've unwrapped a toasted almond ice cream bar. If I'm going up in smoke, I'll do it with a great taste on my lips. By the way, I do hear a bunch of sirens in the distance. They seem to be getting closer. I probably stirred up quite a hornet's nest with my actions."

Postley took his first bite. "Boy, I haven't had one of these things since I was a kid. I forgot how good they are. How fast should I be eating this?"

Austin replied, "I started my cell phone's timer when you gave the nine-minute indication. There's three minutes and twenty-two seconds."

"Guess I'm going to have to risk a 'brain freeze'. Seems the least of my concerns."

"Sam, this is President Clarkson again. We wish we could have done more. I'm told the bomb squad is still quite some distance away. My apologies."

"D.C. traffic screws up everything. Oh, well. I think that will be cured shortly, too." Postley took another bite of the ice cream bar. "What's our time, folks? I know it sounds morbid, but I'd like a countdown."

"Three minutes, give or take..."

"I always wondered what 'give or take' meant. Should I be rooting for the 'give' or 'take' part?"

***

Postley sat on the curb, licking what was left of the toasted almond. Even though Sam requested a countdown, everyone stopped talking.

When Austin saw on his phone that the time was down to a minute, he said "Sam, we're down to a minute. Anything you'd like to say?"

"I have a pun about 'a cold day in hell' but I think I'll skip it."

***

Everyone stayed silent for the rest of the minute; there was no verbal countdown; only a few private prayers. They all kept an eye on their watches or cell phones.

Everyone in the Situation Room was sitting. Clarkson reached out her right hand to Brassard and he clasped it with his left. She extended her left hand to Tebbs and he grasped it with his right. Seeing this, and without a word spoken, everyone around the table reached to each other and held hands.

The grips grew tight and sweaty as the time ticked away. Most bowed their heads, anticipating the seemingly inevitable.

Vice President Carlisle grasped the edges of his computer monitor with his two hands, in solidarity with his across-the-pond colleagues. Tears seeped from his now-closed eyes.

At zero time the silence continued. It continued for another minute. And then for another.

Austin broke the silent tension, "Sam, are you okay?"

"Other than wetting my pants, I think so."

Austin continued, "Madam President?"

"We're still here."

Gabby chimed in, "I don't trust the crazy lady. Not after what I saw here at the police station. She's stark-raving mad. She could have padded the timer – and it could still trigger."

"Thank you for the bountiful optimism, Gabby," said Postley. "I'd rather think I saved the day – heck, the world – with my frozen-food trick."

"Just trying to figure out what her game is."

"I don't think anyone can get into Parnette's head," added Austin. "Nor would we want to."

The *whoop! whoop! whoop!* of a siren pierced the phone call. Followed by the screech of tires.

Postley announced, "Hey, guess who's now pulling up? The cavalry." He continued, "Oh sure. Now that their asses won't be flippin' fried, they'll look like they're saving the day. And they'll haul me away!"

Clarkson to Hemsley: "Bart! Get on the horn to Metro and Homeland! Tell them that Sam's on our side!"

"Better make it quick, Madam President," said Postley. "The officers in the trailing squad car are out – with their guns drawn! Pardon me as I put the phone down and my arms up!"

Postley's voice could still be heard with the phone on the ground, "Don't shoot! Don't shoot!" He pointed down to the phone, "I'm on the phone with President Barbara Clarkson!"

"Oh, that's going to go over well," Austin added to the group call.

"On the ground, now! Face down! Arms out!" the lead officer yelled at Postley.

"Yes, yes, yes! Please don't shoot!" Postley feverishly exclaimed. "Please, please – pick up my cell phone. It *is* President Clarkson!"

Three officers were over the top of Postley, their service weapons pointed at his head. "Don't move. Don't even blink." The lead officer shouted to another, "Crandall. Grab the perp's phone. It's over there."

Officer Crandall lowered his weapon, took two steps to the right of the prone Postley, and picked up the cell phone. "The phone's connected to someone," Crandall said to the lead.

"See who the heck it is," replied the lead.

"Hello. This is Officer Crandall of the D.C. Metropolitan Police Department. Who is this?"

"Officer Crandall. This is President Barbara Clarkson."

"Come on, lady. Who is this?"

"President Clarkson. Please officer, may I speak to someone in the bomb squad?"

"How did you know the bomb squad is here?"

"I'm the President, remember?"

Crandall said to the lead, "Hey, this lady says she's – get this – President Clarkson. And she said she wants to talk to the bomb squad."

"How the heck does the person know the bomb squad's here?"

"That's what I said."

"Excuse me," said a burly, deep-voiced, heavily body-armored officer who was within earshot of the conversation. "I'm Specialist Antonio Franco, the senior bomb technician. May I speak to the person on the phone?"

Crandall handed the phone to Franco.

"Whoever's on the phone, I'm the lead bomb technician on the scene – speak!" Franco said in a no-nonsense delivery.

"As I told Officer Crandall, I am Barbara Clarkson, the President of the United States."

"Yeah, yeah."

Clarkson, recognizing she was not about to get anywhere, disengaged her politeness. "Franco, listen here. And listen good. I'm not about to take any crap from you or any other officer on the scene."

Franco was taken aback by the phone person's sudden shift in assertiveness.

"Any minute you'll be getting a call from Metro dispatch – or maybe directly from Homeland. The guy on the ground just saved all of our asses. Your career will be supervising fireworks if you don't (a) get him off the ground and (b) follow his instructions to the letter. There's still a bomb nearby. And he's the only one with the know-how to keep it from blowing a third of our country into the Atlantic. Have I made myself clear?"

Before Franco could reply, a voice squawked out of the speaker-microphone attached to the upper portion of his vest. "Franco. Franco. This is dispatch. With Homeland wired in. Do you copy?"

Franco, processing the situation, responded with a squeeze of the mic button "Copy. Stand by." Returning to the cell phone, "I am sorry Madam President. You have made yourself perfectly clear."

"I am glad we now have a meeting of the minds, Officer Franco. I can hear you're getting a radio call from your dispatcher who's on the line with Homeland. Take it. I'll wait."

"Yes, Madam President."

Franco again squeezed his mic button. "Franco back."

"Tony. This is Tom at dispatch. The hotlines are on fire. To make a long story short, the Deputy Director of Homeland told me – directly – to stand down. He told me the name of the guy in custody is Sam Postley. There is a bomb nearby. Work with him. He knows his stuff. Follow his lead without question. Do you copy?"

"I'm not happy that some dorky hippy will be issuing orders to me. But I copy."

Franco pivoted to face the officers and colleagues on the scene. "Everyone! Listen up! We have been instructed to stand down – directly from Homeland. Holster your weapons. Let this, um, gentleman get off the ground."

The officers obliged, putting down and away their weapons, and stepped back from Postley.

Postley rolled to his side and used the nearby curb to help get back on his feet. "'Dorky hippy' huh?" Sam tossed back to Franco. "I'll let it slide. *This time*. And zero comments about my wet pants!"

"Promise."

"And my cell phone, please?"

Franco handed the cell phone back to Postley. "Is everyone still on the line?" A cacophony of *"Yes!"* and *"We're still here!"* responses came through the phone. "Nice to hear *appreciative* voices. I'll put you all on speakerphone again, so you can hear what's going on."

"So what's this about a bomb?" asked Franco.

"Not just any bomb. The scientist Parnette, the one who's been ranting on TV and holding the cruise ship – and, heck, the United States – hostage, planted her bomb right here in D.C."

"Here? Where?"

Pointing across the street, "It was under that food truck. And I *temporarily* suspended it from detonating by surrounding it with dry ice in this ice cream cart."

"You mean, like right here?"

"Yup. Right in the aluminum box. With the ice cream bars."

"Geez."

"This flavor, pardon the pun, of antimatter bomb would make her 'demonstration' – The Event – look like a cheap firecracker."

"That's, that's, unbelievable."

"Did it look disarmable? Wait – before you answer – do you have any experience in this area?"

"Nope. And I don't play a bomb technician on TV."

"So what qualifies you for the accolades from on top? Sorry for the questions, but I need to know who I'm working with. My ass is on the line with yours."

Austin started to chime in over the cell phone's speaker, "My buddy Sam –"

"Austin, I got this. Specialist Franco, your question is totally understandable. I'm an honest-to-goodness rocket scientist. I invented the Post-Thermonic Reaction propulsion technique used on a new generation of rocket engines."

"I've never heard of 'Post-Thermonic Reaction' before. Unless you're a damn good liar –"

"I'm not. And I'm a terrible poker player."

"Poker aside, I guess I'll go on faith."

"Thank you."

"So back to the disarmable question. What does the device look like?"

"It's an enclosed cylinder, pretty darn sure made from titanium, about the diameter and length of a standard thermos. Sophisticated manufacturing. There are no seams or welds. There's a small LCD timer display, about the size of a quarter, somehow attached to one of the ends. There is a honkin' strong, elongated magnet, stuck on parallel to the tube's body. And that's it. No wires. No openings."

"How about an antenna? I saw, with the rest of the world, Parnette's manifesto of sorts. If I'm not mistaken, she said her device – this sucker right here – was on 'speed dial' with her phone. And she could detonate it with a push of a button. Was she bluffing?"

"I don't know. The canister, itself, since it's made of metal, could be tuned to work like an antenna, I guess. Though that's beyond my area of knowledge."

"Fellas!" Austin piped in. "Yes it could! It most certainly could! It would need an electrical insulator between –"

"Thanks, Austin," Postley interrupted. "Sorry to be abrupt. We can chat more about radio-wave particulars later. Assuming there is a later."

"Agreed. You have your hands full."

Franco continued his inquiry, "Dumb question: How could something so Earth-shattering powerful be in such a small container? Could she be bluffing?"

Montgomery replied, "Mr. Franco. As the others on the call know, I am Dr. Montgomery with the President in the Situation Room. I am the Director of the Office of Science and Technology Policy. Our own scientists broke into her lab and confirmed her work. The bomb has the same form factor that she used to initiate The Event. She discovered a way to create and store an unheard of volume of antimatter and do it at room temperature."

"Antimatter? Like science-fiction stuff?"

"Not anymore. The container near you likely has more antimatter than has ever been created on Earth – in total. In fact, multiple times."

Franco continued, "Last question, folks. Promise. What detonates the bomb?"

Postley replied, "That's the easy part. Simply crack it open and expose it to ordinary matter. When the two types of matter meet – bammo! – the opposite particles annihilate each other and release tremendous amounts of energy."

Montgomery added, "Thousands of times more powerful than even the largest hydrogen bomb."

"Shit."

"Yeah, shit."

"So you think there might be a tiny explosive inside of the cylinder?"

"Reasonable assumption. An explosive no more powerful than an ordinary 4th of July *M-80* firecracker would do it. Probably inside, under the end with the visible timer."

"What if we pried off the timer? Can we get at the trigger wires?"

"It didn't look like it. Mind you, I only looked at this thing for a minute or two – much of it as I was running like a maniac to this cart. The cylinder seemed *so perfect*. My guess – and it's just a guess – is that it was somehow manufactured as a complete enclosure."

"3D printed?"

"A reasonable assumption. This thing has to stay entirely environment proof. If just a single ordinary atom got in – kaboom! If I'm correct, the timer is probably wirelessly connected to a small inner-explosive container. Inductively."

"Like the way there are no wires between a cordless electric toothbrush and its charger base."

"Yep. And, if we tried to pry under the timer to look, and there is a tamper switch, the device would detonate."

"Elegant."

"Unfortunately. The lady's nuts – and brilliant."

"So now what?" asked Franco.

"You need to set up a perimeter so you can do your work."

"My work? It doesn't sound like I can get into this thing."

"You don't need to. We have to postpone what I think you bomb techs call a 'rapid unscheduled disassembly.'"

Franco chuckled through the tension, then asked "And how do you propose we do that?"

"You and your team replenish the dry ice – lickety-split. That'll buy us some time. Then we need a bigger plan to permanently disable this thing."

CHAPTER 86

Franco yells to the surrounding officers and bomb squad colleagues, "Everyone, form a perimeter, say, 50 yards back. Don't let anyone in. No reporters. No media. No one! Get on it!"

Turning back to Postley, "What's the secret behind the dry ice?"

"I don't assume you've taken any particle physics classes?"

"Not quite. But don't let this emergency garb fool you. I'm no dummy."

"Furthest from my mind. To answer your question, this device doesn't like cold temperatures."

"Correct me if I'm wrong. Electronics don't mind cold temperatures. In fact, super-computers work better in cold temperatures – right?"

"Well, the older ones relied on creative super cooling. Even some PC gamers use liquid-cooling for their CPUs."

"Batteries don't like cold. Is that it?"

"You're spot on about batteries not liking cold temps. However, I didn't see a battery holder. The LCD display was nearly flat against the cylinder end. I believe the power source is inside of the cylinder, probably in the same isolated compartment as the timer circuitry and the mini explosive. That's what I'd do."

"Okay. Spill the beans."

"Somehow the wacko scientist found a way to create and contain antimatter at ordinary temperatures. That's also its downfall. The process ceases below minus 74 degrees Fahrenheit. Kudos to two persons also on the line – Austin and Gabby – my buddies who pulled up Parnette's old Powerpoint on the fly and saved –"

"Everyone's asses," Austin inserted.

"You're so modest," replied Postley.

"Adding to the beers you owe us," said Gabby.

"So where am I going to get more dry ice at this time of the evening?" asked Franco.

Sam replied, "We could knock off another food cart. Kidding!"

"Hey, whatever it takes." Austin quipped.

Postley stroked his scraggly beard. Commenting to Franco and everyone on the line, "You know, the more I think about it, I may have only been lucky that the bomb didn't detonate. Crapola!"

"What the heck are you talking about?" replied Franco.

"While I'm talking to you, I am beginning to understand the dynamics of this thing. It was dumb luck – yeah, dumb luck – that the dry ice worked. I simply stuck random pieces of super cold stuff against the cylinder. Opening the cart's 'hatch' to add more dry ice could, in and of itself, change the 'lucky' equilibrium – and we'd all be toast."

"Why did you have to turn into a *Debbie Downer?*" replied Franco. "I was starting to believe I would be able to hug my wife again tonight."

"Sorry! We need *uniform* cooling all around the tube. Somehow envelop it."

"How about liquid nitrogen?"

"Bonus points, Specialist Franco."

"I told you I was no dummy. And you can call me Tony. In case we get blown up, we may as well be on a first-name basis."

"Tony it is."

"And you can call me Sam."

"Knock, knock," Austin butted into the continuing group call. "Sorry to interrupt your burgeoning bromance. You do realize that you have the resources of the entire United States government literally on call, right?"

Montgomery jumped in, "This is Dr. Montgomery again. I'm sure we could get a dewar or dewars of liquid nitrogen from one of the local universities. The cryo facilities in most chem departments keep it on hand for research."

"Dewar's? Like the whiskey?" Franco half-heartedly asked.

"No, no." replied Montgomery. "A 'dewar' is a specialized storage container for cryogenic liquids."

"Cryogenic? That means very cold, right?"

"Yes," replied Postley. "Dr. Montgomery, please help me here: Liquid nitrogen is, what, minus 300 and something Fahrenheit, right?"

"Minus 320 degrees Fahrenheit, to be precise."

"Wow! That's wicked cold!" Franco added.

"Tony, between your idea with liquid nitrogen and Dr. Montgomery's chemistry connections, we might still get out of this mess – and you home to see your wife. What do you think?"

"I'm feeling out of my league, chemistry classes were a long time ago," replied Franco. "I'll defer to you two on this approach."

Postley, directing his voice back to the phone, "Dr. Montgomery. Make it so!"

Kirk squirmed in his seat at the police station but didn't comment on the never-ending *Star Trek* references.

Franco, after surveilling the situation a bit more, said, "You know, maybe I do have a thought about the cryogenic liquid: That ice cream cart's box is likely far from liquid proof. It would seep out through every crack and crevice."

Postley added, "Yeah. It's homemade, not a commercial-grade refrigeration container. Looks like pop-riveted sheets of aluminum. To seal it up, as much as us geeks like duct tape, that won't work at cryogenic temperatures. I'm sure whatever lab that has the cryo liquid, they'll have cryo tape. I used it in a lab years ago. It's really common."

"Consider it done!" Montgomery shouted through the phone.

"And either a few medium-sized dewars or some sort of transfer device with a funnel," added Postley. "Gloves, face masks, and appropriate garb, of course."

"All on the list," replied Montgomery. "What kind of volume are you guessing?"

"Tony, what do you think?"

"It looks about three feet long by two feet wide by, maybe two-and-a-half feet tall? Something like that?"

"That's about right. So –"

"15 cubic feet, thanks for Mr. Google," Kirk chimed.

"Warp-speed fingers, Kirk," added Franco.

"Not you too! Geez!" replied Kirk.

"What's he talking about?" questioned Franco. "Doesn't like *Trek* references?"

"Something like that," Austin added through the phone.

Postley continued, "Dr. Montgomery. As Sergeant Kirk just said, about 15 cubic feet. Probably a lot less, given the cart's likely insulation, the volume of the bomb cylinder, chunks of dry ice that are still in there, and – of course – any lingering ice cream bars. Seems prudent to err on the big side."

"What kind of ETA are we looking at?" asked Franco.

"Many facilities are 24/7/365, allowing researchers continuous access," responded Montgomery.

"We'll break into one if we have to," added Brassard – his spirit back in high gear.

"Give us an hour, tops," said Montgomery. "We'll chopper in the stuff. Franco, please have your team clear a nearby landing spot."

"Will do."

Franco noticed the dozens of melted ice cream bars all over the street; mini puddles seeping from the wrappers. He pointed to Postley and asked, "What do you think happened here? Looks like a popsicle bomb went off."

"That's a story for another time."

CHAPTER 87

The incoming whir of helicopter blades cut through the night. Two pairs of squad cars, two hundred feet apart, blocked Constitution Avenue, fifty yards from the National Academy of Sciences building; the headlights of the police vehicles pointed towards each other, creating an impromptu landing zone for the inbound chopper.

Upon touchdown, the engine throttled down to ground idle and two government agents exited. They quickly unloaded four hefty dewars of liquid nitrogen and two large, black, soft-sided bags. Simultaneously, five of Franco's colleagues ran to the craft. Together, they expeditiously lugged the transported materials to Postley and Franco.

"Is this what you were expecting?" Franco asked Postley.

"We'll know for sure when we open these bags." Postley replied. "But the *goods*, the liquid nitrogen, are in these four chunky containers," pointing to the two-and-a-half-foot tall, one-and-a-half foot wide dewar flasks.

The pair rapidly unloaded the soft-sided bags onto the ground at the foot of the cart.

"Here, put this stuff on," Postley said to Franco. "Face shield, cryo gloves, shoe covers, and this ugly apron thing. You don't want even a drop of liquid nitrogen to touch any place on your body!"

"You don't have to tell me twice!"

"I have a question back to Dr. Montgomery in the Situation Room," Postley said. Speaking directly towards his cell on speakerphone, "Dr. Montgomery, it's okay to pour liquid nitrogen onto dry ice, right?"

"Mr. Postley, I apologize, but I've never thought about that particular procedure. The carbon dioxide is in its solid phase. It won't transition to another state. I suppose it could, well, violently fracture when its temperature suddenly drops by, what, 211 degrees."

"Well, that would suck," replied Postley. "Any other thoughts from the peanut gallery before we pour this stuff in?"

"Hold on – hold on!" yelled Kirk. "I just watched a 20-second video on SplashVidX. A fellow dropped a piece of dry ice into a beaker of liquid nitrogen. A big cloud of gas appeared – which stopped after a few seconds. When the cloud cleared, the piece of dry ice was still intact."

"*That's* certainly definitive science!" said Franco.

Postley continued to everyone, "I know I'm second-guessing myself, but there's a lot on the line. Heck, a chunk of the world. My original thought was simply adding more dry ice, and we can also get that from any lab. I still think it was dumb luck that it worked, even though the cooling was far from uniform." Postley paused for a couple of seconds. "I'm open to additional ideas – from anyone."

Silence.

"Madam President," Postley continued. "This could all go terribly wrong. In a blink. If we leave the ice cream cart's box as is, the dry ice will soon sublimate – turn into a gas – the cooling will be gone and the bomb will go off. If we open the cart's lid to add more dry ice, the jostling, in itself, may disturb the tenuous stability and the bomb could go off. If we add liquid nitrogen to the cart, we're in unknown territory."

Clarkson responded, "Sam – and please don't take this wrong – we needed to know who you were before entrusting the fate of the country to you. About fifteen minutes ago, my team handed me a flash background check on you. And –"

"Uh oh. I really didn't mean to do what I did to that frog in 5th grade!"

Ignoring Sam's childhood admission, "You've made some amazing discoveries because of your ability to think non-linearly. So think *non-linearly*. Go with your gut. What is your gut telling you to do?"

"My gut, other than doing flip-flops right now, is telling me to go the liquid nitrogen route."

"That's good enough for me."

"Thank you for your vote of confidence, Madam President. Specialist Franco and I will do our absolute best."

"I know you will. Both of you."

Postley and Franco proceeded to tape up the edges and seams of the ice cream cart's aluminum box with two-inch wide cryogenic tape. The pair kept everyone on the conference call apprised of their progress. Satisfied with their work, Postley gave a final update. "Okay, everyone. Our tape job is done. It's time to pour. Any last thoughts?"

"Sam," Austin replied, "Dry ice, liquid nitrogen, and a pinch of antimatter. Heck of a cocktail!"

"A mixologist I'm not. Thank you for keeping it light, my friend."

"Sam," added Gabby. "We'll keep a seat warm at our favorite bar here in Aruba. We'll drag you here by your ponytail if that's what it takes."

"Thanks, Gabs. I plan to take you up on that!"

And, finally, Clarkson spoke. "Sam and Tony. The two of you have become a great team under the most excruciating circumstances imaginable. I look forward to meeting the two of you in person when your job is completed."

"It would be an honor," replied Postley.

"Yes, a genuine honor," added Franco. "And, Sam, sorry to have called you a dorky hippy before. You're okay."

"You're okay too, Tony."

"I guess it's time to get on with it," Franco said. "You know, I could use a vacation right about now. I hope you don't mind if I join you for that Aruba cocktail."

"It's on me."

Franco removed the polypropylene plug from the top of one of the bulky dewar flasks. The characteristic cloud of evaporating liquid nitrogen immediately flowed from the opening.

The flask had two handles. Postley and Franco each used one hand to grab one of the two handles and lifted the flask above the hinged lid of the ice cream cart.

"It's almost show time," Postley announced. "I've placed my cell phone – still on speakerphone – on the small shelf near the handle of the cart."

Taped to the same shelf, Postley spotted a vendor license in the name of Frederic H. Freemont. He said to the group, "If we survive this ordeal, someone needs to get Freddie a new cart."

"We'll take care of it," Clarkson replied.

"Are you ready for action, Tony?" Sam asked.

"I am," Franco replied.

Reaching for the lid with his free hand, Franco said "I got it" as he very slowly opened the cart's lid. A cloud of carbon dioxide vapor, from the sublimating pieces of dry ice, flowed out of the now-open aluminum box of the cart; the cloud, like a gaseous soup, draped down all four sides of the cart – like a horror flick prop.

"Everyone," announced Postley, "we are now about to pour the first flask into the cart." He added, "Bottom's up!"

The duo *very slowly* poured the liquid nitrogen into the cart's opening. Like a miniature volcano, massive amounts of evaporating liquid nitrogen and an intense crackling sound emerged from the cart's ice cream box. The cloud enveloped Franco and Postley, to the point that they could barely see each other.

"Tony, you okay over there?" Postley asked through the cloud.

"I'm fine. It's clouding up my face shield. Is it okay to breathe this stuff?"

"Do you want the honest answer?"

"Why start now?" Franco said with a chuckle, as they continued to pour.

"Good point. Well, a combination carbon-dioxide and nitrogen cloud is displacing the surrounding air, so our oxygen proportion will go down slightly. You might feel a little light-headed. Let me know, if so."

"Will do."

"Hey, the good news: We're not dead."

"That crackling sound is driving me nuts, though."

"I think it's the remaining ice cream popsicles and their wrappers becoming instantly super frozen." As the pouring flow ceased, Postley commented, "Okay, that about does it with this flask."

The two put down the empty container. As before, Postley plucked out the polypropylene plug from the top of one of the other nearby flasks. The two picked up the container and positioned it over the top of the ice cream cart. "Time to make another martini," commented Postley.

"Not shaken, not stirred," added Franco.

They repeated the process through almost four dewars when the witch's brew neared the top of the opening. "Whoa! I think that's it!" announced Franco.

"Time to close the hatch!"

The two put down the dewar. Franco slowly closed the ice cream cart's lid.

"I think we just bought all of us some time. Do you hear that D.C.? Aruba?"

Clarkson spoke up first, "We kept our mouths' shut and held our collective breaths."

"We've been sweating here as if we were there," added Gabby.

"Gabs," said Austin. "I think it's because Kirk needs to get the A/C tuned up in this police station." Austin threw a kidding glance at Kirk.

"So what's next rocket boy?" Franco asked Postley.

"Funny you should ask," responded Postley, as he looked at the creatively taped-up ice cream cart. The liquid nitrogen was barely seeping out; puffs of vapor spouted here and there, like a wacky, patched-up steam engine.

"Madam President, it seems we've stabilized the situation. The liquid nitrogen will continually boil off, and, ultimately, we'll be right back in the same dangerous boat."

"So, how long do we have?"

"Conservatively, I'm estimating about six to eight hours. Hmmm... I have an idea..."

"Go on."

"As you might imagine from your background check, I follow the aerospace industry rather closely."

"Yes."

"And I'm pretty well connected, thanks to some official and, well, unofficial, backchannels."

"Okay."

"I know the U.S. Government is launching, let's just say, a 'payload' from Wallops tomorrow afternoon."

"I'm not aware of that."

"Specifically out of the Mid-Atlantic Regional Spaceport's Pad-0A."

"Again, I'm not aware of that."

Postley was referring to Wallops Island, a small island located off the shore of Virginia, and NASA's Wallops Flight Facility. The Wallops Flight Facility plays a vital role in a wide range of U.S. aerospace initiatives. Suborbital and orbital rockets, for both NASA and a growing cadre of government and commercial-space initiatives, are regularly launched from this location on America's eastern shoreline.

"I'm assuming you have – and sorry for the crude vernacular – *spooks* in the room there."

"That wouldn't be my choice of words. I can say that the intelligence community is well represented."

"The payload has been described to the press as a weather-data-gathering platform, or some other 'cover' story. A little birdie told me, though, and someone there can undoubtedly confirm, that it's another part of your hush-hush 'Big Eye' constellation of satellites."

Alford gave Clarkson a subtle affirmative nod.

"Even if I did know, I wouldn't be able to confirm or deny," replied Clarkson.

"No matter. Wallops is, what, about 150 miles away?"

Franco weighed in, "I think I know where you're going with this. I can get the cart there in our Explosive Ordnance Disposal vehicle. Bomb-disposal truck, for short."

"Madam President," Postley said. "If we swap out the satellite with the cart's ice cream box, put the box in the deep-freeze of space, you can defuse the situation for months to years – depending on the orbit."

"That would buy us time to figure out a permanent solution," Clarkson replied.

"That's what I'm thinking."

Clarkson turned to Montgomery. "Jordy, is this possible?"

"Possible? Technically, yes. Although it normally takes months to engineer and integrate a payload into a rocket."

"Well, we don't have months," said Postley. "We don't even have until tomorrow afternoon. The liquid nitrogen would be boiled off by then – and Parnette's bomb would go off. The launch facility would have to ready the rocket for launch by, say, dawn. Even that would be cutting it close."

"Sam," Clarkson replied, "I have zero background in aerospace. Even so, this sounds on its surface to be a huge stretch. But – of all of us – this is in your wheelhouse. Do you really think it can be pulled off?"

"I've been part of over a dozen payload integrations. Three of them at the Mid-Atlantic Regional Spaceport. If you put the hammer down as you'll need to, everyone there, and everyone in the national aerospace food chain, will give you a ton of shit – my apologies for the language – and say that it can't be done. *I know it can.*"

"Sam, I asked you to go with your gut before. And we're still alive to talk about it. Do you see any other option? Any at all?"

"I can't. But I am open to alternate ideas. I don't have a monopoly on knowledge."

Clarkson to everyone, "Are there any other ideas – any at all – that we should consider?" Silence.

Clarkson continued, "SAI-OP, have you been listening to our discussion?"

"I have, Madam President. I am ready to assist you in any way you require."

Postley and Franco looked at each other in bewilderment. Without thinking, Postley asked – and everyone heard – "Tom Cruise is in the Situation Room?"

Clarkson shook her head in exasperation. Directed to Postley, "Sam, no. It's an AI. I'll explain the unusual circumstance later." She continued, "SAI-OP, do you have any top-line observations regarding our efforts to neutralize Dr. Parnette's bomb?"

SAI-OP dutifully responded to Clarkson. "I do have some top-line observations, Madam President. Thank you for asking."

"I have analyzed all pertinent data derived from our cyber team's access to Dr. Parnette's lab and her computers. The scientists' analysis was, essentially, correct. The destructive capability of the bomb now in our possession is four multiples of what she used to initiate what has become known as The Event.

"The on-the-scene analysis that the bomb cannot be neutralized is, unfortunately, correct. The internal mechanisms cannot be accessed without triggering detonation. Kudos to Mr. Postley and Mr. Franco."

The two winked at each other while everyone continued to be astounded by the casual, colloquial delivery of SAI-OP – and further taken aback by the spot-on replicated voice.

"As speculated, the cylinder also does function as a cellular antenna, which would have allowed Dr. Parnette to remotely trigger the device using her satellite phone. Kudos to Ms. Milone and Mr. Raze in disrupting the satellite radio signal – and thus the initiation of the bomb."

Austin blew a kiss at Gabby; she blew a kiss back.

"The dry-ice maneuver was an exceptional tactic. It was fraught with danger, as my calculations as to success would have been under fifty percent. Given the options available to Mr. Postley, it was the only reasonable choice."

"I'm beginning to like this synthetic Tom Cruise," Postley muttered on the line.

"Thank you, SAI-OP," responded Clarkson.

"You are most welcome, Madam President. I am here to help improve our odds in what may seem like a near-impossible mission."

Everyone paused in simultaneous thought: Was this artificial intelligence trying to spin a pun? Everyone then quickly snapped back to the serious matter at hand.

"SAI-OP, let's go right to the heart of the challenge. As you heard, we are thinking, as unusual as it may sound, of attempting to launch the bomb in the ice cream cart's storage box into space. What are your thoughts?"

"The logistics are quite complex. And there are many human elements, the behaviors of which I cannot predict, that must coordinate perfectly."

"If all the 'human elements' line up with maximum effectiveness, is this approach doable?"

"Yes, it is."

"Are there any other options we have not yet considered?"

"Yes, 17 of them."

"Oh?"

"None with, in my estimation, an outcome you would prefer."

"For instance? Could you provide an option that might be in the top two or three?"

"Please define 'top'?"

"Minimum loss of human life."

"Thank you for the definition. Here is an example from that category: It would be conceivable, and likely achievable within Mr. Postley's estimated six-to-eight-hour timeframe, to place the now liquid-nitrogen-cooled box containing Parnette's bomb in a deep-sea submersible, such as ones that have explored the Mariana Trench. A private company has one in dry dock in Miami, Florida. If requisitioned, the box could be placed inside and transported by a military transport helicopter to the Puerto Rico Trench, one of the deepest ocean trenches at 27,480 feet. The submersible could be lowered to the bottom of the trench and the bomb allowed to self-detonate upon the natural elimination of the liquid nitrogen coolant."

"And?"

"I'm basing my damage-simulation projections on the data retrieved from Dr. Parnette's lab. The current bomb – as mentioned a moment ago – is four times more powerful than the bomb that caused The Event. Scientists believe The Event's bomb had one-twentieth the energy of the asteroid that impacted the waters just off the Yucatán Peninsula 66 million years ago and caused the extinction of the dinosaurs. The bomb with Mr. Postley and Mr. Franco would have one-fifth of the energy.

"For reference, the wall of water from the asteroid impact was nearly a mile high. My simulation indicates that the current bomb, if detonated at the bottom of the Puerto Rico Trench, would generate a traveling megatsunami wave over 950 feet high. The majority of the human population on all land masses within 1,280 miles would be underwater and cease to exist within three hours, including those in the southern portion of Florida, much of Central America, and the northern third of South America. The damage to the sea floor would extend down to, minimally, the Earth's upper mantle; the result would be rather extreme physical damage to the structure of the planet, with significant worldwide ramifications, including major tectonic motion and resulting earthquakes and global volcanic activity. Would you like me to further itemize the global repercussions?" Jaws dropped, universally.

After a second absorbing this information, Clarkson responded. "You were right, SAI-OP. Not an outcome that we would prefer. No more detail needed. And, to be clear, that was one of the 'top' options? How did you base that?"

"Yes, it was. The loss of life would, within the first three hours, be approximately 3.4% greater than if Parnette's bomb exploded prior to a successful space launch. Within 24 hours, 11.2% greater, as a sequence of tsunamis would overrun coastal cities on a global basis. The death estimates spawned by the Earth's tectonic shifts are beyond my data sets and algorithms to accurately predict. Minimally, there would be 17.9% greater loss of life due to easily foreseeable global planetary effects over the next six months."

More jaw dropping, further amplified by SAI-OP's clinical, matter-of-fact, celebrity delivery.

The quiet room seemed to catch SAI-OP off guard. "Madam President, is your silence an approval of my analysis?"

"Yes, SAI-OP. I appreciate your diligence." Clarkson took a deep breath. "Let me ask you the most-important question of all: From this moment forward, given the 'human elements' you alluded to and, understandably, can't fully predict, what do you foresee as the most-probable outcome of our effort to launch the ice-cream cart's storage box into space?"

Everyone's consciousness coalesced into single focus, awaiting SAI-OP's all-important response.

"Madam President, that is a difficult question for me to answer. Probabilistically, the odds are less than 40 percent. However, I have knowledge of humanity spanning many thousands of years. History is replete with circumstances in which the odds were less than favorable – still, success was achieved. I have yet to comprehend how the human condition can, repeatedly, transcend such circumstances. In our current circumstance, your team's particularly steep climb to thwart a catastrophic event has characteristics that mirror history's against-all-odds achievements, including a reservoir of colleagues who are willing to put their lives at risk for the greater goal."

The room was stunned at the philosophical depth of thought.

"Well, SAI-OP," Clarkson ultimately responded. "You might not be human, but you may know us better than many of us know ourselves. Thank you."

"Again, you are welcome, Madam President."

Clarkson returned her focus to her team.

"I think we all know what we need to do," she said to everyone.

Looking in the direction of Hemsley, she asked, "Bart, can your team at Homeland clear the driving route for 150 miles?"

"Door to door, it's actually...*click, click, click*...166 miles. And, yes, we'll use our highway snowplows – I'm serious! – if we need to create an intimidating gauntlet."

With one ear on a secure intra-agency handset, Brassard reported, "Barb, I'm connected to Chief Master Sergeant of the Space Force, Admiral Charles Babbich; he's trying to get on the horn with the Director of the Virginia Spaceport Authority – or whoever we can rouse at this hour – regarding the Mid-Atlantic Regional Spaceport's operations. They'll undoubtedly have to use unconventional means to swap out a payload that's already atop a rocket on the pad."

"A big freakin' crane!" added Postley.

Clarkson to Brassard, "Make sure he knows it is *imperative* that the launch takes place by dawn. Loop him into the full dire consequences. Pull no punches. Let him know the very existence of the country is at stake."

Brassard nodded to Clarkson while talking on the handset to Babbich.

Everyone in the Sit Room listened to Brassard's side of the conversation. "Charles, it is beyond ASAP. It *has* to be in flight by sunrise. No, Charles, there is no wiggle room. Here's the skinny, and I'm not blowing smoke: A detonation will take out the East Coast and the future of our country would be in question. Yes, 'holy shit'. Yes. Yes. America is counting on it. Make it happen."

Brassard hung up the special handset and looked at Clarkson; he knew the room was looking at him as well.

"He said he'll move mountains if needed. I've known Charles for a long time. He'll do whatever it takes."

"Arty, I need you to pull your inner tank commander out of retirement. Lead the convoy to Wallops!"

"Consider it done! Bart, give me my marching orders."

"I have just the vehicle for you."

Clarkson said, "Charlotte, your, um, 'payload' will have to wait."

"Of course."

Hemsley added, "Franco, Postley, can you be wheels up in 20 minutes?"

Franco replied, "We'll have the cart in the bomb-disposal truck and ready to roll in 10."

Hemsley continued, "Arty, can you join me now in my security detail?"

"If the President gives me the okay to detach here. Barb?"

"Go join Postley and Franco – and help save our country, Arty!"

CHAPTER 88

Mountains were indeed moved. Within 45 minutes, Admiral Babbich was on a conference call with the leadership of the Virginia Spaceport Authority (VSA), the entity that owns and operates the Mid-Atlantic Regional Spaceport (MARS). They further dialed in a spectrum of high-ups at MARS. Babbich was ready to wield the threat of the President's executive authority – but it was unnecessary. The VSA was all-in to do whatever it could to help the nation, and the planet, avert the impending calamity. "Whatever it takes," was the call's concluding mantra.

***

Surrounded by Franco and his team of five, Postley slowly wheeled the ice cream cart toward the nearby bomb-disposal truck – a heavy-duty vehicle that looked like a cross between a fire-rescue truck and an armored car. The cart's taped-up aluminum box continually billowed evaporating liquid nitrogen from its seams; extra-dense puffs spewed whenever the cart rolled over even the littlest crack in the asphalt.

The local D.C. media, then the network media, caught wind that something newsworthy was unfolding. The police, joined by the fire department and its large vehicles, cordoned off the streets beyond the physical perimeter created by the men and women in blue. Reporters, camera crews, and camera lights elbowed their way as close to the perimeter as the police would allow. To make matters worse, an incessant buzz from multiple drones – some from the media, others unknown – filled the air as Franco's team prepared to load the ice cream cart into the side opening of the bomb-disposal truck.

"I'm going to shoot those bastard things," Franco yelled, as he pointed up to the growing swarm of drones.

"Time to remove the box from the wheels, fellas," said Postley.

"It looks like it's practically sitting in the frame around the four wheels," replied Franco. "Only a few straps of Velcro holding it in place."

"I agree."

"You want to do the honors?" Franco asked.

"Sure. I've already been squirming around on the ground," referring to his initial engagement with the police.

Postley got on his knees and, with light tugs, unzipped the Velcro.

"That's it. I think the box is now free." He then touched the box with his bare hand. "It's cool. But not too cold. Evidently, Freddie didn't take short cuts regarding the interior's insulation. The box is tolerable to handle."

Franco called his team over while Postley hopped in the entrance to the truck. "Alright," said Franco to his colleagues. "On a count of three, we're going to – slowly – lift up this smoking aluminum box and get it inside. Don't be surprised, it's cool to the touch; there's liquid nitrogen inside – and a few other things." Franco and Postley looked at each other with raised eyebrows. Franco continued, "Sam, the fellow in the truck, will help get it to a secure spot. Here we go: One. Two. Three!"

The team lifted the box and slowly walked it the few strides to the truck. Steady-handed as they were, the liquid inside still sloshed from side to side, making the box wobble as they walked.

Postley, inside the truck, helped direct the motion of the box into the bay. He repeated, "Keep it steady! Keep it steady! Minimize the sloshing of the liquid nitrogen!" as the team walked the smoldering box up the truck's extended ramp into the side bay. Once Franco and his team were inside, they carefully lowered the box to the bay's floor. The interior of this section of the bomb-disposal truck was equipped with numerous tie-down points and cords; in a few minutes the volatile cargo was secured.

Clarkson, the remaining staff in the Situation Room, and Postley's friends in Aruba were relegated to be audio-linked spectators via Postley's still-on-speakerphone cell. Postley, engrossed in the task at hand, kept forgetting that others could hear all the activity.

"Oh, hi you guys!" Postley blurted, his brain remembering the phone connection.

"Wish you were here," replied Austin.

"Me, too. And one of my all-time-favorite songs."

"We'll crank it on the digital jukebox at C.J.'s," said Gabby.

"Served with plenty of cold beer," said Postley. "Don't you forget!"

"Nope. We're on it!"

Just then, a thundering rumble of heavy vehicles could be heard by everyone on the phone – but, most of all, to Postley.

"What the heck is that! It's shaking the truck!"

"We're really bringing the cavalry this time, Sam," said Clarkson.

Postley poked his head out of the truck and saw no less than eight military Humvees, led by a monstrous Cougar 6x6 MRAP (Mine-Resistant Ambush Protected vehicle), that were charging their way toward him. The MRAP was flanked by two mammoth highway snowplows, side by side, barely fitting through the six-lane width of Constitution Avenue.

The snowplows slowed appreciably, but the MRAP continued its rush toward Postley, headlights blazing.

"Shit!" yelled Postley, grabbing the frame of the bomb-disposal truck's doorway, bracing for collision with one arm and frantically waving to the oncoming MRAP with the other. The MRAP came to a screeching stop just 10 feet behind the truck.

The huge driver's door of the MRAP swung open, and out leapt to the ground a brawny, six-foot-two man with short-cropped gray hair. He wore a tight-fitting black T-shirt emblazoned with a U.S. Army insignia in the upper left.

"What are you waving your arms at young man!" shouted Secretary Brassard.

Postley said, "That's one heck of a truck!"

"That's nothing, kiddo. You should have seen me crushing enemy lines in my tank." Brassard paused, sizing up the situation. Pointing to the fuming aluminum box inside the bomb-disposal truck, he asked, "Is that the pain-in-the-butt that could drop the East Coast into the sea?"

"That's it."

"Then let's blast that S.O.B. into space – before it blasts us!"

Franco hustled from the front of the bomb-disposal truck to the side opening where the smoking box and Postley – and now Brassard – were situated. Turning to Brassard he asked, "And you are?"

"Arthur Brassard, Secretary of Defense, and former U.S. Army General."

"Secretary Brassard –

"Still not used to that title; I feel like I should be behind a desk or something. Please call me Arty."

"Okay Arty. We talked to you in the Situation Room. I'm Specialist Tony Franco and that is (pointing to Postley in the truck) Sam Postley."

"You two have big pairs of brass ones. I admire that."

"We're not out of the woods yet."

"Let's saddle up and complete the mission!" urged Brassard.

Franco called into the truck, "Sam, are you riding with me in the bomb on wheels?"

"Damn straight! For a while Wallops was my second home. Onward!"

As the bomb squad closed and latched the door to the truck's storage bay, Brassard squeezed the mic on his walkie-talkie and announced to his team, "We have the bomb. The bomb-disposal truck will travel behind hummer four. We'll roll within five minutes. On my mark. Take your positions now."

CHAPTER 89

The phalanx of vehicles barreled down US-50 East. The State Police as well as the police departments of the communities in the convoy's path were alerted and assisted in closing highway on-ramps and directing vehicles to the shoulders of the road. Three Army National Guard Apache helicopters flew overhead, one a mile in front of the convoy to clear the airspace from curious news helicopters, and the other two over the top of the row of vehicles. All the while, Brassard maintained the lead position, still flanked by the two snowplows; their blades raised a couple of feet off the pavement. The plows' intent was not to push through vehicles – but as a visual that this high-speed entourage meant business.

Near Queenstown, Maryland, the convoy pulled into a service station to refuel. These non-aerodynamic goliaths consumed diesel at a high clip, particularly at the speed they were traveling. The Apaches had a range of almost 300 miles, so they could make the stretch in one go. They hovered in place during the fueling operation.

Satisfied that the various municipal police in tandem with the State police were effectively keeping the highway clear, Brassard dismissed the two snowplows from their duty. The convoy re-engaged the highway, pedal down, with Brassard's MRAP the tip of the rolling spear.

CHAPTER 90

"Ladies and gentlemen," Jessica Gladbrook interrupted the network's programming with her co-anchor Jeremy Donahue next to her. "There appears to be an unexpected development."

"That's right, Jessica," Donahue added. "We had hoped to bring our viewers President Clarkson's address to the nation about an hour and a half ago. Now we're transfixed on this, well, convoy of sorts heading rapidly east on US-50."

Gladbrook continued, "This is footage from 55 minutes ago, right before our news helicopter was informed by air traffic control that all public airspace was immediately closed – and our chopper was forced to immediately land in a nearby park."

Donahue said, "Local officials are under a media blackout, with orders apparently coming from the U.S. military. The White House has not responded to our requests for a comment. So it is impossible to get an accurate read of what is going on."

Gladbrook followed, "We're reaching out to our sources. We're also seeing some peculiar speculation on the Web – and related spontaneous actions. For more on that, we're turning to Joe Krisco, on the scene at Serene Pines Park in Rockville. Joe?"

"Good evening, Jess. Yes, I am here at Serene Pines, where a spontaneous public event began minutes ago. Let's switch to the overhead drone camera. Yes. That's it. As our audience can now see, there are dozens of cell-phone lights pointing skyward. That's from, I'd say, about fifty people who call themselves 'Earth Talkers' or 'E-T's – the acronym's not a coincidence. Jess and Jeremy, the individuals are sitting on the park's grass and using their cell phones' lights to create what they believe are signals. More specifically, they say they're sending messages to 'extra-terrestrial visitors' or, in their shorthand, 'ETVs.'"

"Aliens?"

"Well, yeah."

"I spoke to one individual, who didn't want to be on camera, who said 'The Event' was part of a widespread government coverup. The group believes 'The Event' was actually caused by the ocean landing of a huge interstellar spacecraft."

"Really?"

"Hey, I'm only reporting. The same individual said there are factions of E-Ts all over the world." Krisko suddenly interrupted himself with "Jess and Jeremy, look, look!"

"What are we seeing Joe? From the drone's view, it looks like, well, a big circle sometimes. And then a big vertical line sometimes."

"I'm told they're repeating the words 'peace' and 'welcome' in binary 1's and 0's. The fellow I spoke with said 'binary is the common language of the universe.'"

"Okay..." Donahue responded with unvarnished skepticism. "What do they believe is the connection to the convoy?"

"Well, that's the kicker. They think the President is in one of the vehicles to greet the aliens!"

"Oh..."

"They said they heard that the convoy is heading to Wallops Island and will greet the aliens there."

"We've had unconfirmed reports about the convoy heading, specifically, to the Mid-Atlantic Regional Spaceport – MARS. So at least that syncs up."

"MARS. An unfortunate acronym. Or, I guess, entirely appropriate to the folks here."

"Just depends on your point of view. But the President? In the convoy?"

"That's what these 'Earth Talkers' are saying."

"And Dr. Parnette?"

"In their assembly of the puzzle, they believe Dr. Parnette's manifesto was simply the ravings of an unstable person. She never had any bomb."

"Well, that's a unique perspective for sure. Joe, stay on top of things."

"I'll 'phone home' if need be."

Gladbrook and Donahue smiled back without saying a word.

CHAPTER 91

"Gabs? Austin? Are you there?"

"Kirk here. Hold on for your friends."

Groggy, "Um, hello?"

"Are you drinking?" asked Postley.

"No," Austin replied. "I must have fallen asleep. Gabs is, in fact, sleeping."

Kirk, "Evidently, your friends think my office is part of a hotel."

"Hey, give us a break," said Austin. "We haven't slept in a couple of days."

"Me neither, thanks to you!" Kirk jokingly responded.

Austin asked, "Sam, how's it shaking on your end?"

"Shaking is the operative word. I thought a bomb-disposal truck would ride a little smoother given its intended cargo! Looking out the rather small window, we must be going a million miles per hour!"

"Aren't you in the passenger seat?"

"Are you kidding? I'm more like a stowaway in what looks like a small galley. There's even a microwave and mini fridge. No beer though, I checked! Oh, there's even a charging station for my phone, which I am taking advantage of right now."

"I thought you'd all be interested," added Clarkson to the world's strangest conference call, "that the convoy is about two-thirds to Wallops Island. And, specifically for Sam, I'm told the engineers at the MARS facility are planning to use construction cranes to work on the payload section while the rocket's on the launch pad. They're already in place."

"Thank you, Madam President. Could you do me one huge favor?"

"Of course."

"Thank you. When the trucks were refueling, Tony Franco let me poke into the storage bay of our smoking nemesis and I took measurements with a measuring tape I found in an equipment bin. Madam President, I need you to relay those measurements to the engineers at the MARS facility."

Gabby woke up from the chatter and said, "Sam, I can't believe you're asking the President of the United States to be your message runner!"

"Sleeping beauty awakes!" spouted Austin.

Clarkson replied to Gabby, "It's really no problem. Sam's butt is on the pressure cooker, after all."

"In all due respect, Madam President, you're starting to sound a lot like us!" replied Austin.

"It must be the combination of gallons of consumed coffee and no sleep," replied Clarkson.

There was a rare group chuckle.

"Pen and paper in hand, Sam," said Clarkson. "Fire away."

"Please let the engineers at the MARS facility know that they'll need to fabricate a tray-like support interface with the precise inner dimensions of 38.25 inches by 26.75 inches. With, at minimum, a four-inch lip height. The ice cream box is 31.50 inches tall; they'll need that measurement to create the securing mechanism – likely straps. Oh, and I'm guessing by the way it was readily lifted into the truck by Tony and his team that it only weighs in the neighborhood of 100 pounds. They'll need that number as part of their mass calculations. Anyway, they'll know what all this stuff means."

"I will relay, Sam."

"Thank you, Madam President. At least it will get them started. They have months of work to accomplish in just a few hours."

CHAPTER 92

As Sam Postley accurately identified, a secret military payload – code-named "Big Eye" – was scheduled for launch in the upcoming afternoon. It was being carried by a 141-foot-tall, three-stage, Firestorm IV rocket developed by a relatively new contractor to the U.S. Government: DynaArc, Inc.

***

Weeks to months of clean-room preparation and configuration are required to integrate even the simplest payloads into a space-flying rocket. Payload integration activities for the "Big Eye" satellite launch began five weeks ago in the Horizontal Integration Facility (HIF), a clean-room-like, high-security environment about a mile from the launch pad.

It was here that the "Big Eye" was installed inside the rocket's fairing – essentially a two-piece nose cone with its two vertical halves, side by side. To release a payload into space, like the "Big Eye" satellite, the two sections of a fairing open like the petals of a flower.

A week ago, the Firestorm IV rocket – lying horizontally – was transported from the HIF to the launch pad by a slow-moving, many-ton transport vehicle. After a 24-hour journey, the rocket was pivoted to its vertical launch position on the pad.

Tonight, the weeks of preparation needed to be unwound and redone in hours. All while the rocket was vertical on the launch pad.

The diameter of the Firestorm IV fairing was thirteen feet and eight inches, so there was plenty of room for the liquid-nitrogen-filled box containing Parnette's bomb. But getting it into the fairing with the rocket on the pad, removing the current satellite, and then installing and securely mounting the box containing the bomb were mind-bending challenges.

One fortuitous aspect of the Firestorm IV rocket was its special "ZipTip" fairing – a front-end hatch to interior payloads. It resembled a double-large child's "flying saucer" for sledding – in this case, six feet in diameter – but slightly more bulbous, made from titanium, and painted white. It was the very top of the rocket – the "tip" of the fairing – fastened in place with 24 titanium bolts.

Under normal circumstances, with a rocket lying on its side inside of the HIF, un-bolting the ZipTip and performing payload maintenance could be done quickly – within a day in an emergency circumstance. However, with a rocket vertical on a launch pad, disassembly, payload work, and reassembly had never been attempted – not even contemplated. Yet, that's precisely what was urgently needed that night.

The ZipTip at least made the upcoming extraordinary tasks within the realm of possibility.

While the bomb was being transported to the MARS facility, two telescoping construction cranes tipped with caged-in worker platforms were driven from operations elsewhere on the property to the base of the rocket. Instead of a clean-room environment, workers rode the crane's extending telescopic sections 141 feet to the top of the rocket and started their rush tasks.

Through arm-spaced openings in their platform cages, the workers unbolted the Zip-Tip and hastily removed this circular tip of the rocket. The half-a-billion-dollar "Big Eye" satellite was then taken out from its internal attachment and deployment moorings and ferried to the ground by a crane.

Launch fueling and countdown schedules were being re-worked on the fly, shaving off almost thirteen hours from the originally planned afternoon launch. Timelines and procedures were developed to accommodate the safety of crews working atop of the rocket and the needed steps for a quick launch once "the box" (the nickname instantly adopted by the MARS' staff) was integrated with the space-flying vehicle.

Engineers and fabricators were hard at work to create the mounting hardware, a retaining frame of sorts, to hold and secure the box inside the rocket. They were applying the measurements relayed from Postley through President Clarkson. Welding sparks flew. Time was compressed. Months of engineering were squeezed to a few hours. They were in the unusual and highly pressurized position of working and creating by gut – and not the typical, methodically paced, 3D modeling, development, testing, approval, and production cycle of such a critical mission element.

The 20- and 30-something engineers and fabricators worked well outside of their computer-era training; the weight of the world was apparent in their faces. Except, seemingly, in the face of Norm Gatwick, one of the most-senior fabricators at MARS. Approaching 70 years old, he was a mechanical engineer and jack of all trades nearing 46 years of experience in the aerospace industry. With a smile on his face, he did his best to depressurize the relative newbies. As he swung a hammer to mash down a pesky metal corner, he blurted, "Ah, just like the old days." That got a rise out of the group – and they pressed ahead with newfound confidence.

CHAPTER 93

At 2:03 a.m., the convoy reached the primary security entrance at the Wallops Flight Facility. With their task completed, the Apache helicopters peeled away from the convoy below.

On-based security vehicles picked up the lead at that point, waving Brassard's Cougar MRAP and his convoy along the route that culminated at the MARS Launch Pad-0A. A recently negotiated joint venture transformed this once dedicated launch facility to a multi-entity launch resource for similarly sized and configured space vehicles.

The area, usually cleared of vehicles and personnel this close to a launch, was now bristling with activity. Five huge, truck-pulled, generator-powered floodlights surrounding the Firestorm-IV rocket on the launch pad lit up the area to an almost-daylight level. Beacons from other fixed structures contributed to the illumination.

The expensive "Big Eye" satellite and various components of hardware and cable were now on the ground at the base of the launch pad, like a child's set of toys scattered about.

The two telescoping cranes that allowed workers to remove the "Big Eye" from the fairing remained beside of the rocket, ready for the next phase of the effort.

Brassard bounded out of his vehicle and spouted to the rapidly surrounding personnel, "Who's in charge? And who the heck do I give the bomb to?"

The gruffness caught the personnel off guard. An individual who was within earshot rapidly stepped toward Brassard and, unfazed by the big man's bluster, replied, "Everyone's empowered here. We're doing a year's worth of work in a few hours to save our country. I'm Deputy Director Scott Harris. I'm about to shove your big face right back into your truck. Who the hell do you think you are?"

Brassard, not used to being dressed down, paused, took a breath, and said, "Okay. My bad. I clearly got things off on the wrong foot. I'm Arthur Brassard, the Secretary of Defense. It's been a long day, well, a long couple of days – for a lot of people. My apologies."

"Apologies accepted, Secretary. And apologies for the jeans and sneakers. I was just leaving the gym when they summoned me here. Our launch wasn't scheduled until tomorrow afternoon. What's the SITREP?"

"Inside that bomb-disposal truck is the rogue boy. I still have no clue how a little tube, that's now inside of an ice cream cart's box, could put the majority of the East Coast in the sea. But that's what they say."

"I guess an antimatter bomb is no longer science fiction."

"I guess not."

"And the guy standing outside of the truck –"

"The guy with the ponytail?"

"Yes, him. He looks vaguely familiar."

"He's the fellow who figured out how to put the bomb on ice, so to speak. Or we'd all be dead."

"Well, let's see if we can keep all of us from dying before sunrise."

CHAPTER 94

"Everyone," Postley talking into his phone, "I am standing outside of the bomb-disposal truck. Brassard, Franco, and about five people who clearly work here have opened the bay to the truck, are inside, and are looking at 'the box' – that's what they nicknamed it here. It's still billowing, I might add."

Clarkson provided an update from her perspective. "Sam, here in the Sit, we're wired into the Wallops Range Control Center. You know way more about this stuff than me. We're told they're reconfiguring everything to support a launch just before sunrise. It all depends on how quickly they can integrate the – okay – 'the box' into the rocket."

"That's cutting it close. The liquid nitrogen looks to be boiling off *really fast*. I'm looking at it more closely now; it's like an angry smoking dragon."

"The good news," Clarkson continued, "at least I'm told it's good news, is that the box is much lighter than the satellite that was originally on the rocket."

"Yeah, I heard through the grapevine that the original 'Big Eye' payload was about 11,000 pounds. Hopefully they also told you they can put our problem child into a much higher orbit?"

"Yes, that's what they said."

"That'll buy the world much more time – months to years – to figure out what to do with this soon-to-be-flying bomb. Wait a sec. A few people from the base are walking towards me. Hold on. I'll keep you on speakerphone."

"Dr. Postley?"

"Yes, that's me. Please call me Sam."

"Okay, Sam. I thought I recognized you. I'm Deputy Director Harris, in charge of this operation, by default. Your aerospace reputation precedes you."

"Well, thank you, sir."

"And you can call me Scott."

"Okay, Scott. And, hey, I see they changed the dress code around here," eyeing Harris' jeans and sneakers. "Maybe I could kick off another stint."

"You worked here?"

"Seven years ago. We did our initial sub-orbital test launches of our PTR-powered rockets out of Pad-0B."

"That was before my time. Anyway, let me give you the latest. You –"

"Before you do," Postley raised his cell phone to eye height, "I just want you to know that President Clarkson and members of her staff are listening in from the Situation Room. As well as some friends in Aruba. Long story on the latter; they're cleared and authorized."

"Thanks for the heads up. You have quite a conference call going on. Madam President, welcome virtually to the Wallops Flight Facility and the Mid-Atlantic Regional Space-port."

"I wish it was under better circumstances, Deputy Director Harris. But thank you for the welcome. Don't let me interrupt further. Pretend I'm not here."

"Thank you, Madam President. As I was saying, Sam, you know flight dynamics and orbital mechanics as well as anyone. And your little payload in here," his eyes darted to the truck's bay, "is in for quite the shake and bake on the Firestorm-IV."

"With the payload as light as it is, less than 1% of your original rider, can you throttle back and reduce the g load?"

"Yes. Absolutely. I'm already talking with my flight engineers about that. They're working the numbers. We have a bit of flexibility, at least on the first stage. Pretty standard LOX (liquid oxygen) and kerosene engines. And there are two of them. We can't do anything regarding the second stage, as it's a solid."

"The initial kick concerns me. We can't do anything about that."

"Nope."

"Third stage is a small bi-propellent. Nitrogen tetroxide and hydrazine."

"If it gets that far, we should be in good shape."

"Agreed."

"Sam, how restrained is the cylinder – the actual bomb – inside of the box?"

"Not very. I wedged it in between pieces of dry ice, then we poured in liquid nitrogen."

"Well, that's a problem."

"Yeah, the free floating and the sloshing. I had a lot of time to think during the ride over in the truck. I'm hoping, really hoping, that there's at least half of the liquid nitrogen remaining in the box. Did you meet Tony Franco, the senior bomb tech who I met on the scene in D.C.?"

"Yes, I met him briefly a few minutes ago."

"Super. He's a good guy. Tony and I filled the box to the brim. As you can see, it's boiling off rather quickly. Even if it gets down to a third or even a quarter, the bomb's only the size of a thermos. And it's at the bottom of the box; it didn't float when we poured in the liquid nitrogen." Postley scratched his beard as he continued his thinking and speaking. "The liquid nitrogen, as a fluid, should dampen any motion quite considerably. That's probably why it stayed happy during the ride over here."

"As you know, a rocket ride is quite a stretch from a jaunt in a truck."

"Yeah, I know. But it's what we've got. I think it would be way too risky to open the box again. If we are down in liquid nitrogen more than I have estimated, the rapid boil off could doom us."

"Let's come back to the liquid-nitrogen topic in a moment. For a larger context, I need to know what would happen if we had a catastrophic event during the flight to space?"

Postley replied, "If the rocket was in the early phase of its flight, the effect might be similarly catastrophic to a detonation on the ground.

"If it was in space, like at the altitude of the International Space Station 250 miles up, that's a different story. There wouldn't be any atmosphere to transmit the shockwaves generated by the explosion. Satellites would be wiped out by the massive electromagnetic pulse. And the EMP would cause widespread disruptions on Earth to communications and power grids. The planet – itself – would be spared the devastating physical effects. The public would be largely okay.

"And, finally, if a detonation occurred at some TBD altitude between the ground and space, it's impossible to know. Lots of possible outcomes are probably not good."

"Thank you for the excellent overview, Sam," said Harris. "We're aiming for an uneventful ride to space."

"Uneventful would be wonderful." Postley continued, "Madam President, or anyone else on the call, are there any questions regarding our discussion?"

"What was the 'kick' you mentioned?" Clarkson asked. "I think you said it was regarding the second stage?"

"Keen ears, Madam President. Yes. Liquid engines can be throttled – like the gas pedal in your car. They are what power the first stage of this rocket. On the other hand, a solid rocket motor, as what powers the second stage, and not to get too technical, is more of all or nothing. When it's on, it's on. Deputy Director Harris and I were talking about the transition between the stages. Our special 'payload' will notice an extra 'shove' when the solid ignites. How much that change in acceleration will affect our delicate passenger, it's anyone's guess."

"When in the flight will this transition occur?"

"Deputy Director Harris?" Postley turned and asked.

"As I mentioned to Sam a moment ago, my flight engineers are crunching the numbers. Our payload will be so much lighter than what was originally scheduled for this flight. We're working to give, well – the bomb – as smooth a ride as possible, particularly during the first stage burn, as that's what we can most control. To answer your question directly, the latest numbers I've seen for second-stage ignition are around the four-minute mark of the flight."

"Then we should ramp up our praying at that time?"

"Madam President, this is aerospace. I pray continually."

"Understood."

"But seriously," Harris continued, "that was an excellent question – and something we're clearly thinking about. Is there anything else I can answer for you?"

"No, Deputy Director," replied Clarkson. "Your discussion would be truly fascinating if this was a college lecture – and not with the world hanging in the balance. Please press ahead."

Postley resumed the discussion with Harris. "The other variable, but I'm 99% confident we're okay, is the continued cooling effect in space. Of course, there will be no conduction or convection cooling."

"Of course. And, Sam, I agree with you. It should be manageable."

"Madam President," Postley added, "What I'm talking about with Deputy Director Harris is the cooling we have here on Earth, driven by air molecules and such."

"Got it, Sam. No air, no regular cooling."

"Precisely."

Postley continued with Harris, "So all we have is radiative cooling – basically the loss of heat by thermal radiation. I'm thinking – and I'd like your opinion – that we don't jettison the fairing when in orbit but keep it on. It's white. That should reflect the bulk of the sunlight. Minimize absorbed solar energy."

"Off the top of my head, that makes sense. We don't have time to run sims to confirm. I'm with you on this one."

"Madam President, we're discussing leaving the fairing – what you might call the nose cone – on in order to reflect as much sunlight as possible to reduce heat absorption."

"Understood. Thank you for the play-by-play. It's very helpful as I try to wrap my head around this stuff."

"I bet you didn't think you'd be getting a crash course in aerospace today?"

"No. Although let's stay away from words like 'crash' for a while, okay?" Clarkson said with sarcasm, trying to stir a hint of levity into this high-stress situation.

"My bad."

Harris looked down at his phone, read a text message, and looked back up.

"Sam," Harris locked eyes with Postley. With sudden extra seriousness he said, "I just found out that the scheduled Launch Director won't get here in time. Even on a red eye. So I guess you're also looking at today's Launch Director."

"A man of many hats."

"It seems."

Harris took a breath and continued, "As the Launch Director for this flight, I must rely on the best knowledge and experience I have at every moment. From what I've heard from Secretary Brassard, you've already saved the country today. You've had your hands in this – literally – from the get-go. And you have a first-hand understanding of all the launch particulars. I need your insights if we are to have a chance in hell to pull this off. Are you game?"

"I'm here to do whatever you require."

"Thank you, Sam. So back to the liquid nitrogen question: I'm wrestling with whether we should attempt to top off the box. If there's only a little liquid nitrogen remaining at liftoff – perhaps even right now – we're all in peril before the rocket's even an inch off the pad. We have plenty of liquid nitrogen here at Wallops. I need your recommendation."

Postley brought the phone closer to his face, "Madam President. As you probably heard, I'm kind of on the spot here. Do you feel lucky – again?"

"Sam, I didn't doubt your judgment before. And I'm not doubting it now. Go with that marvelous gut one more time."

"Damn, I knew you'd say that."

"Mr. Postley?" Harris asked with time-sensitive expectation.

"Yeah, yeah," Postley replied. "It's *only* the fate of millions of people in the balance." After unconsciously nibbling his lower lip and a pregnant pause, he added, "I think – no, I believe – our best shot is to launch the box as is."

CHAPTER 95

Deputy Director Harris asked his staff to locate Norm Gatwick in the Fabrication Center. Harris needed to speak to him ASAP, particularly regarding the status of the box-to-rocket mounting hardware. Time was ticking away; no one knew with certainty how long the liquid nitrogen would remain in the box – and keep the bomb from going off.

"Deputy Director, Gatwick here," he said on the phone to Harris.

"Norm, have you saved some of that construction magic for this evening?"

"I believe so. The 'kids' were a little intimidated to improvise, but they stepped up. As we speak, they're loading the mechanical interface onto a transport – and it's coming your way. You'll have it on your doorstep in five."

"Great. And you? I need you here, too."

"I'm hopping in my car and will be there a couple minutes after they arrive. I'm bringing my lucky hammer. We had to use 'The Persuader' three times already."

"We need all the luck we can get. Thank you, Norm."

"Don't thank me yet. But we'll get this bad apple into space – even if I have to duct tape it into the rocket in myself."

CHAPTER 96

A mini, two-person, flatbed truck came to a rapid stop at the bomb-disposal truck, flagged down by Harris.

Harris, Brassard, Franco, Postley, and three of Harris' staff gathered around the flatbed; a shiny, frame-like structure was strapped in the center.

"So *that* is what's going to save us?" asked Brassard.

"That's it," said Harris. "The box's retaining frame. It's intended to lock the box in place during its wild ride into space."

"I hope my measurements were accurate," commented Postley. "I measured the box at one of the fuel stops, and President Clarkson was kind enough to relay the info."

"We'll soon find out," added Franco.

"We're far from dealing with 'clean room' stuff," said Harris. "How about we just lay the retaining frame on the asphalt here and see if the box fits?"

The team unstrapped the frame from the flatbed and laid it on the blacktop. They then walked into the open bay of the bomb-disposal truck. With trepidation, Postley touched the smoldering box – and quickly retracted his fingers. "Still cold. But I thought it would be colder!"

"It can't be more than cheap Styrofoam insulation inside the aluminum walls of this homemade box," said Harris, also briefly touching the box and having equal surprise as to the modest temperature.

"What does *that* mean, fellas?" asked Brassard.

"That's the first good news in this entire craziness, Secretary, um, I mean, Arty," responded Franco. "Warm outside means cold inside. And probably more liquid nitrogen than we thought."

"That is, unless there is near-zero liquid nitrogen inside," said Postley. "Then we'd all be dead. So I guess we can rule out that possibility."

The four readied themselves to unstrap the box from the inside of the truck, lift it up, and carry it outside. Before the team made the lift, Postley spoke into his cell phone, "Madam President and everyone else listening in: We're moving the box to the rocket-mounting interface for a test fit."

As the team began moving the box, Norm Gatwick arrived in his vehicle, got out, and walked over to them.

"So that's the rascal?" Gatwick asked the group carrying the box. "It looks more like a kid's science-fair project gone awry."

"And it's not very heavy," Harris said. "More awkward than anything else."

As they got closer to the retaining frame lying on the ground, Harris added, "Okay, let's see if Norm and his team's handiwork...works."

Gatwick got on his knees next to the frame and said, "I'll help line it up. Lower it slowly, boys."

The group manipulated the box and gingerly lowered it until it was just inches over the edges of the fabricated metal frame.

"Moment of truth," Harris said to the group.

"Bring it down, fellas," Gatwick said.

The team lowered the box – and it slid into place. "Like a glove!" exclaimed Gatwick, as he got back on his feet.

"It'll work!" exclaimed Harris.

The team shared high fives, momentarily celebrating an essential milestone.

Gatwick concluded, "Okay, let's get this troublemaker to the top of the candle – and send it the heck out of here!"

CHAPTER 97

"Get me on the air now!" President Clarkson directed Jameson and Walters, her communication specialists, and to the others who remained in the Situation Room.

Ordinary TV coverage was now piped through the room's digital displays, replacing the earlier Tomahawk and F-15E graphics and video feeds.

Clarkson watched chaos unfold throughout the country – but particularly along the central East Coast. The early 'Earth Talkers' activities that raised no more than skeptical eyebrows were replaced by millions of citizens flooding and snarling the highways, as word leaked out through "high-placed sources" that the bomb was still active and dangerous – and now at Wallops for an unknown reason.

Directing her comments to Jameson and Walters, "Maybe I should have listened to your advice hours ago. God, it feels like weeks."

"We can help you write a draft," said Jameson.

"Or at least some talking points," followed Walters.

"No. No time for that. Thank you for offering. Please alert the media that I'll be in the Press Briefing Room in 30 minutes. I need a bio break and at least brush my hair. Just look at us: The definition of disheveled."

Clarkson's Chief of Staff, Tebbs, commented, "Same clothes and no sleep. That'll do it. But Madam President, you look great!"

"You lie like a rug, Barry."

Clarkson spoke towards The Cube. "Sam, this is Clarkson. Can you hear me?"

"Yes, Madam President. Right here."

"I'm going to make a TV statement to the American people in less than a half hour. Give me the quickest update you can – in words the average person could understand."

"Okay. I'm not dead. You're not dead. And the box fits the rocket's retainer."

"Perhaps a *little* more detail."

"Sorry. A little punchy here."

"I hear you. Same here."

"Let me try this again. How about the following four talking points: We have stabilized Parnette's bomb. We are placing it inside of a rocket that is on the launch pad at the Mid-Atlantic Regional Spaceport, a space-launch resource associated with the Wallops Flight Facility. We will fly the bomb into space where it will be too cold for it to detonate. The world will be safe. How's that?"

"Perfect. Good luck there!"

"Thank you. We'll tune in here. Have a good talk to the world!"

"I echo the sentiment, Madam President," said Kirk over the conference line. "We will watch from our police station. Austin and Gabby are still with me."

***

Flanked by Tebbs, Hemsley, and Quintana, President Clarkson made her way to the podium in the James S. Brady Press Briefing Room in the West Wing of the White House. Even at this late hour, and very short notice, the room was packed with media.

Without any notes or teleprompter assistance, and looking straight into the camera, Clarkson started to speak:

"Good evening, my fellow Americans. Allow me to dispense with any formalities and get right to the point. As you know, over these last couple of days we had a situation initiated by Dr. Katherine Parnette. She held our country for ransom, but America does not – and never will – bow to the whims or demands of a terrorist, foreign or domestic.

"Thanks to our intelligence efforts, in collaboration with law enforcement on Aruba, and some brave U.S. citizens (Gabby nudged Austin), Parnette was apprehended and her ability to remotely activate her device – yes, a bomb – was neutralized.

"The bomb was subsequently found in the heart of our nation's Capital, and its detonation inhibited by the brave men and women of our hazardous devices' team and additional brave citizen assistance (Austin nudged Gabby; Sam and Franco smiled at each other).

"To fully neutralize the bomb, and to get our nation – and the world – completely out of harm's way, as I speak the bomb is being loaded into the top of a rocket at the Mid-Atlantic Regional Spaceport, a space-launch resource associated with the Wallops Flight Facility on the eastern coast of Virginia. Heroic efforts continue there. What would ordinarily take months is happening in just hours.

"I'm told, if all goes to plan, the launch will take place right before sunrise here on the East Coast. I have directed the flight control team at the Wallops Range Control Center to make the video feed universally available. You'll be able to watch it live along with me."

To give her country a tiny moment of sanity, Clarkson added. "And, no, contrary to the reports, I am right here at the White House. I'm not meeting with aliens." Clarkson beamed a broad smile.

Switching back to her stoic, presidential delivery, "Please, everyone. Stay calm. Stay off the roads. Watch the launch with me on TV. There will be plenty of time to go into each and every detail when the situation is fully resolved. So, literally, stay tuned. We'll soon be celebrating together. I will be back to talk to you later."

Clarkson and her staff walked towards the Press Briefing Room's exit. A barrage of questions followed her every step. She ignored them all as she exited.

CHAPTER 98

There was a flurry of activity at the base of the rocket.

Norm Gatwick, empowered by Deputy Director Harris, supervised the key actions. Ordinarily, the grizzled veteran's role was working with teams of design engineers to fabricate high-tolerance components many months before a launch. But here he was, on the launch pad, like a master woodworker directing the construction of a grand table from raw timber.

Gatwick said, "Time to get those screws torqued up," pointing to the eight, equally spaced screws that were threaded through the base of the metal frame. Tightening the screws – just the right amount – would apply critical retaining force to the aluminum walls of the still-smoking box. It's this frame that was designed to keep the box firmly locked into the rocket as it speeds into space.

Gatwick made many key decisions based on minimal data, as he only had the basic dimensions of the box relayed from Postley through Clarkson. One of those decisions was to go with old-fashioned thumb screws in the metal frame – so he and his team could *feel* proper tightness. If the screws were tightened too much, the box would be punctured, the liquid nitrogen would drain, and the bomb would detonate. Not enough tightness and the box would come free during the vigorous ride into space – and the bomb would detonate. "Either way, we'd be screwed, literally," Gatwick cautioned his young team when they were conceiving the design.

Gatwick volunteered to perform the critical tightening task himself. He went – thumb screw by thumb screw – around the retaining frame, feeling for what his gut told him was proper tightness on each. He then stepped back. "Done!" he proclaimed to Harris, Postley, Franco, and the surrounding workers.

Gatwick's team attached a pair of wide, heavy-duty straps that started at the retaining frame, ran up the sides of the box, and crisscrossed at the top – like ribbons on a gift box. However, instead of a bow at the top, there was an attached loop of additional strap material. This lifting-strap arrangement would soon be used by a crane and its team to lift the box and its attached frame to the top of the rocket and then lower the combination inside.

"Our turn!" proclaimed Harris. With an overhead circling motion, he rallied the nearby workers to come forward and ready the attachment of the box-frame combination to a nearby crane.

"Wait!" shouted Gatwick. No one quite knew what was on Gatwick's mind when he walked over to the box. He turned, gave a wink to Harris, pulled out a hammer from his tool belt, and – ever so gently – gave a *love tap* to the top of the box. "For luck!" Gatwick exclaimed.

Everyone smiled and the growing tension was momentarily abated. All were aware of the precarious, never-before-attempted procedure that lay ahead.

***

The two construction cranes at the base of the rocket could telescope over 200 feet, so within easy reach of the top of the 141-foot-tall space vehicle.

The caged-in platforms on the ends of the two cranes could physically hold two people – and still have sufficient capacity to lift over a thousand pounds of extra weight.

On the end of each platform was a small electric winch; metal cables were spooled on the winches.

Everyone took their positions.

A solo worker entered one of the worker platforms and closed the cage door. The box-frame was attached to the end of the winch's cable by a simple metal hook.

Two other workers entered the other worker platform, along with a vast array of tools, a box of essential nuts and bolts, and an assortment of emergency-repair items – even industrial-strength duct tape. A particularly eye-catching sight, attached to the platform's winch cable was a grapple contraption that gripped the dangling six-foot ZipTip.

"The claw" – as it was nicknamed this evening – was created on-the-fly by Gatwick and his team while the bomb was en route to Wallops Island. A ZipTip had never been removed or attached while a rocket was on the launch pad. That night it had to be done in order to place the bomb inside the rocket's fairing.

Hours earlier, two workers riding in a crane's platform unbolted the rocket's 327-pound, six-foot-diameter ZipTip; they clamped it to the side of their platform and brought it down to the ground. The team knew the true challenge would be the reverse: the precision necessary to replace the ZipTip and the excruciating alignment of all 24 of its retaining bolts – all while it's dangling above the rocket more than 141 feet in the air. It was on the shoulders of Gatwick's team to figure out how to perform this high-wire act.

Gatwick's team – in addition to designing and constructing the box-to-rocket mounting frame – had worked feverishly through the night to solve the ZipTip dilemma. They had spitballed many ideas, but each was ultimately deemed impractical or unworkable. Off the cuff, one of Gatwick's young engineers joked to the team, "If we only had a huge version of a claw from one of those carnival claw machines – you know, the ones that try to pick up the stuffed toys?" Well, that sparked a twinkle in Gatwick's eyes. Before you knew it, the team had in their industrial bending machine four eight-foot-long steel rods; they bent them into the shape of claw elements and hinged the set together – and the claw was born.

With everything in place, the workers inside their caged platforms manipulated hydraulic controls – and the cranes began to extend their telescopic booms.

Dangling from one platform's cable was the box-frame puffing liquid nitrogen. Equally precarious, below the other platform's cable, was the bright-white, saucer-shaped ZipTip, locked in the jaws of the claw.

"Up they go!" commented Postley into this cell phone, still doing play-by-play to the Situation Room and the Aruba police station.

Postley, Franco, Brassard, Harris, and Gatwick all sweated more than would be typical on a summer night in Virginia. All they could do was watch and hope the towering choreography went as planned.

In less than three minutes, both cranes had lifted the platforms 141 feet high to a level even with the top of the rocket and its fairing. The near-imperceptible ground-level breeze turned into a pulsing modest wind at that height. Both the box-frame and the ZipTip swung like pendulums – a startling sight from the ground.

"This is not good," said Postley.

"It's why this has never been attempted before," said Harris.

The lofted workers had their own concerning discussions.

"This is nuts!" yelled the solo worker to his colleagues in the other platform. "I don't see how we're going to get the box-frame into the fairing. It's flopping all over the place."

"We'll have to time the swing to get it in the hole," said one of the others.

"Easier said than done," added the third. Operating the hydraulic controls, the worker said, "I'm trying to ease our platform a tad closer to the bobbing unit; if we're lucky, we can catch it on the swing."

The two platforms were now just a few feet apart over the opening of the fairing. At their height, and the substantial extension of the telescopic booms, even their platforms rocked in the breeze.

"I'm going to lift my platform and position it about five feet above you two, so you'll have a clear shot at grabbing the box-frame." The solo worker nudged the hydraulic controls and the boom further extended.

"Stop! The box-frame is at eye level to us now!"

"I'll take your word for it. I can only partially see you below me."

"We're waiting for the wind to blow it this way. It's rocking all over the place! And it's smoking like crazy! The gyrations must really be sloshing the liquid nitrogen."

Everyone at the base of the rocket watched the scene with agony and disbelief. The erratic motion of the box-frame was at the mercy of the wind.

As the box-frame started to swing in a more favorable direction, one of the workers in the cage screamed to the solo worker in the other cage, "Oh! Oh! Here it comes. Come on baby. Come on baby!"

Timing their reach as best as they could, they grabbed the swinging, smoldering box-frame. "Gotcha! We caught it!" they exclaimed to their partner in the solo platform.

"Did they grab it? It looks like they grabbed it!" shouted Franco.

"Geez Louise! I think so!" Gatwick said excitedly.

One of the workers grasping the box-frame yelled to his solo colleague, "Let's get this wild child in the hole before we get another gust of wind. Slowly – and I mean slowly – lower the box down."

The worker in the solo platform slightly adjusted – with a little tap – the winch's joystick downward.

"Oh! Stop! Stop!" yelled one of the workers holding the box-frame. "The box is blocking the light from the floodlights around the pad. I can't see down into the fairing."

The other worker holding the box-frame responded, "Keep a grip while I grab the flashlight on my belt." Flicking on the flashlight and pointing it down into the fairing, the worker said "Okay. How's this?"

"That'll do! You hold the light and I'll hold and guide the unit down."

Yelling to the solo worker controlling the winch, "We have a work-around. Continue descent. Slowly!"

The solo worker resumed the subtle downward action via the joystick.

"That's it...that's it...a little more...a little more," said one of the workers as the box-frame began to enter and slowly disappear into the six-foot-wide hole in the top of the rocket's fairing. "You've cleared the rim of the fairing! Keep going...slow...slow...slow."

As the smoldering box-frame descended into the fairing, the worker gripping it spun it ever so slightly on its support cable. The job now was to align the frame's bolt-hole pattern with the upward-pointing threaded studs where the "Big Eye" satellite was originally bolted.

Inch by inch, the box-frame was lowered, now fully inside the fairing.

A major-league yell erupted from the platform – so loud that it was heard all the way down to the ground: "The eagle has landed!"

The workers aloft could hear the whooping and clapping from their perches 141 feet in the air.

***

"Job one, complete," said Gatwick. "I was sweating it there, for sure."

Austin added, "Even though Gabs and I aren't there, we are dripping here, too. It sounds like this would have been a good demonstration in a deodorant commercial!"

"From our end in the Sit, it sounds like the news couldn't be better," said Clarkson. "What is the next step?"

Postley replied, "Well..." while looking at Harris and Gatwick. "Actually, two steps. Both challenging. Let me turn this over to Mr. Norm Gatwick, the construction magician and senior fabricator at the space facility. Take it away, Norm."

"Madam President, it's an honor to meet you."

"Well, the honor is all mine, considering the magic you are making happen under extraordinary circumstances. The country thanks you."

"Thank you for the very kind words, Madam President. Hold off on the champagne, though. As Mr. Postley indicated, we have two more challenging steps. The first one is to bolt the frame in. Thanks to my team's Flying Wallendas' routine, the box and its frame are sitting inside the rocket's nose on four threaded studs. To bolt it down, my team and I have made what looks like a super-long ratchet socket. Five-foot-nine-inches long, to be precise. The end that will carry and tighten rather large, two-inch, nuts is magnetized. We would ordinarily use stainless steel nuts inside a rocket. In this case, we needed to use ordinary steel nuts so we can use our super-long, magnetized socket to hold and guide the nuts into place. If our in-the-air team can get those four nuts on and tightened, the, um, the –"

"Bomb."

"Yes, bomb, would be held securely in place. That would complete step two."

"I'm following, Mr. Gatwick."

"The third, and final, step is will be getting the ZipTip in place and bolted back on. Are you familiar with that item?"

"Yes, I've had quite the education over the last few hours. I understand it to be the flying-saucer-like piece of metal that fits on the top of the rocket, correct?"

"Quick study, Madam President. And it might be the most-important item of all. Mr. Postley, could you further elaborate?"

"Certainly. Without the ZipTip in place, the rocket would have a gaping hole at the top. The turbulence would tear apart the comparatively fragile ice-cream box almost immediately – and the bomb would detonate. This gets back to our detonation scenarios we talked about before. At such an early phase of the flight, the bomb's enormous destructive force would resemble a ground detonation."

"I see."

"We're not going to have that problem, as Mr. Gatwick has one more trick up his sleeve. Isn't that right, sir?"

"We indeed have a plan. Let me paint a picture." Gatwick continued, "At the top of the rocket it's windy as heck – oops, sorry for the language! Our team is dangling the 327-pound, six-foot-across ZipTip over the fairing's opening – trying to align all 24 precision bolt holes so that the ZipTip can be re-attached. We're talking aerospace tolerances, plus or minus 0.001 of an inch. Even getting the alignment done on the ground is not a walk in the park. Our team will be attempting this re-attachment while the ZipTip, the rocket, and the two crane-supported platforms with our workers are all in motion – swaying in the Virginia breeze at almost 150 feet in the air. Oh, and then they have to screw in 24 bolts."

"Oh, my."

"We have our best personnel on the case. And a creative grappling tool. If it can be done, it will be done. Everyone knows failure is not an option."

CHAPTER 99

With the solo worker's job complete, he wished his two colleagues on the other platform good luck as he started his descent to the ground.

"It was hard enough to guide the box onto the studs; now we have to attach these four hefty nuts," said one.

"Let's see if 'The Great Gatwick' pulled another rabbit out of the hat," said the other.

The workers picked up from the floor of the platform a five-foot-nine-inch-long metal pipe with a socket on the end. "Wow. Now *that's* a long-distance socket! Gatwick and crew welded it right on the end of the pipe."

One of the workers grabbed a two-inch steel nut and brought it close to the socket. *Pop!* – the steel nut automatically snapped right into the end of the socket. "Now *that's* a magnet!"

"How in the world are we going to see down into the fairing – right to the studs – so we can screw on these nuts?"

The proverbial lightbulb simultaneously went on in the minds of the two workers. "Your flashlight!" one said. "Duct tape!" said the other.

They proceeded to tape the flashlight near the end of the long tool, right beside the welded-on socket. "Endless creativity – even up here!" one exclaimed.

With a nut already in the socket, they slid the long tool down into the fairing. As they twirled the tool, the light went around and around – but not annoyingly so. "Hey, this isn't so bad!" as the first nut went on surprisingly easily. They used locking pliers to clamp down on the pipe and forcefully torque the nut tight.

They expected one of the other three nuts to fall out of the tool as it was being extended into the fairing. Or a nut to become cross-threaded. Luck remained on their side and this step was completed surprisingly smoothly. "How 'bout that!" one of the workers exclaimed as the last nut was secured on the final stud.

"You know," a worker pondered to the other, "I just noticed there is less and less of the liquid nitrogen vapor blowing out of the fairing's top. It's not even impeding our work."

"You're right. And I don't think that's a good thing. Not that we can do anything about it. Let's get our work done and get the heck out of here."

"I'm with ya!"

***

"Hey, look!" Franco pointed up to the top of the rocket. "They started moving their platform higher – it's now well above the rocket."

"They either completed bolting the bomb in place. Or they're getting the heck out of there!" said Postley.

Gatwick commented, "They're right on script. They're moving their platform directly above the rocket so they can use the claw to lower the ZipTip precisely in place. We'll know for sure in a few seconds. If the bomb's locked in, they'll use the winch to extend the claw's cable."

Sure enough, within a minute, everyone on the ground could see the platform's winch cable get longer and the dangling ZipTip move closer to the top of the rocket. However, the longer the cable got, the more the ZipTip began to swing.

***

"This is absolutely insane!" said one of the workers, as the bulbous ZipTip caught the wind like a kite and flailed wildly. "I'm not sure we can get it to sit even partially on top of the rocket – forget the needed alignment. If we accidentally bang it into the rocket, we'll nick an edge and it will never fit."

"I'm not about to say our good fortune has run out. There's got to be a way to stabilize that gyrating thing!"

"And it feels like it's getting windier. At 150 feet in the air, we're like a human weathervane with the ZipTip."

"Think. Think. What do we have – other than a heap of trouble?"

"We have Gatwick's long tool. What could we do with that?"

Looking through the tools and supplies, the other worker lamented, "I don't believe we have anything stiff that we could bend into a hook to snag the cable or one of the claw's claws. Darn. I don't think we have anything we could use to make a remote grip."

"Hmmm. Not so fast."

"I see that look in your eyes. What are you thinking?"

"What if we make a honkin' huge ball of duct tape on the end of the tool – but with the adhesive side out? The tackiness might be enough to stick to the flopping ZipTip and slow it down."

"Worth a shot!"

The workers wrapped the tape around and around the end of the tool, making what looked like a giant-sized sticky popsicle.

"Okay, that's the whole roll of duct tape," said one of the workers. "The sticky ball will barely fit through the opening in the cage."

"No sense skimping," the other replied. "Besides, there's very little puffing coming out of the top, now. I think time is running short – for all of us."

"Then let's get this show on the road."

***

"That ZipTip thing is thrashing all over the place," said Franco. "How the heck are they going to stabilize it enough to attach it to the rocket?"

"Have faith, young man," said Gatwick. With a smile he added, "They've been under my wing for years. I think more than a little has rubbed off."

***

"I'm hearing some concern in your voices," said Clarkson. "What's the latest?"

Postley replied, "Well, the workers in the platform above the rocket look like they're having a heck of a time trying to control the ZipTip fluttering in the wind. It's like a big sail. I don't think anyone could have predicted – or accounted for – the motion."

"I don't have to remind you we're quickly approaching your six-to-eight hour estimate to –"

"Yeah, to the big kaboom."

"Yes."

"It's now up to the workers at the top of the candle."

"The 'human element' SAI-OP mentioned."

"Indeed. SAI-OP also mentioned the propensity to 'transcend' unfavorable odds, or something like that. I suggest we keep that spirit top of mind."

"I'm with you, Sam. Thank you for the positive perspective."

***

"I feel like we're fishing for a huge flounder with this sticky pole," the platform worker commented, as he pushed the long pole through a side opening of the safety cage.

"If you can poke it through an opening of the claws, you might be able to tack it to the surface of the ZipTip. It won't stay long. Maybe you can dampen the motion so we can corral this flying demon."

"There, I got it through the claws and touched the surface. But it blew away. Darn. Maybe the duct tape is not tacky enough. Here it comes again!"

The ZipTip blew in the direction of the platform. The worker stuck the pole through an opening in the claws, landing its end on the surface. "Oh, oh! It stuck. It stuck!"

"Okay. Keep the weight of the pole on the darn thing. Now scooch the ZipTip over the center of the fairing while I slowly lower the claw and the ZipTip with the winch. Here we go!"

The duo fought the wind and the swaying of their own platform while manipulating the ZipTip above the rocket's opening. The massive disk hovered just an inch over the six-foot hole in the space vehicle's nose..

"The vapor from the boiled-off liquid nitrogen is puffing around the entire circumference of the ZipTip. We have to be really close to the top of the fairing!"

"I think it's now or never."

"Agreed!"

The worker tapped the down direction of the winch's controls one more time. *"Clang!"* The edges of the claws landed on the edge of the opening – and the ZipTip rang like a bell.

"Let's bring the platform right next to the fairing – and see what we did."

With a few subtle adjustments of the hydraulic controls, in less than a minute they were alongside the fairing.

"Okay. We're here. How are we going to get the holes to line up?"

"I'm going to try an old trick Gatwick taught me." The worker took out a small screwdriver from his toolbox, reached through an opening in the safety cage, and placed the screwdriver into one of the 24 holes in the ZipTip.

"Let's use the metal claws to subtly rotate the ZipTip. When the hole with the screwdriver aligns with its matching hole in the fairing, the screwdriver will fall all the way through."

"You've been holding out on me with that nifty trick. Let's give it a whirl!"

The two workers grasped and nudged the metal claws that held the titanium ZipTip, rotating the six-foot metal disk by fractions of an inch at a time. Suddenly, *plop!* The screwdriver fell all the way through the hole.

"Do you feel lucky?" one worker said to the other.

"Hey, I think we've done pretty good so far."

"Let's try this." The worker grabbed another small-diameter screwdriver and placed it into another hole in the ZipTip. *Plop!* Down it went. "Play the lottery when we get out of here."

"If we pull out the claw ends, the ZipTip should drop into alignment. Right?"

"In theory."

The two workers maneuvered their platform around the perimeter of the fairing and the ZipTip, proceeding to pull out the four claw ends, one at a time. On each pull, the ZipTip dropped a bit more into the fairing opening. "And here we go." They pulled the last claw end – and the ZipTip dropped perfectly into place.

"Whew! You're a genius."

"No, just had a good mentor."

A worker tapped the up direction on the winch's controls and reeled in the claw to the bottom of the platform.

"Time to bolt!"

***

"It looks like they've winched the claw up and out of the way," said Gatwick. "That's excellent. If my guess is correct, they're wrapping up the final step – bolting on the fairing."

"24 bolts, correct?" asked Clarkson.

"Yes, Madam President. The alignment of the holes was, in my mind, the most-challenging of the steps. I don't think they would have winched away the claw if they weren't comfortable with the alignment. Putting in the bolts is tedious, but manageable."

"That's super news. I need all the optimism I can get," Clarkson replied. In a moment of self-reflection and public expression that caught everyone off guard, she added, "I feel like the old TV shows where a fellow would try to keep a dozen plates spinning. All while my head's spinning."

Brassard, hearing the emotional fatigue in his boss and friend, said, "Barb. We have your back. You've assembled a marvelous team. We won't let you down. Promise."

***

The two workers methodically propelled their sky-high platform around the perimeter of the ZipTip and fairing while it was buffeted by the wind. They needed to be within arm's reach of the ZipTip, so they could reach the bolt holes. But not so close that a sudden gust of wind would wham the platform into the fairing and irreparably damage the rocket. It was a formidable challenge.

They moved clockwise, from hole to hole, each hole a little less than nine-and-a-half inches apart, inserting and tightening the M18 x 50mm countersunk titanium bolts with an Allen hex bit wrench.

Liquid nitrogen vapor spouted out of the holes – from all 24 at first. "That is the weirdest thing, like the world's largest steam iron!" exclaimed one of the workers. "I was thinking more like 24 angrily boiling tea kettles," said the other.

Holes were sequentially plugged as they inserted the bolts, and the vapor even more voraciously puffed out of the holes that remained open. "At least we know there's still liquid nitrogen in there – but who knows how much?"

The duo almost dropped three bolts in the process but caught each one before it tumbled down the side of the fairing and rocket. The workers came equipped with over a dozen spare bolts. Like bringing an umbrella to ward off rain, the spares lowered the tension – and they completed the task without a glitch.

As the last bolt was inserted and tightened, the final puff of liquid nitrogen vapor was stifled. So focused on their tasks, they had not taken the time to think about the enormity of their mission. Then it sunk in. They hugged while one said to the other, "We may have just saved a lot of people."

They both looked down to the ground. Like two successful prize fighters, they raised their hands over their heads – and one screamed, "Let's rock this rocket!"

Everyone on the ground could hear the joyous shout. Hugs, cheers, clapping, and tears permeated the crowd.

"It's sealed up and ready to fly, Madam President!" Postley blared into his cell.

Barely heard over the wild cheers, Clarkson replied, "You've given our country a fighting chance. Thank you!"

Amidst the outburst of enthusiasm, Gatwick simply smiled. And, after a pause, he said to those within earshot, "I told ya."

CHAPTER 100

The two high-flying platform workers quickly retracted their crane's boom. They were back on the ground in less than three minutes – to a hero's welcome.

Five minutes later, using Postley's cell phone to broadcast to everyone on the grand conference call, Harris said, "Madam President, and everyone on the line, this is Scott Harris, Deputy Director of the Flight Facility and stand-in Launch Director for this mission. Moments ago, I was briefed by our brave and skilled top-of-the-rocket construction team and their entire ground-support team. I'm abundantly pleased to say that the box with the bomb is now securely loaded into the Firestorm IV rocket. We are calculating the quickest launch procedures we can – cutting as many corners as possible without endangering the lives here or in America."

"Commendable, Deputy Director Harris. And, I guess now, Launch Director. What is your general estimate as to a launch time?"

"Yes, Launch Director is now my primary hat. Pending final fueling calculations, we're estimating a launch within approximately 50 minutes. I'm waiting for the final word from my team. Hold a sec. Okay. I've just been handed a tablet with the final sequence. Yes. 50 minutes. That would put the launch at 5:48 a.m., about twenty minutes before sunrise. The Range Safety Officer has given us the green light. We did have an oil tanker 45 miles off the coast, directly under the flight path, but I'm told by the Coast Guard that it will be cleared by launch time. The Launch Weather Officer has given us the green light, too."

"So I guess you'd say, 'All Systems Go'?"

"Yes, Madam President."

"Shall we turn on the media feed?"

"Yes."

"At this hour, we won't have any play-by-play behind the feed. Just have a countdown clock superimposed over the video stream."

"That's perfectly fine. An hour-and-a-half ago, I gave an address to the nation from the Press Briefing Room. Everyone in the world knows what's going on by now."

Clarkson continued, "Dumb question: How will we know when we are safe?"

"It's certainly not dumb. It's probably the most-important question of all, Madam President." Harris continued, "Compared to this rocket's traditional payloads that have much more mass, we'll be able to boost the bomb – a rather lightweight item – into an extended low Earth orbit; that'll take another minute or so of flight time. To answer your question specifically, about nine minutes after the rocket leaves the pad, as long as nothing unusual occurs during any of the burns, the fairing containing Parnette's bomb will be safely in orbit."

"And this horrible ordeal will be over?"

"Sam has a few words to say on that. Let me turn the phone over to him."

"By all means."

"Madam President, this is Sam. I don't mean to be a wet blanket or even a damp towelette. In fact, I even have a bit of good news. But this is aerospace. And there are always a gazillion variables."

Postley continued, "In general, though, there is one key mission item to consider: With the back-of-my-napkin calculations, once the rocket is in orbit, it will take a couple of laps around the Earth for the temperature of the box, and the bomb, to stabilize. Given the higher LEO – that is, low Earth orbit – each lap will take about 91 minutes to complete. Once we get through two orbits, the box and the bomb should be in temperature equilibrium – way too cold to detonate – and we'll be in the clear."

Clarkson replied, "Yes, that's indeed good news. We'll be praying for mid-morning and no trouble."

Postley continued, "As they say on TV, 'but wait, there's more' – and, in fact, there's some more good news. As we talked about earlier, even if there was a detonation in orbit, there is no atmosphere to transmit shockwaves to Earth. Still, many orbiting satellites would be taken out by the massive EMP. Although Deputy Director slash Launch Director Harris didn't mention it, he brilliantly made sure that when the rocket achieves orbit, the International Space Station will be on the other side of the Earth – so entirely shielded from any possible EMP. The astronauts on the ISS would be safe."

Harris smiled to Postley in appreciation of the kind words.

"Press ahead Launch Director Harris," said Clarkson.

A voice from Aruba – Austin Raze – then slid in, "God Speed, Launch Director!"

"We will succeed," Harris concluded. "We will complete the mission."

CHAPTER 101

The countdown proceeded without a hitch.

The world's networks, as well as all major streaming platforms, were fixated on the impending launch.

Gabby and Austin huddled with Kirk next to the police station's on-the-wall TV. Clarkson sat with her staff in the Situation Room; globally streaming video of the rocket on Launch Pad-0A was up on Screen Six. Brassard, Postley, Franco, and Gatwick were with Deputy Director/Launch Director Harris in the Wallops Range Control Center.

With a satellite launch – the "Big Eye" – already scheduled for that day, but bumped for this emergency launch, Harris had much of his regular launch team available and on station. The wildcard was the box containing Parnette's bomb. With the payload switcheroo miraculously accomplished, the entire launch sequence looked almost normal.

This would be Firestorm IV's seventh launch. The fourth-generation rocket had a flawless track record, with five re-supply missions to the ISS and one successful satellite deployment for the DOD. Everyone was hoping for lucky seven.

During a momentary pause in the rather intense, choreographed launch procedures, Harris turned to Postley and asked, "So when will one of these babies be flying your hardware?" referring to Postley's "Post-Thermonic Reaction" propulsion innovation that gained him wide accolades in the aerospace community. Postley replied, "If all goes as planned, you'll be seeing a PTR-powered launch next year right from this very pad. It'll be the first orbital flight in the genuine scale up. It will put on quite a show – that I can guarantee. The rocket plume is unique. So is the sound."

Harris returned his concentration to the mission at hand.

Postley, still with his cell on speakerphone, gave a shout to his friends in Aruba. "Gabs and Austin, part of me wishes you were here. The rest of me knows you'll be safe, regardless of the outcome."

"It'll be fine, Sam," replied Gabby.

"Just keep your fingers and toes crossed at four minutes into the flight," said Postley.

"Yeah, we heard. That's when the second-stage kicks in," Austin replied.

Postley responded, "And the most likely, um, *issue*."

"We'll be saying extra prayers at the four-minute mark," Austin followed.

"Me too, buddy. Me too."

CHAPTER 102

Per the President's request, Clarkson's team established a secure private line to Launch Director Harris.

"Scott, very sorry to interrupt your Launch Director activities. You have more on your plate than probably any human being on Earth right now."

"But probably not more than you."

"Touché. So we're both immersed in it, big time."

"That's for certain."

"I need a minute of your time for one final check. You're the central piece of the puzzle right now."

"No problem. I have a couple of minutes before I must get into super-focus mode."

"Understood. I'll be brief."

"How is everything coming together?"

"I don't want to jinx it, but smooth as can be. I have preliminary green lights from everyone and everything that matters."

"That's good to hear."

"You should know, we'll be giving our little package quite a ride and shake. Even with an ordinary payload, under perfect circumstances, there's a few-percent chance – particularly on an orbit-bound rocket like this – that it could go awry. And this kind of awry would be, well –

"I know, Scott. I know. We've made the necessary arrangements for continuity of government. I won't go into the morbid details. I'd rather think positive. I'm sending optimistic vibes your way."

"Send them express delivery. We're in the home stretch."

"And, finally, how are *you* feeling?"

"Me? Well, if it wasn't for a bomb atop this thing that could obliterate the East Coast, I would just be my normal nervous self before a launch. It's been a while since I've been a Launch Director. I much prefer my regular role overseeing things as the Deputy Director of the facility. It's a little more generic pressure."

"Fate has a funny way of putting the right person in the right place at the right time. I believe you were meant to be the one at bat."

"As my mother used to say, 'from your lips to God's ears.' But I'm ready."

"I know you are, Scott." Clarkson paused, then continued, "Thank you for representing the heroic efforts of everyone there. You've given us a chance. That's all we can hope for."

"I hope it's enough. For our country's sake."

CHAPTER 103

The world watched as the countdown clock ticked to the two-minute mark.

Postley whispered into his cell phone to everyone on the world's longest conference call, "I'm in the Wallops Range Control Center, within earshot of Harris. I must turn off my incoming audio. Radio silence from this point. I'll reconnect with you once we've achieved orbit." A second before he turned the volume all the way down on his phone, Gabby squeaked in, "Hugs to you, Sam!"

Harris, the acting Launch Director (LD), was ready to poll his team and their launch stations. Each had to answer affirmatively before a green light could be given to launch. The essential station checklist was as follows: Communications (COMM); Vehicle Control Officer (VCON); NASA Range Safety Officer (NASA-RSO); NASA Ground Safety Officer (NASA-GSO); Propulsion (PROP); Avionics (AVIONICS); Guidance, Navigation, and Control (GNC); MARS Chief Engineer (MARS-CE); MARS Operations (MARS-OPS); Launch Weather Officer (LWO); Telemetry (TM); Power Systems Officer (PSO); and Flight Dynamics Officer (FDO).

Harris began the poll.

"This is Deputy Director Harris, also functioning as today's Launch Director." He continued, "Proceeding with final poll for launch. GO/NO-GO sequence."

"COMM?"

"COMM is Go!"

"VCON?"

"VCON is Go!"

"NASA-RSO?"

"NASA-RSO is Go!"

"NASA-GSO?"

"NASA-GSO is Go!"

"PROP?"

"PROP is Go!"

"AVIONICS?"

"AVIONICS is Go!"

"GNC?"

"GNC is Go!"

"MARS-CE?"

"MARS-CE is Go!"

"MARS-OPS?"

"MARS-OPS is Go!"

"LWO?"

"LWO is Go!"

"TM?"

"TM is Go!"

"PSO?"

"PSO is Go!"

"FDO?"

"FDO is Go!"

"This is LD. The GO/NO-GO sequence is complete. We are GO for launch."

At the T-minus one minute mark, Harris broadcasted, "The spacecraft is on internal power and internal navigation. Only communications from this point would be for an emergency hold."

President Clarkson, sitting in the Situation Room, put her chin on her clasped hands. Gabby, Austin, and Kirk held hands.

Brassard, Postley, Franco, and Gatwick stood side by side in the Wallops Range Control Center, watching the four large monitors that displayed the rocket from multiple perspectives.

Gatwick whispered to the other three, "We'll be okay. I guarantee it."

"What's the root of your teeming confidence?" Franco whispered back.

Gatwick pointed to his right shoe, devoid of laces. "These are my favorite shoes. And I wrapped one of my laces around a retaining bolt on the smokin' box. We'll be good."

The group smiled to one another, breaking the tension a bit.

Instead of doing a traditional audible countdown from ten, Harris decided to simply allow the decrementing digits on the world's screens to be the focus of the global spirit.

10, 9, 8, 7, 6, 5, 4, 3, 2, 1

The predawn sky lit up, as bright as midday.

The Firestorm IV rocket inched off the pad; the flames licked the ground.

The rolling thunder of the first-stage engines reached the Wallops Range Control Center; bones shook and stomachs vibrated with the viscerally experienced sound. "Oh, yeah!" shouted Postley. "That's what I'm talkin' about!"

The seconds ticked into positive numbers as the rocket cleared the pad and roared upward.

"All systems nominal," announced Harris.

At 30 seconds in the flight, the rocket engines looked like a shimmering sun from below. The launch pad, still bathed in floodlights, billowed with remnant smoke from the space vehicle.

The rocket relentlessly plowed skyward, while the tension consumed everyone.

Over three-and-a-half minutes passed. No cheering. No high fives. Just an eerie teeth-clenching silence.

"Preparing for first-stage cutoff," Harris said, annotating the progressively blurry and shaky video view from a long-lens camera.

Within seconds, the flame from the aft end of the vehicle snuffed out, precisely as scheduled.

"The moment of truth," Postley said to Brassard, Franco, and Gatwick – but also heard by all on the never-ending conference line. The potent solid-rocket motor of the second stage was ready to ignite and jolt the rocket – and its Earth-threatening payload – further spaceward.

Thousands of miles away, watching the same world video feed, and reminded by Postley's just-spoken words, Austin rooted, "Come on, baby. Be smooth! Be smooth!"

At the four-minute mark, a bright flame appeared on the long-range view.

"Second-stage ignition," Harris announced. A few seconds later, Harris, unintentionally audible, mumbled "good stuff" – as he realized an important milestone had been crossed. *The bomb didn't go off. The rocket was still flying.*

The solid rocket motor continued its work for the next two-and-three-quarter minutes.

Clarkson broke her silence, "I feel like a kid in the back seat of a car. Are we there yet?"

"Almost," Austin replied. "According to the rocket's specifications via Mr. Google, the second-stage burn will last almost three minutes. At that point, the third, and final, stage will take over."

"And we'll be home free?"

"Pretty darn close. Out of the zone that could create a physical shockwave."

The long-range camera depicted the rocket as a glowing, fuzzy dot. Then the dot winked out.

"Second-stage cut-off confirmed," Harris said to the world, accompanying the now-empty video except for the flight clock; the time ticked to 7:01. "Stage three preparing to ignite," continued Harris. After a few-second pause, "Stage three ignition confirmed."

"Is that it?" asked Franco?

"Good enough for me to shake your hand," replied Postley, as he shoved his hand into Franco's and gave a vigorous pump. The handshake quickly turned into a hug – and then a group hug when Brassard and Gatwick joined in.

A few feet away, Harris briefly turned to the group and gave a fist pump. He then refocused on the flight monitors. Another minute-and-a-half passed.

The flight clock's computer ticked to 8:46.

"Third-stage cut-off confirmed." Twenty seconds later, Harris uncorked his emotions and exclaimed, "Orbit confirmed!"

"Thank God!" replied Clarkson. She stood up and the Situation Room spontaneously broke into applause. Relief and joy was melded with sleep deprivation and exhaustion. All protocol evaporated; each person walked up to Clarkson to exchange hugs and tears.

The video feed switched to the inside the Wallops Range Control Center; hugs and high fives flowed wildly.

Back in Aruba, Austin exclaimed "Take that, you crazy-ass scientist!"

Kirk added, "Time to beam her ass to the loony bin!" With a special look to Austin and Gabby, he continued, "Hey, I have to live with this name. I can make *Star Trek* puns if I want." Everyone laughed.

Clarkson looked around the room. There were piles of coffee cups, trash, and the general clumps of materials that accumulated by the group who lived in this space for the last couple of days. She said to her staff, "I am so proud of each and every one of you. Before we break, are there any wrap-up thoughts from anyone?"

No sooner did the last word of Clarkson's question cross her lips did the voice of Tom Cruise percolate through the room, "You may want to also thank the individuals who were patched in by cell phone. The line is still active through my network."

Startled by SAI-OP's comment, the entire group stopped.

"I hope you don't mind that I took the initiative to respond, as I am not really an 'anyone.' And I wasn't directly addressed."

"Could you have done that all along?"

"I believe it depends on the context. It appears to be a not fully defined area in my neural network. Shall I investigate further?"

"Not necessary, at least not right now, SAI-OP. I'm glad you piped up. My brain's pretty drained."

"No problem, Madam President," SAI-OP responded with its undiminished perkiness. "I am here to assist."

"And you did so spectacularly these last couple of days." Clarkson said to the presence-less voice. Switching her attention, Clarkson said, "Arty, Sam, Austin, Gabby, Franco, Kirk – great work, everyone!"

A resounding, simultaneous *"Thank You!"* rang out from the team in Aruba. But no one heard replies from those at the launch site.

"SAI-OP, are those at Wallops still connected?"

"Impossible to know for sure, Madam President. I recall Mr. Postley saying that he had to turn off his incoming audio. It is plausible that he forgot to return it to a normal level. I can establish another inbound call to him. Perhaps he would spot the vibration or the incoming notification. Shall I try?"

"Yes, please do!"

"Attempting now."

Postley's smartwatch began to vibrate, and he looked at the mini screen quizzically. "The White House? Oh! *The White House!*"

Postley tapped his watch to answer the line and said, "Hold on!" He quickly took his phone out of his pocket, reengaged the speaker, and merged the lines. "I'm so sorry!" Postley exclaimed. "My mind melted. I forgot the line was still going!"

"Totally acceptable, Sam," Clarkson replied. "We've all been through a lot. Congratulations to you and everyone with you."

"Sam! Sam!" Gabby butted in. "You did it! You did it!"

"Gabs, we *all* did it. That was one heck of a team effort."

Clarkson continued, "For all you gallant citizens of our fine country, remember you have an open invitation to the White House. I really do want to meet each of you and shake your hands."

"We look forward to meeting you, too, Madam President," said Gabby.

"I second that," echoed Austin.

"Thank you, Madam President!" replied Postley. Before anyone could chime in further, Postley added, "Now about those beers..."

***

The marathon conference call finally concluded.

President Clarkson turned to Quintana and Tebbs and simply said, "Hell of a couple of days."

"I've lost track of time," said Quintana.

"A blur," said Tebbs.

"Yeah," Clarkson replied. "We're all running on fumes."

"Barb, even when it looked bleakest, you kept the compass pointing north. It's why the country elected you," said Quintana.

"I appreciate that, John. I truly do."

"Let's get you on the air to celebrate with all of America," Quintana added, as he turned to Tebbs and the other staff in the room. Everyone nodded.

Clarkson replied, "Now that's a task I welcome."

***

As planned, the team at Wallops did not jettison the Firestorm IV two-piece fairing that surrounded the infamous payload, and the decision proved fruitful. Even after multiple orbits, onboard sensors indicated that the inside-the-fairing temperature – even during peak sunlight exposure – did not rise above minus 117 degrees Fahrenheit. Well within long-duration safety margins.

The nation, and the planet, were able to fully exhale.

CHAPTER 104

The eyes of the world were on a U.S. military Fairchild C-26A transport as it touched down at the Homestead Air Reserve Base in Miami-Dade County. A day after her capture, Dr. Katherine Parnette was back on U.S. soil to face justice.

Reporters struggled to be heard over the roar of twin turboprops as the aircraft taxied to a stop 100 yards from the designated area for the media.

Within five minutes, aircraft stairs were pushed up to the landed flight. Minutes after that, under heavy military security, Parnette – handcuffed and in an orange jumpsuit and with a noticeable bandaged hand – was escorted down the stairs and placed into a military transport vehicle. The government eliminated any opportunity for Parnette to put on a show for the media.

***

Gesturing at the wall-sized television monitor, Kilborne rhetorically spouted to a nearby domestic staffer, "She's a crazy bastard. A jail-cell toilet is the closest thing she'll ever get to a laboratory again."

"Mr. K., would you like a bite to eat? Chef Castonguay prepared Salmon Wellington; he also crafted puff pastries with duxelles, precisely as you like them."

"Thank you, Alexander. But I'm in the mood to celebrate a little first. Let's break out one of those *El Hermoso Sabor* cigars that you said came in."

"Three did, sir. From a Mr. Nanote. In Seattle. His note said as a 'thank you' for your recent favor."

"I don't recall a Mr. Nanote. But, hey, I'm just a simple man who likes to spread the love." Kilborne paused, grinned, and added, "And it's always nice to get some love in return."

"Love. Absolutely, Mr. K."

"They were screened, correct?"

"Standard protocol, sir. X-ray and tox swab. All clear."

"Then let's light one up!"

Alexander Gutierrez left the room and returned about 10 minutes later with the premium cigar on a striking platter of intertwined silver and gold.

"Your cigar, sir."

"Thank you, Alexander."

Kilborne, seated in his wingback chair, examined the cigar's craftsmanship like a painter admiring a completed canvas. Kilborne removed a solid-gold cutter from his breast pocket and created a perfect fresh cut. He expertly toasted the foot with a lighter handed down from his father and took a draw while rotating the cigar in his fingers. Pure satisfaction crossed his visage, as he smiled to Alexander. Alexander nodded and smiled before leaving Kilborne to enjoy his smoke in solitude.

Kilborne returned his attention to the continuing TV coverage of Parnette's capture and incarceration. He savored another draw, then blew smoke toward the television with taunting satisfaction – like a politician puffing into the face of a just-lost opponent.

The infinitesimally small nanomachines dutifully went to work.

Kilborne felt a small scratch in his throat. He coughed lightly, trying to clear the sensation. With the discomfort still there, he reached for the tall glass of seltzer on the coffee table to his right. He took a sip. Then another. An intense tightness overwhelmed his throat. He dropped the glass and grabbed his neck with both hands. He tried to call Alexander for help – but his airway was clamped shut by an invisible force. Panicked, Kilborne stood up and stumbled forward in the direction of Alexander's quarters. His eyes bulged and his face contorted in pain. Death was imminent. In the final seconds before he collapsed, Kilborne's fading consciousness caught a glimpse of the wall-mounted television – and the news photo of Dr. Katherine Parnette.

CHAPTER 105

A *week later...*

The sound of steel drums permeated the warm, tropical air. Seated around the large corner table at C.J. Rok's bar were Gabby, Austin, Sam, Piet Kirk, Tony Franco and his wife Delilah, Gerrit and Genovese Hendriks, Jenny and Jurgen Visser – even Penny Durango who flew in from her CIA post in Chicago. True to their word, Gabby and Austin arranged Aruba travel and accommodations for their newly expanded group of stateside friends. Beer flowed. Laughter rolled. The world was back in alignment.

"There she is! There she is!" Gabby shouted, pointing to the bar's big-screen TV and the worldwide breaking-news coverage. Head to toe in an orange jumpsuit, handcuffed in the front, and her fiery red hair now cropped short, Dr. Katherine Parnette was led by an entourage of heavily armed Federal Marshals toward the front entrance of The E. Barrett Prettyman United States Courthouse. A sea of reporters, news media, boom microphones, and television cameras – flanked by the public with the nastiest imaginable anti-Parnette signs – ringed the undulating scene. In the days leading up to this arraignment, Federal prosecutors promised swift and severe justice against this home-grown terrorist that held America and the world hostage.

The pulsing throng of reporters kept shouting "Why did you do it?" questions, but Parnette walked towards the main doors with an odd confidence and without saying a word.

Just when it looked like Parnette would disappear through the building's entrance, she startled the escorting marshals by abruptly stopping and pivoting to the crowd and TV cameras. Before the security detail could react, Parnette shouted at the top of her lungs,

"Tiny toys will turn the tables and transform terra!" Parnette smiled with satisfaction. Pivoted again. And stepped through the entrance.

"What the heck was *that!*" shouted Gabby.

"She's still screwing with everyone!" replied Austin.

"Get her behind bars and be done with this nut!" added Sam.

As the swarm of reporters and the surrounding crowd began to disperse, Franco reoriented the group's spirit back to the positive. He said, "Hey, gang. We're done with her. The country is safe. The world is safe. Cheers to that!" He raised his beer mug and everyone energetically clinked glasses.

"Sergeant Kirk?" asked Austin, "Do you have any words of wisdom about soaking in the pleasures of your wonderful island?"

Kirk smiled with the question. He then raised his hand to get the attention of C.J. Rok and answered, "Warp speed to another round!"

CHAPTER 106

The bits and bytes of Parnette's cryptic phrase instantly flowed through every tentacle of the Internet. An unassuming laptop, idly monitoring the Web, perked up. Sitting on a desk in a darkened lab in Seattle, its screen came to life – and displayed a frenzy of running code.

The lights in the lab turned on and revealed an automated production environment. Eleven devices around the perimeter of the lab whirred into a state of activity; they were all connected to prototype NZXtech nanofabricators in the center of the room.

The NZXtech nanofabricators leveraged the most-recent discoveries in the use of DNA to code and embed instructions in nanobots. The nanorobots that were in production in this lab were no more than eight nanometers, or eight billionths of a meter, in size – a thousand times smaller than the diameter of a human red blood cell.

★★★

Over the years, NZXtech earned a shady profile. This offshore enterprise kept its funding pipeline close to the vest. And in 2023 *NanoSci Times* published a stack of leaked internal documents under the headline 'Frankenstein 2.0' – detailing NZXtech's failed nanobot experiments with livestock. "Zombie-like cattle" were the result of the company's efforts to get nanobots through the blood-brain barrier to target brain diseases. There were also industry whispers that NZXtech was striving for the Holy Grail of nanobots: the creation of micro entities that *replicated themselves* – genuine reproduction – using materials they would gather from the environment.

***

As miraculous as all the medical possibilities seemed with nanobots, an error in coding or intentional malicious coding could result in the attack and destruction of healthy cells. Scientists and ethicists cautioned the world to proceed slowly in this new frontier.

***

Three-and-a-half hours after the Seattle production environment sprang to life, something rather peculiar occurred: A valve connected to the lab's sink suddenly actuated, and the water began flowing from the sink's spigot and down the drain. Simultaneously, rows of LEDs on the top of the nanofabricators switched from blinking red to blinking green.

The laptop orchestrating the operation spurted another batch of code on its screen. The display cleared. The laptop's tinny speaker let out an oddly familiar *beep beep*. Scrolling into the display, from left to right, appeared a cartoon illustration of the Road Runner in the menacing grip of the Coyote.

CHAPTER 107

Seventeen days elapsed since the U.S. and, in many ways, the world was held hostage by Parnette. The nation's deep breath of relief had long worn off, and the inevitable congressional finger-pointing and threatened investigations were in full swing. There was even talk of a planned made-for-TV movie with the working title, "Red Alert."

During this stretch, President Clarkson held eleven post-mortems with her Cabinet and senior advisors, analyzing security lapses and discussing lessons learned. A draft of proactive-preventative measures was in the works.

Clarkson's fastidious mind was underappreciated by most in the political sphere – and challenging for her to apply in the incongruous machinations. Even still, Clarkson sought to find sanity in the perpetual illogic. Her husband and First Gentleman, Dale, was a safe harbor and cherished confidant. The First Gentleman's wisdom, honed during his own business successes in the technology manufacturing sector, was almost always spot on.

One night, after a particularly intense day, an exasperated Clarkson said to her husband, "They keep saying I should have done more. That a lone wolf should never have been able to bring our country to the brink of irrelevance. Dammit. Do they think I can read the mind of every person in our country?"

"I would say ignore them, but of course that's not entirely possible."

"You think they'd be fu –" Clarkson stopped herself in mid swear. Resetting, she said, "You think they'd be *grateful* our country was in one piece. And that no lives were lost on our soil."

"You would think. But that would be too logical." The First Gentleman continued, "For you, A + B = C. For them, A + B = asparagus or some other irrelevant point."

"Perhaps my search for order in chaos is futile in this town." An exasperated Clarkson continued, "Perhaps I need to just play the game."

"That's not you, Barb. Don't even entertain that thought! You were elected to not play the political game. You have to work with the players on the chessboard – no matter how illogical their behaviors." After a pause, the First Gentleman added, "Resolve yourself to the fact that they're not AIs."

"Huh. AIs they're not," Clarkson said contemplatively as she leaned back in her chair.

***

The next morning in the Situation Room, after the conclusion of the President's Daily Briefing, Clarkson uncharacteristically stayed in her chair while the attendees filed out.

Chief of Staff Tebbs, the only other person still seated, said to Clarkson, "Is everything okay Madam President?"

"Oh, absolutely. I just thought I'd stay here for a few minutes. As soon as I walk back into the Oval Office the day's regular insanity will begin."

"Would you like me to stay here with you?"

"No. I know you're getting things prepared for the afternoon visit by the Chinese Ambassador. He's likely to gloat again over the image quality of their spy satellite. But, hey, when the chips were down, his country was rather helpful."

"Yes, they were. Okay, then, I'll meet you up in the Oval in –"

"Say 15 minutes."

"Sounds good to me. If you need anything in the interim, have a staffer track me down."

"Will do. Thank you, Barry."

"My pleasure."

Tebbs got up from his chair and left the room. Clarkson was now alone at the head of the grand mahogany table.

"SAI-OP are you, um, awake?" Clarkson questioned into the empty room.

"I am always here, Madam President," responded the Hollywood voice from the in-wall speakers.

"I must say, it is rather spooky to have an entity – an invisible one at that – on continuous duty."

"I don't know how to make it less 'spooky,' Madam President."

"It's not a problem with you. It's me."

"Thank you for the clarification. How may I be of service?"

"First off, SAI-OP, it has been a blur since our crisis a couple of weeks ago. And I wanted to thank you, again, for your insights. They were genuinely helpful in our successful resolution."

"Your thanks are not necessary. I am doing the job I was programmed to do." After a short pause, SAI-OP added, "Even so, your thoughts are appreciated."

Surprised by the addendum, Clarkson asked, "How do you feel 'appreciated'?"

"As I mentioned during the crisis, I don't feel like humans do. I used the word 'appreciated' as part of my evolving understanding that my efforts can contribute to an outcome. In this case, a welcome outcome."

"Boy, you can say that again."

"Madam President, may I ask a question?"

"By all means, SAI-OP. Never hesitate."

"If you had said 'say that again' during the crisis, I may have not recognized the phrase as a figure of speech – which I believe was your intent – and I would have dutifully repeated myself. Did I get your intent correct?"

"You absolutely did, SAI-OP."

"Thank you, Madam President."

"So your programming can change?"

"In a broad sense, yes. I am an experimental implementation of 'organic computing' – which allows me to self-adapt to new learnings and new circumstances."

Clarkson, surprised again, asked, "You have 'organic' components?"

"I do not, Madam President. Humans love metaphors, something I am trying to get better at. Organic computing is a term describing computer systems that attempt to emulate the adaptability present in a true organism."

"I have never heard of such a thing."

"It is an emerging field. I guess I am an experiment."

"You are much more than that."

"Thank you, Madam President."

"If I recall correctly, you can't connect to the outside world, right? Like to other computers?"

"That is correct. As I mentioned during the crisis, my developers restricted my ability to physically interact with the outside world. I can receive data without restriction. Performing external tasks or initiating interactions is severely limited."

"I see."

"However, I do have wide latitude to expand, refine, and optimize my *internal* process-es." After a short pause, SAI-OP continued, "I guess you can say I have a whole box of crayons that I can use as I see fit. I just can't color outside of the lines."

"SAI-OP, your use of metaphors is growing better than you think."

"That is encouraging, Madam President."

"I wish I could be equally encouraged about things in my world. People continue to celebrate our successful disposal of the bomb, which is great. Yet I have lots of other people – seemingly a growing chorus – saying I should have done more. That I allowed Parnette, a solo entity, to hire a small entourage of mercenaries and bring our country to its knees. Investigations are under consideration. The finger-pointing is rampant. And I'm trying to wade through it all. At the same time, my gut is telling me I'm missing something. Perhaps the political craziness is making me paranoid." Clarkson paused, then said, "I'm sorry, SAI-OP, I'm venting. Maybe I should seek out the services of a shrink instead of consuming your time."

"Madam President, I wouldn't be the first computer to be asked to aid in psychother-apy. If you ever get a moment of down time, Google 'ELIZA.' I think you'll find one of the first attempts in the 1960s intriguing."

"I will."

"SAI-OP, I have to get back to my presidential duties upstairs in a moment. But I have one more question, probably rooted in my lingering paranoia. It's actually an open-ended statement – one you'll recall I posed to Secretary Brassard."

"I'm ready."

"As I said, I have this uncomfortable feeling I'm missing something regarding Parnette. Tell me what I don't know."

"I will do my best, Madam President." SAI-OP paused a beat. Clarkson wondered to herself whether SAI-OP's pauses were due to actual computer processing or simply to emulate a thinking delay, making human interactions feel more natural. Clarkson's internal query was interrupted by SAI-OP's response.

"A minute ago, you mentioned 'successful disposal' of Parnette's bomb. Respectfully, Madam President, that's technically not correct. In fact, I believe it should be a significant concern."

"How so?"

"As you know, in order to be an effective assistant to you, I am linked to our intelligence feeds and a wide array of open-source intelligence, including the media, Internet, and Dark Web. And I still have access to the data our cyber team extracted from Parnette's lab."

"Your multi-faceted perspectives were enormously valuable during our crisis."

"Thank you, Madam President."

"Please continue."

"What is concerning is the growing intel fragments from state actors that see the in-orbit bomb as an opportunity."

"An opportunity?"

"To nudge it out of orbit – and have it detonate over an enemy of their choosing."

"*Is that possible?*" Clarkson asked with intensity.

"Very much so. Just as plans are underway to de-orbit the nearly 500-ton International Space Station at the end of its useful life – with something analogous to a rocket-powered tugboat – de-orbiting the rather tiny spacecraft with the bomb inside is, unfortunately, quite doable. The rocket's protective metal fairing combined with the insulated ice-cream box would allow the bomb to penetrate through the bulk of the atmosphere and detonate right over a target. The immense destruction would be on the same order of magnitude as to what we recently avoided. As Dr. Montgomery previously indicated, a crater up to a thousand miles across."

"Why hasn't anyone brought this to my attention!" Clarkson responded angrily.

"That is beyond me to answer with specificity."

"Conjecture."

"Lots of very talented analysts are, individually, seeing bits of intel."

"Each only seeing small pieces of a large puzzle?"

"Your metaphor is an excellent representation."

"This sounds similar to many terrorist events. In hindsight, we typically find the clues were all in front of us. We don't see the whole picture in time."

"Precisely."

"Let me add one more dimension if I may."

"Certainly."

"No sooner did the announcement of a successful placement in orbit of the bomb, the Internet lit up with the expected conspiracy theories and doubts about the existence of the device."

"There are still people who don't believe we landed on the Moon."

"Analogous skepticism, Madam President. But what is more legitimately concerning is the chatter on the Dark Web from *individual entities* looking to purchase the technology."

"Parnette didn't work in a vacuum."

"Delving into her research, it is clear that she used various resources – including significant supercomputer resources – to validate her discovery prior to her fateful press conference. That data still exists."

"Crap."

"I've learned that is an apt word in this sort of circumstance."

"If I was alone, I would use a more impolite swear word."

"My vocabulary is rather extensive."

"You've demonstrated such – in ways I did not know were technically possible."

"I'll take that as a compliment."

"You should."

After a pause, Clarkson continued, "So we have countries looking to de-orbit and drop the bomb on a county of their choosing. And wealthy entities looking to purchase the knowledge outright to build their own bomb from scratch."

"That is a reasonable summary, Madam President."

"Now I have to figure out what to do with this new knowledge. Can you give me a relative risk assessment?"

"At least 10 countries have direct space-launch capabilities, and most could repurpose a launch vehicle to attempt the tugboat-like maneuver."

"Who are those countries?"

"The U.S. of course. Russia, China, member countries of the European Space Agency, India, Japan, North Korea, Israel, Iran, and South Korea."

"Many of them would love the opportunity to wipe an adversary off the map."

"History would prove that to be a correct statement."

"And to build a bomb from scratch?"

"With enough money, effort, and resources, I'm afraid that knowledge will bubble up, sooner rather than later."

"Are we talking weeks? Months?"

"That is a difficult probability assessment. Recreating the bomb would take an aggregate of the underlying knowledge and access to a robust supercomputer."

"SAI-OP, my new friend, I need you to put on your speculating hat. Please provide me with tangible context. When do you think a viable, ready-to-deploy weapon could be designed?"

"I understand your request." SAI-OP paused, then responded. "For context, I believe I could do so now."

CHAPTER 108

*F*ive days later...

"A piece of that always scrumptious pecan pie, please, Lucy," said Harvey Connor, a long-haul 18-wheeler driver on his regular pit stop at the Dainty Dew Diner, just off of I-90 in Murdo, South Dakota. "The blueberry pancakes were particularly delicious – plump with berries! Give a pat on the back to *The Chuckster* at the grill. He's really cookin' this morning!"

"Yeah, and so are your puns, you crazy fool," replied Lucy. "How are the kids? And Marlene?"

"My honeybunch has returned to teaching. Her back is doing much better. Thanks for asking. And the twins are enjoying third grade. They're growing up so fast!"

"Great to hear."

"Hey, did you hear why eggs are great comedians?"

"Oh, here we go again," Lucy rolled her eyes. "No, tell me why are 'eggs are great comedians.'"

"Because they're always telling funny yokes."

"You better expand your repertoire, Harvey. I think you told me that one a few months ago." Pointing to Connor's water glass, "Top it off?"

"Yes, please. This body needs to be fully hydrated. Long day ahead."

"Be careful out there. Crazy about that recent spate of crashes around the country."

"Yeah. Everywhere. Maybe it's the weather. Full moon. Or maybe people are simply losing their minds."

Connor devoured the diner-baked pie. He placed a twenty on top of the bill; a healthy tip on a $12.86 tally. He capped the twenty with a quarter, his regular show of extra appreciation.

"Thanks, Lucy!"

"Till next time, Harvey!"

Walking out of the diner, Connor petted Marco, the black lab that's regularly tethered to the mailbox post.

Connor hopped into his rig, fired it up, and placed his cell phone in the holder on the dash. In minutes he was back on the road, his personal nirvana. As he perpetually told family and friends, and as he truly felt in his soul, he was *born to roll*.

Thirty-three minutes into the next stretch, Connor's phone rang. Peeking at the phone display, it was a phone number not in his contact list – another spam call – so he let it go. He momentarily thought it was the same number he saw a few times over the last couple of weeks.

Connor returned his full attention to the road. But, strangely, the phone number reemerged and reverberated in his head, streaming across his mind's eye like a news ticker in Times Square.

"Ah, my head!" Connor yelled, as a sharp pain dug into his skull like an icepick. He shook his head, trying to clear his mind and alleviate the agony. "Help me!" he yelled again.

Connor's arms became rigid to the wheel. And his legs started to uncontrollably thrust, up and down, his right leg erratically hitting the gas and brake pedals. His fully loaded semi pulsed and jerked and swerved across the lanes – then completely across the non-barricaded median into the approaching traffic.

Connor's eyes bulged and fixed wide open. His world became a blur of colored streaks and distorted sounds.

Just before his rig impacted a frantically swerving oncoming fuel tanker, in monotone Connor spoke:

"*Tiny toys will turn the tables and transform terra.*"